The Hero Virus

What doesn't kill you makes you stronger

By

Russell Dumper

The Conrad Press

The Hero Virus
Published by The Conrad Press in the United
Kingdom 2024
Tel: +44(0)1227 472 874
www.theconradpress.com
info@theconradpress.com
ISBN 978-1-916966-79-6
Typesetting and Cover Design by: Levellers
The Conrad Press logo was designed by Maria
Priestley.
Printed and bound in Great Britain by Clays Ltd,
Elcograf S.p.A.

For my wife, Anna, and her endless patience. For my boys, Lucas and Jacob, who do their best to be quiet (and often fail). For all my friends and family, the support of whom I could not possibly manage without.

1

Click. The hollow sound of the hammer hitting an empty chamber bounced around the room. The chambered bullet escaped him again. The click was the first thing he had heard for the last 112 days.

Some mornings the gun was in his hand before he woke up, the cold muzzle between his lips before he even opened his eyes.

It was becoming instinct.

Besides, it was easier that way. He could pull the trigger before his brain clicked into gear.

This was one of those days.

It was always more difficult on the days where he was fully awake. He would snatch the Magnum .357 from the bedside cabinet, spin the cylinder and squeeze the small apostrophe of metal, anyway, but shards of doubt were stuck all through his mind, as if each one were embedded in a different memory.

He hated these days. It gave him the chance to consider it. On several occasions, he had sat upright in his bed for several minutes, weapon in-hand, wondering what Herodotus would do if he died. His parents had died when he was six and his last blood relative had died years ago, so Herodotus was the only family he had left. But he had decided that God would look after the faithful Labrador.

Because, if God wanted him to take care of Herodotus, the hollow click would resonate around the bedroom.

That click was the first thing he had heard every day for the last one hundred and twelve days.

God, Allah, Destiny, or whoever controlled the universe, obviously had a purpose for him.

One hundred and twelve days since the accident. It was a long time to wonder what that purpose might be. Every hour that went by was another hour he had dragged himself through life by the collar.

He had hated every, single one of them.

The loneliness was crippling. He was insulted by the forced sympathy from all those around him. He loathed the muted conversations and looks of pity.

One hundred and twelve days of cornflakes and microwave meals.

One hundred and twelve days of... nothingness.

He spent several moments eyeing the gleaming weapon in his hand. It was a strange sensation not to have respect for life any longer.

Chris Taylor sighed heavily and placed the gun back on the bedside cabinet. 'Morning, Herodotus.'

Hearing his voice, the buoyant, golden-furred canine bounded through the half-open door and leapt onto the bed, his long tongue covering Taylor and the bed sheets in an affectionate slobber. His tail wagged furiously, betraying the excitement he had always greeted people with, whether he had been alone in the house for ten minutes or all day.

Herodotus attacked him with joy. Taylor stroked him and told him that he was a good boy, almost feeling guilty as he swung his feet out of bed, stabbing them into his slippers.

He ambled through to the bathroom to splash cold water on his face and studied himself in the mirror over the sink. His posture seemed to be sagging, but he was still tall and broad. His blonde hair had thinned considerably of late and his blue eyes were increasingly opaque. Where he would have considered himself athletic a few months ago, he could not recall his last visit to the gym. His aquiline nose was blotchy and his thin lips were dry. He had always thought that he had quite a small mouth, but it looked to be shrinking. His cheeks sagged and the wrinkles had grown from grooves to crevasses, which only seemed to make his skin seem paler. Indeed, he could see the life draining from him with every passing day.

He sloped down to the kitchen, yawning as he flicked on the kettle and took a bowl from the draining board. The corn flakes were still on the side from the previous morning, so he tipped some into the bowl. Reaching into the refrigerator, he took the carton of milk from the pocket inside the door and splashed it all over them, snatching a spoon from the drawer as he flicked on the television.

Plonking onto a stool at the breakfast bar, he looked around the kitchen and eyed the empty, pine table and four matching, lonely chairs. He recalled the day the new, pine kitchen had arrived and how much he had disliked it. He was about to let himself slip into a memory when something on the television piqued his interest.

There had been some violent tremors during the night, leaving a trail of destruction all over the country. Some of it was surprisingly severe, leaving property devastated, and dozens of people seriously injured. No part of England had escaped damage.

Leaning forwards, he peered out of the window. The house next door had a broken window and their garden furniture had toppled over. His eyes moved down the street, from crooked street lamps to a pile of bricks on top of a van, where a chimney had collapsed.

How strange, he thought, that he had not felt anything in the night. He shrugged his shoulders and returned his attention to the television.

He saw more during his morning walk with Herodotus. Very few houses had managed to escape the effects of the tremors. He followed the same route as every morning. As he left the small residential area and ventured towards the countryside, he became increasingly surprised at how Mother Nature had ravaged the trees in the area. Herodotus did not seem to mind. He managed to find a whole host of new places over which he could cast his scent.

Taylor often wondered if Herodotus ever cared that Jane was not taking him out. Ever since he was a puppy, she had taken him out every morning. If he did care, he did not show it. He sniffed, barked, chased and urinated as zealously as ever.

Sometimes, Taylor thought he saw a twinkle of sadness in his eyes, though, especially in the evening, when it was time for food. Jane had always fed Herodotus in the evening. Then she would curl up with him on the sofa and watch *EastEnders*. Taylor was certain his canine friend missed that. The theme tune had become the signal that the house was winding down for the night. At the end of the show, Herodotus made his way upstairs to the floor of the bedroom, where he would position himself on Jane's side of the bed.

He suspected that Herodotus missed her most at night, just as he did, and he knew that the dog could sense when he was struggling. Herodotus would come and sit down next to him, perhaps placing his head in Taylor's lap, or nudging his hand for some affection. It was strange that an animal could empathise with him more than any other human could. But Herodotus was part of the family. Only he knew their routines and the small, but myriad, idiosyncrasies of living in their house. Only he could appreciate the void left by her absence.

Walking slowly up the hill towards the copse at the top, he sucked the spring air in through his nostrils, the sweet aroma of blossom tickling his senses. The trees were sprouting leaves and the morning dew heightened the scent of freshly cut grass. The shrill harmony of morning birdsong filled the air.

Reaching the top of the hill, he let Herodotus off his lead and watched him bound off into the trees. Taylor sat on a trunk that had fallen in the night and looked back over the small town of Towcester, that he lived on the outskirts of. The hill afforded him an excellent view of the town he was born, and had grown up, in.

There was an industrial estate on the far side, where he worked, and the town centre towards the middle. The rest of the view consisted of patterns created by the roads meandering through the housing estates. Some were circular, others straight and there were several zigzags. There were splashes of green dotted around the town, with tall trees standing guard over them and a few, large buildings, such as schools and the hospital. Running around the left-hand perimeter of the town was a serpentine river, which suddenly swept in through the middle and dissected the town, before trailing away over the right-hand horizon as it passed the famous racecourse.

He often liked to relax his eyes and allow images to form. Several businesses on the industrial estate formed together to make a giraffe. One housing estate looked like David Schwimmer. Most mornings, though, the parish church drew his eyes to it. The tall spire seemed to pierce the clouds and he could not help but sit, stare and wonder.

He had never been a religious man, despite the fact Jane had visited church regularly. But he had found that to be changing of late. He had caught himself looking to the heavens for an explanation. He was not really sure why, but it seemed to help a little. Indeed, if there was not something up there, his loss was senseless. As long as he subscribed to the theory of a higher power, he could believe that there was a plan. He could believe that Jane was not gone, but had merely moved on and that he would see her again.

He *had* to believe that. He did not know what other option there was. Indeed, if he started to think that Jane was taken from them for no reason other than sheer bad luck, he might be inclined to put more than one bullet in the Magnum.

Taylor had endured many long, dark hours and, no matter what he tried to acclimatise to his loss, his chest felt hollow. It was as if everything that made him who he was had died with her, leaving a void where his personality had been. But the weeks of introspective reflection had managed to reveal one fact to him.

Losing her was a tragedy, but it was an inevitability of life. Such melancholy was the risk one took when being happy. Indeed, to feel such misery was not possible without first experiencing such overwhelming joy. That she was gone was not what ate away at his soul.

It was the way it happened that crushed him. And the events afterwards made the bile rise into his throat.

Fearing he might vomit, Taylor tore his thoughts away from it and checked his watch. He was going to be late for work if he did not hurry.

Jumping up, he called for Herodotus. A few seconds passed and there was no sign of the Labrador emerging through the trees, so he called again. After a minute, there was still no sign of his faithful, and usually obedient, companion. That was most peculiar.

He looked at his watch again. He had only been back a week. He did not want to be late already.

Striding purposefully into the copse, he caught a glimpse of some gold amongst the green. Walking towards it, he could hear a lapping sound and the faint trickle of running water. Having walked through these trees hundreds of times, he knew there was no stream or creek, so approached with a cautious curiosity, unsure what he would find.

He was relieved to reach Herodotus and find him drinking from a small trickle of water sprouting from the ground and dribbling down the hill. Intrigue quickly took control as he noticed the steam coming from the water.

Taylor arrived next to Herodotus, who greeted him with customarily feverish tail wagging, and attached the lead to his collar as he crouched down to inspect the hot spring. He was certain it had not been here before, so was perhaps another effect of the tremor. Pulling Herodotus away, he did not think any more of it.

Had he known what was in the water, he might have.

'How are you, Chris?'

He glanced up from his desk, looked askance at the woman who had interrupted his thoughts, and forced a smile. 'Fine, thanks. You?'

Bernadette did not even try to hide the pathos in her eyes, or the sympathy etched into the creases in her cheeks caused by her uncomfortable smile. Taylor loathed this almost as much as the loneliness.

Bernadette was a middle-aged woman, sporting neck-length blonde hair with grey roots. She always wore tight blouses to highlight her ample bosom, apparently unconcerned that it also displayed her flabby arms and swollen stomach. It was not the fact that she was being overly nice to him that was so annoying, but she had never really spoken to him before, aside from the occasional, perfunctory greeting. He hated that so many of his colleagues suddenly pretended to care. Most of them had not even met Jane during their six years together, so how could they care that she was gone?

Several people treated him as they always had done. They were casual, work acquaintances and, though he could see the condolence in their eyes, they did not pretend to be anything more. He could respect them, at least, for being genuine.

But these people were few and far between. A large part of his working day had become consumed by the sycophants, leaving him with less time to do his work. All he wanted was to get on with his job. Anything to distract him for a few minutes, to take his mind away from what he had lost. Didn't these people understand that they nullified the exact reason he had chosen to return?

'Chris!'

This time when he looked up, he saw Nate standing in the open doorway to his office, beckoning him in. 'Can I have a word, please, mate?'

Nathan Tyson was one of the few who did truly care. Although Taylor's boss, as the Factory Manager of the building that produced record numbers of salads for the supermarkets, they were also close friends.

Nate had suggested the Production Planner role to him when they played rugby together a decade before and, despite the fifteen-year age gap, with Nate now fifty, they had grown close.

Taylor walked into the office and sat down opposite his friend, eyeing him studiously. Nate looked his age these days. His chocolate skin looked weathered and his large, brown eyes were dull. His thick crop of black hair was just a memory, the remnants sitting atop either ear and leaving the rest of his head to reflect the bright halogen lights in his office.

Nate had retained his moustache, though, ignoring the silver flecks spread throughout it, and his bulky physique, although it was more fat now, than it was muscle. His smile had not changed, though. He had huge, rabbit teeth that gleamed every time he flashed them, a sight that Taylor had always found oddly compelling.

He was not smiling now, however. His face was grave and his eyes frigid. 'Are you sure you should be back already?'

Taylor looked around the office before he replied. It was quite small, only around four feet wide and eight long, but Nate had somehow managed to squeeze a desk, five chairs, a circular table, a filing cabinet and six shelving units in there. The room always smelt of Nate's overpowering aftershave. 'What else should I do?'

Nate shrugged his shoulders. 'I don't know. Take a bit more time, perhaps?'

He scoffed acerbically. 'And do what with it? Rattling around an empty house doesn't help much. At least here I can take my mind off things a little. Don't worry, I'm fine.'

'You don't seem fine. You're quiet, withdrawn.'

His eyes flashed with white-hot rage. 'That's probably because my pregnant wife was recently killed.'

Nate's expression did not soften. 'What's happening with the other driver?'

14

'Nothing,' Taylor replied, forming fists and placing them in his lap as the surge of anger threatened to overwhelm him. 'The breathalyser was faulty, so the police can't prosecute. He's got a smart lawyer. I guess that's why it's useful to have rich parents.'

Nate's face transformed to one of outrage. 'That can't be it, can it? So many witnesses said he was drunk. There must be some physical evidence. They could use blood or urine to test him.'

'Not over a day later. They tested his breath at the scene and he passed. They didn't even notice that their equipment was faulty until the next day. The alcohol was out of his system by then.'

'That's disgusting! I'm so sorry, mate. Life is cruel. What's his name?'

'Jeremy Clarke.'

'Do you want me to...you know?' He made a fist and punched the air.

'That won't bring her back, Nate.'

'No, but it might...'

Taylor scoffed. 'Do you think it hasn't occurred to me already? Do you have any idea how much time I've spent thinking about it?' *Every morning*, he thought. When the hollow click resonated, he always considered taking the Magnum to the post office and waiting outside.

'You're right,' he replied sombrely. 'I'm sorry for bringing it up, mate.'

Taylor nodded, fighting the ire in his gut. 'Can I go back to work now?'

The ensuing silence lasted almost a minute and was awkward for both of them. When Nate finally broke it, emotion choked his voice. 'Well, you know where I am if you need anything, even if it's just a chat.'

'Thanks, Nate,' Taylor replied, unclenching his fists and smiling morosely. 'Don't worry, I'll be fine.' He stood up and left the room without making another sound. He knew he had just seen Nate at his most emotional. What he did not really understand is why it irritated him so much.

He sat back at his desk, opening the spreadsheet for projected labour requirements on his computer. Even moving back through the office, he could feel the eyes upon him. He hated all this sympathy. He hated that conversations suddenly stopped when he entered the room, the pity in the eyes of people he barely knew, as if he was a three-legged puppy. He just wanted everyone to treat him the same way as they always had.

Staring at his monitor, he decided to test the parameters. He would spend the afternoon making deliberate mistakes to see if anyone would bring it to his attention. He knew Nate would not have any qualms about highlighting his errors, but he was curious to surmise whether, or not, his colleagues; many of whom were vipers that would usually relish the chance to bad-mouth a cohort; would behave as he would expect them to.

To his disappointment, nobody said a word. They simply corrected his mistakes for him without uttering a sound. Perhaps returning to work was a bad idea. Until others moved past his tragedy, he did not see how he could. Their behaviour was a continual reminder of his loss.

Not that he blamed them. He did not even try to hide his melancholy, which obviously made them uncomfortable. It was his fault, really, for putting them in a position they could not fully understand or cope with. He knew it would make the situation better for everyone if he could just bury his despondent torment and return to the man he used to be.

However, even if he knew how to do that, he did not want to. If he hid his despair, it was as if he was already forgetting her.

By the time he was sitting behind the wheel of their old Ford Mondeo, driving home, the memories had ambushed his mind. Everything seemed to inspire the recollection of his previous life: Jane sitting in the passenger seat doing her make-up, Jane outside the Post Office, Jane waiting for him outside the school where she had taught.

All that managed to do was highlight the pointlessness of the half-life he was currently living. He was in limbo, no longer Chris Taylor, but a shell where once a man had been.

Parking in the driveway of their three-bedroom, detached house, he cast his eyes over the garden and silently reproached himself for letting the weeds overrun the flowerbeds and the bushes grow out of control. Even the small, ornate, cobbled path was covered in patches of green. Jane would never have let her garden run into such a state. He would fix it at the weekend.

Feeling much lower than when he had left that morning, Taylor felt instantly better when he opened the front door and he heard the scramble of activity in the kitchen. He closed the door behind him as Herodotus bounded down the hallway towards him.

The Labrador collided with his master's legs, as he did every day in his desperation to rub himself on his master, but Taylor suddenly found himself sprawling.

Looking up at the ceiling, he realised that Herodotus had hit him with such force that he had knocked him over. The dog, noting the fact that Taylor was now at his level, leapt on him joyously and Taylor welcomed him with a sense of confusion.

Herodotus was unusually strong today. Or perhaps the tribulations of the day had made him weak.

Taylor got to his feet and prepared food for them both. He produced two microwave meals; one for each of them, although the meal for Herodotus would be minus the carrots he openly detested. While he waited, he sent a text message to Nate, San and Tim to confirm what they, no doubt, already suspected. He did not feel like going to the pub to play pool tonight.

Sitting in front of the television, both wolfed their meals down and settled down for the evening. Taylor slumped in the same chair he had used for a decade and Herodotus settled down next to it. They both cast forlorn looks towards the empty sofa, where Jane would stretch out to watch *X-Factor* and a host of others shows Taylor hated.

The room seemed desolate without her. She had specifically chosen the velour, navy three-piece suite to match the grey carpet and ghost-coloured walls. He recalled spending hours fitting the 42-inch LCD television over the closed fireplace and marble mantelpiece. In the corner next to the bay window was Jane's small, square, teak table, with two matching chairs, where she would spend her evenings working. There were potted plants in the corners either side of the sofa, which housed two dying Yucca plants. The scent of lavender, from the air fresheners Jane hid around the house, was starting to fade. He might have replenished them if only he knew where they were.

Other than that, though, the room was devoid of all the small things that used to make it so cosy. Jane's shoes, Jane's handbag, Jane's magazines, Jane's jewellery, Jane's books, Jane's make-up, Jane's clothes. It had taken him weeks to tidy it all up, but it had gotten to the point where he could not look at it any longer. As long as it all sat there, he expected her to walk back in at any moment. He had needed to get on with his life and that simply was not possible until he tidied it. Now, however, it seemed sterile.

Taylor watched the news for only a few minutes before his eyes migrated to the photograph on top of the mantelpiece. Jane smiled brightly, her brilliantly white teeth highlighting her light blonde hair and azure eyes. He was grimacing as Herodotus, still a puppy at the time, gnawed on his foot.

He rested his head back on the chair cushion as a serene expression covered his face, almost as if some drug had consumed him. A smile creased his lips at each corner as his brain slipped back in time.

Jane walked in the front door. It was during the brief period of time she had experimented by having her hair cut in a bob. She strode into the living room and tossed her handbag on the floor with a growl.

Taylor sat in his chair and smiled in her direction, but she did not notice the dog bed in the corner, nor the tiny ball of golden fur hiding at the side of the sofa. Instead, she launched into a five-minute diatribe about one of her lazy colleagues who, Jane contested, remained only in a job because of her loose morals.

During the entire speech, Taylor merely sat and nodded, watching her intently as she marched back and forth, gesticulating wildly. She was so sexy when she spoke with passion. He wondered if it was inappropriate to take her on the settee, knowing that the puppy was there. He decided it was.

She was mid-expletive when she spotted the little ball of fluff, with enormous, brown eyes, peeking out at her from the corner of the sofa. She forgot her anger in a flash, as her jaw dropped. She gaped at her husband, then back at the puppy, before dropping to a crouch and assuming a high-pitched voice that Taylor had never heard before.

The puppy seemed to like it, though. It took Jane mere seconds to coax him from his hiding place, creeping out inch-by-inch until she was able to sweep him into her arms. They were inseparable from that moment onwards.

Taylor's mind suddenly leapt forwards to that evening, as they lay in bed, with the tiny golden fur ball at their feet. He recalled listening as Jane deliberated over names. Having studied Archaeology, she had fallen in love with the Persian Empire and that lead her to The Histories. It was her favourite piece of ancient literature and the seminal work of a man called Herodotus. That was the first time Taylor had ever heard the name, although Jane went on to explain that Herodotus was 'the first real historian' and one of her heroes.

Taylor opened his eyes when he felt the warm saliva on his face, finding a fully-grown Herodotus astride him. He ruffled the fur behind his best friend's ears, which was always welcome, and moved his blurred vision to the clock on the wall.

It took a few moments for his brain to register the fact that it was three in the morning and that the timer on the television had already switched it off.

Dragging himself upstairs, his apathy towards even the most rudimentary hygiene standards meant he could not find the motivation to wash his face. He fell onto the bed in his clothes and thought about how much he hated Jeremy Clarke until he fell asleep.

Had Jane been there, he probably would not have fallen asleep and, if he had, she would have forced him to wash his face.

Had Jane been there, there was every chance the world would not have changed.

2

Taylor woke before the alarm, reaching out and feeling for the Magnum with his fingertips, a reflex action he no longer considered. He just did it. Before he even opened his eyes, the hollow click bounced around the room.

It was almost as if that was the sound that triggered his eyelids every morning.

Clearly, Destiny still had a use for him.

'Morning, Herodotus,' he said, through a sore throat, realising that he had slept in his clothes again.

After twenty seconds, the door remained ajar and he was beginning to wonder if his faithful companion might be involved in one of his more mischievous antics.

Then he heard a whimper.

Leaping out of bed, he sprinted out the door to see Herodotus lying outside the bedroom, much as he had most nights since Jane had been taken from them. Every morning he bounded through the door the moment he realised Taylor was awake.

This morning was different, though. Herodotus did not lift his head or wag his tail. His huge, brown eyes met Taylor without the usual joy. Instead, they were full of pain and fear.

Taylor knelt down next to him. 'What's wrong, buddy? Are you sick?'

He inspected the Labrador, quickly realising he did not even know what to look for, and rubbed the stomach. Herodotus managed a single, faint wag of his tail.

'Don't worry, I'll get you some help.'

Taking the stairs three at a time, and almost toppling down them, he landed next to the telephone table and snatched it from the charging dock. Simultaneously, he grabbed the plastic folder on the table. It was Jane's, filled with cards, on which were the contact details for every possible requirement any human might have. He recalled how regularly he had mocked her organisation.

Now he ripped the V section from it and threw the folder on the floor. It landed in a cloud of cards, as they covered the beige carpet he had always hated. He located the card entitled 'Vet' and tossed the remainder onto the others.

Locating the out-of-hours number, he dialled it as quickly as his shaking hands would allow.

'Hello?'

'I need help!' he croaked. 'It's my dog. He's sick.'

'Calm down, sir,' the voice replied, as if this were just any normal telephone call. 'Can you tell me the symptoms?'

'Not really, no. He's just lying there, whining. That's not like him at all.'

'No lumps or bumps at all?'

'I don't think so.'

The veterinarian continued in his composed tone. 'Has he vomited at all or has he eaten anything you would consider unusual?'

'I don't see anything,' Taylor replied, his voice becoming a high-pitched squeak.

'Okay, I think I need to see him. Do you know where the clinic is?'

'Yes.'

'Get there as soon as you can. I'm on my way.'

'Okay, thanks.'

He hung up and threw the telephone on the floor, rushing up the stairs and coming to a halt on his knees next to his best friend. 'Right, buddy, we're going to get you some medicine now, but I have to pick you up, okay?'

He slid his hands under Herodotus slowly at first, but sped up when the Labrador did not protest. He staggered down the stairs, grabbing the keys from the hook as he waddled past, trying to move as quickly as possible, without dropping his faithful companion. He managed to balance his friend against his torso with one hand and use the remote to open the car, as he waddled out of the house. Once he got Herodotus in the boot, he leapt into the driver's seat. The clinic was twenty minutes away.

Nine minutes later, he skidded into the small car park and saw that the wiry frame of Dr Adams was already waiting for him.

Taylor leapt from the car and raced to the boot, struggling to open it because his hands were shaking so much. He left the doors open, staggering swiftly through the door the veterinarian was holding open for him and heading straight for the examination room.

By the time he gently laid Herodotus on the table, he could not tell if his face was wet because of sweat, or if the tears he was fighting had escaped. He wiped his eyes.

They were tears.

Dr Adams arrived next to him and started to inspect his patient by lifting the flaps of the mouth and checking the gums. 'I'm sorry, Mr Taylor, but you weren't making much sense over the 'phone. Can you try to explain the symptoms to me now, please?'

Taylor realised that his throat was parched, turning his voice to a squeak. 'I don't know what's wrong with him. He's normally so lively, but he won't even move.'

Herodotus let out an anguished cry.

'And he keeps doing that. I've never heard him make that noise before.'

Dr Adams continued to examine the Labrador, carefully feeling around the body. 'Do you know if he took a fall, perhaps? Or maybe he ate something unusual? You didn't leave any medicine lying around, or a container open, maybe?'

'I don't think so.'

A silence fell upon the room as the surgeon continued with his work, methodically feeling his way around the patient. After a few minutes, he started to concentrate on the stomach.

Taylor watched intently, his face pallid and clammy. His chest was starting to ache and his eyes felt like he had washed them with Tabasco sauce. His mind was a tumult of terrifying images. He could feel a lump of anguish in the back of his throat.

Not Herodotus!

Please!

He could not fathom what he would do without his golden-furred friend. He knew Herodotus was the main reason he had managed to survive the last one hundred and thirteen days.

They had been torture but, somehow, Herodotus had given him hope. When they were together, everything seemed slightly better.

He could not lose him.

He needed him.

Taylor watched Dr Adams carefully and it seemed that he had been examining the Labrador for hours. Taylor's head was throbbing and the pain was excruciating.

Eventually, the veterinarian looked up, a sombre, yet confounded, expression on his face. 'I can't seem to find anything wrong with him.'

He shook his fist in the air. 'What are you saying? He's not sick? Look at him! Of course he's sick!'

'Calm down, Mr Taylor. I can see he's not well, but it's not a physical problem.' He took a small torch from his pocket and checked the eyes. 'He's not responding to stimuli, though.'

'What does that mean?'

'It could be a brain-related affliction.'

'Please, help him! Please! There must be *something* you can do.' Taylor could hear the desperation in his own voice. It was at such a high pitch, he did not recognise it as his own.

Dr Adams seemed uncertain. 'Well, that would depend on diagnosing the actual illness and, then, on how advanced it is. We could do an MRI, but it's not something I would normally recommend because it's very expensive.'

Taylor felt the hope wash over him, although he still sounded prepubescent. 'That's fine! Money's not a

26

problem. You do whatever you can to save him. Whatever it takes, whatever the cost. I can't lose him!'

A little surprised, the surgeon shrugged his shoulders. 'Okay. I'll make the arrangements.' He turned and walked briskly out of the room.

Taylor looked down at Herodotus, a lethal cocktail of rage and misery welling up inside of him. This was the only creature in the world that understood how empty his life was. This Labrador was all that was left of Jane. If he died, there was nothing left of her.

He refused to exist in a world that had no remnants of Jane in it.

Herodotus closed his eyes and whimpered loudly, causing Taylor to bend over and squeeze him, burying his face in the golden fur. 'You'll be okay, buddy,' he whispered. 'You'll be okay.'

Turning his head, Taylor looked up at his companion's face. Herodotus was looking back at him through half-open eyes. Taylor felt the faint wag of a tail behind him and smiled.

Suddenly, Herodotus lurched powerfully, emanating a mixture of strident whines and guttural growls. Taylor jumped up, his heart thumping against his chest, the panic gripping his soul.

The Labrador's legs and head were jerking violently and his squeals were deafening. He seemed to be having a seizure.

'Help!' Taylor cried, diving onto Herodotus in an attempt to stop him from falling from the table.

The veterinarian rushed in. 'Don't try to restrain him!' he ordered, rushing to the cabinet on the wall. 'You'll hurt him more!'

Taylor let go and fell backwards, his horrified gaze passing between the surgeon and the canine.

Dr Adams snatched a bottle from the cabinet and jabbed a syringe into it.

Herodotus started to cover the table in urine. It quickly filled the table and started to form a waterfall as it splashed onto the floor.

Dr Adams sucked the sedative from the bottle with the syringe.

Herodotus evacuated his bowels onto the table.

Dr Adams darted over and tried to stab the needle into the Labrador's neck, slipping on the urine-covered tiles and missing the target.

Herodotus began to spit blood everywhere. It flew in every direction, spewing from his mouth in huge crimson splashes.

Taylor sobbed. A slice of pink flesh landed next to him and he recognised it as his best friend's tongue.

Blood flowed from the table, mixing with the pool of urine on the floor. Dr Adams was already rushing back to the cabinet on the wall, searching for a dose of something to stop the carnage.

Then, as suddenly as it had begun, the horror stopped. Herodotus flopped down onto the table, his eyes closed and his body limp. A last breath escaped his body.

Taylor looked up and saw his friend at peace.

The room was silent, except for the quiet plopping sound of blood dripping from the Labrador's mouth and onto the table.

Taylor could not move. He sat on the floor, his knees to his chest, and buried his head in his hands, ignoring the pool of bodily fluids creeping his way. The grief was too heavy. It held him down and gripped his heart. The tears flowed and his body convulsed with every sob.

Dr Adams cast his eyes over the macabre scene and shook his head ruefully. His eyes landed on the weeping man on the floor and he felt his heart twinge. Every once in a while, he had a patient whose passing was mourned the same way a parent would mourn a child.

He walked out of the room and towards the bathroom. He needed to wash before he could get some breakfast.

Taylor sat sobbing, rocking back and forth. His mind was a whirlwind of despair. He just wanted the darkness to consume him, but knew that, no matter how tightly he closed his eyes, daylight awaited him.

The crushing sense of loneliness filled him quickly. What would he do now? Herodotus was all that remained of her. His very personality was an imprint of her that lasted beyond her life. And now it was gone.

What would he do now?

He was truly alone.

Taylor had no idea how long he sat in a ball, sobbing quietly. People came and went, starting the unwelcome task of cleaning the room for other patients. Eventually, Dr Adams crouched down and placed his hand on Taylor's shoulder.

'I'm sorry, but we have to take him away now. I'm obliged to have him cremated immediately because we can't be certain that his disease isn't contagious. I can't put other animals at risk, Mr Taylor.'

Looking up slowly, Taylor felt the daylight burn his swollen eyes. He got to his feet and moved towards the table apprehensively. Herodotus lay there peacefully, his mouth now closed. It was as if he were sleeping.

Taylor rubbed the fur behind his ears and began to unbuckle the leather strap around his neck. As he removed the collar, he felt a resurgence of tears, so buried his face in the golden fur and said goodbye.

He walked from the room in a somnambulant trance, getting into his car and driving around.

It occurred to him that he should probably call work, but his telephone was at home. He could not go back there.

Not yet.

He drove around for most of the morning, lost in his despair. He drove down country lanes and motorways, through villages, towns and cities and he passed by his house a dozen times. It was as if he thought he could navigate his way out of his misery, as if he could reach happiness by driving at eighty miles an hour. The sun was high in the sky by the time he conceded that the distance between him and overcoming his grief was not one that could be measured in miles.

He pulled up outside his house and sat at the wheel for several minutes, trying to summon up the courage to venture inside and confront the terrible, silent emptiness. When he finally succeeded, he stormed through the front door, slamming it behind him as he stomped straight up the stairs.

His eyes stung and his vision was blurry from the incessant flow of tears, but they quickly locked onto his target.

The Magnum.

He snatched it from its bedside resting place with a grunt and spun the cylinder, placing the muzzle between his lips as he waited for the whirring to stop. He placed his finger on the trigger.

The whirring stopped and he flexed his forefinger.

The hollow click seemed louder than ever before, as if magnified by the desolation.

Taylor dropped the gun to the carpet and fell to his knees. Looking up at the ceiling, he screamed at the light fitting. 'What do you want from me?' He stood up, his fists clenched and raised above his head. 'Do you keep me alive to torment me, is that it?'

He fell onto the bed and buried his face in the pillow, letting the grief consume him.

The telephone woke him. He sat up sharply and rubbed his face confusedly. How long had he been asleep?

Stealing a glance at the radio alarm clock, realising that it was just after three in the afternoon, he reached over for his telephone and checked the number.

Nate.

'Hello, Nate,' he croaked, recalling the events of the morning and fighting back the resultant tears.

'Are you okay, Chris?'

'Herodotus died this morning.'

'Who?'

'Jane's dog.'

'Oh, shit,' Tyson replied, his voice gentle and even. If anyone else understood the significance of the late Labrador, it was Nate.

'Do you want me to come in? I know it's late, but I can still-'

'No, no!' he replied sharply. 'Take as long as you need, mate.'

'I'll probably be back tomorrow.'

'If you feel up to it. Don't worry, if not.'

'Okay, thanks.'

An uncomfortable silence seemed to increase the static on the line. After several seconds, Nate spoke softly. 'I'm so sorry, Chris. If there's anything I can do...'

'Yeah, thanks, mate.'

'I won't bother you about work. We'll see you when you're ready.'

'Thanks, Nate. I'll talk to you soon.'

Taylor ended the call and got up slowly, ambling through to the bathroom. After his shower, he decided to go for a walk in the desperate hope that it might help raise his spirits.

Putting the collar in his pocket, he took the lead from the cupboard and held it tightly in his hand as he strolled casually along the same route he took every morning.

It no longer seemed tranquil. Without company, it just seemed eerie.

He fought away the dismay by filling his head with memories, playing them over in his mind. Jane running along the path, with a tiny Herodotus chasing after her. Herodotus chasing rabbits and barking at them once they had vanished underground. Jane kissing him whilst Herodotus skipped through the copse.

The copse.

He suddenly snapped out of his reverie to realise that he was already there. Treading carefully, he made his way into the trees and took the collar from his pocket. He found the place where his best friend had last been. The spring was gone, but the ground was still slightly moist, making it easy for him to dig a hole with his fingers.

Taylor raised the collar to his lips and kissed it gently as he choked on the sadness. It was like a lump at the back of his throat that stifled his breathing. He felt the heat behind his eyes and the tears formed, dripping into the hole he had just made.

Taylor placed the collar in the ground and swept the dirt back over it. With a last, lingering look, he stood up and walked back home. Every step of the journey seemed laboured, as if the tears made his feet heavier somehow.

He was cold by the time he reached his house and could feel the tickle of a cough in his sore throat. It had been a difficult day and had drained him. He decided the best course of action was to get a good night's sleep. Had he felt hungry, he might have prepared himself something to eat, but he was too miserable to eat. He thought about how much he hated Jeremy Clarke until he fell asleep, exhausted by his rage.

When he awoke in the morning, both he and the bed sheets were drenched. For a moment, he wondered if Herodotus had spilt a glass of water, but the events of the previous day came flooding back to him and he realised that it must be sweat.

Then the shivers hit him. He felt freezing. Taylor tried to move, but every muscle was on fire. He closed his eyes and tried to sleep, but that only made his head throb. Within minutes, it felt like a mallet on either temple.

Dragging himself from the saturated bed, he crawled to the bathroom and rummaged through the medicine cabinet until he found a box of paracetamol. His throat felt like sandpaper. He downed four and at least a litre of water before crawling back to his bed.

He was asleep within seconds.

Day one hundred and fourteen: the first day he had not put the gun in his mouth.

Day one hundred and fourteen: the start of his transformation.

3

The shrill melody of Vivaldi pierced his ears and jolted him awake. Taylor reached out from the warm duvet and snatched the telephone from the bedside cabinet, pulling it under the sheets and answering it in the warmth.

Had his fingers so much as grazed the Magnum, he might have remembered it was there.

'Hello?'

'Chris, are you okay?'

He recognised Nathan's gravelly voice instantly. 'Yes, fine.' He paused and sat up sharply. 'Actually, I feel great today.'

He did. He really did.

Taylor took a moment to consider how terrific he felt. He could not recall the last time he had started the day with a sanguine feeling in his gut. It would have been months ago.

Nate let out a relieved chuckle. 'I'm glad to hear it. I was starting to get worried. Where have you been?'

He let out a loud, genuine laugh. He could not remember the last to escape his lips. 'I felt a bit rough, but I'm okay now.'

'As long as you're okay, mate. I know I said I wouldn't bother you, but it makes me nervous when I don't hear from you for a couple of days, let alone four.'

Taylor felt another unstoppable laugh erupt from inside of him. 'Nate, I spoke to you yesterday.'

He paused for several seconds. 'Chris, I last spoke to you when Herodotus died. That was Wednesday.'

'Yes, and today is Thursday.'

'No, Chris,' he replied, slowly and cautiously. 'Today is Monday.'

Taylor suddenly felt his spirits dip. 'No, it can't be.'

'Are you *sure* you're okay, mate?'

Summoning up enough composure to suppress the panic, Taylor forced out a reply as his mind whipped itself into a tornado of jumbled thoughts. 'I'm fine, Nate. Don't worry. Sorry, I've got to go. I'll call you later.'

'Make sure you do.'

Taylor dropped the telephone on the bed as he leapt out of it. He dove on the television remote control and stared at the clock on the morning news show. It took several seconds to sink in.

It *was* Monday.

What the hell had happened to the last four days?

Was he sick? He vaguely recalled feeling ill after getting home from burying the collar. Perhaps he had been delirious.

Marching out of the bedroom, he strode into the bathroom and noted the glass on the side of the sink. The pile of medicine on the floor drew his eyes next. The memory of him crawling through and taking the paracetamol filtered through to his mind.

A search around the rest of the house revealed nothing else out of place. Could he really have been asleep for four days?

He turned on the television in the kitchen and stood watching it vacantly for twenty minutes, racking his brain for another explanation. There was not one.

Perhaps he *had* been very ill. Yet he felt fine now.

Was it really possible to lose a section of your life? Was it really feasible that somebody could go to bed one night and wake up four days later with absolutely no recollection of what had happened in between?

If he thought his life was a void before today, he actually now had a segment that really was filled with nothing.

He decided that a shower might help untangle the mess of thoughts in his head. As he washed, he started to wonder if he might have slipped into a coma. The more he considered it, the clearer his memory of Thursday morning became.

He had felt awful. He had been feverish. His head was thumping. He had crawled to the bathroom, drank water and swallowed tablets, before crawling back to bed. That was all, was it not? Nothing else.

Had he been out and about, living and breathing, but with no memory of it?

No. There would be some evidence. He would have tidied up the mess in the bathroom. He would have put the glass back. Something, anything else, would be out of place.

Stepping from the shower, he walked past the mirror and caught a glimpse of his reflection through the misty glass. He held his breath and moved back a step, not daring to believe what he had seen.

Being ill seemed to agree with him. He looked trim and muscular. His body had not looked like that since his early twenties, perhaps not even then. He had not gone back in time. His illness, whatever it was, had stripped the body fat from him.

He flexed his arms and admired the taut biceps. He contracted his stomach and watched all eight of the fleshy tiles appear in his abdomen. He had never been so defined.

He must have been very ill. That was the only explanation he could conjure for such a dramatic change in appearance. Perhaps his eyes weren't working properly. Or, more likely, his mind.

Smiling to himself, he spent several more minutes enjoying the view before deciding to get dressed and eat some breakfast. As poured his cornflakes, he silently vowed to return to the gym and sustain this, somewhat fortuitous, side effect of this alarming turn of events.

He had lost four days. The evidence was irrefutable.

Taylor half-concentrated on the news as he ruminated about his situation. He could so easily have died. There was nobody here to call an ambulance, nobody to check that he was still alive. He was no expert, but he imagined that any illness that could render him unconscious for four days was potent enough to take his life.

He was lucky, really. For the first time in months, something had gone his way.

And another peril of his loneliness became clear to him.

He knew the only reason Nate had not checked on him earlier was because Herodotus had died and he knew Taylor well enough to leave him alone to deal with the pain. But that could have killed him had this mystery illness been slightly more virulent.

But it was not.

As it transpired, he felt incredible. The fog had lifted from his mind and his thoughts were crisp and clear in a way he had forgotten they could be. Plus, he looked great. He had always wanted to look that good.

He was lost in his thoughts when it happened. Shovelling the cornflakes into his mouth, with his eyes fixed on the television, but his mind trying to locate fresh memories from the past four days, he bit down on the spoon accidentally.

And it bent.

Taylor had misjudged enough bites to know that this one should have hurt, perhaps even chipped his tooth. He took it back out of his mouth and examined it, shocked at what he found.

There were several dents in the metal. Tooth marks.

He ran his thumb around the spoon. It was definitely steel. Putting down his bowl, he ran his fingers over the dents several times before repeating the motion with his nail.

How had he managed to do that?

He put the spoon on the breakfast bar and opened the drawer. Carefully removing another spoon, he inspected it carefully, twisting it around in the light to be certain that it did not contain any blemishes or weaknesses.

Then he put it in his mouth and bit down.

He could feel the steel give way to the sharp bone. Removing it from his mouth, he eyed the arced row of dents suspiciously, noting how the concave curve of the spoon was now indented with a ridge, following the line of the tooth marks.

He turned it over several times, scrutinising it from every angle.

How had he managed to do that? Was the cutlery defective? If it was, why had he not noticed it before?

Maybe it was different cutlery. Had one of his forgotten tasks, undertaken in the past four days, been to replace all the cutlery?

It looked the same. This set was a wedding present and, whilst an exact replica may have been difficult to find, it must be possible.

Yet, if he *had* done that, why could he not remember it?

He did not know a great deal about the subconscious, and how or why it repressed memories, but it seemed logical to him that, of all the traumatic events in his life over the last few months, buying new cutlery was not near the top of the list.

He carefully gripped the spoon between his forefinger and his thumb. He squeezed. The steel bent over so the handle and tip of the spoon were now touching.

And it was effortless for him.

Taylor gasped and tossed the spoon on the breakfast bar in disgust, staring at it with incredulity for several minutes.

What was going on?

40

Composing himself, he feverishly thrust his hand into the cutlery drawer, bending spoons, forks and knives with the same level of ease. He ruined sixteen before he realised that they were all from the same set. If these were defective, then surely the others would be, also.

Slamming the drawer shut, trying to suppress the panic welling up inside of him, he scanned the kitchen desperately for something else to test him. His eyes locked on to the microwave.

He was next to it with two strides and he slipped the fingers of one hand under it. Inhaling deeply, he raised it several inches. Again, it was absurdly and inexplicably simple to lift.

The shock gripped him and he dropped it with a loud crash. He jumped backwards, his wide eyes glued to the metal, rectangular cuboid and his mouth gaping.

He looked down at his hands, turning them over several times, as if the answer might be written on them somewhere. He clenched both fists and flexed his arms. His muscles were doubtlessly a little larger and much more defined, but that would not explain his sudden strength.

Powering back up the stairs, he whipped his tee shirt off and studied the reflection again. His previous admiration had not done him justice. There was not an ounce of body fat on his torso. The striations and bulges of muscle covered every inch of his entire body. He looked like a bodybuilder, yet he had not lifted a weight in months. He walked through to the bathroom and stepped on the digital scales.

He was fourteen and a half stone. He was not entirely certain what his weight had been before, but he conservatively estimated that he was a stone heavier than four days ago. That was over six kilograms. And it all seemed to be muscle mass.

He ran back down to the kitchen, as he decided to attempt something more challenging. Bending down next to the cooker, he lifted it with one hand. He barely had to strain. He dropped it with a deafening crash.

It did not matter how much time anyone spent in the gym, or what they could bench-press, nobody could lift that weight so effortlessly.

What had happened to him? Why was he so strong? How could he have lost four days and woken up stronger than ever before?

Slipping a fresh tee shirt over his head, he darted out of the house with one question in his head: how much could he lift?

He leapt in the car and raced to the quarry where he and Jane had enjoyed many days hiking. It was several miles from anywhere and there were no other cars parked nearby. He sat and looked over the quarry, primed for any sign of movement.

Nobody had worked in the quarry for at least a decade. It was a huge hole in the ground, with trees and shrubs dotted around the crest. The pit itself sloped down to the centre, where a small pool had formed with years of rainwater, with rocks and boulders randomly strewn across the ground.

Taylor had spent hours appreciating the remote serenity in the past, with the rich variety of wildlife and the kaleidoscopic array of blooming flowers against the backdrop of grey, orange, red and yellow rocks. Yet, today, he did not stop to enjoy any of that natural beauty.

Today he focused only on the rocks. He stopped counting at forty, but there were more than enough, in a variety of shapes and sizes, to test his newfound brawn.

He watched the quarry for half an hour and, once satisfied that he was alone, he found the small track and made his way down into the pit. The first rock he came to was about half the size of him. He looked at it for several minutes, studying it carefully.

It was oval-shaped and a mixture of light grey, white and beige in colour. He stroked the uneven surface, feeling the grit coming away under his fingertips. He guessed it was around the same size as the washing machine in his kitchen.

And far heavier than anything he could expect to lift alone.

Moving so he was directly in front of it, he bent his knees and placed his palms on opposing ends of the underside of the rock, digging his nails into the crumbling surface to secure his grip. He straightened his back and flexed his arms, feeling every sinew tighten as he tried to judge the correct amount of tension he needed to pick the rock up. His toes scraped on the ground as he tried to push himself up with his legs.

To his surprise, he shot upwards, his legs driving him upright with such speed that he could not keep his grip. The rock tumbled out of his hands and rolled onto the ground in front of him.

Pulling his feet backwards, as the rock landed with a dull thud, he gaped at it in disbelief. It had been no more difficult to lift than if it had been made of polystyrene.

Taylor moved to a slightly larger rock. This time he was more prepared, however, and managed to lift it steadily, without almost dropping it on his feet. This one had almost required a bit of effort.

He moved around the quarry, constantly scanning the area to ensure he remained alone, picking up boulders of an ever-increasing size. It was not until he began lifting huge rocks, which must have weighed several tonnes, that he began to struggle.

Noticing the bright sun high in the sky, he wiped his brow on his tee shirt and checked his watch. It was already almost noon.

Strangely, that revelation troubled him almost as much as the fact he was able to lift boulders that only a crane should be able to move. It also bothered him far less than the realisation that he had barely thought about Jane or Herodotus so far this morning.

What had happened to him? How was any of this possible? Was he even awake? He pinched his arm to be certain.

He sat down on the boulder that had been a struggle to pick up and looked around the quarry. Without ripping chunks from the quarry wall, there was nothing larger to test himself against.

Taylor looked down at the rock he sat atop of, guessing he was at least eight feet from the ground. It must weigh the same as a truck, he thought to himself.

Could this be real? There were many fantastic tales in the world, but he had never heard of anyone being able to lift a truck clear off the ground.

It did not make any sense. Something had changed him and he could only imagine that it had occurred in the last four days.

Of which he could only remember a few, blurry minutes.

One thing he was convinced of was that fact that he did not have the answers to the multitude of questions swirling around in his head.

He needed to talk to someone, but he knew he had to be careful about who that was.

If everyone found out about him, he knew he would become the object of frenzied attention, from the press and scientific community alike. They might even subject him to the sort of horrific tests that he saw on television and read about in books.

He could not stomach that. He would normally talk to Nate, but he knew Nate would call San, who might be professionally obligated to alert the authorities. They would not act out of malice, but rather because their nature was to worry about him, even if it was a tad misguided sometimes.

There was only one person he could think of who might understand whilst, at the same time, respecting his wish for secrecy.

When Tim opened the door, his haggard appearance shocked Taylor to the point where he stole a glance at the house to be sure he had the right one.

Tim Bulling had lived in the same red-bricked, terraced house for years. The weeds in the front yard had grown so much that the patio was barely visible and the fence looked more battered than usual, but it was certainly the correct house.

It was Tim.

Tim had once been as tall and broad as Taylor, but had become hunched in the five years since they turned thirty, at which point his waist had begun to expand and soften. His mane of dark hair, no longer impeccably groomed, was dishevelled these days, with random curls springing out in every direction, and the bright, green eyes were dull. The handsome features that were once the envy of everyone in the school rugby team had become sallow and weathered. It seemed that he had not shaved in several days, his stubble showing tiny streaks of silver. Even his teeth were turning yellow, afflicted by stains left by too many cups of coffee and rolled cigarettes.

Taylor briefly wondered if his bachelor lifestyle was still his choice, or if it had become enforced. Tim's blog had become more vehemently anti-government over the past, few years and, even though Tim took great care to keep it anonymous, his closest friends were starting to avoid inviting him to events after reading some of the more anarchistic posts.

'Chris?' It took Tim several moments to recognise the man on his doorstep. 'What the hell are you doing here? Are you okay?' His initial expression of shock quickly transformed to worry.

'Don't I look okay?' he returned with a smile.

Tim opened the door fully and gestured him inside. 'You look fantastic. That's what worries me.'

Taylor walked inside, following the small hallway towards the kitchen, treading over and around the clothes and shoes in his path. 'Don't ever let it be said that you're not charming.'

Tim closed the door and walked behind him. 'You didn't answer the question, mate.'

Taylor reached the small kitchen/diner and looked around. There were open tins and boxes all over the counter, with dirty plates, dishes and cutlery stacked up in the sink. The small dining area housed only a table and four chairs, buried under papers and books. The only slight space was where his laptop sat open. The faint aroma of marijuana tickled his nostrils.

'How's the writing going?' Chris asked, sensing that he already knew the answer.

'I've got some manuscripts out, and I have a few sponsors on the blog and the website, so we'll see how it goes,' he replied in a perfunctory tone. 'I'm pretty optimistic. You want a cup of tea?'

'What sponsors?'

'Don't worry, those Nazi guys won't fool me a second time. You want a cup of tea, or not?'

Taylor nodded, so Tim filled the kettle, flicked the button and then set about finding a couple of mugs in the sink, which he rinsed out. 'Why are you here, mate?'

A little surprised by the directness of the question, Taylor watched his host locate a couple of tea bags before he answered. 'Can't I just visit my best friend?'

Tim laughed sardonically. 'I've seen you twice since the funeral, bud. You've become a hermit.'

'Sorry, but we still text and I should say thanks for all the late-night chats' he replied, with a nod. 'It's just been a tough time lately.'

They both fell quiet and Tim smiled, conveying his pleasure to see his friend with a knowing look. The kettle switch clicked off and he made the tea. 'So, are you going to explain why you look so good? I would've expected you to look like crap.'

Taylor laughed. 'There's that famous charm again.'

Tim proffered the steaming mug of weak tea. 'You didn't come here to give me compliments, mate. After what you've been through, you can't just waltz in here, looking like a million pounds, and expect me not to raise an eyebrow.'

'You're just jealous because you look like you slept in your clothes.'

Tim grinned. 'I *did* sleep in them. More importantly, though, you're here for a reason and, although I don't know what it is, I'd be willing to bet a book deal that it's got something to do with the fact you look like you've been sleeping in anti-aging cream and had peck implants.'

Taylor took a sip of his tea as he chuckled, almost firing it back out through his nose. 'You really *do* have a way with words, mate. You should think about writing a book, or something.'

Tim was no longer smiling, his grave countenance piercing his guest. 'What's going on, Chris?'

Taylor put the mug on the sideboard and looked around the room. 'It's probably easier if I just show you.' His eyes met the table, mostly hidden by the mountain of papers and books, and he walked over to it. Crouching down, he gripped the nearest table leg.

His eyes met Tim's, who did not bother to hide his bemusement, and then Taylor stood up, raising the table with him.

Papers and books slipped onto the wooden floor by the dozen, but Tim did not seem to care. His jaw dropped and the tea dribbled from it onto his creased, grimy plaid shirt but, other than that, he was frozen.

Taylor smirked, recalling his own reaction, and heard the wood starting to creak loudly. Afraid it was about to snap, he carefully placed the table back on the floor.

'Holy fu-' Tim began, his voice failing him.

'I know.'

'How did you do that?'

'I've no idea,' Taylor replied, shrugging his shoulders. 'I woke up this morning to discover I was incredibly strong.'

Tim grinned mischievously. 'Can you do it again?'

He did so and Tim began to chuckle excitedly, unconcerned about the increasing piles of paper, books and magazines on the floor. 'That is awesome, mate! What else can you lift?' His voice had become loud and squeaky.

'I'm not sure what my limit is, but I went down to the old quarry and was lifting some pretty huge boulders.'

'Boulders, huh?' Tim replied with a thrilled grin creasing his lips. 'What about cars?'

Taylor shrugged his shoulders nonchalantly. 'Probably, but that's not the point, is it? Why am I so strong? How did it happen?'

'Who cares? This is a gift, mate. It's about time something good happened for you. Nate told me about Herodotus.'

A sullen shadow fell upon his face. 'Are you so sure it's a gift?'

'Of course!' he returned joyously. 'Every boy dreams of being Superman. You actually are!'

Taylor laughed nervously. 'Well, I can't fly.'

'Maybe you should just enjoy it, rather than worry about it.'

'It's not that simple, Tim. Something's happened to me. I got sick and slept through the last four days. I can't remember anything.'

'That's when this happened, is it?'

'It must've been.'

Tim paused, suddenly less jubilant. 'You lost four days? Without doing drugs?'

'And I think I was really ill,' he replied with a nod. 'I'm worried there might be something seriously wrong with me.'

'You should go and speak to San.'

'I don't know,' Taylor said hesitantly.

'Why not? It's San.'

'I don't want this getting out, Tim. You know what he's like. He'll refer it if he finds anything amiss. He might have to by law, or something. And you know San.'

Tim glowered at him. 'Hey, it's San. You can trust him.'

'What if there's something seriously wrong?'

He let a mollifying grin cover his face. 'You're over-thinking it, as usual. If you were ill, you'd feel ill. As wonderful as this is, it's very weird. If you're worried about it, go and see a professional. San's nothing, if not professional. He'll know what to do.'

Taylor paused and gave his friend a sombre look. 'Tim?'

'Yes, mate?'

'You'll keep this between us, won't you?'

'Of course, mate.'

'You know, just in case.'

'Just in case of what?' Tim asked, confused.

'I don't know yet. I just get the sense this isn't the miraculous gift you think it is.'

4

Taylor looked around the office and sighed. If only his co-workers would treat him as normal. The perfunctory platitudes were starting to wear down his patience. They were so careful not to say the wrong thing. It made him feel as if his grief actually drained the joy from the room.

He found himself longing for an inflammatory remark. Even a joke or an observation. That would do. Anything to suggest he was still part of the human race. The irony of it was that, by trying to be considerate, these people made him feel more ostracised than ever before. Of all the negative effects his tragedy had on his life, he had never expected to become a social pariah. At the time when he most needed to be part of the team, he felt like an outcast.

The fact he found himself glancing at the clock every few minutes only heightened his querulous disposition.

Two hours and twelve minutes before his appointment with San.

He noticed the people filtering out of the office and towards the boardroom, which jogged his memory to attend a meeting about summer staffing levels. He took his photocopies of the annual forecast and made his way through with the others.

The meeting lasted an hour and seventeen minutes. That was the only part of it that he paid attention to. If anyone asked him about the decisions made, he would have no idea. If he was honest, he did not care much, either.

When he returned to his desk, the first thing he noticed was that his bottle of water was missing.

'Has anyone taken my water?' he asked, at such a volume that it made those closest to him jump.

The entire office stopped and everyone met him with blank looks.

He repeated the question. This time, however, he shouted it, as he felt the heat of rage behind his eyes, although he could not understand *why* he was so angry.

The others in the office exchanged vacant expressions amongst themselves. Nobody offered an answer.

When Taylor asked the question for the third time, he hollered it. His voice was so loud, it hurt his throat.

His colleagues' faces changed. They were no longer blank. They were utterly confounded.

The commotion drew Nate from his office. He stood in the doorway and met his friend with a steely glower. 'What's going on out here?'

Taylor turned towards him, so irate that spittle flew from his mouth when he spoke. 'Somebody stole my water!' he yelled. 'I want to know who it was!'

Nate furrowed his brow. 'So what? Why don't you just get another from the 'fridge?'

'I want mine!' Taylor was perfectly aware of how he sounded like a brat having a tantrum, but he did not care.

Nate walked to the refrigerator in the corner and took a bottle of Volvic from it. He then walked over to Taylor and tried to hand it to him.

Taylor swiped it from his hand viciously, crashing it against the wall. 'No! I want my bottle and I want to know who took it!'

Nate took a step back, his face contorted with confusion. 'Calm down, Chris! It's just a bottle of water.'

'Exactly!' he retorted, the vitriol clear in his eyes. 'Why steal *mine*? There's a 'fridge full of them there!' He thrust his hand out, pointing at the corner of the room.

'Are you okay?' he asked softly, placing his hand on his friend's shoulder.

Taylor slapped it away angrily, before shoving his friend in the chest. 'No!'

Nate flew backwards, colliding with the filing cabinet with a loud, metallic thud. He let out a pained grunt before sliding to the floor.

As he landed on all fours, he whimpered loudly. His anguished wail seemed to snap Taylor out of his rage. Suddenly, he realised what he had just done and who he had done it to.

Taylor rushed to his friend's side. 'Oh, shit! Nate, I'm so sorry! Are you okay?'

The manager was struggling to breathe. Taylor helped him to his feet and to the nearest chair. 'Just breathe, Nate. One breath at a time, mate. You're winded, that's all.'

Taylor knew that might be a lie. With his sudden robustness, there was no telling what damage he could have done. He had not even hit Nate hard. He was grateful for the small amount of restraint he did manage to show.

He could feel the eyes on him and looked up. Everyone watched him, their faces frozen in astonishment. Nobody dared say a word. The only sound in the office was that of the manager's wheezing.

After a couple of minutes, Nate was breathing normally, although he winced in pain as he stood up. 'Jesus, Chris, you don't know your own strength!'

'I'm so sorry!' he said, the compunction on his face and in his tone. 'Are you okay?'

'No, I'm not okay!' he bellowed, his eyes ablaze. 'You've crossed the line! Get your arse home and seriously ponder whether, or not, you're in the right frame of mind to continue working here.'

'Nate, I--'

He held up his hand to halt the protest. 'No, Chris! You're not ready to be back and it's clear you should seek some help before you are. Go home. I'll get H.R. to get some names for you. They'll be in touch.'

He hung his head in shame. 'I don't know what to say.'

'Don't say anything,' he replied, lowering his voice. 'Just go home and don't come back until you've sorted your head out.'

Taylor looked around the room. For the first time in one hundred and eighteen days, he did not see pathos in their eyes. He saw confusion. He saw anger.

He saw fear.

He shuffled out of the door and made his way to his car.

Nate watched him drive out of the car park from the window in his office. He looked down at the half-empty bottle of Volvic in his hand, that had once been his friend's, and shook his head as he put it to his lips and tipped the bottle up.

Taylor did not go home. He drove straight to San's clinic and sat in the waiting room, ruminating. He played the events out in his mind, allowing the memory to stew, turning it over and over until the ire returned as a dull heat behind his eyes. He could feel the anger polluting his soul.

What was wrong with him?

By the time his name flashed up on the board, his acrimonious ponderings had engulfed him, to the point where the receptionist had to urge him to attend his appointment.

Sanjip Namib was one of the few friends Taylor had who had never been interested in rugby. Indian people played cricket, he had once explained matter-of-factly. They played cricket, worked hard and loved their family.

Taylor vaguely remembered San from when they were children, growing up on the same street. The Indian was thirteen years Taylor's senior, so they had not been friends back then, but Taylor vividly recalled the fact that they were about the same height by the time he was ten. San had been a keen follower of local rugby and that had, inevitably, led him to Nate, Tim and Taylor.

By that time, San was almost a doctor. He was also just as short and rotund as he had been as a teenager. And still was today.

Taylor found himself strangely intrigued by San's thick, black hair. He swept it into a side-parting every

56

morning, just as he had every morning from the age of fifteen. He was also an unfeasibly hairy man.

He had to shave twice a day and had even managed to grow thick hair on his knuckles. Taylor had seen him in a vest top and his skin was almost imperceptible beneath the hirsute exterior. Indeed, when they had been to the beach together, it was difficult to tell if he was topless or wearing a black, wool jumper.

Walking into the dusty office, redolent of an old antique shop, he sat down in the chair opposite his friend and looked around. The desk, chairs and examination area were all comprised of dark wood furniture, which combined with the dark brown carpet and burgundy walls to make the room seem much darker than it actually was. 'Alright, San?'

The diminutive Indian gave him a quizzical look. 'I'm good, thanks. How are you?'

'I'm good. Great, actually.'

San raised his eyebrows curiously. 'You'll have good days and bad days. It's important to focus on the good ones and remember why you thought they were better than the others.'

'Sage advice, San, but that's not why I'm here.'

The doctor sat up sharply. 'Really? Is something the matter?'

'I have to show you something?'

This clearly piqued his interest and he leaned forwards with a look that suggested consternation for his friend, tapered by the zeal for something a little different to colds and gout. 'Okay. Go on, then.'

Taylor smiled softly. 'Don't be afraid, San. Just go with it, okay?'

'Okay,' he replied, the confusion etched in the creases around his eyes. He sat back and waited patiently.

Taylor stood up and walked over to him. Bending down, he reached out with one hand and picked up San's chair with the Indian still in it.

The doctor gripped the armrests, his eyes wide and his mouth open, as his friend held him aloft for several seconds, before carefully placing him back at his desk. He then calmly walked back to his seat and plonked himself in it.

San did not say anything for a while. Instead, he cast his friend a bewildered glare. Taylor thought he could actually hear his friend's scientific mind whirring, trying to conjure an explanation for what had just happened.

Taylor smiled awkwardly, held his hands out and shrugged his shoulders.

'How did you-?'

'I've got no idea,' Taylor interrupted. 'All I can tell you is that I got sick, fell asleep for four days and woke up as He-Man.'

The doctor shook his head, trying to clear the fog. 'You were asleep for four days? Are you sure?'

'Well, I don't remember any of it. I recall feeling a bit rough and going to bed on Wednesday night. I have a vague recollection of waking up and taking some paracetamol at some point. Other than that, I simply woke up yesterday morning capable of bench-pressing cars.'

'That's a bad sign, you know?'

Taylor rolled his eyes and smiled. 'I guessed as much, mate, which is why I'm here. Can you explain any of this?'

'A four-day fever? Well, that's perfectly feasible, but I would expect a longer recovery period than just a few hours. Do you feel dehydrated at all?'

'I was a bit thirsty when I first woke up, but I feel fine now. If anything, I feel better than I have in a very long time.'

San sat back in his chair and rubbed the thick stubble on his chin. He shook his head fervently. 'No, that doesn't make any kind of sense. Do you have any kind of medicine in your system at all?'

'Just paracetamol. That wouldn't explain the strength, though.' He was pleased that the doctor was handling the news with apparent calm.

San exhaled loudly. 'Nothing explains that, Chris. There have been many recorded incidents of terrific strength, but they're usually associated with a more extreme, moribund situation.'

'How does that affect it?' Taylor asked, perplexed, yet intrigued.

'Well, you must have heard about the woman who lifted a car because her child was trapped under it. It's not just an urban legend. It was caused by a surge in epinephrine, the body's reaction to an extreme situation.'

'But I'm not in an extreme situation.'

'I realise that, Chris,' he riposted swiftly. 'But I'm afraid there isn't any medical evidence to explain superhuman strength. You could be experiencing an elevated level of epinephrine as a reaction to an infection, or some other kind of illness. I don't know. All I can do is take some blood and test it. Then we'll see if that shows us what made you ill. It might give us a starting point for our inquiry.'

'How long will that take?'

'If I call in some favours, I can probably get the results back tomorrow.'

Taylor sighed. 'What should I do until then?'

San smiled comfortingly. 'You should enjoy it. I'm almost certain that it's just a temporary thing.'

Taylor left the clinic a few minutes later, with those words rattling around in his mind. If this was a temporary situation, he felt that he should make the most of it.

He grinned to himself as he realised that there was only one thing he would use his strength for.

And that one thing was called Jeremy Clarke.

5

Taylor pulled his collar up to keep the chill from his neck and stuffed his hands back in his pockets.

The cold swept in with the darkness and he was not properly dressed for it, in a thin, white tee shirt and beige summer jacket. He was tempted to head home and give up on his quest, but his curiosity drove him on, as he made his third tour of the town centre.

He tried to clear his head and enjoy the crisp, night air, but there were too many thoughts swirling around for him to suppress. What was happening to him was the stuff of fantasy. It did not happen in real life, did it?

Well, he was living proof that it did.

He could not shake the feeling, though, that San's optimistic outlook was for his benefit. The theory that this was some kind of side effect from his body's reaction to a mystery illness seemed fanciful. It was more likely, considering his luck, that he had an exotic, but deadly, disease.

That was more like it.

Taylor had considered dying many times recently, but this was not how he imagined it. He quite liked the drama of the Magnum, even if Destiny was determined to keep him around.

Maybe this was why.

He found it curious that every time the hollow click had sounded in the morning, he felt a little relieved that he was not going to leave Herodotus alone yet, since the

Labrador had died, he had only tested Destiny's resolve once, later that same day.

In truth, he had been too preoccupied. It had not even crossed his mind.

Perhaps that was the first stage in dealing with the tragedy. Maybe he was moving on.

Not that he minded dying. It did not scare him. As long as Jane and Herodotus were waiting for him.

The more he considered it, the more he succumbed to Tim's theory. This might just be a gift from God, or whoever. Presumably, whatever power had chosen to bestow this upon him, there was a reason for it. He doubted this gift was an act of charity.

They wanted him to use it for something.

For one hundred and thirteen days in a row, he had placed a gun in his mouth, spun the cylinder and pulled the trigger. Every day the odds were one in six that it would be his last. He did not know the odds of his continued survival, but he knew there must be a higher power at work.

This *must* be the reason he was still alive, the reason for his pain.

It was all a test.

Taylor had never put much faith in higher powers, but he was starting to reconsider his philosophy. He found some comfort in thinking that God took his loved ones for a reason. If it was preordained then, somehow, it was not as terrible.

He had often contemplated exactly why this made him feel better. He suspected he drew some comfort from believing that there was some order in the chaos. It was as if this meant that the universe was not such a cruel, unforgiving and merciless place.

Taylor knew that he did not want to live in a place where anarchy reigned supreme. He did not want to exist in a universe where terrible things could happen to anyone, regardless of their character. It did not matter if you were kind or evil, good and bad luck were not rewards or punishments. They were at the mercy of chance.

Life was a roulette wheel.

Yet, he was starting to think that this might not be the case. If there was a higher power at work, and they had a purpose for him, everything made some kind of sense. Maybe whatever he needed to do was immense and he needed to be alone to do it.

Maybe whoever, or whatever, was pulling the strings had taken Jane and Herodotus to a better place and had now given him this gift. But, why?

There had to be an explanation and, where this would have troubled him normally, he found that he had faith that the answer would present itself.

Faith.

An alien concept to him just a few weeks ago.

But he had pulled that trigger one hundred and thirteen mornings in a row and was still here. There had to be a reason for that.

He wanted the reason to be Jeremy Clarke. Surely, though, the universe had bigger problems than one scumbag.

Even if it did, however, that did not stop him from enjoying his gift. After all, he had earned the right to do a little something for himself.

And for Jane.

Besides, what if San was right and this was a temporary gift?

This was an opportunity he dare not waste. First, however, he needed to test it.

Suddenly, raised voices snapped him from his reverie.

He needed several seconds to recognise his location. He was slightly outside the town centre, down a side street that led from the main shopping district to a small collection of pubs and restaurants. The buildings were high and the road was poorly lit, making it seem quite imposing, although he had walked down here hundreds of times alone at night and never once felt threatened. The aroma of a dozen different ethnic cuisines wafted down the street, making him feel hungry even when he knew he was not.

Tonight, though, there was an uncomfortable, almost eerie, chill in the air. His eyes strained to discern the source of the cacophony. There were five, young men haranguing a young woman. Their voices carried down the street with clarity and he could hear the slurring associated with severe inebriation.

'Alright, luv?'

'Want to come and party with us?'

'Don't be rude, luv.'

'We can have a good time.'

The girl was alone and could not have been much older than nineteen or twenty. She shuffled away from them hurriedly, but they followed close behind. When ignoring them did not work, she asked them to leave her alone. Then she tried to make her escape, but they chased her. After a few seconds, she started shouting at them and broke into a run. By this time, Taylor could see her face. She was terrified. The tears were already flowing down her cheeks.

Suddenly, the reason for his gift became clear to him. Witnessing this made him angry. He could feel the knots in his stomach and the muscles in his neck felt like they had frozen stiff.

Yet, in his mind, he felt a surge of peace. His thoughts contained a clarity that he had not experienced in months. Years, maybe.

The world started to make sense again.

His life, his existence, made sense again.

Taylor stormed over towards the group of young men. Each stride felt full of power. He could feel the strength in his veins. He could feel the force behind his eyes. He was ready to use this gift.

He was ready to embrace his reason for living.

His divine quest.

He marched across the road, his arms pumping at his side, his hands clenched into fists. 'Hey, lads!'

They had not noticed him until this point, despite the fact he had deliberately stomped his feet as loudly as possible. One of them stopped and looked, and then the others mirrored him. They fell silent as their profane badgering stopped at Taylor's presence.

The young girl glanced at him gratefully as she hurried past and away into the night.

Taylor had successfully diverted their attention towards him and it caused a strange, warm glow inside of him. He expected to feel afraid or, at the very least, intimidated.

Yet, he was ebullient with a sense of confidence that was unfamiliar to him. Indeed, no matter what happened, victory was already his. The young woman was scuttling away to safety behind him, so Taylor had achieved his goal.

What happened next was irrelevant.

His gift had given him the confidence to intervene and, perhaps, save a young woman from something very unsavoury.

He had not felt this good since Jane had passed away.

He studied the faces of the five men before him and guessed they were around seventeen years old. Only one of them was even close to his size, yet they looked at him with disdain in their eyes.

Taylor smirked. He had also been arrogant at that age. Invincibility was a delusion reserved for the young.

They studied him, no longer offering expletives, but examining their inchoate foe with curious eyes. He was an entirely different prospect to a defenceless young girl. They spread out slightly and started to engulf him. Once they had all assumed their enfilade positions, the largest of the group chose to address him.

He was a bit taller than Taylor, but not as broad. He had an acne problem and crooked teeth. His shaven head was almost egg-shaped. 'What's your problem, mate?'

Taylor controlled his nerves, forcing his voice to sound flat and even. 'I just wondered if you fancied bothering me, instead of that poor girl.'

He sneered. 'We're just having a laugh, mate.'

'It didn't sound very funny to me,' he retorted swiftly.

'Maybe you ain't got a sense of humour,' he answered, his tone querulous.

'Or maybe you guys should try talking to girls instead of harassing them.'

The skinhead paused for a moment, the brain churning behind his frigid eyes, searching for a witty riposte. When he failed, he spat on the ground, only inches from Taylor's shoe. 'Maybe you should mind your business.'

'It's odd, isn't it?' he asked with a chuckle.

'What is?'

'How you're not talking to me the way you were talking to her. Are you afraid of me?'

'No, I ain't!' he returned instantly. 'I'll take your head off, old man.'

Taylor laughed loudly. 'Will you, indeed? Go on, then.'

The young man paused and stared at him blankly. 'What?'

'Take my head off,' Taylor replied in a sardonic tone. 'I dare you.'

'I don't want to hurt you, old man.'

'You won't.'

'You're an old fella.'

Taylor laughed and cricked his neck. The sound of his bones cracking together echoed down the street. 'I'm young enough to teach you boys a lesson in manners. Take a swing, if you've got the balls.'

One of the smaller men grabbed the skinhead's arm. 'Come on, Gaz. Just leave it, yeah?'

Gaz yanked his arm away viciously. 'Hold on, Dev! This bloke thinks we're cowards.' His cold glare bored into Taylor. 'Don't you, mate?'

Taylor indicated the other four, young men with a sweep of his arm. 'Looks to me like they follow your lead, son. That would make *you* the coward, I guess.'

Dev exhaled sharply and muttered under his breath. 'Oh, shit. Please shut your mouth, mate.'

Gaz ignored his friend. 'You think *I'm* a coward?'

Taylor smirked. 'Why else would you pick on girls?'

'I'm not afraid of you,' he replied with a sneer.

Taylor could see that his opponent had clenched his fists tightly. 'Of course you're not, but that's because you're either arrogant or stupid. Which one is it?'

'You're starting to wind me up, pal.'

'Just starting?' he retorted quickly, chuckling. 'I've been trying really hard, too.'

'You want to fight me?' Gaz asked through gritted teeth.

'Would it just be you?'

He smirked. 'Probably not.'

'I'll tell you what *I* want,' Taylor returned tersely. 'I want you to apologise to that girl for what you just put her through.'

'We were just messing! Anyway, she's already gone.'

'So apologise to me instead.'

68

Gaz chortled sardonically and turned his head away to look at one of his cohorts. Then he spun back, stepping forwards and swinging his fist around as he did so.

The punch caught Taylor by surprise and crashed onto his chin. Taylor staggered backwards a step, but noted that the blow had not physically hurt him.

He was dazed, however, stunned by the speed of the unexpected attacked. Gaz waded in with several more punches, connecting with a few before Taylor managed to get his hands up to act as a shield.

Gaz kept going, pushing forwards and kicking out at Taylor's stomach. Taylor caught his foot and pushed him backwards. Gaz flew back and landed on the ground, several metres away.

Seeing his friend dumped on the cold concrete, one of the other young men jumped in, hurling a fist in Taylor's direction. It struck on the shoulder ineffectually. Taylor barely even noticed it. Had it not been for the blur of movement in his peripheral vision, he might never have noticed it. It was no more painful than if a butterfly had just flown into him.

Taylor spun and jabbed out his fist. It was a reflex, with little direction and even less force. He felt his knuckles crunch into the ribs and heard a yelp as several cracked. The young man collapsed to the ground in a heap.

Gaz was getting to his feet, as the remaining three friends spent a moment studying the prone form of their companion. They exchanged a look and silently agreed on a course of action.

All three pounced in unison, like a trio of cumbersome cats. Taylor held the palm of his hand out on front of him and Dev leapt into it with a thud. Taylor's arm barely moved. He had not even needed to lock the elbow joint. It should have buckled under the weight of the body that landed on it. Yet, it did not.

Dev's solar plexus connected with the heel of his hand and the young man's jump simply stopped in mid-air, his own momentum making the blow a powerful one. He fell to the ground with a pained wail.

The other two were in flanking positions and their attacks arrived within a second of each other. The fists landed on either side of Taylor's face, one near his temple, the other on his cheek.

Taylor felt these blows. But only just. His entire face should have exploded with pain. Yet the flying punches felt about as uncomfortable as a playful nudge. His head should have been thrown about, whipping his neck in one direction, then the other, but it barely moved.

He tossed both fists out in opposite directions. They were weak attempts at a defence, barely glancing the intended recipients. The young men screamed in agony as one set of knuckles brushed a jaw and the other flicked past a kidney.

They both dropped to the ground, in almost identically prostrate positions, burying their faces and muffling their wails.

Gaz looked at the trail of suffering and let out a roar, charging at Taylor with wild eyes and a flurry of fists. Taylor raised his hands to cover his face instinctively, deflecting several blows before his adversary changed his trajectory of attack.

The punches landed in his abdomen, kidneys, liver and chest. Taylor knew they had struck him, but there was no pain. There was a faint disturbance of his flesh, but no shooting agony. He could see Gaz's face, contorted with rage, through his arms. He could see the effort his foe was thrusting into every blow. Gaz was squeezing every ounce of strength he had into his attack.

Taylor spent a moment in shock. Gaz was probably not as powerful as he was a few days ago, but he was certainly formidable enough to cause damage with such a concentrated offensive. He dropped his arms, which Gaz noted swiftly, moving his strikes up to Taylor's face. His head moved a few inches with each blow, but there was still no pain. More intriguingly, there did not seem to be any damage.

He looked at Gaz, starting to falter under the effort of his attack, and saw some blood. It was from his opponent's knuckles. Thrusting his hand out, Taylor snatched one of the punches from the air and squeezed. His hold caused Gaz to howl in pain.

Taylor held the wrist tightly and could feel the bones straining as he clenched. He knew he was on the cusp of breaking it. All he needed to do was apply a little more pressure for the bones to snap and crunch. He studied the young man who had launched the attack and was now limply hanging from his arm.

Gaz was bawling, the tears running down his face. Taylor considered breaking his arm for a moment, but decided against it. That was a spiteful thought and he needed to rise above such pettiness. He let go.

Gaz fell to the ground with another shriek. Taylor paused and surveyed his handiwork. All five young men were writhing around in agony. He had inflicted this upon them.

Some of it had been accidental, as he acclimatised to the limitations of his strength. But it was not all unintentional. He had wanted to hurt them. He had wanted to teach them a lesson. But he never expected to be so unscathed.

And he had seriously injured these young men.

Suddenly afraid, not just of the consequences to his actions, but what he was capable of, Taylor turned and ran into the night.

He did not even look back once.

6

At first, Taylor thought he was ill again. Thud, thud, thud. The pounding in his head sounded like the throb of blood he associated with a headache.

Then he woke up and realised that the stabbing pain was absent.

He had been dreaming. Yet, the banging noise was real. It was coming from downstairs.

The front door.

He swung his legs out of bed and stabbed his toes into his slippers, dragging himself down the stairs. He half-expected to see uniformed officers waiting outside, so he was relieved to see the familiar silhouette of San through the patterned glass of the front door.

He opened the door with one hand as he covered a yawn with the other. 'Morning, mate.'

San had a look of concern on his face, although Taylor knew he carried the same worry whether he was about to inform a patient they had a terminal illness or his wife that they were out of milk. 'Sorry to come 'round so early. Can I come in?'

Taylor shrugged his shoulders, turned around and shuffled towards the kitchen. 'You want coffee?'

San walked inside and closed the door behind him. 'If you're making some.'

'I need coffee,' he grunted, vanishing from view.

The doctor followed his host through to the kitchen and set his eyes upon the pair of mugs and the huge jar of

Carte Noire from which Taylor was shovelling granules. 'Where's the filter machine?'

Taylor waved it away as he rubbed the sleep from his eyes. 'I tried using it a couple of times, but it tasted like warm piss. Jane was the expert.'

San nodded knowingly, despite the fact he struggled to believe that any coffee could taste like urine. 'How are you doing?'

Taylor paused as he reached the refrigerator door. 'How do you take it again?'

'Milk, one sugar.'

He smiled. 'Ah, yes. It's obviously been too long since you last visited.'

San frowned. 'You've cut yourself off, Chris. Besides, I wanted to give you some time.'

Taylor slopped some milk into each mug and returned the plastic carton to the door of the refrigerator. 'I know, mate. Don't worry, I'm not annoyed, or anything.'

'You didn't answer my question.'

He took the sugar jar and spooned one into San's mug, but none into his own. 'Which one?'

'How are you doing?'

The kettle clicked to indicate that it had boiled and he started to fill the mugs. 'Don't muck about, mate. There must be a reason that you're here at the crack of dawn and, given that you're my doctor, I'm guessing it's not good news. So, why don't *you* tell *me* how I'm doing?'

San watched him stir both cups before taking receipt of one. He blew the steam from the beverage, but did not take a sip once he felt the level of heat on his lips. 'I've spent all night doing research into your condition.'

Taylor sat at the table and indicated that San should do the same. 'Condition? I'm starting to think it's a gift.'

The doctor chose a seat and dropped into it. 'Perhaps. The results won't be back from your blood work yet, but I did some digging into recorded instances of superhuman strength.'

He sat up sharply. 'And?'

'The basics can be found with a Google search, but there is more information available, if you know where to look. There are urban myths, most of which involve desperate situations. For example, a man once held up half a building when it fell on him. There are, literally, hundreds of similar accounts, but none of them are empirically documented.'

'None at all?'

San furrowed his brow. 'No. There are eyewitness statements, but no scientific evidence or explanation for the events.'

Taylor slurped his coffee. 'And nobody has any idea how these feats were possible?'

'That's not entirely true. There's a lot of speculation and educated guesswork. Most experts seem to believe it involves an overwhelming surge of adrenalin, or epinephrine, or whatever you want to call it.'

'So, basically what you said yesterday,' he said dryly with a roll of the eyes. 'Hasn't anyone looked into it a bit further?'

San blew the steam from his mug again and, this time, took a small sip. 'There have been experiments, of course. From what I read, however, it's almost impossible to replicate an emergency situation under controlled, laboratory conditions. The surprise of the predicament is thought to be a key factor.'

'Why don't they just do the experiments, but not tell the subjects what they're involved in?'

San laughed. 'Those kinds of things are illegal almost everywhere, certainly in any country where they have money spare to investigate these incidents and the theories behind them.'

Taylor cast his friend a quizzical look. 'There must be at least *one* person in the world who's investigated this further.'

'Probably, but I couldn't find them. My guess is that, if there is, it's not a research project that's sanctioned by any recognised authority and the paper isn't likely to reach the mainstream medical industry. I haven't stopped looking, though. I might find something.'

'When do you expect the test results back?'

'This afternoon.'

He sighed loudly. 'Do you think they'll tell us anything?'

San took another sip from his mug. 'If your body has undergone a physiological change, we'll be able to see it in the blood.'

'What if the tests don't show anything?'

'Then we'll do more tests. Believe me, there are plenty more tests we can do. Irrespective of what we find, regardless of whether it provides answers, or not, I've ordered an emergency MRI for tomorrow morning in the city. I'll find out precise details today.'

'The city? Northampton or Milton Keynes?'

San paused apprehensively for a moment. 'London, actually.'

'London!' Taylor scoffed. 'You seriously want me to go all the way to London just to visit a hospital?'

'It's not the sort of hospital you're thinking of,' the doctor returned swiftly. 'A friend of mine works at a university hospital. They do more research than treatment. I'm hoping the unique and interesting nature of the case will convince him to slot us in.'

Taylor thumbed the handle of his mug uncomfortably. 'Look, San, I don't want to sound ungrateful, but I'm not prepared to become a guinea pig.'

Suddenly, his expression became grave and his voice stern. 'Do you want answers?'

'Of course.'

'This is how you get them,' he retorted querulously. 'You're not obliged to do anything you're not comfortable with, but I'm concerned about your health and, as your friend and doctor, I think we should investigate further.'

Taylor held up his hand. 'I feel fantastic, San.'

'And I want to know why.'

'Can't we just leave it at that?' Taylor entreated.

He looked at his watch and finished his coffee. 'No, we can't. Don't take this the wrong way, but you should feel like crap. I'm worried about you. If I'm right, this is just a side effect from your body's reaction to this illness. Hopefully, it will dissolve in the next few days and we can forget all about it.' He glanced at his watch again. 'Look, I need to get to work. I'll call you later with more information.'

Taylor sighed. 'Okay, San. Thanks.'

He watched his guest leave and sat for a while, considering what he should do next. He had a gift. He did not want it explained by science. He wanted it to be divine.

He certainly did not want it to be temporary.

However, if San was right, he needed to use his gift while it remained. He could not waste it.

Jane would know what was best. She always did. Somehow, though, he suspected she would not approve of what he was about to do.

Decided on his next move, he leapt up, washed, dressed and snatched his jacket from the closet as he stormed out of the house.

He was outside the Royal Mail sorting office within twenty minutes. He was there for just under an hour before he saw him leave.

The man who ruined his life.

Jeremy Clarke.

Taylor was now pleased he had spent so much time following Clarke around in the weeks after the accident. He knew Clarke's routine meticulously and, most importantly, he knew the registration number of Clarke's van by heart.

He followed the large, red Transit around as Clarke began his day at work. He delivered parcels all day, every day. Driving for a living. It made Taylor feel sick.

Clarke was a huge man, but his size owed to his diet more than time spent in the gym. He was nearing seven feet tall, so his huge, overhanging stomach was less apparent than it would be on a smaller man. He had broad shoulders and hands the size of shovels. His short, sandy brown hair seemed at odds with his dangerous grey eyes, which did not bear the creases of his fifty-one years. He had tattoos of eagles, bears, skulls and half-naked women on his arms and neck. Taylor did not want to imagine what ink he had in more intimate places.

He never really fathomed why he had spent so much time following Clarke around. Perhaps he was trying to understand the man who had taken everything from him. Maybe he hoped to find some modicum of forgiveness once he knew more about the subject of his intense enmity. It had not worked. Taylor simply drove around a safe distance behind him for ten hours a day.

He did not really know why he had stopped stalking Clarke, either. One day he woke up and the desire was gone.

He suspected that it had something to do with the events on the last day he spent trailing the postal worker. Clarke had been to the pub at lunch and enjoyed three pints of bitter. One might argue, Taylor supposed, that a man of Clarke's size could easily absorb three pints without really feeling it.

He may even have been able to accept such a hypothesis had this man not just murdered his wife.

And now he knew that it *was* murder.

Perhaps that was why he had stopped following Clarke around all day, every day. Because now he knew that Clarke was guilty. He *did* drink and drive. He *did* kill Jane and *was* without compunction. Somehow it made his loss easier to manage. He had a focus for his anger.

Now Taylor knew that forgiveness was not an option, he might be able to get on with his life.

Or maybe not.

The police had only managed to make things worse. The faulty breathalyser was bad enough, but his call to inform them of Clarke's drink-driving habits was summarily, if politely, dismissed.

Now, as he watched Clarke enter the same pub he visited most lunchtimes, he knew he would have to act. He had to. The anger was back, an irrepressible rage that made his stomach tighten and his eyes bulge.

He had witnessed the fact that Clarke had stopped drinking for a short while; evidence that he knew that he had done something wrong. As far as Taylor was concerned, his return to drink was proof that the remorse had passed.

Taylor's life was in tatters, as Clarke sipped his bitter with complete disregard for what he had done, and what he might yet do. All because he liked a drink.

How long before he destroyed another life? Or several?

Someone needed to stop Clarke before it was too late. *He* had to stop Clarke. Nobody else was going to. It was *his* responsibility and God, Destiny, or whoever, had given him the means to do it.

Taylor parked up in the supermarket around the corner and walked to the pub car park, where he stood next to the van and waited, his eyes fixed to the rear entrance only ten metres away.

It was almost an hour before Clarke emerged. Initially, he was concentrating on the cigarette he was lighting, but he noticed Taylor as he stuffed the lighter into his trouser pocket. Recognition was instant. He ambled over with a crooked smile on his face. 'You again?'

Taylor's glare was icy. 'Enjoy your drink?'

He tossed his thumb towards the car park exit. 'Fuck off, pal.'

'Didn't you learn your lesson when you killed my wife?'

'Look, fella, I told you and the police already: I weren't drinking.'

'Like you're not today,' he retorted with a scowl.

Clarke took a step forwards and fixed Taylor with a steely glare. 'The police cleared me, so fuck off.'

Taylor looked up at the monstrous anathema towering over him. He felt more emboldened than at any point in his life. He felt no fear. He felt heroic. 'The police don't know you like I do.'

The gargantuan moved even closer, casting all of Taylor in shadow, with a confused smile. He flicked his cigarette a few inches from his intended target. 'Do you reckon I ain't seen you following me around? I felt bad for you before, but now you're making me angry.'

He shrugged the remark off. 'Why do you do it? Don't you care that you'll hurt other people?'

'Leave me the fuck alone!' the colossus exploded, shoving Taylor in the chest with both hands.

Taylor flew back several metres, landing on his back with a dull thud. For the first time, he began to appreciate the power of his adversary. That had hurt. His chest ached and his back throbbed.

He plucked himself from the concrete and got to his feet. 'You'll have to do better than that.'

Clarke's face was scarlet, as he failed to hide his surprise that Taylor had picked himself up so quickly. 'Fair enough.' He waded towards his adversary, fists clenched. His first swing was on the move: powerful, but cumbersome.

Taylor ducked under it with the ease he would if someone were swinging a breezeblock at his head. He did not have time to strike out, however, as Clarke turned quickly, throwing a back-fisted punch towards him.

Taylor needed to leap backwards to evade it, shocked by the speed of Clarke's reactions. The next attempt, though, was absurdly lethargic, as if he were pushing his hand through porridge. Taylor had all the time he needed. He parted his legs slightly, bent his knees and braced himself as he raised his hand.

He would need all his strength for this to appear as effortless as possible.

Opening his hand, which only just covered Clarke's fist even when fully extended, Taylor caught the punch and stopped it dead.

He felt a slight stab of pain in his shoulder, but nothing more, so allowed his lips to crease into a sardonic grin.

Clarke's previously aggressive expression transformed into bewilderment.

Taylor squeezed. He could feel the bones starting to bend within Clarke's fist.

The delivery driver squealed in pain, pulling his hand backwards sharply. Taylor's hand was not large enough to sustain a tight grip and it was plucked from him before he could break any of the bones.

The giant rubbed and shook his hand, staring at his foe in confusion. 'What the-?'

Taylor smirked. 'I said you'd need to do better, Jeremy.'

'Who the fuck *are* you?'

'You know who I am,' he replied in a menacing tone. 'You're asking the wrong question.'

Clarke clearly could not comprehend what had just happened. The rage was erupting inside of him already. 'Am I? What's the right fucking question, arsehole?'

'What am I going to do to you?'

He lost control. Nobody threatened *him*. Nobody. *Not ever!* He let out a roar and jumped at Taylor, his fists flying.

Taylor deflected the first and blocked the second. The third, however, landed in his ribs and he felt a sharp pain. The fourth and fifth were wayward, easily avoided with a sidestep.

Clarke offered him no respite, lunging at him again. Another strike hit the target, this time on the underside of the chin. Taylor's head snapped backwards, stretching his neck beyond its tensile limit.

Taylor dropped to the ground. The last attack should have broken his neck. Yet, besides a little ache, he was virtually unscathed. He knew, though, that it was time to end this. The longer he toyed with Clarke, the greater the very real risk of getting hurt.

Clarke was powerful and dangerous.

He stood up just in time to repel another ferocious attack, blocking Clarke's fist with his forearm. This time, however, he fought back. His fun was over. It was time to get to his reason for confronting the giant.

Taylor tossed out a fist and it landed square in Clarke's chest. The delivery driver yelped like an injured puppy, flying backwards to the ground. Taylor did not move. He stood motionless, fists clench by his sides, and glowered at his fallen foe.

Clarke could not understand what was happening. His anger faded, quickly replaced by fear and confusion. He may not have been an especially intelligent man, but he knew what was possible and what was not. This was not possible.

He scrambled to his feet and rushed to his van. He leapt inside and locked the doors, stabbing the keys into the ignition.

Taylor nonchalantly ambled over and stood in front of the van. After a few seconds of looking through the windscreen and enjoying the sight of Clarke wide-eyed with fear, he placed both hands on the bonnet.

Clarke started the engine and lowered the window slightly, craning his neck to move his lips up to the crack. 'I'm not fucking stopping for you!'

Taylor grinned, trying to hide the worry that this might be a step too far for his newfound power.

'Get out the fucking way!' Clarke screeched through the gap, revving the engine.

He bent his knees and cricked his neck.

Clarke clunked the van into gear and began to inch forwards.

Taylor braced himself and locked his arms at the elbows.

The van did not move.

Clarke increased the revs and, when it still did not move, he began to panic. Terrified, he slammed his foot on the accelerator.

Taylor watched the rear wheels of the van start to spin. Smoke poured out, obscuring his vision. The acrid smell of melting rubber burnt his throat. But the van still did not move.

He needed to keep his body rigid, but could barely believe how easy it was for him. The stasis only lasted a minute, before he tried to push. Digging his feet into the ground, he bent his arms and heaved.

The van flew backwards into the wall a metre behind it.

Taylor marched towards the door, thoroughly enjoying the fact that Clarke was cowering behind it. With one hand, he ripped the door from the hinges.

People were starting to rush out of the pub, reacting to the loud crash that had fractured the brick wall. Taylor ignored them and Clarke's whimpered pleading, snatching a fistful of shirt and yanking him from the vehicle, tossing him onto the ground.

Clarke began sobbing and Taylor watched the dark patch forming around his groin with satisfaction. His smirk grew as he walked towards his broken foe.

Taylor found that his focus was starting to waver. He had fantasised about this moment so many times, but now he did not know what to do with it. In his dreams, he pummelled Clarke's face to a bloody pulp. He realised that it was suddenly different.

Now he actually could crush Clarke's skull, he did not want to. He looked down at the urine-soaked giant and his smile vanished. He felt nothing but disdain and, inexplicably, pathos.

Then his 'phone rang. He looked down at Clarke, who was covering his face with his hands and peeking through his fingers. 'You're lucky, Jeremy. I don't feel like ruining your life today. I'm going to give you what Jane never had: a second chance. But, if I catch you drinking and driving again...'

Taylor turned and strode away without finishing the sentence. He took the 'phone from his pocket, leaving the other drinkers in silence, staring at the inconceivable sight of Clarke in a ball, sobbing and broken. Taylor looked at the 'phone.

San.

'Did you get them back already?'

'Yes.' His voice was shrill. 'Where are you? Can you get to the clinic?'

The tone in the doctor's voice alerted him to the fact that something was wrong. 'Is there a problem, mate?'

'Kind of. Can you get here?'

Suddenly, Taylor's tone filled with urgency. 'Do you know what's happening to me?'

'Chris, can you just get here, please? I also need to know what contact, if any, you might have had with other people.'

'What are you talking about San? Did you find you why I'm so strong?' he asked, suddenly perturbed.

'It's a virus, Chris. Your strength is the result of a virus.'

7

Nathan Tyson opened his eyes and felt the drenched bed sheets first. Next, he realised that his pyjamas were also sodden. Sitting up, he looked across at the clock. He was running late.

Touching his arm, he looked around for a glass of water, or anything else he might have spilt during the night. Unable to see anything, he assumed Debbie must have it taken away and jumped out of bed.

He walked slowly down the stairs, realising that he felt a bit giddy. Actually, he felt a little bit weak, like he had not eaten in several days. He grasped the banister tightly and eased himself down. Halfway, he paused and took several, deep breaths. They made him feel better.

Continuing down, he walked through to the kitchen and saw Debbie.

She was standing at the sink with her back to him. She was tiny, only a little over five feet, and was just as slim as she had been on their wedding day, fourteen years ago. He pictured her dark brown eyes and light coffee-coloured skin. Her lips were thick and luscious. Her hair curled down to her shoulders and he spent a moment enjoying the view of her bottom before greeting her.

She spun around with a gasp, dropping the cup she was washing and ran towards him. Throwing her arms around him, she squeezed tightly. 'Oh, Nate, are you okay?'

He hugged her briefly and chuckled confusedly. 'I'm fine. I'm hungry.' He indicated his soaked pyjamas. 'I'm a bit wet, though. Did I spill something in the night?'

She pulled away from him slightly and glared at him blankly. 'Honey, do you have any idea how long you've been in bed?'

He felt his stomach turn. 'If you say four days...'

She glared at him, perplexed. 'No, it was two days. Don't you remember?'

His heart was already thumping against his chest. 'No. Was I unconscious?'

She stifled her tears with a gulp. 'No, Nate. You were wide awake. You've been lying in bed, staring at the ceiling and refusing to get out of bed for the last two days. Are you going to explain why?'

Taylor pumped the nervous energy into his legs as he dug his toes into the stained carpet and shook them continuously. Tim sat next to him and cast another querulous glance in his best friend's direction.

'Chris?'

He turned towards Tim. 'Yeah?'

'Can you stop that?'

'Stop what?'

He flicked his eyes towards Taylor's legs. 'That.'

'Oh, sorry.' He placed his hands on his knees, as if they were the source of his movement. He turned to San. 'So, is it contagious?'

'It's not airborne,' the doctor replied firmly, tossing his finger first towards Tim, then at himself. 'If it was, we'd both have it already.'

Taylor could feel the cold sweat on his brow and shivered. 'How serious is it, then?'

San shrugged his shoulders. 'The lab. wasn't specific, but they're sending a virologist here, which they've never done before. That suggests to me that they're taking it seriously.'

Tim sucked a lungful of air through his teeth. 'That can't be good, can it? That means it's really bad.'

'Not necessarily,' San replied sharply, holding his hand up forcefully. 'They couldn't give me a name, so it's quite plausible that we're talking about a new strain of an existing virus, or...'

'Or?' Taylor prompted urgently.

'Or it's a new virus,' he finished slowly.

'Oh, shit!' Tim exclaimed. 'Will he die?'

'Hold on a moment!' the doctor instructed firmly. 'Nobody is thinking about a fatality here. You're meant to be here to help and you're not helping, Tim! The fact is that if his body were deteriorating, there would be signs. That's not happening.'

A long pause ensued, eventually broken by Tim. 'Do you think there might be a cure?'

San smiled awkwardly. 'We can't cure any virus. All we can do is treat the symptoms.'

'What symptoms?' Taylor scoffed. 'I feel better than I've ever felt in my life.'

San nodded knowingly. 'Exactly. That's probably the most curious aspect of this virus. You're not showing any ill effects whatsoever. Indeed, it's quite the opposite. That's why I'm convinced you're not in mortal danger.'

'Any idea where I caught it from?' asked Taylor, chuckling awkwardly.

He shrugged his shoulders. 'I'm afraid you're more likely to know than I am.'

Tim cleared his throat noisily. 'What makes you so certain it's a virus? Like you said, he's not even sick.'

San raised his eyebrows in astonishment. 'You can see it in the blood, Tim. That's how it migrates around the body.'

'Are you sure?' he asked again. 'He doesn't look ill.'

The doctor harrumphed loudly. 'That's obviously not how this virus works. Each one is different. For example-' His telephone buzzed, interrupting him. 'Hold on a second.' He picked up the receiver and put it to his ear.

San listened for a few moments and placed it back down again. 'They're here. I'm sure they can tell you more than I can.'

As if by rehearsal, the door burst open at exactly the same time as he finished his sentence. A team of people dressed in masks swarmed into the room, wearing navy blue windbreakers, with large, yellow letters emblazoned on the back. H.P.A.

San cast them each a stern glare as they poured in, before tersely declaring his annoyance. 'You don't need the masks!'

A man, with silver hair neatly swept into an immaculate side-parting, barged his way to the front. His tailored, charcoal suit seemed at odds with his windbreaker. 'We'll judge that for ourselves, thank you, Dr Namib.'

He stood up sharply. 'Look, I don't know why there are so many of you. I was informed that one virologist would be coming here. This is a medical practice, not a circus!'

The silver-haired man was tall and thin. He shook his scaphocephalic head. His cold, blue eyes veered away from the irate Indian and landed on a woman directly behind him. 'Seal the entire surgery. Test everyone.'

San shook his fist in the air as his eyes bulged in their sockets. 'What? The virus isn't airborne!'

He took a step towards San and glowered down at him, the wrinkles around his eyes straightening out. 'How do you know that, doctor?'

He indicated himself and Tim. 'Because we're not infected. Neither of us is even slightly ill.'

Silver bobbed his head towards Taylor. 'He's not sick, either. Yet.' He turned back to the woman. 'Do it now, please!'

She nodded obsequiously and hurried from the room.

Taylor watched quietly, but the anger was bubbling inside of him. He stood up. 'Do you have any idea what it is?'

He laughed conceitedly. 'If they knew what it was, they wouldn't have sent *me*.'

'Who *are* you?' San demanded irritably.

'Dr Mike Norbury.'

Tim and Taylor exchanged a blank look. San gasped, the anger in his expression quickly replaced by reverence. '*The* Mike Norbury?'

He nodded seriously. 'Can I assume that means you understand how seriously we're taking this?'

He nodded and sat down, gawping in awe at the silver-haired man before him.

Taylor turned to the Indian and whispered. 'Is he important, then?'

San nodded slowly, his eyes glued the man he so patently idolised. 'You could say that. I suggest we sit here quietly and let him work.'

'Seriously?' Tim asked, his brow furrowed.

'Seriously,' the doctor retorted sternly.

Norbury moved in front of Taylor and peered down at him. He suddenly seemed even taller and thinner. 'Do I have your undivided attention now?'

He looked back up and nodded once.

'Excellent,' he replied, a crooked smile creasing his lips. 'Do you have *any* idea how you might have contracted this virus?'

Taylor shook his head pensively. 'None at all.'

Norbury plucked a notebook from his inner jacket pocket and spent a few seconds studying it. 'You fell ill on Wednesday, is that correct?'

'Yes, but-'

'Where did you go on Wednesday?' the virologist interjected brashly.

Taylor paused and took a deep breath. 'What does HPA mean?'

Norbury grinned. 'Health Protection Agency. Where did you go on Wednesday?'

'Why is the Health Protection Agency here?'

He chuckled. 'I can see that you're going to be one of those cases, Mr Taylor. Or can I call you Chris?' Taylor nodded, so he continued. 'You see, Chris, you have a very potent and previously undiscovered virus inside you. That's of interest to a huge amount of people but, for the time being, we need to prevent a pandemic. That's our first priority.'

'What about curing me?'

He shrugged his shoulders. 'That's a long way down the list. You already have the disease. We want to stop others getting it. To do that I need you to provide me with certain pieces of information that will allow myself, and my team, to ascertain what it is we're dealing with and how best to go about stopping it. So, I'll ask again: where were you on Wednesday?'

'The vet's surgery.'

'Why?'

'My dog died.'

'What's the name of this veterinarian?'

'Adams. He's not far from here.'

Norbury spun to the man next to him. 'Get to that clinic, seal it and find out what the vet knows.' The man darted away.

Taylor stared at him blankly. 'Do you want the address?'

'No need. It's on your credit card statement.'

He exhaled sharply. 'My what? What does that have to do with my health?'

The icy glare flowed from Norbury's eyes. 'Everything. They help formulate a history of your life. Where did you go on Tuesday?'

'I got ill on Wednesday.'

'Duly noted,' he returned swiftly. 'Yet I fear you aren't an authority on the incubation period of this mystery illness. Tuesday, if you please, Chris.'

He paused as he considered it. 'Nowhere, really. A walk with the dog and work.'

Norbury laughed loudly. 'That's not nowhere. That's two places, on top of your home. I have teams on their way to your house and your work already. Where did you go for a walk?'

'The same route I've walked every day for ages.'

'Did you notice anything different, or were you bitten by anything?'

Taylor paused as he racked his brain. 'No, but...'

The room waited for him to continue, until Norbury impatiently urged him on. 'What, Chris?'

'Herodotus, the Labrador I was at the vet with,' he explained slowly, accessing the memory painfully, 'discovered a hot water spring I'd never noticed before. I'm pretty sure I hadn't noticed it before because it wasn't there, but I couldn't guarantee that. Even so, it was gone the next day.'

'Immediately after the tremor, yes?'

Taylor screwed his face up in consternation. 'Yes, actually.'

Norbury spun around on one heel. 'Right, listen closely!' he announced, his voice suddenly loud enough to address a huge, outdoor crowd, despite the fact the GP office was little more than twenty feet wide and fifteen long. He paused for half a second to ensure he had the attention of everyone in the room.

'We have the source. Now we enter the containment phase. Team Alpha is already en route to secure the home. Team Bravo will secure the workplace. We have a team here to monitor the clinic. You need to second another team from the NHS and send them to the coordinates that Mr Taylor is about to give us. Notify the Department of Health that we have a situation and prepare a room where I can brief the minister.'

He finished speaking and studied the masked faces before him. 'What are you waiting for? Go!'

There was a flurry of windbreakers and, within ten seconds, only the trio of friends and Norbury remained.

Tim was staring at Norbury incredulously. 'Did you just say you have to brief the minister?'

He turned and scoffed loudly. 'Yes, I did, Mr Bulling.'

'Why would you need to brief any ministers?'

'The situation has escalated!' he snapped. 'If the origin of this virus is extraneous to the human body, it may be able to permeate the local wildlife. If that happens, we have no way of controlling it. Even I can't stop birds from flying.

The initial tests suggest this may be the most potent virus we've ever seen. I'm treating this as I would a full-scale emergency.'

8

The melody sounded tinny through the cheap speakers erected around the edge of the field. They sat atop tall poles, which doubled as anchor points for the crepe paper and plastic banners. There was a kaleidoscopic array of colours, of both types of banner. Each one whipped around in the sharp breeze that accompanied this cloudy day. A storm was brewing on the horizon, but hopefully it would not arrive until after the festivities.

The school field was neatly divided into sections. The far side was the competition area, where the young athletes would prove their mettle in such harrowing events as the egg and spoon race or the fifty-metre sprint. The parents had erected a small dais over the left-hand side of the field, which would display the talents of each class in a well-rehearsed rendition of an Easter tale. The right-hand segment was an array of small stalls, where one could choose between a raffle or hoop-la, an apple dunk or bouncy castle.

Nate always enjoyed the Easter Fete at the school. Travis was entering his last year at the school and James was now in Year 2, so he had come to know many of the other parents well and this was one of the few chances he had to spend time with these friends.

But anyone who thought this was all about the children was sorely mistaken. After the kids' competitions, the parents were called into action. The fifty-metre sprint suddenly became an event of Olympic importance. Nate had won it every year since his sons had matriculated to this school. He was not about to give up his title without a fight, no matter how much Debbie worried about his health.

He cast his eyes over the other fathers, noting several young upstarts who might fancy their chances. At his age, they were all contenders, but he had the element of surprise in his favour. He was still fast, despite his girth and years.

Debbie nudged him. 'Are you sure you're okay, honey?'

He chuckled, continuing to scrutinise the opposition. 'Honestly, I'm fine. Stop worrying, will you, please?'

'Why don't you remember anything from the past couple of days?'

'I don't know, honey. Some way to spend my holiday, huh?'

She rolled her eyes. 'It's not funny.'

He touched her arm tenderly. 'I was probably delirious.'

'Maybe,' she scowled. 'I still think you go should to the GP and let him have a look at you.'

'If I feel rough, I'll call San.'

'Why don't you just call-'

'I'm fine, Deb!' he snapped. 'Could you please just leave it alone now?'

'Fine,' she sighed, looking around. 'Where are the boys?'

'At the apple dunk,' he replied, disinterested. 'I thought you were having a go?'

'I'm not in the mood.'

He turned to face her. 'Come on, Deb,' he appealed, in the most mollifying tone he could muster. 'We don't get out as a family that often. At least *try* to enjoy it.'

She looked into his eyes and smiled. 'You *are* looking good, actually. You have a glow about you.'

He chuckled. 'I think that's sweat.'

She pushed herself up onto her toes and kissed him on the cheek. 'Still a handsome devil.'

He grabbed her waist and pulled her tight, kissing her passionately. 'And you're a temptress! Are the boys staying at Scott's Saturday night?'

She grabbed his hand, but suddenly pulled away. 'Holy f-'

'What?'

'I just got a shock from you!' she declared, rubbing and studying her hand.

He looked at her confusedly, then at his own hands. 'Really? I didn't feel anything.'

Debbie's large, doe-like eyes were full of suspicion as she tentatively reached out towards him and brushed his hand. Once again, she yanked it away, exclaiming painfully. 'That's not static, Nate.' She indicated the redness on her skin. 'I'm burnt, look. What's going on with you?'

He did not even try to hide his annoyance, throwing his hands up in the air. Before his response left his lips, however, a bolt of lightning seemed to escape from his fingers and vanish into the cloud above.

He watched as it burst out from his hands. It appeared to move in slow motion, although he knew it actually took less than a second to disappear from view.

He gawped skywards for several seconds, before turning to his wife.

Her expression confirmed she had seen the same thing he had. Their eyes locked in a gaze of bewilderment. For several seconds, they stood looking at each other, open-mouthed, their brains trying to rationalise what they had seen. However, no matter how many options their minds raced through, the fact was that what they had just witnessed defied explanation.

'Was that...?' she began, so dumbfounded she could not even finished the question.

'I-I-I think it was.' Even as the words came from his mouth, he could barely believe it. He looked around to see if anyone else had noticed it. If they had, they did not show it.

'How is that possible?' Debbie asked, her eyes alight with a mixture of fear and confusion.

'I...' he started, but an explanation eluded him. 'Erm, maybe...'

Before Nate could formulate anything resembling justification, shrieks began to emanate from the stalls. They both spun their heads to see a commotion erupting at the apple dunk. The cacophony of screams and wails pierced the air as their eyes locked onto the sight of two boys convulsing on the ground.

Their faces were terrifyingly familiar and both parents exchanged a look of dread, the inexplicable event of moments ago instantly forgotten.

Nate charged away, his wife close behind him.

Taylor, San and Tim sat silently in the back of the HPA Jeep, staring vacantly out of the dark windows, despite the fact they could not see anything through them.

Norbury was sitting in the passenger seat and had cast them stern glowers each time any of them spoke. It seemed he was not content with dragging them away from the surgery. He insisted that they make the enforced journey in total silence, whilst he spent the entire time acerbically barking one order after another into his telephone.

The vehicle was so dark that, when it screeched to a halt, the passengers were completely disorientated. They were shocked when the door opened and they realised they were outside a local primary school.

Norbury did not offer a reason for bringing them here. He leapt from the Jeep and demanded a cordon from the first person he saw.

The trio got out of the Jeep and Taylor noticed that they were actually the lead vehicle of a convoy. He stretched his neck to see all the vehicles, but stopped counting at twenty. There were six Jeeps like the one they had arrived in, but the majority of the traffic seemed to be personnel carriers.

Full of armed soldiers.

'This is serious,' San whispered.

'You think?' Tim scoffed sardonically.

Taylor said nothing. He could not tear his eyes from the startling scene before him.

There were people everywhere. The HPA windbreakers were suddenly less prominent when compared to the array of weapons carried by the men and women in fatigues. Civilians were being gathered into a group and jostled angrily against the police presence, to no avail.

There were several people who appeared to be doctors, judging by their white overcoats, and they were huddled around the bonnet of a black Jaguar, peering at a MacBook Air resting uneasily on top.

The soldiers and HPA officers scurried around busily, their symphony conducted by Norbury, who was shouting, pointing and gesticulating exigently. He seemed to relish pulling the strings.

Taylor watched the spider in the centre of the web keenly, and followed his hand gestures to the ambulance on the edge of the school field and the team of paramedics next to it. He tried to discern what was happening, but it was too far away and there were too many spectators blocking his line of sight.

'Where's the goddamn head teacher?' Norbury yelled.

A meek, small, young, spectacled woman held up her hand tremulously.

'Get me a list of attendees this instant!'

'There isn't a list,' she whimpered.

Norbury scowled, the vitriol seared into his eyes. 'Then get me list of every student enrolled here.'

'Why?' the head teacher asked, producing a surprisingly brazen tone.

'Do I look like I have time to explain, lady?' he shouted. 'Get me the fucking list!'

Sufficiently crushed, the head teacher shuffled away to do as she had been instructed. Norbury did not savour his victory. He summoned the closest subordinate, although, Taylor noted, that appeared to include everyone here.

The doctor indicated the school field. 'Nobody in and nobody out. Start setting up some testing stations over there. Park the truck in the car park.'

Taylor looked left and right. He did not see a truck.

'What about the student list, sir?' another HPA officer asked.

'Go with her and get it,' Norbury snapped. 'Establish who's here and who isn't. Then bring the rest of them here!'

Taylor walked towards him slowly. 'Dr Norbury?' Finding himself summarily ignored, he raised his voice. 'Norbury!'

He turned to look at him. 'I don't really have time for a chat, Chris.'

'What are you doing?' he asked through gritted teeth.

'This is a containment situation. Please don't interfere.'

Taylor did not try to disguise his disgust. 'I'm no lawyer, but I'm pretty sure you can't detain a bunch of seven-year-olds, just in case they have a bug.'

'Actually,' he retorted swiftly, his head snapping around, 'I can do anything I deem necessary. I need to ascertain any and all potential carriers.'

'They're not carriers. They're kids.'

Norbury pointed at the ambulance with a scoff. 'They're walking Petri dishes. Any person who will eat what they find in their nose is a potential carrier, irrespective of age.'

'You can't treat them like criminals,' Taylor insisted vehemently. 'Don't you think you might be overreacting slightly? This isn't a terrorist attack.'

'No, it's not,' he replied, in a disquietingly low voice. 'It's much, much worse.'

The two men stood a foot apart, locked in a cold glare, before Norbury shattered the impasse by pushing past Taylor and rushing away.

He turned back to his friends, who stood watching silently. 'This is madness. It can't possibly warrant all this fuss.'

San shrugged his shoulders nonchalantly. 'Mike Norbury knows what he's doing, Chris.'

'Does he?' Taylor retorted venomously, sweeping his arm through the air. 'Look at this. You would think they'd found a bomb in the school.'

San laughed dryly. 'There is, potentially. This is a biological bomb. If *he's* worried,' he said, indicating Norbury, 'we should be, too.'

Tim was ignoring them. He was straining his neck to see what was happening near the ambulance. 'There's something weird going on over there.'

Suddenly, a bolt of electricity shot into the sky.

The strident screams echoed down the street. People hurried away from the ambulance. They walked at first, but soon started to run. Within moments, adults and children alike were pushing and falling over each other to get away from the scene. The rushed into the barrier of police, who struggled to contain them, trying to steer them towards the playground where they had managed to assemble a large number of the other patrons.

'What the hell was that?' Tim gasped, exasperated. He looked up at the clouds. 'Where did that come from?'

The large assembly of onlookers around the ambulance had almost entirely dispersed. Another bolt of lightning fired into the cumulus hovering overhead.

The few people that remained fought to get away. They were shouting and yelling, barging their way to safety, only to collide with the human barrier of police, who were quickly assuming postures usually reserved for riot control. It left gaps for Tim to look through.

'Chris?' he called out.

Taylor turned to his friend. 'What?'

'That lightning...'

'What about it?'

'Did you notice it was going up, not coming down?'

'Was it?' He chuckled. 'Are you sure?'

'It's coming from someone over there?'

Both San and Taylor laughed heartily. The doctor spoke. 'Don't be absurd, Tim!'

'That's not all.'

They both turned to ridicule their friend, but saw him frozen with fear, his face pallid. Suddenly, they knew something was very wrong.

Taylor grabbed Tim's arm. 'What else is there, mate?'

'The person the lightning came from.'

'What about them?'

'It's Nate.'

9

Taylor barged through the crowd with the ease of a musk oxen pushing through a tulip garden. He brushed aside men, women and children alike, with Tim and San hurriedly following in his wake. Many people cast him irate looks, but nobody challenged him, preoccupied by the fact the police and army were rounding them up like cattle.

Taylor noted, with some intrigue, that nobody seemed to question how it was that he was able to barge them all out of his way with such consummate ease.

They reached Tyson to find him crouched down, Travis in his arms. The paramedics had already loaded Debbie and James onto stretchers and were taking them to the ambulance. They heard the word 'critical' used several times.

They watched in horror as three burly men in HPA jackets intercepted Nate's wife and son. Norbury's subordinates were guiding them to a hastily erected tent in the very centre of the school field.

Their eyes moved to their friend. Nate was oblivious to the commotion around him. He cradled Travis, the tears streaming down his face and his pained wails piercing all those around him.

Taylor studied him for only a moment, instantly recognising the expression, so contorted with despair. Only one thing could cause that.

His eyes moved towards Travis, who lay dead in his father's arms.

Nate wailed. 'I made him sick! I did this!'

Taylor felt his eyes watering. 'Oh, Nate.'

He looked up and there was a moment of recognition in his eyes before they returned to the boy in his arms.

Norbury suddenly appeared next to them. 'Get the boy to the truck!'

The trio of HPA agents obediently moved towards Nate and started to ease Travis from his grip, but he fought them away. They looked towards Norbury, who indicated that they should continue.

The largest man placed a large, strong hand on Nate's shoulder, causing him to turn around to investigate who it was touching him. As he did this, the others moved in and tried to snatch the boy away.

When Nate realised what was happening, he growled and snapped around. With a guttural snarl, he grabbed the man behind him with one hand and thrust the other out towards the duo in front of him.

Taylor was about to intervene on behalf of his friend, but barely completed one step before he stopped dead, his mouth gaping.

Nate's hands glowed for a moment, an ethereal blue colour, before the large man suddenly flew backwards, thrown from his feet by an invisible force, accompanied by an ear-splitting crack. Simultaneously, a crackle of electricity burst from the hand in front of him, zapping the duo and hurling them to the ground several metres away. All three men squealed in pain and landed in crumpled heaps.

Nate did not seem to worry about the fact he had been able to electrocute three people, nor did he seem to care that there were dozens of witnesses. He simply turned back to Travis and continued weeping.

Taylor stared vacantly at Tim and San, who reciprocated.

'Did you see that?' San whispered.

'I told you!' Tim exclaimed triumphantly.

Taylor was less enthused. 'What the hell is going on?'

Norbury did not seem intimidated by what he had just seen. He shook his head ruefully at the men who were prostrate on the ground and moved towards Nate with caution. 'I'm very sorry, but we need to take him away.'

Nate looked up, fire in his eyes. 'Leave him alone! Leave us alone!'

'No,' he returned defiantly. 'I can't do that. If we can get the boy to my doctors, they can perform a post-mortem straight away. If that can help us establish the behaviour of this illness, we might be able to save your wife and other son.'

Even in the turmoil of his misery, Nate understood. His features mellowed slightly and he relinquished his grip on Travis. Slowly, he extended his arms and offered the corpse to the nearby soldiers. Norbury clicked his fingers and they whisked Travis away, leaving the father to fall to the ground, in a crumpled ball of dejection.

Taylor felt the tears running down his cheeks, the memories flooded his mind. Taking the boys to play football at the park, or them jumping on him or waiting for Uncle Chris to build Lego sets.

He watched the soldiers carry Travis across the playground, towards a huge truck that was pulling into the car park. He took a moment to study the enormous vehicle.

It was unlike anything he had ever seen before. Easily forty feet long and fifteen high, it was white and had small domes all over it. It looked to him like someone had wrapped it in metallic bubble-wrap. On top of the cab was a satellite dish, whilst the trailer was covered in small cameras and huge solar panels. HPA was emblazoned down the side of the trailer in huge, blue letters.

Turning back to his friend, Taylor walked over and crouched beside him. Consumed by despair, Nate could not stop crying. He acknowledged the presence of his friend by leaping at him and holding him in a tight embrace.

'What actually happened?' Tim asked quietly, moving close enough to be heard without raising his voice.

Nate needed several seconds to control the overwhelming grief. 'I don't know,' he croaked, the horror strangling his voice. 'The boys were at the apple dunk one minute and then, suddenly, they were having violent convulsions.' His eyes locked onto San. 'What kind of illness does that?'

San shook his head ruefully. 'I don't know, mate. I'm so sorry.'

'How are you firing electricity from your hand, Nate?' Tim asked eagerly.

He shook his head. 'I don't know. What's happening to me? What's happening to my family?' He lurched forwards, held tightly by Taylor, and the convulsive sobs took control of his body once more.

Norbury was hovering intently just behind them. He looked down at Taylor. 'I think we can safely assume you *did* manage to pass it on.'

Nate's head snapped around. 'Pass what on?' He looked around, noticing the commotion around him for the first time. 'Who are all these people? What's going on?'

Norbury sighed and calmly explained the situation surrounding Taylor's virus.

When the doctor finished speaking, Nate stood up slowly and locked his red eyes on his friend's. 'The bottle of water?'

Taylor recalled his outburst vividly and allowed himself a single, atrabilious nod.

Nate launched himself at his friend, grabbing his collar angrily. "Why didn't you warn me?' he screamed, spit flying from his mouth in every direction.

San jumped between them. 'He didn't know, Nate! Let him go!'

Taylor bowed his head in shame and Nate kept his grip.

'Let him go!' San shouted, pushing them apart. 'Nate, why don't you go and spend some time with your wife and son? They need you.'

Nate seemed to come to his senses and shook his head violently. 'You're right, you're right. I'm sorry, Chris.'

As he moved away, Norbury stepped across him, placing his hand on Nate's chest. 'I don't think that's a good idea. Until we can establish the nature of this virus, and if we have any medicine that can treat it, I would prefer you keep your distance.'

Nate pushed his hand away. 'I don't care what you prefer. San's right. I should be with them.'

He barged past Norbury and stormed towards the trailer, San jogging to keep up with him, declaring that he might be able to help.

Tim was not paying attention to the scene between Nate and Taylor. He was watching the soldiers erecting a mesh fence around the perimeter of the school. 'What are they doing over there?'

'We need to make this school a secure compound,' Norbury explained matter-of-factly.

'Why?'

He rolled his eyes querulously. 'Do I really need to explain?'

Tim chuckled. 'Is it just me, or is it starting to look more like a prison than an emergency medical facility?'

'These people aren't criminals,' Taylor chimed in, forcefully.

'Maybe not,' he replied knowingly. 'But until we establish more facts about this virus and, more importantly, how it spreads, nobody is leaving this compound.'

Taylor indicated himself and Tim. 'Does this rule extend to us?'

'Are you in the compound?' he snapped.

'Technically, I would say yes, but we did enter voluntarily.'

Norbury scoffed acerbically. 'Then it includes you.'

Tim noticed a news van pulling up outside the school and pointed to it excitedly. 'I wonder what *they* will make of the illegal imprisonment of several hundred people.'

He threw his arms up in the air in frustration. 'Shit!' He turned and aimed his vitriol at the nearest subordinate. 'Intercept them. Tell them we'll issue a statement shortly. Whatever happens, don't let them in here! And get the biohazard signs up, for Christ's sake!'

The young man seemed uncertain. 'Wouldn't a spokesperson normally do that?'

'Congratulations!' Norbury snarled. 'You've just been promoted!'

Taylor laughed. 'I guess you're not quite as untouchable as you think you are.'

He cast Taylor a frigid glare. 'Press interference was always inevitable. The only surprise is how swiftly they picked up the scent. If you'll excuse me, I've got patients to attend to.'

As he tried to rush past, Taylor grabbed his arm and gripped it tightly. 'Why haven't you asked to see the effect the virus has had on me?'

He grimaced slightly and tried to yank arm free. His attempt was futile. 'I've already seen the CCTV footage of you and the postal van. That was the man who killed your wife, wasn't it?'

Taylor squeezed the arm. 'So, you should know that we'll leave if and when we choose to?'

Norbury pulled his arm away again and Taylor released his hold. He met Taylor's glare with a formidable one of his own. 'I have patients who need me.' With that, he marched away.

Tim stared at his friend worriedly. 'They've put that fence up quickly and there are more soldiers appearing every minute.' He was watching the procession of armed personnel carriers as they unloaded their payload and drove away. 'Do you think we should check on Nate?'

He cast his eyes over the trailer that both Nate and San had rushed towards and shook his head despondently. 'We can't help him. San's with him. He'll be more help than we will. But we should probably try to stop Norbury from trapping everyone else here.'

'That's a nice idea,' he replied with a smirk. 'However, I feel obliged to point out the small army that will probably try to stop us.'

Taylor nodded his head towards the television cameras being hastily dragged from the ever-increasing fleet of news vans. 'Maybe it's time for these people to see what I can do.'

He walked towards the gate, Tim trailing him excitedly. The police and army had managed to calm the rebellious crowds, having rounded them up into smaller groups. The tents were up in the field and the soldiers were lining up the people outside of them, all under the close supervision of teams of people in HPA windbreakers.

Taylor was quietly impressed how quickly Norbury had managed to get the scene organised. He was also thankful that the officials on the scene were completely preoccupied with the fete patrons. It meant they ignored him.

He watched a small team of marines guiding another huge truck into the car park as the armoured personnel carriers continued to drop their cargo outside the school. Teams, each consisting of around a dozen people, continued to construct the perimeter fence, which was at least twelve feet high. Taylor noted the razor-sharp barbed wire at the top and the armed men and women already patrolling it.

There was a larger team at the car park entrance, connecting wall panels together. He could see people shipping equipment from one of the smaller vans. The pneumatic drill helped them secure the gatehouse walls, the alligator ramps and the enormous bollards.

'They're getting this up quickly,' Taylor remarked, as they walked casually towards the construction site. 'If we don't leave now, we might never get out.'

'If we can get to those reporters, they might be able to help us put a stop to this madness.'

As they got closer to the newly erected gatehouse, a group of seven armed soldiers approached them bearing admonition. 'Turn around, guys.'

Tim brought out his most charming smile. 'We were just curious, but this looks pretty serious, so we'll get out of your way.'

'Get in line, sir,' the lead marine instructed, pointing to the row of tents.

He waved his hand in the air. 'No, no, no, you've got it all wrong. We've got nothing to do with whatever's going on here. We wandered in to see what was happening. We're inquisitive like that, I guess.'

Tim recognised the two, brass stars on the marine's epaulettes and tried to increase the charm emanating from his grin. He could see that it was not working.

'That's unlucky, gents,' the lieutenant replied dryly. 'Nobody comes in or out without permission from Dr Norbury.'

Tim adopted his most stricken look. 'Seriously? Why?'

The lieutenant shrugged his shoulders coldly. 'That's not my concern. Those are my orders.'

Tim's smile faded and he exchanged a look of consternation with his friend. Taylor, however, had a strange half-smile and a glint in his eyes that Tim knew all too well from their formative years together. He took several steps backwards.

Taylor took a single step forwards and met the lieutenant with a steely glare, folding his arms across his chest as he spoke in a deadly quiet tone. 'You know that you're not going to shoot any unarmed civilians in front of the press.'

'What makes you think we need bullets to stop you leaving? I think we can handle you without deadly force.'

'Really?' he scoffed. He lunged at the lieutenant, grabbing the lapels on his uniform and picking him up effortlessly. He held the soldier aloft for several moments, before tossing him into the new fence.

The other soldiers froze, their mouths gaping as they stared at the lieutenant lying on the ground. The crowd of reporters noticed, also, and they rushed towards the fence, digital and video cameras aimed at Taylor. Suddenly, a cacophony of questions came through the mesh.

The six men and women turned their gazes to Taylor, who was smirking victoriously. Overcoming their shock swiftly, they charged at him. He swatted them away like flies, their assaults bouncing off harmlessly.

Their colleagues near the gatehouse recognised the sight of a threat and joined in the attack. Taylor swung his fist towards the first to arrive. He could hear a bone crack over the yelps and watched the recipient fly through the air, crashing into several on-rushers. He looked down at his fist. He had not even hit them hard.

Reinforcements were arriving quickly. Taylor made a conscious decision to try to avoid striking them. He had no real concept of how powerful he truly was and might do some irreparable damage to one of them without even trying. That was the opposite impression to the one he wanted to convey in front of so many lenses. Besides, he had no desire to hurt these people. They were only doing their jobs.

They came at him two or three at a time, but he pushed and hurled them away, confident he would not cause any lasting damage using this tactic. In the midst of the scramble, he managed to steal a moment to catch Tim's gaze. His expression was a mixture of joy and awe.

'Go,' Taylor mouthed. Tim needed several seconds to realise what his friend was saying. Once he did, he darted out through the half-constructed gate. Nobody even noticed him.

Taylor watched the crowd envelop him and then turned back to the swelling mass of uniforms around him. There were easily twenty soldiers. He noted that none of them had guns and that their blades remained sheathed.

He had been right about them not wanting to use deadly force in front of the news crews.

Taylor continued to barge, push, shove, toss, hurl and throw for several minutes, before the waves of attacks suddenly stopped.

The soldiers still surrounded him, but he used the abeyance to catch his breath. Throwing people around was tiring work. He spun around and around, the faces before him a blur. He did not even know if he had already faced these people. If they were getting up and coming at him again, he would need to find a way to incapacitate them without severely hurting them. Otherwise, he would tire and they would be able to wear him down.

Suddenly, he felt a sharp pain in his leg and he thought someone had managed to stab him. When he looked down, though, he saw a metal dart sticking out of his thigh.

He did not even have time to recognise the significance of the object before he descended into sleep and collapsed to the ground.

10

Frank Davet could not remember the last time he had been ill. He had not had a single sick day in twelve years. His manager, Nathan Tyson, had even arranged a meal to celebrate this fact.

It was not so much that he loved his job. It was just who he was. He was the best Machine Operator the factory had, but he had no real passion for it. He loved Scalextric. The design of the track, the precision of the surroundings, the graceful speed with which his cars negotiated it. It was all about detail. Everything needed to be perfect.

His house was full of it. His current track consumed every room, which might have been one of the reasons he was still single. Not that this particularly concerned him. Internet porn made a woman much less necessary and, besides, his hand did not nag or need cuddles. Conversely, he could not afford a cook or a cleaner.

He felt great. Short, thin and, as several people had told him, damn fugly, he had never been a confident man. His short, ginger crew cut probably had not helped, much like his huge, green, frog-eyes and his yellow, crooked teeth. But, somehow, he felt as if he could take on the world. And win. In all his forty-seven years, he had never felt this good.

He had no idea where he had caught this from, but he knew he had managed to lose three entire days because of it. And that had caused him to miss the Scalextric show in Romsey, which really pissed him off. He had spent weeks preparing the track and had already put it in the back of the van.

When he had first started to feel better, he had been bemused. He had been angry. But, knowing what he now did, he realised it could be a blessing in disguise.

Now he could really make something of his life.

How, or why, this had happened, he did not know. He also did not care. The fact was that he had managed to predict correctly the score of every sporting event that had occurred since he woke up six days ago.

Football, rugby, tennis, cricket, darts, motor racing, horse racing, even tiddlywinks.

Davet had no clue how he knew this. But he did know that he was going to make the most of it.

He looked over the screen on the laptop and flicked between the different tabs. He knew better than to use one website for all his bets. He split them between a dozen sites and all three bookies in town. He also knew to lose on one site every day, but make a healthy profit across the others. He lost in the bookies, also, having formulated a roster to decide which shop to lose in that day.

By ensuring he never won an obscene amount of money with a single bet, and by losing regularly, he hoped to avoid raising suspicion. He had seen *Casino*. He knew what happened to those believed to be cheating the system. Although, he had spent a fortune discovering that his talent did not extend to poker, roulette or slot machines.

So, he guessed, he did not have to worry about aggrieved mobsters, but he did not know how deep the ties were between bookies and organised crime. He did not want to risk it. This was one secret he was determined to keep. He had seen enough of the news to know he needed to keep it from everyone he knew.

He had a long-term plan. If he could squirrel his winnings away over a period of several years, he would be able to retire and live in the lap of luxury. In the meantime, he would go to work, come home, place some bets, masturbate and go to sleep. He would keep filtering money into his new account at Credit Suisse until such a point that he could buy a home in the Algarve for cash. Then he could quit his job, sell his house and get out of this shithole.

He perused the odds for Fulham v Blackburn on Paddypower.com and put thirty pounds on 2 – 1. Next he moved to Ladbrokes.com and put five pounds on Fulham to win, before visiting Skybet.com and placing five pounds on Blackburn to win.

He moved from website to website, clearly marking down on a piece of paper those with which he was placing losing bets. Once he had finished, he calculated that he should make a £4,356 profit for his afternoon. He was just putting his jacket on, preparing to visit all three bookies and increase that, when he saw a shadow flicker past the window.

An instant later, the front door crashed open. A line of heavily armed soldiers, all in full battle gear, streamed into his living room, demanding that he lay face down on the floor.

Davet flopped to the carpet like a dead fish. Somebody forced his arms behind him and secured his wrists with a cable tie. When he opened his eyes, Davet saw a smartly dressed man, with silver hair, standing over him.

He crouched down and smiled into Davet's face. 'Good evening, Frank. My name's Mike Norbury. You and I need to have a little chat.'

Tess Walters had never enjoyed her life as much as in the last week. Her teenage years had been horrible, but they had taught her one, essential life lesson.

People were nicer to attractive women.

Unfortunately, she was not part of this elite group. Large breasts only helped if they protruded further than the stomach, she realised far too late to benefit. By the time she was eighteen, chocolate, crisps and ice cream were not so much snacks, but daily essentials. They were her only, real friends. She was certain her human friends only spoke to her because she made them feel better about themselves.

That was until she met Giles. He may not have been a hunk, but he loved her for her. He did not care that her blonde hair was dyed and wiry. He did not care that her brown eyes were opaque most of the time. He did not care that opening her legs did not part her thighs. He loved her.

Of course, that was until they found out that she was sterile. After they discovered they would be denied adoption on account of their health and age, he had fallen into a deep depression. The last days of their marriage were the worst of her life. Finding him hanging from a ceiling rafter by his belt was an image that had seared itself into her mind. Nothing could erase it.

That was, until the past week. She was often sick, so the fever was nothing new. What did come as a surprise, however, was waking up two days later.

Her boss was not a forgiving man. Kevin was a handsome, muscular thirty-three year-old bank manager and she had imagined his hands on her hundreds of times. Her job as a financial advisor was not glamorous or exciting, but she liked dealing with people and she was good at it, maybe the best in Milton Keynes.

But she had been warned about her attendance several times, so her invitation to Kevin's office came as no shock when she returned to work. What was a shock, however, was when he told her how good she looked. Obviously being sick agreed with her. As he began his reprimand, she sensed that he was flirting with her. Could it really be?

She left the meeting and rushed to the toilet to inspect herself. She still looked forty-three, as far as she could tell. She might have lost a pound, or two, but losing twenty would barely alter the rolls on her stomach. What was Kevin talking about? Maybe he just felt sorry for her.

Her shock was compounded, then, when he asked her to stay back after the branch had closed and help him check some figures. They were in his office, working at the table in the corner, when his hand grazed her leg. Their eyes met and he asked her if he could tell her a secret. She acquiesced and he confessed that there was something about her he had always found attractive.

They had sex on the sofa in his office. Her first, ever multiple orgasm. Her previous forty-three years had been pointless. Her life started now.

After leaving, she discovered that it was not just Kevin. On the way home, several men ogled her as she walked past. Two wolf-whistled. She had not been on the receiving end of a lecherous wolf-whistle in her entire life.

Back at home, she stripped off and studied her body. She was still fat. She was still pale. She still had the mole cluster on her back.

She jumped in the shower and, before she had finished drying herself, there was a knock on the door. It was Brian from next door. He was about fifty and used to be handsome, before marriage and three children had drained him. She answered the door in her robe and his eyes bulged when he saw her. When he asked her to borrow some milk, she was a little suspicious. There was a shop at the end of the road. When he told her that his wife had taken the children to the cinema, she caught him looking her up and down.

She decided to put it to the test. She dropped her robe in front of him and he leapt on her. They had sex three times on the kitchen floor. Then he left before his wife returned.

Back in the shower, Tess could not work out what was happening. Two men that she had often fantasised about had thrown themselves at her. She went to bed feeling great about herself.

The next day, Kevin was not at work. When she got home, there was a police car outside the house next door.

Brian had driven into an oncoming bus. The following day, at work, she discovered that Kevin been hit by a train. They were accidents, but both seemed intentional. Since neither man had any history of depression, the police were ruling out suicide.

Tess sat and pondered the situation for days. Then she decided to test it. She got dressed up and headed down the local pub. Stuart was a twenty-one year-old barman who she had fancied ever since locking her eyes onto his beautiful, smooth, tanned features. Within an hour, they were back at her house, Stuart inside her. They had sex five times that night and he went home in the morning, when she left for work.

When she went back to the pub that night, the landlord told her Stuart had died of food poisoning.

Tess ran home in tears. She did not dare test it again. It seemed she was some type of siren. Any man she found attractive was available to her, but they died afterwards. It was a matter of time before people realised what was happening. More importantly, how could she condone what she was doing?

She sat on her bed and looked at the naked, young police officer sleeping soundly. The poor boy was no older than twenty-five and had only knocked on her door to ask a couple of questions about Brian's family. It was not his fault he was handsome. It was not her fault she wanted him. She had spent a lifetime yearning for beautiful men and they had completely ignored her. She could not stop herself.

Once the young officer had finished pleasuring her for the sixth time, she let him go to sleep and then took his service gun from the holster strewn on the floor. She held it in her hand and studied it, knowing that this young man would also die in a terrible accident the following day.

She had to stop. Yet she knew, without a single scrap of doubt, that she would not be able to. All she had ever wanted was to be beautiful. This was her dream. It was better than she could have ever expected it to be. And it had turned her into a killer.

Tess sat on the bed and put the gun to her temple. She closed her eyes and thought about the beautiful men she had enjoyed over the last week. Maybe this would save the last one.

She pulled the trigger just as Norbury pulled up outside her house.

David Harper considered himself an unlucky man. All his life, whoever was in charge of the universe had screwed him over. Why they hated him, he had no idea.

His blue eyes were too far apart and his blonde hair began falling out twenty years ago, at the age of nineteen. His nose was enormous and droopy, whilst his skin was oily, acne-scarred and saggy. He had quite a lot of muscle, but could not get rid of the layer of fat that covered it up. His belly hung over his belt, no matter what he ate or how much he exercised.

He was a smart man, but had been overlooked for promotion on four separate occasions in the last five years. In every case, the job had gone to people less capable, or less qualified, than he was. They were all now his superiors and it made him feel sick.

He did not regret joining the police force, but he had expected it to be more rewarding, both financially and mentally. He was not poor, but he should be wealthier. He did not hate his job, but he did not feel like he was making a difference, either.

Until three days ago.

He suspected he got sick during the furore at the school last week, but he could not be certain. Either way, the HPA doctors had tested and cleared him, so they allowed him to leave.

He had felt a little rough that night, but took some Beechams and went to bed. When he awoke five days later, he knew it was serious. He watched the news for ten minutes and understood what was happening to him.

Under any other circumstances, being able to melt metal with his hands would have unnerved him. The fact he could not melt anything else seemed strange, but he was not about to complain. The fact he had survived suggested that his luck had changed. He thought about what he should do with it for around thirty-two seconds.

He should fix the wrongs in his life.

And to do that he needed money.

Nobody had any idea about his newfound talent, so it was easy for him to sneak into the Reading branch of HSBC late at night, disable the security and melt the safe door without anyone ever suspecting him. He spent a great deal of time making it seem like the criminals had employed the use of lasers to melt the metal and hoped the ruse lasted long enough for him to get out of the country.

Burying a little under four million pounds in cash and valuables under his shed was not his greatest plan, but he had not considered it carefully. It would suffice until he worked out an exit strategy.

He could not just deposit the money in the bank and expect nobody to notice. The police had called in the government's help with the investigation but, fortunately, the outbreak kept the larger law enforcement agencies too occupied to dedicate significant resources to it. Whilst four million was a lot of money, the viral pandemic was the priority.

He had briefly considered whether, or not, he would suffer from guilt.

The fact that his superiors denied his request to join the task force only confirmed to him that he had done the right thing.

For the past twenty hours, he had been sitting in front of the computer, trying to unearth a foolproof method of getting him and his cash out of the country before the borders were closed. Forty minutes ago, he made his decision.

Car.

The ferry to Calais booked, he was currently exploring ways to hide his haul all over the vehicle. He could take most of the panels off and stuff most of it in the bodywork, he guessed. His Vauxhall Vectra was probably large enough.

Tomorrow, he would vanish and nobody would ever see him again. That gave him the night to work in the garage and hide everything in the car.

He was hard at work, stuffing piles of cash in the passenger door, when he heard the garage door sliding up. He leapt out of the car to the sight of a gun muzzle. He grabbed and melted it, but suddenly there were ten more.

His face dropped and his heart sank. Somehow, they had found him.

It confused him when the silver-haired man strode up to him. He had seen the MI5 agents in charge of the case and he was not one of them. Harper stared up at him blankly, his mouth gaping.

The silver-haired man smiled as he looked around at the pieces of car on the floor. His eyes then moved to the piles of cash and bags full of valuables, ranging from gold and diamonds, to watches and necklaces.

He grinned as he looked back at Harper. 'It looks like you're planning a trip, Dave. Unfortunately, I'm going to have to ask you to delay it.'

Harper fought back the tears. His life was over. 'Am I going to prison?'

Norbury scoffed. 'No, Dave, I'm not going to tell MI5 about this. As long as you do me a favour.'

'What?'

'You come with me to a research facility so I can learn more about you.'

'Will you let me leave?'

He laughed. 'Of course! It's not a prison. You can even keep all your loot.'

Harper could barely believe his ears, but he was going to jump at any chance to keep his riches *and* avoid incarceration. Former police officers did not last long in prison. 'How long do you need me for?'

Norbury paused for a few moments. 'I can't say for sure. Not long. As soon as I have the answers I need, you can leave. Does that sound fair?'

Harper nodded zealously. 'Yes, it does!'

'Great. If you would be kind enough to follow these men to the van outside, they will take you there.'

Jack Cole had always planned to do great things with his life. He was an exceptional student, incredible athlete, unfeasibly handsome and incorrigibly charming. He had everything.

And he knew it.

His path through school and university was almost too easy. He scored top marks in everything he did without even trying. He left a string of model girlfriends behind him before meeting his model wife, who was the only woman he knew who challenged him.

He had no idea how he had got ill, but suspected it had something to do with the girl who had come to London for the interview at his company last week. He was sure she was from Towcester and that was the place that had been on the news all week.

He almost regretted sleeping with her. But she was attractive and he knew he could. The fact she thought it might help her land a job on his board was irrelevant. It would not, but it did not harm her chances.

Somehow, he had lost two entire days. Diane was in Dubai on a photo shoot, so he would not have to inform her about what had happened. Surely, though, she would notice the change in him.

He did not understand how, or why, but he was suddenly less impressed with himself. Even he knew how narcissistic he was, but he suddenly did not worry about his hair being perfect, or completing two hundred stomach crunches every morning.

He did not even care about his clothes. Only yesterday, he had left his penthouse flat wearing brown Gucci loafers with a grey Armani suit. How ridiculous!

A week ago, that would have been unthinkable.

He did not care, though. Whether, or not, his apathy was a result of the fact he could transform himself into a silverback gorilla at will, he was not certain. He guessed they had to be connected somehow.

Interestingly, he had mused, his metamorphic ability did not worry him. He woke up in the morning covered in dark fur, but had not even been especially surprised. His bed was broken from his sudden weight and he noticed his hands first. The stubby, grey fingers poking out of the thick dark arm hair. It took him less than three hours to master his new talent.

It also did not concern him that his entire attitude towards life was now different. Usually, whenever Diane was away working, he would take the opportunity to sow some oats. His wife knew about it. She would be doing the same. It was one of the things that made their marriage work.

He did not want to now, though. He had an inexplicable urge to help others.

Every fibre of his being pulsed with altruism. He was giving money to homeless people and wanted to set up a foundation for sick children.

Where had this benevolence come from? Prior to his illness, there had not been a magnanimous bone in his body.

And last night, it got worse. He found himself out on an estate. *An estate!* He had never even driven through one before.

Yet, there he was, hiding in the shadows. The moment he heard a group of youths haranguing an elderly lady, he sprung into action. The silverback gorilla gave those kids a beating they would never forget. Now the police were hunting an escaped gorilla, although no zoos had reported one missing.

Cole sat in his silk pyjamas and watched the news, as the reporter camped outside the school in Towcester tried to find any scrap of information about the effect of the virus they were investigating there. He smiled. He knew why they were trying to keep it a secret, but that was never going to work. More importantly, it was wrong.

He whipped open his laptop and it took him seven minutes to design the website. He needed fifteen minutes to locate and hack into the server they were using to collate the data being collected at the school. He downloaded it to his computer.

For the rest of the evening, he sipped bourbon and launched his new website.

Theherovirus.org was born and he linked it to Usenet. Within minutes, it was all over Facebook, YouTube and

Twitter. It took him almost half an hour to get it to the very forefront of any Google search on the words 'new virus' and 'Towcester'.

He sat back as his computer uploaded the recordings of what people could do to the host server. They would all be available for consumption by the public and he knew there were only ten or fifteen people in the world that might be able to break through his security to stop it. The videos became available on the site as soon as they finished uploading.

A contented grin spread across his face. He knew he was doing the right thing. People needed to know the truth and the fact was that the virus's effect on him had been so profoundly positive, he knew the world would be a better place if everyone caught it.

He closed his eyes and dreamed of a world where people only sought to help others. A world where people were kind and generous. A world that was not ruled by money, greed and hate.

He did not even get a chance to look at the clock when the door crashed open and the armed soldiers piled in. He knew he was still in his living room. Transforming into Silverback, he threw the intruders around like toys, but he was heavily outnumbered and outgunned. His fight lasted only a few minutes before they cornered him in the kitchen, a dozen weapons aimed at him, each with an itchy finger on the trigger.

But they did not move to fire. He did not really understand the reason why until a silver-haired man began to weave his way through the mass of soldiers, all dressed in full tactical gear.

'Can you talk normally when you're like that, Jack?' he asked casually, his roving eyes studying the gorilla.

Cole did not know. He had not thought to try. He tried. 'I'm not...yes, I can, it seems.'

'You revealed the virus to the world, Jack. Have you any idea about the shit storm you've started?'

'It's a good thing,' he insisted. 'People deserve to know what it can do.'

'Of course, you have fully perused the information you stole from our server, yes?'

Cole scoffed. 'I glanced at it.'

'So you know who I am?'

'Norbury?'

He clapped his hands. 'I suppose that saves me from introducing myself. Did you also happen to glance at the part of our research explaining that exactly half of the people infected actually die, as their bodies can't support the virus?'

Cole's face sank as he turned back into a man. 'What?'

Norbury smirked. 'You didn't see that part and, I suspect, none of the videos on your website will depict just how dangerous it is. Am I right?'

He shook his fist in the air. 'You're lying!'

'I don't need to lie. This illness is deadly. Not everyone is as fortunate as you.'

'I don't believe you!' he shouted.

'Be that as it may,' the doctor replied with a sigh. 'I'm going to have to insist that you come with us and help us with our research.'

Cole became Silverback and stood tall. 'You'll have to force me!'

'So be it,' Norbury uttered, as he clicked his fingers.

A dozen tranquiliser darts ensured Silverback was fast asleep in less than a second.

Tim Bulling finished typing the credit card details and hit 'enter'. The website chimed and the new window opened with the live footage already playing. He was pleasantly surprised. He had expected it to be grainy.

He maximised the window and connected the cable to his television. Now he could watch the fight in fifty inches of high definition.

He cast his eyes over the crowd and briefly wondered how they knew where the event was being held. This was only the fifth night, but everybody already knew that it was impossible to find it. The police had tried. The government had tried. Overseas agencies had tried.

Shrouded in secrecy, these fights were now the most watched broadcast anywhere in the world. Rumour had it that even the most capable hackers in the world had not been able to penetrate the website's security. Nobody knew who owned the site or where it was broadcast from. They tracked it as far as mIRC and then lost it.

He checked the names at the bottom of the screen as he moved the pizza boxes from the sofa to the floor and sat down. Flea v Claw was not a duel that anybody would have been excited about a week ago. But theherovirus.org had changed the way the world thought in only a week.

Tim watched zealously as the buzzer sounded and the competitors leapt into action. The draw of this event was mainly the fact that nobody knew what to expect.

Flea, a tiny, thin woman who looked about fifty, bounced up in the air, jumping several metres, landing in a crouch directly behind her foe. Claw, a burly man easily twice her weight and half her age, could not spin in time to avoid a fist to the groin.

She sprang away, somersaulting out of reach as he attempted to retaliate. His nails extended to over six inches and Flea was only just out of reach...

Claw sliced across her forearm. She bounced away again, powering up and to the side. Her feet touched the ground for a split-second, as she committed Claw to his attack. She was gone before he sliced the empty space, landing behind him and ramming her knuckles into his kidney.

He spun, swiping his talons at thin air. Flea was already gone. She sprang up in the air, twisting so she landed, feet first, on his head. Claw crumpled under the propulsion of her attack, but managed to catch her with the tip of his claws as she bounced back up in the air.

Tim watched it eagerly, his saccadic eyes almost pounding with excitement. The next bout was Brick v Icicle, so he knew he had a great night of entertainment ahead of him. He envied the possibilities these people now had in their lives. He was not sure he would be prepared to gamble his life for claws, but they had survived the challenge of The Hero Virus, so their options were limitless.

He wondered what it would be like to have options in life. It had fallen in Taylor's lap. Many of these people had chosen to contract the virus. Tim believed that made them braver than his friend. Exchanging fluids with a host was not easy to achieve.

He doubted he could ever be that courageous. Maybe. He might try, one day.

He banished the thought from his head, knowing that his life was not *so* terrible that he needed a virus to improve it.

He sank into his seat and enjoyed the spectacle on the television.

11

Taylor heard the gentle bleep of a heart monitor first. Then he heard the others. He had no idea how many there were, but it was a lot.

His head was throbbing and his mouth was dry. He did not try to open his eyes for several minutes. He merely absorbed the sound. Dozens of heart monitors, shuffling and talking some distance away. It soon became clear that sound would not help him discern where he was.

He opened his eyelids very slightly at first. The artificial light that entered through the slit was far milder than daylight or sunlight, but it still felt like a needle in his eyeball. He winced and shut his eyes again for a few seconds, before daring to try again. The daggers behind his eyes returned, but began to fade after a few moments. Once it had finally subsided, he opened them fully.

He was lying on his side and the first thing he saw was a bed. There was an elderly woman in it and she was fast asleep, with hosts of tubes pouring out from her mouth, nose, ears and arms.

He rolled onto his back and looked up at the ceiling, which was at least ten metres above his bed and made of white tarpaulin. He was in a tent.

Groaning, Taylor sat up and gasped at the sight before him. He was in a trolley bed in the middle of several dozen trolley beds. Every one of them had someone sleeping in it.

He rubbed his eyes, hoping it might ease the hammer inside his skull. His chest felt tight and he had plasters all over his arms. Looking around again, trying to make sense of his situation, he started to recall why he was here.

The soldiers. The dart.

As he scanned the room, he noticed an empty bed. Then another. The tent was not full. Yet. His eyes landed on a plump, short, brown-haired nurse walking around the beds and checking the screens attached to each heart monitor. He watched her for several minutes until she noticed him and scurried over.

'Don't get up too quickly!' she admonished firmly.

'What happened?' he croaked.

'You've been undergoing tests,' she explained in a perfunctory tone, touching the monitor next to the railed headboard and examining it. 'To help us fabricate a cure.'

'Tests?' he asked hoarsely. 'What tests?'

'Oh, the normal,' she continued, studying the screen. 'Blood, saliva, urine, MRI...that kind of thing. Dr Norbury will go through it with you in detail.'

'Norbury,' he murmured, containing a flash of anger. He watched her working for a few more moments before the curiosity got the better of him. 'Are all these people asleep?'

She smiled sweetly, piercing the patient with the kind eyes of a woman who placated people professionally. 'They're sedated, sweetheart. Some of the tests are a bit invasive and very uncomfortable, so it's better if the subjects are asleep. Besides, it's the only way to suppress their abilities.'

His jaw dropped as he looked around the others. 'They *all* have abilities?'

She spoke slowly and deliberately, enunciating every word carefully. 'Yes, my dear. They all have the virus.'

'How many?' he asked, staggered.

'We have one hundred and forty-two accounted for, so far.'

'What can *they* do?'

Her grin vanished and she shifted from foot to foot uncomfortably. 'I really think you should talk to Dr Norbury about this, my dear.' She poured him a beaker of water and handed it to him.

'Thanks,' he said, snatching it from her and gulping it down gratefully. The cool liquid soothed his parched throat.

'Sips!' she instructed sternly. 'Take small sips!' He paused and did as he was told. When she was satisfied that he was behaving, she continued. 'I'll let the doctor know you're awake. When you feel up to it, your clothes are under your bed. The soldiers on the door will escort you to Dr Norbury's office.'

She gave him another professional smile, before turning and walking away. Taylor watched her leave and switched his focus to the exit on the far side. He had not noticed the duo of armed sentinels before. He checked the entrance on the near side of the tent and saw two more guards posted there.

He spent several minutes sipping water, using the time to collect his senses. He slipped his clothes on and tested his strength on the leg of his metal trolley bed. He crushed it with one hand.

Walking casually towards the nearest exit, the soldiers eyed him suspiciously. He asked them to take him to Norbury and they summoned an armed escort, consisting of two, young marines, who cautiously took him out of the tent.

Taylor tried to survey as much as he could during the short journey. He was surprised to see he was still at the school. He left the cavernous, white marquee, which covered most of the school field, and walked across the grass. He looked over at the perimeter. The fence was up and topped with barbed wire. He also noted the teams of armed patrols strolling around and the protestors outside. The teenagers with machine guns guided him into the main school building.

Taylor entered the classroom that Norbury was using as his office and the doctor held his hand up to stop them as they entered.

The young marines grabbed an arm each and held Taylor at the entrance as Norbury talked to the huge screen on the wall. The patient cast his eyes around the room. They had piled all the desks in the corner, except for that of the teacher, which Norbury was using. On it were several computers and piles of folders. There were filing cabinets against the wall behind the desk and half a dozen maps on the wall: one of the world, one of Europe, one of Britain, one of Northamptonshire and one of the Towcester region. In each one, Norbury had stuck pins. There were too many to count in the local map, at least a hundred in the county map, several hundred more in the British map, several in the European map and a few in the map of the globe.

They all recognised the man with whom Norbury was conversing. He was rotund, tall and imposing, with more wrinkles than a man of fifty-eight should have, but also a thick mop of light brown hair, which seemed dyed, though he insisted was not. It was the Prime Minister. They watched in silence.

'I'm asking if the situation is contained,' Hodgkin demanded angrily. 'Stop dodging the question.'

'We can't be sure yet, sir,' Norbury replied, letting out an exasperated sigh.

'If it isn't airborne, I'm told that makes it manageable.'

'Sir, with all due respect, HIV isn't airborne, either-'

'Okay, okay, I see your point,' the PM interrupted brashly. 'However, you must appreciate the perception of this situation. You have turned a primary school into a prison complex. I'm watching the next election slip from my grasp with every passing day. In high definition, no less.'

'Sir, I think we have more pressing concerns than next year's election.'

'Look, doctor, I fear I'm not being entirely clear. Contain this outbreak and find a resolution. Do it swiftly.'

'We've established that it hasn't spread to the local wildlife, sir. That's a big step, but we can't rush this, or-'

'Swiftly, Norbury. Or I'll find someone who can.'

The Prime Minister disconnected the call and Norbury sighed loudly, beckoning Taylor over. The doctor slumped in his chair as the marines waited for Taylor to sit opposite him before leaving.

Taylor smiled uneasily, noting the staggering difference between the rigid, immaculate doctor who commanded complete obedience from a platoon of soldiers and the drained, withered man before him. Norbury had huge, black bags under his red eyes. His face was sallow and gaunt. His hair was in complete disarray and it looked like he had been sleeping in his clothes for several days. He had not shaved in a while and his body was limp and hunched. 'Hard day? You look like crap.'

He nodded sombrely. 'They're all hard at the moment.'

The patient scoffed. 'I hear the hardest days are those that start with a prison full of kidnap victims.'

'Don't be so pithy.'

'How long have I been here?'

'You?' Norbury leaned back in his chair and interlocked his fingers behind his head. 'Two weeks.'

Taylor hid his surprise and anger that they had stolen a fortnight of his life from him. He focused his ire on a more pressing outrage. 'You've kidnapped all these people, Norbury. I can't believe they let you get away with this.'

'Would *you* have voluntarily let us run tests on you?' he asked tersely.

'Of course.'

'No, you wouldn't,' he scoffed.

'You didn't even ask.'

The doctor smiled knowingly. 'You need to appreciate exactly what we're dealing with here. We have hundreds dead and hundreds more with abilities they don't understand and can't control. Our priority *has* to be containing it.'

'You could have asked,' Taylor returned defiantly.

'Maybe, but I can't risk refusal here.'

His eyes flickered to a series of aerial, thermal and close-up images of the copse. 'Any luck finding it?'

The doctor shook his head. 'We've excavated the entire area. Whatever you saw is long gone now.'

An awkward pause followed. Taylor shattered it. 'Where are San and Nate?'

'Dr Namib offered his assistance, but isn't qualified to work within this facility. He left several days ago.'

'I want to speak to him.'

'Don't worry, Chris,' he replied with a mollifying wave of his hand. 'He asked to be kept apprised of developments and receives regular status updates on you and Mr Tyson from my staff.'

'What happened to Deb and James?'

The expression on the doctor's face told him the bad news.

He started crying. 'Is Nate in the tent?'

'He's still undergoing tests.'

'What tests? What are you doing here, Norbury?'

'We're studying the virus, Chris,' he retorted venomously. 'Did you think this was all for fun?'

'Have you learnt much, at least?' he pressed quickly.

Norbury nodded excitedly. 'A vast amount. For example, it all began with you.'

Taylor scoffed. 'I guessed that much already. Have you figured out anything new?'

'Well, it's definitely a virus, for a start. However, it doesn't behave like other viral infections. It has a very strange effect on people.'

'You mean their special talents?'

He shook his head slowly. 'Not really, no. This is an incredibly advanced and unique agent.'

'You sound like you admire it.'

'In a way, I do. I guess it was always inevitable that nature would eventually produce something to balance us.'

'Balance us?'

'The planet is ridiculously overpopulated, Chris. Nature has found a way to combat that, whilst stimulating an evolutionary change at the same time. This virus will kill you or advance you. It's that simple.'

'And you can't develop a vaccine?' Taylor asked angrily.

'That won't work,' the doctor replied with a rueful shake of the head. 'It will give the patient an ability. We *did* think of that, believe it, or not.'

Taylor glowered at the man opposite him. 'So, you've imprisoned all these people and still have no idea how to treat them?'

Norbury leaned forwards. 'That's not a surprise. It can take months to develop a treatment for a previously unknown virus. Believe me, I would rather pursue my research in a proper facility, but the way this is affecting people makes that impossible.'

'What's so different about this that you need to study it in a prison?'

'You keep calling it a prison,' Norbury stated irately. 'This isn't a prison.'

Taylor scoffed. 'Really? Why else would you need towering fences and armed guards?'

Norbury glared at him confusedly. 'I don't think you understand. We need those to keep people out.'

He paused and shook his head. 'Why would anyone *want* to get in here?'

The doctor smiled awkwardly. 'To get the virus, Chris. They all want it. It's more valuable than gold.'

12

Taylor sat in stunned silence for a few minutes. During that brief time, several thousand thoughts swirled around in his mind. He understood instantly. They wanted to be powerful.

They had seen what he was capable of and wanted it for themselves.

When he snapped back to real life, he saw Norbury's satisfied smirk and scowled. 'Is it true that the virus kills some of the people who contract it?'

'Uh-huh.'

'Like Herodotus?'

'Your dog? Yes, we think he was ground zero but, without his body, we can never be totally certain. You are the original carrier.'

Taylor could not get his mind around the concept. 'Why would people *want* this virus if it has a good chance of killing them?'

The doctor shrugged nonchalantly, rubbing the stubble on his chin. 'It would seem that many people are quite prepared to gamble with their lives.'

'What are their odds?'

Norbury jutted out his bottom lip and tilted his head slightly. 'We haven't yet compiled enough data to be certain, but we estimate around fifty-fifty.'

'But, why?' Taylor demanded vehemently. 'Please tell me you have some idea how this virus works.'

'Of course!' he proclaimed, his expression suggesting disappointment at having been asked the question. 'How familiar are you with the workings of a virus?'

'They make you ill. We can't cure them. That's about it.'

Norbury smiled wryly. 'I'll try to explain it in layman's terms.'

'I'd appreciate that,' Taylor chuckled.

The doctor took a deep breath. 'A virus is, basically, an organism that survives by infecting a host cell with a genome, a bit like a parasite.'

He held up his hand sharply. 'What's a genome?'

'It's all the genetic information held by any given organism, within DNA or, in the case of this virus, and other viruses, the RNA. Do you know what that is?'

'That DNA is our genetic map, isn't it?'

Norbury smirked. 'Well, that's a simplistic way of putting it, but you could say that. Anyway, the virus infects the cell and feeds on the protein in it, using the cell's own metabolism to replicate and spread to other cells.'

'What happens when the protein runs out?'

'The virus kills the cell, which is why it migrates and spreads. It wants to survive. Well, that's true of most cases, at any rate.'

'But not this one?' Taylor asked, raising his eyebrows.

'It's not true of all cases. Some cause no obvious damage, or even change, to the host cell. It can continue to function normally. In this instance, our virus actually stimulates the cell. I suppose the simplest means of explanation would be to say that this virus acts as an accelerator.'

'Okay, but even I know enough to understand that the body has natural defences against an infection.'

'Right,' he replied with a knowing grin. 'The body produces antibodies, which usually attack the virus. However, *this* virus can, somehow, bind with an antibody to evolve. It uses the bloodstream to travel to the brain, where we're finding the vast majority of infected cells.'

'The brain? It's a brain disease?'

'No. It would seem that it seeks neurotransmitters, such as epinephrine or serotonin. It's not satisfied by standard cells. It wants these. Whatever cells it infects to start with, it abandons them and heads for the brain. The other cells are a means to an end.'

Taylor screwed up his face, perplexed. 'Why would it do that?'

'Because it's advanced, Chris. These are high-functioning cells. The virus feeds on these to enable it to grow quickly. It's also complex enough to stimulate the neurotransmitters. The more there are, the stronger it gets.'

'I won't pretend to know exactly what that means, but it sounds very advanced. How can a virus know to do that?'

Norbury held his hands out to either side, palms upwards. 'We have no idea. If it wasn't so terrifying, it would be magical.'

Taylor paused to allow the information to seep into his brain. 'Is that why it produces an ability in the host?'

'Kind of,' he replied with a head bob. 'But not always. When it accelerates the neurotransmitters, it inevitably ventures into parts of the brain that we don't really use a lot.'

'Is that also why it kills so many people?'

'Indeed. Each person has a unique chemical balance in their brain, which might be the reason they're good at maths, sports or art. This is also what determines our personality. Because of this, the virus either produces an ability or-'

'It kills them.'

'Correct.'

'Forgive me, but I thought we only used about ten percent of our brains? Is the virus tapping into unused parts?'

Norbury waved the remark away. 'Forget that nonsense. You only use between ten and twenty percent of your brain *at any given time*. You use all of it at different times, depending on what you're doing. For example, you use a different part to talk than you do to run, a different part to taste than you do to listen.'

'Okay. So why does it kill people, then?'

'In around half the subjects, the ones that died, we found toxic levels of these chemicals. Their brain poisoned them. We're seeing known illnesses, too. This virus can trigger an aneurysm or encephalitis, for example.'

'You're saying that some people just can't handle it?' Taylor remarked, intrigued.

'More specifically, the inherent chemical mixture in the brain can't sustain the virus. We don't understand

149

why. It seems bizarre that an organism of such majestic complexity and sophistication would allow its host to die. That kills the virus, too. And it's not easy to transmit. You need ingestion or prolonged exposure to contract it.'

'Maybe it's not so smart, after all?'

Norbury scoffed loudly. 'I've researched every virus known to medical science. I've discovered seven new ones. One thing they never do is commit suicide. I'm missing something. I just don't know what.'

Taylor took in a lungful of air and pushed it back out. He scratched his head. 'None of that explains why people *want* it. Why flip a coin for your life?'

'People are flying here from all over the world!' he exclaimed with a sarcastic chortle. 'All they want is a dose of this virus. I guess they want to be special.'

'It doesn't seem worth risking your life for.'

'What makes it even stranger is that, even if they survive, their new talent might be useless.'

'How so?'

'You've seen a couple, haven't you? You're inhumanly strong and your friend, Mr Tyson, can manipulate and magnify the electricity in his body. Some of the other talents we've seen have less blatant uses.'

'Such as?'

'We have one patient who came here from Yemen and managed to ambush an infected girl whose parents were bringing her here. He shot the parents and drank the girl's blood whilst she was still alive before executing her, too. All of this to get an ability where, if he touches you, it forces you to urinate. That's it.'

150

Taylor gasped, his expression aghast. '*Why* would anyone do such a thing?'

He shrugged his shoulders. 'Why do we do a lot of things? Our race isn't nearly as civilised as we often believe it to be.'

'He killed a kid so he can make people piss themselves?' he muttered, barely able to believe the words.

Norbury nodded sadly. 'She was nine. The world is going crazy, Chris. That's why we need to contain this virus and find a way to either treat, or reverse, the effects. One woman got into the compound, injured four people and can now force flowers to bloom.'

'What use is that?'

His face lit up in illumination. 'Precisely my point! It's impossible to predict what this virus will do to the host.'

'I assume not all the talents people now have are as pointless?'

'Far from it,' he replied, indicating the wall next to them. Taylor had not noticed it before, but it was covered in images of people, with notes scribbled on them detailing their abilities.

Norbury stood up and moved to the photograph of a young woman. 'We've seen a wide variety. This woman's name is Helen Taylor. She heals herself. We haven't tested the full limits of it, but she can grow a finger back.'

He pointed to a picture of another young woman. 'This girl became a genius and had managed to develop a theory for a perpetual energy source. We were bringing her in when a Russian oil oligarch had her assassinated.

She had not yet managed to write down the theory. It's lost forever.'

He moved along the wall to a boy, no more than six years old. 'Telekinesis.' The next picture was an elderly man. 'Telepathy.' He moved along the wall, stating the talent manifested inside the person belonging to the image. 'Clairvoyance, clairsentience, clairgustance, mammalian mind control, amphibiousness, aqua-kinesis and, literally, dozens of others. We caught one guy who could turn into a gorilla.'

He needed a few seconds to get over the shock. 'Are all these people in that tent?' he asked, tossing his thumb over his shoulder.

'For the moment, but new subjects are appearing daily.' He sat back down in his seat heavily. 'We're no longer sure. Every time we think we've got them all, we get reports of more cases. We bring in the infected and anyone they've been in contact with during the incubation period, which is twenty-four hours. It shouldn't be spreading.'

Taylor pondered the problem for a moment. 'Herodotus caught it. Maybe it's the animals.'

Norbury shook his head fervently. 'No, no. Your Labrador was an isolated case. He ingested the original strain. We're assuming it was far more potent, although we haven't yet found it to prove that theory. We've tested random creatures of every type, from every group of the animal population. We've got nothing.'

'And it's definitely not airborne?'

'Not that we can tell and we've tested it as thoroughly as science allows.'

'So, how is it finding new hosts?'

'That's the mystery, Chris.'

Taylor paused again. He had absorbed a huge amount of information in a very short space of time and his mind felt like it was swimming in novocaine. 'Can I help at all?'

Norbury nodded eagerly and slammed his hand on the desk. 'You're the primary host. Every time it moves to a new host, it seems to dilute.'

'It gets weaker?'

'The rate of acceleration in the host neurotransmitters is far lower. Third generation hosts have much less power than you, the first generation host.'

'So, you're hoping it will peter out?'

He shook his head. 'It will, eventually, but we can't rely on it. We're bringing in fifth generation carriers capable of pyro-kinesis. It could be a long time before the virus is so weak it can't produce a dangerous ability or kill the host. We can't afford to wait that long. Besides, it could mutate. If that happens, we'll have to start all over again.'

'So, how can I help?'

'Just let us test you.'

Taylor did not hesitate for an instant. 'No problem. I'm all yours.'

'Some of the tests are quite invasive and unpleasant, but it's our best hope of discovering how it's still spreading.'

'It's fine,' he asserted. 'Just don't sedate me.'

'It might be better for you if-'

He held up his hand. 'Don't sedate me. If you try, I'll withdraw my consent and fight you to the bitter end.'

He sighed. 'We won't sedate you, Chris.'

He stood up sharply. 'Now that's settled, am I free to walk around the compound? I feel the need for fresh air, having been asleep for two weeks.'

Norbury motioned towards the door and nodded his head. 'Feel free.'

Taylor grinned and walked out of the classroom, feeling the crisp air in his lungs.

Norbury motioned towards the guards by the door. 'Keep a close eye on him. One wrong move and you know what to do.'

Taylor had no idea how long he was walking around. He did his best to ignore the commotion outside the fence, but the noise blocked out all others. The crowd he had previously believed to be protestors were actually clamouring to get inside. He shook his head in disbelief.

The complex no longer looked like a school. The huge marquee covered the majority of the field, but there were other, smaller tents dotted around the grounds. Three huge trailers rested in the front car park and the army had finished erecting the gatehouse and five other temporary buildings on the playground. Doctors, nurses and soldiers scurried around busily and Taylor realised that he had not yet seen anyone inside the compound who was not wearing an overcoat or uniform.

He strolled casually around the perimeter, trying to block out the begging from the swarms of people on the other side of the fence. The army had troopers standing at static posts, as well as several patrols and he noticed the large signs warning of the voltage surging through the metal mesh. He could see the CCTV cameras swinging back and forth atop the poles. Nobody would enter this compound without Norbury's permission.

He was walking past a plywood hut, trying to peer in the window, when he heard the familiar voice calling his name.

He spun around and his eyes locked on to Tim, jostling for position on the other side of the fence.

Taylor rushed to his friend. 'What you doing here, mate? Are you okay?'

'I'm fine,' he replied, barging away the sudden rush of people clamouring to get Taylor's attention. He had to elbow an old woman in the ribs to avoid being pushed into the electricity. 'They won't let me in to see you.'

'Did you tell the press what was happening here?'

'They already knew everything,' he shouted, pushing away a young man who was fighting to steal his position. 'Are you okay?'

He nodded, ignoring the guards who had run over to shout at the surging throngs. 'I'm going to help them with their research.' He indicated the people around his friend. 'Are you sure it's a good idea to be near all these crazies?'

'I'm glad you're okay, mate, but that's not the only reason I'm here.'

'Really?' Taylor was intrigued, suspecting that his friend was probably writing a freelance article and wanted an exclusive.

'I need a favour.'

155

'If I can, mate. What's up?'

Tim did not pause, or even blink, as the words escaped his lips. 'I need you to give *me* the virus.'

13

Taylor's efforts to convince the soldiers to let Tim in failed and he needed Norbury to grant his friend access. Despite his fury at being dragged away from work to allow a civilian into a secure compound, Taylor eventually forced him to concede by saying he would refuse all the tests they wanted to do on him.

After half an hour, he and Tim were sitting in the teacher's lounge, now used as the canteen for the medical staff, drinking disgusting coffee. It was a small room with a few desks and chairs around them. A well-worn, green sofa sat in the corner, facing out into the room and the wall was covered in motivational posters about how best to influence young minds.

They sat in an awkward silence for a few minutes, before Taylor finally spilled what was on his mind.

Taylor was staring at his friend, horrified. 'Why do you want it?'

Tim took a sip from his mug and winced as he swallowed the bitterest coffee he had ever tasted. 'Look at my life, Chris. I'm a total failure.'

He shook his head fervently. 'No, you're not. You're an inspiration to the rest of us. You're living life on your own terms.'

'I'm a failed writer,' he spat angrily.

'You're chasing your dream.'

'I can't find a woman.'

'You're playing the field.'

'They're going to re-possess my house.'

'We all have cash flow problems sometimes, Tim.'

'I'm completely miserable, Chris.'

He paused and studied the expression on his best friend's face. How could he not have noticed this before? 'I had no idea. I thought you were happy. We all did.'

He shrugged his shoulders and his lips creased into a sullen smile. 'That's what I want everyone to think, mate. I'm ashamed, so I act like everything is just how I want it to be. I haven't been happy in years.'

Taylor absorbed this information from the man he had once perceived to be the happiest and most confident he knew. 'I'm sorry to hear that, mate, but how would getting the virus help?'

'It's being called The Hero Virus,' he returned, in a tone that suggested the answer was obvious.

'Why?'

'Because it turns people into heroes, Chris.'

Taylor glowered at his friend over the mug as he took a sip. 'It might also kill you.'

'I read that the odds are fifty-fifty,' he replied dryly. 'I'll take the chance.'

He grimaced at his friend's lackadaisical attitude. 'You would really risk your life so easily?'

'Damn right!' he retorted vehemently. 'My life isn't worth anything. It's a joke. I'll happily gamble it for the chance that something special might happen to me. This could make me great, Chris.'

Taylor held up his hand. 'This is absurd! Even if you live, your ability could be useless.'

'Maybe. I'll never know if I don't try, will I? Besides, from what I've read, I'd get a 2nd Gen ability if you give

158

me the virus. That's got to be better than one of the 8th Gen abilities I could buy.'

'You can buy them?' he asked incredulously.

He nodded as he finished his coffee. 'Uh-huh, if you have the money and contacts.'

Taylor shook his head ruefully. 'That's ridiculous.' He ruminated over the concept for a few moments. 'What did you mean by 8th Gen?'

'That's what they're calling the diluted abilities. They're judged by how many times the virus has been passed on.'

'So, what am I?'

'You're the 1st Gen, Chris.'

'How much does an 8th Gen ability cost?'

'About a hundred grand.'

Taylor gasped and leaned back so far in his chair he almost fell. 'That's preposterous! And you have that kind of money?'

'Of course not!' he laughed. 'But I can get it, even if the lender is highly questionable. But it seems absurd, especially when you think an 8th Gen ability is weak compared to yours. Who wants to be able to see in the dark? I want something awesome.'

Taylor could not control his outburst of anger. 'You don't get to choose, Tim!'

'I know that!' he retorted querulously. 'But it increases my odds to get a 2nd Gen.'

He let out an annoyed sigh and rubbed his temples. 'Tim, this is lunacy. I'm not giving it to you.'

'Please, Chris,' he implored, using his most pathetic look. 'How many times have I been there for you?'

'What's that got-'

'It's got everything to do with it!' Tim interjected tersely. 'When your entire life fell apart, who was there for you? Who was on the end of the 'phone all those times in the middle of the night?'

Taylor bowed his head. 'You were,' he muttered ashamedly.

He pressed his advantage. 'You've said, several times, that you wouldn't have made it if not for me. Is that still true?'

He could not look his best friend in the eye. He simply stared at the table. 'Yes, it is.'

'Now I need *you*, Chris. I need this.'

'You might die,' he stated weakly.

'I know the risks,' Tim retorted firmly. 'I'm an adult. I choose to take the chance. If it goes wrong, I absolve you of all responsibility.'

Taylor looked up with fire in his eyes. 'That doesn't mean anything, Tim. I would still have killed you!'

'I could die, anyway. I'll get the virus, no matter what it takes. Do you really want me at home on my own ingesting it?'

'How can you be so cavalier with your life, Tim? I mean, I'm trying to understand, I really am, but I just don't.'

'You told me, after Jane died, that you felt empty inside. Do you still feel that way?'

Taylor furrowed his brow. 'What's that got to do with it?'

He held up his hand. 'I'm trying to explain it to you, mate. Just go with it and answer the question.'

Taylor thought about it for a moment. 'I still feel that way. It's even worse since Herodotus died, because I've lost another link to her. It's less painful. Not a lot, though. Just slightly. I guess the best way to describe it would be to say that I'm learning to cope with the pain. It doesn't cripple me like it used to.'

'Do you think it will ever go away?'

He shook his head slowly. 'I doubt it. I hope it doesn't. As long as it's there, I know that she's still part of me. Does that make sense?'

'It makes perfect sense. Do you appreciate *why* your sense of loss is so overwhelming, Chris?'

Taylor stared at his friend blankly. 'Because I lost so much.'

'Indeed. You had a lot to lose. Whilst it's tragic that it was taken from you, you had it in the first place. Think of your happiness as a bottle of water. You were with Jane and, although you drank from it every day, the fact you were with her replenished the contents. Are you following me?'

He was a little confused, but nodded anyway.

'Now,' Tim continued, 'when Jane died, the bottle ran empty and you couldn't fill it back up, because she was no longer here, hence your emptiness. Imagine if you had never met Jane and the things that used to fill your bottle up vanished a long time ago. You would have had an empty bottle, much like you do now, only for much longer.'

'But you have loads of things in your life that make you happy.'

'Do I?' he scoffed. 'Do you mind telling me what they are?'

'You have freedom. You can do whatever you want, whenever you want.'

'I have nothing,' he returned tersely, 'because I don't have anyone to share it with. My work is a joke because I can't get anything published. Going out, getting pissed and taking some young bird home no longer does it for me. I want a relationship. I want a family. I want a life. My bottle has been empty for years, mate. That feeling you have inside of you might be a lot more potent than my own, but I've had it for years.'

'If you don't like your life, Tim, then I'll help you get whatever you want. But not this. You could die. That's not going help anything.'

'Don't you think I've tried? It's not that simple, Chris. This is a chance for me to have something amazing. I might be able to do something incredible. This is the opportunity I've been waiting for.'

'There must be another way.'

'There isn't. I haven't taken this decision lightly. I've thought about nothing else for days. This is my shot at happiness.'

'What if you die, Tim? I can't willingly give you a virus that has a fifty-fifty chance of killing you. I just can't.'

His face was expressionless. 'I'll get it one way, or another. The only aspect of my decision that you have influence over is how I achieve it. This is a chance for you to help me. If you say no, I'll start exploring my other options and who knows where that will lead me?'

He studied his friend carefully. He could not recall ever seeing such determination in him before. He turned it over in his mind for several minutes as both men sat in silence, staring at each other. He listened to the sounds from outside. He could hear boots on the tiled floor and muffled voices fading as they moved further away. He heard the growl of an engine and, once that subsided, the ticking of the clock on the wall began to resonate, amplified by the silence.

Eventually, he took a deep breath and ran his fingers through his hair. 'Only if it's in this compound.'

Tim almost jumped from his seat. He punched the air elatedly, his face stretching into a huge grin. 'Whatever you want, mate!'

He stood up sharply. 'I'll talk to Norbury. *If* I can convince him that the idea has scientific merit, he will give you the virus. Wait here for me. It could take some time.'

Tim rushed around the table and embraced his best friend. 'I don't know what to say, mate! Thanks so much! You have no idea what this means to me.'

He returned the hug unenthusiastically. 'He hasn't said yes yet.'

Suddenly pulling away, Tim's face filled with alarm. 'What if he says no?'

'Then I'll make him an offer he can't refuse.'

'Absolutely not!' Norbury bellowed angrily, slamming his fist on the desk and knocking a glass of water over a pile of papers.

Taylor smiled wryly. 'Think about it carefully. You can research the whole process. You will get the opportunity to actually observe the point of infection.'

'I'm starting to regret letting you wake up. All you seem to be doing is wasting my time. You drag me out of the lab. to get your friend in the compound and now you want me to give him the bloody virus.'

'He wants this. I'm going to do it, anyway.'

Norbury chuckled and met Taylor with a ferocious glower. 'And if he dies?'

'Do you think I don't understand the risks? It's what Tim wants. I realise that you don't know him, but I'm telling you he'll get the virus if he really wants it. At least this way we can control the environment. You can ensure nobody else is infected accidentally.'

'I *thought* I made it abundantly clear that there is no way to control this virus.'

'Did you know that people are selling infection?'

Norbury rolled his eyes. 'Most of it's fraudulent.'

'Most? Not all.'

'We're on top of that,' he snapped venomously.

'Or so you think,' he said with a smirk. 'Let me put it to you another way: Tim wants the virus and I owe him more than I can explain to you. He's never asked anything of me before.

One way, or another, if this is what he truly wants, I'll do it for him, with or without you. I didn't come here for your approval. I came here for your help.'

He sighed wearily. 'Don't make me confine you, Chris.'

'Don't make me fight you, doctor.'

Norbury paused for several seconds, considering the proposal with a grave face. 'This goes against all logic.'

Taylor grinned cheekily. 'It's going to happen. Accept it. All you can do is use the situation to your advantage. You'll get the chance to observe the actual infection process, which might help you understand how it's still spreading.'

'That's true, I guess.'

Taylor hid his delight. 'Does that mean you'll do it?'

'Under protest.'

'Duly noted. But is it a yes?'

Norbury took a deep breath and forced the air from his lungs. 'I'll get a room ready. You go and get your friend.'

14

Taylor stuffed the scrambled eggs into his mouth zealously and dipped a slice of toast in the juice before he tore a strip away. He chased it with a gulp of tea, barely pausing for breath before his filled the fork with more eggs and rammed them into his mouth.

Such was his focus on his third meal in a row that he did not notice the soldier walking in. The young man waited for almost a minute before announcing his presence with a hack into his hand.

Taylor looked up and cast the soldier an inquisitive look. He stopped chewing and waited.

'Mr Bulling is awake, sir,' he declared.

Taylor swallowed his mouthful in one gulp and dropped his fork, leaping out of his seat and racing away. He rushed straight past the soldier without even a word of thanks, dashing down the corridor to a former archive, now a makeshift recovery room, with a single bed, some monitoring equipment, one visitor's chair for him and a strong stench of disinfectant. Barging in, he found his friend sitting upright and a young, male nurse feeding him sips of water.

'How you feeling, bud?' Taylor inquired, suddenly feeling the knots in his stomach loosening.

'Good,' he replied with a weak smile. 'I made it.'

'It was touch and go, but you pulled through.'

Tim swallowed a sip of cold water. 'Did it help Norbury figure out how it's still spreading?'

'I've no idea. I've been in here with you most of the time.'

'How long was I out?'

'Three days.'

Tim allowed himself a smile that spread from ear to ear. 'I made it, Chris.'

Taylor nodded joyously. 'Do you feel different?'

'No. Did you?'

'Not really.'

'Did I get an ability?'

He shrugged his shoulders, his discomfiture apparent. 'Norbury says we won't know until it manifests. It's different for each person.'

'They can't scan for it, or something?'

Taylor chuckled. 'They can scan to see if you have the virus, which you do, but they can't predict which ability you'll get. We'll just have to wait and see.'

The nurse handed Tim another cup of water. 'Remember to drink it slowly, sir. I'll leave you guys to it.'

He took another sip and rubbed his eyes with the knuckles on his free hand. 'How do I use it?'

'It will just happen,' he replied in an assured tone. 'Just have patience, mate.'

Tim swung his feet out of bed unsteadily. Taylor took his hand to help him. When he stood up, his legs were shaking. 'Am I meant to feel this weak?'

'It will pass. You need to rest and you need to eat and drink plenty to regain your strength.'

He took a few, small steps. 'It's passing already.' He closed his eyes and took several deep breaths. 'I don't feel any different at all.'

Taylor laughed loudly. 'Neither did I and I found out about my new talent by accident. So will you, don't worry.'

With his friend's aid, Tim ambled wearily out of the recovery room and towards the huge marquee. He moved slowly at first, but was soon walking normally. He stood in the entrance and looked over the rows of beds, which increased in number hourly.

The plump nurse, who Taylor had since learned was called Hooper, appeared next to them. 'Are you okay, gentlemen?'

'Are they all asleep?' Tim asked reverently.

She smiled and placed her hand on his arm gently. 'Yes, they are. It's the only way to suppress their powers. Most people have no idea how to control their ability. It scares them and they become a danger to themselves and those around them.'

He eyed Hooper suspiciously. 'Are there any other cognizant people with powers in the compound?'

'A few,' she replied warmly. 'Those with talents that aren't likely to harm others, ranging from 2nd Gen to 9th Gen.'

'9th Gen?'

Taylor answered the question, despite the fact he directed it to the nurse. 'We've had several new arrivals in the last couple of days. It looks like the virus diluted again.'

'What are their abilities like?'

Taylor searched his memory for a few moments. 'One of them is a healer and is surprisingly powerful.'

Tim met him with a sceptical glare. 'I thought the power of the virus got progressively weaker with each passing generation.'

'It does, usually. It's a bit of a twist, but Norbury insists that one instance doesn't mean much. It could just be an anomaly and we need more data before we start jumping to conclusions.'

He surveyed the beds. 'How many 2nd Gen are here?'

'One.'

He looked at Taylor with melancholic eyes. 'Nate?'

He nodded sullenly. 'Yes.'

Tim's expression of excitement suddenly transformed into a sombre wince. 'He's still here?'

'He can't control it,' Taylor explained, his voice strained with emotion. 'They don't trust him not to hurt anyone.'

'Can I see him?'

'Sure,' he replied, moving away.

Taylor guided his unsteady friend through the maze of beds carefully, but purposefully. It was a familiar journey. Tim gazed at the peaceful faces in every bed with a mixture of fear and wonder. So much potential that might never be realised. He started to become very aware that this was what might await him if he developed a power that Norbury deemed lethal and he could not master it.

When they reached Nate's bed, Taylor carefully lowered him into the plastic chair next to it and stood there silently, his arms folded as he watched his friend sleep.

'What happened with Deb and James? Did they make it?'

He shook his head ruefully.

Tim collapsed forwards onto the bed and buried his face in his arms. When he looked back up, his eyes were red. He took Nate's hand. 'I'm so sorry. I miss you. I hope you'll be okay soon.'

'I come here every day and tell him the same thing,' Taylor remarked with a forlorn smile. 'I like to think he can still hear me.'

Hooper had appeared behind them and commented that she believed the same thing.

Taylor turned to her. 'When's his next test?'

She moved towards the bed and pressed several buttons on the screen. 'Next week.'

Tim looked from his friend, to the nurse, then back to his friend, the confusion evident. 'What test?'

'Everyone gets a chance to prove that they can control their ability,' he explained. 'There's a control room in the school. If they can't control their power, they're sedated.'

'How long for?' he inquired overtly concerned.

'That depends on how many people are arriving. At the moment, they can test about four people a day. There's a roster and the number of people on it keeps increasing.'

Tim scowled. 'How can they be expected to master their power if they're asleep?'

'At least they get a shot, Mr Bulling,' the nurse retorted firmly. 'We've had seven people pass this week, so they're allowed to live in the compound.'

He chuckled sarcastically. 'That's nice, although you have to wonder why a 9th Gen healer can be considered a threat.'

Hooper met him with a stern glower. 'She actually asked to be cured. Know your facts before you condemn us. This woman was rescued from kidnappers who wanted to use her to sell the virus. She is asleep whilst we perform some tests. Some of them are quite uncomfortable.'

'So, if Norbury decides that the ability isn't dangerous, he lets them stay awake?'

Taylor nodded and placed his hand on his friend's shoulder. 'You don't yet appreciate the scope of this crisis, Tim. The Hero Virus is selling for big money. You can get fifty grand for an 11th Gen sample.'

He tilted his head slightly. 'And what are the abilities like at 11th Gen level?'

'Mostly useless, but some people have reported low-level telekinesis, precognition and magnetism. They're quickly learning not to advertise their infection. If they're lucky, they'll only be swamped by the press and people who want to contract the virus.'

'If they're lucky?'

'Uh-huh,' Taylor replied knowingly.

Tim could feel his chest tightening. 'What if they're unlucky?'

'Yesterday, a young, pregnant woman was murdered. They drained her blood and cut her baby from her.'

His face drained of colour and he stood up sharply. 'What? Why?'

'They wanted the virus.'

He staggered away from the bed and Taylor grabbed his arm to stop him from falling. He fought the nausea. 'That's horrific.'

'That's why we're much safer in here than we are out there, Tim.'

He nodded eagerly, as he swayed on his feet. 'I think I should go back to bed.'

'I think that's a tremendous idea, mate,' Taylor replied firmly. 'You should rest before your test tomorrow.'

Taylor watched the screen intently. Tim stood in the middle of the square, metal room and stared at the metal table in the centre. On the table was a variety of objects, from plastic cups filled with water, to wooden bowls filled with ball bearings.

Taylor watched his friend via the camera images. Tim was glaring blankly at the table, seemingly bewildered. Taylor moved the microphone to his mouth, but did not yet say anything.

Tim knew he had been standing there for a long time. He did not know how long they would leave him for, or even if there was a time limit. But he did not know what to do. How could he manifest an ability if he did not know what it was yet?

The entire exercise seemed pointless and he could feel himself getting angrier. He stood before the table with his fists clenched, eyeing the yellow, rubber duck. What could he do with that? He did not understand.

He tried to clear his head, just as they had told him to, but there were too many thoughts. He knew Norbury was watching and what was expected. But he did not know where to start.

How could he test something he did not know existed?

This was ludicrous!

Taylor's voice suddenly crackled from the speaker in the wall. 'Just relax, mate.'

He looked up at the camera in the corner. 'Nothing's happening.'

'It will come. Just let it happen naturally.'

Tim could feel the agitation growing within him. 'I haven't got anything.'

Taylor looked across at the others in the observation room, formerly a broom cupboard. He focused on Norbury, who urged him on with a series of strange hand signals. He turned back to the microphone. 'You have, but you can't force it. Stop trying.'

'I'm telling you, there's nothing in me,' he retorted irately.

'Stop forcing it!' Taylor instructed firmly. 'Sit down.'

He did so obsequiously. 'I don't see how-'

'Be quiet!' he ordered.

Tim visibly shrank. 'Okay.'

'Close your eyes and clear your mind.'

He did so.

'Take deep, slow breaths.'

He sucked air in through his nose and blew it out through his mouth. It felt cathartic.

'Don't think of anything. Clear that cluttered brain of yours.'

He sat for several minutes, breathing in and out. Taylor watched the monitor intently, along with the other people in the tiny room.

Eventually, Tim opened his eyes and looked up at the camera. 'There's nothing-'

'Shut the fuck up!' Taylor barked. 'Sit there quietly and clear your mind. Be patient!'

'And do what?' he snapped back.

'Nothing!' he screamed. 'You're waiting!'

Tim closed his mouth, shut his eyes and placed his palms down on the table. He concentrated on breathing in and breathing out. He started counting the seconds. Fifteen minutes passed when his eyes flicked open.

He started to grin. 'There's something there, but I lost it.'

'That's because you're still trying to force it!' Taylor bellowed. 'Don't!'

He returned to counting the seconds. Ten more minutes passed before he opened his eyes again. The excitement was almost too much for him. 'There's something there!'

'Let it happen naturally,' Taylor urged him softly.

Tim closed his eyes and returned to his state of meditation. He did not count the seconds this time, but guessed it was only a few minutes before his fingers started to tingle and burn. He opened his eyes and sparks were coming from his fingertips. He had no control over the small electrical bolt that fired into the wall.

'Holy shit!' he exclaimed.

The entire observation room gasped. They watched Tim as his fingers sparked and crackled.

Taylor turned to Norbury. 'The same as Nate?'

The doctor leaned forwards and scrutinised the screen. 'It would certainly *seem* that he has the same ability as your friend, Mr Tyson. This would be the first time we've seen a duplicate ability.'

Taylor stared at him confusedly. 'Are you serious?'

He continued to stare at the monitor. 'We've seen similar powers, but they always vary slightly. No two cases of telekinesis will be exactly the same. There will always be a slight difference. And we've certainly not seen the same ability in the same generation.'

Taylor spent a few moments watching his elated friend throwing lightning bolts into the wall before turning back to the doctor. 'Really? Do you think that has some kind of significance?'

He opened his mouth to answer, but the door burst open, stopping him before any words came out of his mouth. It was Nurse Hooper.

She scanned the room and her eyes locked on to her target: Norbury. 'Doctor, we've got a situation.'

Norbury and Taylor exchanged a worried glance before the doctor asked the question. 'What's the problem?'

She was panting heavily and needed several seconds to find the words. 'It's Mr Tyson. You had better come and see for yourself.'

15

When they arrived in the marquee, Taylor could see the crowd of medical staff gathered around Nate's bed. He was able to judge the severity by the volume of the voices.

They were loud.

Norbury charged through the tent and barged his subordinates out of the way, Hooper beside him. Taylor and Tim followed behind, panic gripping their hearts. Soldiers stepped in their way as they moved towards the bed.

'Let them do their jobs, gentlemen,' a mature-looking soldier said dutifully.

They struggled slightly, but Taylor quickly became aware that he was throwing people around the tent. He paused and looked at the three people he had already injured. The mature soldier held a pistol to his head and Taylor held his hands up in surrender.

Tim's fingers were crackling and sparking as he primed himself for battle, but he stopped when he felt a tight grip on his arm. Spinning around, his ferocious glower met his friend's calming smile.

Taylor shook his head gently and Tim's finger stopped crackling. 'This isn't the way to help Nate.'

He nodded his head once. 'You're right, mate.'

They stood and watched the commotion around Nate's bed. Norbury barked a series of instructions over the panicked voices, but they could not see what was happening to their friend for all the people blocking their view. They could not concentrate on what he was shouting. The strident screech of the flat line from the heart monitor was far too loud.

An army medic rushed past and Tim stopped her. 'What's happening?'

'We don't know yet,' she returned sharply, yanking her arm from his hand violently. 'He just started convulsing and his heart stopped. Now, excuse me, please.'

Norbury was hollering and his staff scurried around with horrified expressions on their faces.

Taylor grabbed the medic's arm again, before she could leave. 'Is he going to be okay? Is there anything we can do?'

She glared at his hand until he released his grip. 'If there's anyone who can save him, it's Dr Norbury.' She rushed away and joined the panicked masses surrounding Nate's bed.

They listened to Norbury's voice as it became more high-pitched. Neither man had ever heard him sound worried before. It did not fill them with confidence.

The medical staff continued to scurry around to the sound of the flat line bleep and Norbury's yelled orders for several more minutes. Finally, his voice became even. 'Call it, people!'

Another doctor announced the time of death.

The friends exchanged a look of dread.

'That can't be it!' Taylor screamed, swaying on his feet.

The throng began to disperse and Tim grabbed a doctor as they walked past. 'What the fuck are you doing?'

'I'm sorry,' she replied ruefully, slightly afraid.

Taylor grabbed her arm and squeezed. 'Get back over there! You're not finished!'

She screamed in agony.

Norbury appeared, diving in and trying to snatch Taylor's hand away. 'Chris, let her go this instant!'

He obeyed, using the hand to grab Norbury's collar and pull him close. He lifted the doctor in the air with one hand and shouted in his face. 'That can't be it! I won't allow that to be it!'

Clearly worried, Norbury placed his hands on Taylor's shoulders and spoke in a soft, soothing tone. 'Let me go, Chris. Nate's gone. I'm so sorry, but he's gone.'

He let Norbury go and sank to his knees, fighting back the tears. 'What happened?'

'I don't know yet,' he replied apprehensively, shaking his head sullenly. 'But I promise I'll find out.'

Tim did not fight the melancholy. The tears streamed down his ashen face. 'He was fine this morning.'

'I'll find out what happened,' Norbury promised assuredly.

Taylor stood up slowly. 'Can we help?'

Norbury looked at them in turn, his eyes frigid. 'Yes. You can stay calm and give us time to investigate.'

'You haven't got any idea what could have caused it?' Tim croaked poignantly.

He turned on him furiously. 'No, I don't, Tim! That's what I just said, isn't it? If you would let me get to the laboratory, I can analyse some data and run some tests. That's the only way we'll find anything out. If you want answers, gentlemen, you need to let me get to work.'

Taylor sat next to Tim in the canteen, staring at the news on television vacantly. He peered at the clock as it ticked past the six-hour mark. Still no answers.

Tim had barely looked at the television. Indeed, Taylor was starting to worry about him. He was obviously in denial, as he had barely mentioned Nate's death the entire time.

All he had done was sit on the tired sofa, making his fingertips crackle. Sometimes he fired small bolts of electricity around the room.

If not for Nate's death, they would be testing him right now. As it was, Norbury had more pressing concerns. Whilst Taylor understood that his friend needed to master his newfound talent, he did not think now was the time.

Nate was gone. Gone. Just the like rest of his family and Herodotus. They were gone. The virus had taken them. It was taking everybody. The fact he was so strong would never compensate him for losing so many people. It was not worth it.

He wished he could go back in time and stop Herodotus drinking from that hot spring. Better still, he would stay in bed. He would not take Herodotus out at all.

Maybe then Nate would be alive. Debbie, Travis, James and Herodotus, too.

He could not help but feel responsible, despite the fact he knew there was nothing he could have done. It felt like the guilt was choking him. He tried to think of things he could have done differently. Could he have saved them?

He did not give Nate the water. Nate actually took it. He even tried to get it back.

There was very little he would do differently. He could not have foreseen the virus hidden in the ground. He could not have known Herodotus would contract it and pass it on to him.

Perhaps he should have been more suspicious of the feverish loss of four days and his sudden strength. Maybe he should have gone to San sooner. Would that have helped?

Probably not. So, why did he feel responsible for everything?

Tim formed a small ball of azure electricity in his hand and made it hover several inches above his palm. 'Is it normal to feel like my head might explode at any moment?'

Taylor shook his head sombrely without taking his eyes from the screen. 'Not for me, but it's different for everyone, so...'

Tim shot the ball at the wall and it fizzled out against the paint, causing some of it to flake. 'It hurts slightly less every time I use it.'

He scowled loudly. 'Ask Norbury about it.'

'Is there something wrong?'

Taylor fixed his friend with an angry glare. 'Actually, yes there is. Our friend just died, or hadn't you noticed?'

He scoffed. 'Of course I noticed. What's your problem?'

'Do you really think it's an appropriate time for you to be practicing that?'

'Why not? You said I have to be able to control it, or they'll sedate me. I really don't like the sound of that.'

Taylor shook his head, disgusted. 'Nate's only been gone a few hours and you're acting like nothing happened.'

'Give it a rest, Chris!' he retorted angrily. 'I'm upset, too. We can't help Nate now and it hardly aids the situation if they put me to sleep, does it? It's not like I'm dishonouring him.'

'I think you are a little bit.'

'When I go and piss on his corpse, you can get upset. We're stuck here waiting for news, so I'm using the time constructively. If you don't like it, you can fuck off. Quite frankly, the suggestion that I'm not hurting is insulting.'

They fell quiet for a few moments until Taylor broke the silence. 'You're right. I'm sorry, mate.'

Tim smiled at him. 'That's okay. It's been a crap day. I'm pissed off, too.'

'I know, but I shouldn't take it out on you.'

'No worries,' he replied casually, flicking sparks in the air. 'Do you think the virus will kill us eventually?'

Taylor turned towards him, alarmed. 'I don't think this was the virus. I got it before Nate did and I'm fine.'

'For now,' he returned swiftly. 'Maybe the full effects of the virus materialised in him swifter than they have in you.'

He waved the suggestion away. 'I doubt it. Norbury's looking into it now. He'll come up with something.'

Tim seemed transfixed by the sparks as he made them dance across his palms. 'Don't you think it's weird that I got exactly the same ability as Nate and then he suddenly died?'

He shrugged his shoulders. 'I hadn't really thought about it,' he lied. It was *all* he had thought about. 'It's probably just a coincidence.'

'Probably. What if it's not, though?'

'What are you suggesting?' Taylor asked acerbically, snapping his head around to face his friend. 'That you're somehow responsible?'

'Perhaps.'

'You can't think like that.'

'Maybe the virus only allows one host per ability.'

'How would it know, Tim?'

'Maybe it communicates somehow.'

'Come on, Tim!' he snapped irately. 'That's absurd. It's a fucking virus. It's a basic organism.'

'They're already saying that it's more capable and advanced than anything they've ever seen before.'

'This is getting ridiculous!' he shouted. 'You're talking shit, Tim! This is not the time to be talking shit.'

He did not hear a word Taylor said. He simply continued with his train of thought. 'They don't even know how it continues to spread. I think this virus is far more capable than we can imagine.'

Taylor paused briefly as he considered it. 'I think subliminal communication between the viral cells, when they're in different hosts, is a little too advanced.'

'Maybe. I guess we'll find out soon enough, won't we?'

As if on cue, the door opened suddenly and Nurse Hooper strode in. She eyed them both sprawled across the sofa. 'There you are.'

Taylor leapt up. 'Any news?'

'Dr Norbury wants to see you both.'

He looked down at Tim. 'Maybe sooner rather than later, huh?'

They walked into Norbury's office with their demeanours at odds. Taylor was so nervous he was shaking and his stomach was tied in knots. Tim, on the other hand, was still playing with the sparks on his fingertips excitedly.

Taylor plonked himself in one of the seats opposite the drained doctor. Tim made his way over casually.

'Let's get straight to the point,' Taylor began sternly, casting a surreptitious and irritable, sideways glance at his friend. 'What killed Nate?'

'It's only been a few hours, Chris,' he replied through a yawn. 'We don't have any definitive answers yet.'

'So, why call us in here, then?' Tim chimed in, apparently paying attention, despite the fact he was causing the tiny sparks to slither over his hands.

'Actually, I was after Chris, but you might be able to offer something,' he replied, looking at Tim suspiciously before turning back to Taylor. 'You've spent an awful lot of time with Mr Tyson lately. Did *you* notice anything different at all?'

'Such as?' he inquired uncertainly.

'Anything different. Anything at all. Even the slightest change, no matter how irrelevant it seems, could be the key to understanding his untimely and confounding demise.'

Tim finally looked away from his hand and turned to his friend. They exchanged a confused glance before Taylor responded. 'If you excuse the fact he's been asleep for the entire time, then, no.'

'Are you certain? Think carefully.'

Taylor could not hide his irritation. 'Yes, we're sure. Why don't you just explain what it is you've found?'

Norbury lips expanded into an uncertain and crooked smile. 'Well, it's the strangest thing, actually.'

'What is?'

'The virus in Nate...well, it's, erm...it's dead.'

'Dead?' Taylor repeated slowly.

'Yes. Dead.'

'It's gone?' he inquired, confounded. 'Are you saying you cured him before he died?'

'No, no, no,' Norbury replied, shaking his head fervently. 'Not at all. It's still there, in his blood stream, but it's no longer active. It stopped stimulating the neurotransmitters in his brain. It simply became inactive. The cells creating his ability seem to have died. I'm guessing that's what caused the seizure.'

Tim held up his hand and forced a small flash of electricity to gain their attention. 'So, the virus *is* gone?'

He slammed his fist on the desk and shouted. 'No! You're both missing the point. Listen to what I'm saying! The virus is still there. The cells are dead, but it's there. The only thing that's missing is his ability.'

16

Tim sat in the small examination room, partitioned from the others by nothing more than a screen, and adjusted the gown again. The young nurse, Yuri, carefully slid the needle into his vein and drew the blood from it, before slowly withdrawing.

'Is that the last test?' Tim asked, wincing as he moved the gown again in a futile attempt to make it less uncomfortable.

Yuri chuckled and Norbury replied from next to the screen. 'There are a few more I'd like to conduct, Tim.'

He eyed Taylor, who stood next to Norbury with his arms folded. 'Does everyone endure such scrutiny?'

The doctor nodded. 'More or less. Most of our subjects are asleep, but you can control your ability and insisted on avoiding sedation. And, since your ability manifests itself in the form of electricity, I dare not put you in the MRI machine we have here.'

'Why not?'

'It might stimulate your power involuntarily.'

Taylor sighed loudly. He was only half-listening to their conversation. It annoyed him how quickly they seemed to have forgotten the tragic circumstances surrounding them. It did not shock him that Norbury did not care, but he wondered how Tim was able to block it out so effectually when visions of the dead plagued his every waking moment and haunted his dreams.

He switched back to the present, forcing the melancholy out of his mind. 'Are you honestly saying that you think his ability had something to do with what happened to Nate?'

Norbury met him squarely with an icy glare. 'Are you honestly saying that your curiosity isn't piqued by the fact he developed the same ability as Mr Tyson, who then died?'

Taylor raised his eyebrows quizzically. 'Are you saying they're linked?'

'Are you honestly suggesting you're not intrigued?'

He snorted loudly. 'It was always inevitable that the virus would eventually develop the same results, within the same generation.'

'Perhaps, but this is the first time we've seen it, so I would be remiss not to investigate thoroughly. Add to this the fact that you infected both of them and we might be seeing the start of a pattern. If that proves to be the case, we might have a breakthrough.'

'A pattern?' Tim asked confusedly.

Taylor harrumphed. 'He's suggesting that the hosts give the same ability to whomever they infect, although that directly contradicts his earlier theory that every talent is unique to the individual.'

'We could be wrong!' Norbury riposted brashly. 'If we are, it changes the way we fight it. At this moment, it's unsafe to make any assumptions.'

'In what way?' Taylor fired back.

'If we can predict the behaviour of the virus, we can probably formulate some kind of blocker.'

Tim was rubbing his forearm, where he now had a small plaster with a picture of a cow on. 'Blocker? What's a blocker?'

'It would nullify the effects,' the doctor explained superciliously. 'In layman's terms, it would stop the virus from creating an ability.'

'A cure, then?' he pressed.

'Not a cure,' he replied with a harrumph. 'We can't cure it. People would still contract the virus; they just wouldn't get an ability with it.'

'Meaning people wouldn't want it any longer,' Taylor clarified.

Norbury nodded imperiously. 'Not if their talent is gone with the prick of a needle or the sting of a dart.'

Yuri handed Tim a small, plastic cup. 'Whenever you're ready.'

'What's this for?' he asked, perplexed.

'A semen sample,' he replied with a smirk. 'Take your time.'

He grimaced. 'Seriously? That's more invasive than the brain needle.'

'Speaking of which,' Norbury said to himself, swiftly striding to the nearest telephone and dialling three digits. 'Bishop? Do you have the results from Mr Bulling's cerebrospinal fluid test? I told them I wanted it as a priority.' He fell silent and waited for a few moments. 'You do? Excellent. Have you uploaded them? Good work, Bishop.'

He put the receiver down and turned to the laptop on the desk next to the telephone, starting to tap the keys.

Tim was eyeing the cup suspiciously. 'Hey, how would you have got this semen if I was asleep?'

The doctor smiled. 'Trade secret, Mr Bulling.' He studied the screen.

187

Taylor walked over and looked over his shoulder. 'Is that what you took from his ear?'

'It is.'

'What does it tell you?'

'It will tell me the chemical balance of his brain and I will be able to compare it to Mr Tyson's.'

'And if they're the same?'

'If the virus reproduced exactly the same reaction in Mr Bulling as it did with Mr Tyson, it means we have the start of a pattern, but only if the infected brain has the same blend of chemicals.'

The room fell silent as Norbury concentrated on the screen, flicking from one piece of data to another. Taylor watched over his shoulder, unable to understand any of it.

After a few minutes of watching the doctor studying the alien language, Tim's impatience got the better of him. 'And?'

'They're different,' he replied dejectedly, his shoulders slumping.

'What does that mean?' Tim asked eagerly.

He leaned back in the chair and let out a resigned sigh. His eyes landed on Tim. 'That you don't have the same ability as Mr Tyson.'

Taylor gasped. 'But he does. We've seen it with our own eyes.'

'I know,' he replied, rubbing his chin pensively for a few moments, before his eyes suddenly lit up. 'No, he doesn't. He has a very different ability. A very unique one. Why didn't I realise it before?'

Tim and Taylor exchanged a confused glance before asking their question in unison. 'What?'

Norbury sprang up excitedly. 'I can't believe I didn't think of it before.' He began striding away from them. 'Come with me!'

Tim jumped off the bed and snatched his tee shirt from the back of the chair, slipping it on as he struggled to keep up with Norbury. Taylor followed close behind, calling the doctor's name.

Norbury ignored them both. He powered through the facility and entered the marquee, stopping at the head of first bed he came to. He started tapping his finger on the screen and looked up as the duo arrived next to him.

'What the hell's going on?' Taylor demanded irritably.

He waved his hand over the sleeping woman. 'This is Miss Lewis. She has a 6th Gen ability, which allows her to move objects with her voice.'

'Telekinesis?'

'No, not in the traditional sense,' he explained. 'She asks objects to move and they do. Her voice controls them somehow.'

'Okay,' Taylor said uncertainly. He looked down at her. She was young, perhaps twenty-five years old, and beautiful, with white, porcelain skin and flame-red hair. 'What does that have to do with Tim?'

Norbury's voice was shrill as the excitement started to take over. He turned to Tim, his eyes wide and hands shaking. 'Touch her.'

'What?' he asked, shocked. 'Why?'

'Just do it,' he squeaked. 'Please.'

Tim cast his friend a confused look, who shrugged his shoulders. He turned and looked at the young woman, sleeping peacefully. He reached out slowly. Gently taking her hand in his, he looked back up, now focusing his bewildered expression on Norbury.

The doctor ignored the pleading eyes and looked at his watch eagerly. His eyes flicked between the conjoined hands and his watch for a minute, before they moved up and rested on Tim. 'Can you feel anything?'

He shook his head, no less perplexed. 'No. Should I?'

He ignored the query and turned back to his watch for three minutes more, during which time Taylor and Tim stared at each other blankly. He looked up again, his focused gaze full of expectancy. 'Anything yet?'

He shook his head and opened his mouth to reply, but paused. His mouth gaped, yet no words escaped. He screwed his face up in surprise, first looking down at the young woman, then at Taylor, his eyes finally resting on Norbury. 'I feel it. I feel it!'

Taylor's gawp moved back and forth between the two men. 'Feel what?' he shouted, when neither of them explained the mystery. 'What's going on?'

Tim started to chuckle excitedly. After a few moments, it escalated into a loud, obstreperous cackle. 'I can feel it!'

'What the hell can you feel?' Taylor yelled, his face turning red from the frustration of his ignorance.

Tim pulled his hand away and the laughter died down. He studied it, turning it around in front of his face. His smile covered his face. 'Watch! I'll show you.'

He looked at the pen in Norbury's shirt pocket. He concentrated on it for several moments. After twenty seconds of focusing, he spoke gently. 'Come to me, please.'

Nothing happened. Tim looked at Norbury blankly, then at Taylor with the same expression.

'Try again,' the doctor whispered.

'What are you doing?' Taylor asked.

Tim's face became contorted as he glared at the pen. His eyes started to bulge, his face turned scarlet and the veins popped out of his neck. He gritted his teeth, but spoke softly. 'Come here, please.'

Again, nothing happened. He looked up at Norbury, disappointment in his eyes. 'It's not working.'

Norbury shook his head. 'No, no. You're forcing it. Don't force it. Remember what Chris told you before.'

Taylor's confounded expression passed between them. 'What are you two trying to achieve here?'

They ignored him again, as Tim closed his eyes and took several, long inhalations. He held out his hand and slowly opened his eyes. He stared directly at the pen and whispered. 'Come here, please.'

The pen leapt from the pocket and sped towards him. Tim caught it, snapping his hand shut and cheering. 'That's awesome!'

Norbury smiled contentedly and Taylor's jaw dropped. 'Did he just...?'

'Catrina!' the doctor shouted, beckoning the small, plump, attractive nurse from the far side of the tent with a series of frantic gesticulations.

She shuffled over. 'Yes, sir?'

He indicated Miss Lewis. 'Nurse Hooper, wake this patient up immediately, please.'

Taylor still stared at the two men in turn, his mouth gaping. He could not explain what he had just seen. 'What just happened?'

Tim gleefully summoned a chair to him and sat down, grinning triumphantly.

Norbury turned to Taylor, his smile only slightly smaller than Tim's. 'Don't you see? Mr Bulling absorbed her ability.'

'He did *what?*'

'He absorbed it. His ability is that he can absorb the power from other hosts. When he visited Mr Tyson, he touched him, yes?' He turned to Tim. 'Have you got both now?'

He crackled his fingertips and nodded fervently. 'Looks like it!' He formed a small sphere of azure electricity in one hand as he eyed an empty cup on the table next to the bed. 'Come here.' It shot into his grasp. 'This is awesome!'

Taylor looked down at the sleeping woman. 'How do you know that it won't kill her?' he asked in a disgusted tone.

Norbury looked at him victoriously. 'We don't. We'll find out shortly. Catrina will wake her up and then we'll know.'

'How can you be so blasé about someone's life?' he spat.

The doctor rolled his eyes. 'How else do you suggest we find out?'

Taylor stammered for a few seconds, but failed to find a response.

'Precisely!' Norbury exclaimed, pointing in the air at nothing in particular. 'This is science, Chris. This is how we make discoveries. Maybe she will wake up and be fine. Maybe not. Maybe we will figure out a way to save her. Whatever happens, it means we can stop worrying about a cure, a blocker, or a workable vaccine.'

'What?' Taylor inquired, staggered. 'Why would you think that?'

'Why?' Norbury scoffed. 'Isn't it obvious? Because Tim *is* the cure.'

17

Taylor considered that Norbury's office seemed somehow brighter. It did not look any different, although the bright sunshine outside may be playing a part in his perception, he noted. The scent of freshly brewed coffee and toasted crumpets probably helped, too. More importantly, he suspected it felt like it was brighter because of the demeanour of those sitting around the desk.

Norbury was chirpy, Tim was elated, Miss Lewis was alive and well and even he felt a sanguine twinge in his gut.

He was desperately trying to take stock of what was happening. Was Tim really the answer to this crisis? Could he really curb the flow of this outbreak?

Norbury seemed convinced that this was the case. Tim was revelling in his role as saviour and Taylor realised that he hoped, more than anything, that it was true.

Maybe the fact he had infected the man who could stop the spread of this virus would outweigh his guilt at infecting Nate and, by association, his family. His decision to give Tim the virus might prove to be the turning point in their battle with their microscopic assailant. If they could cure people, which was how it now seemed, then perhaps the world could go back to normal.

'Power crimes' were overrunning the police, Parliament were rushing through 'The Hero Virus bill' to help them. The military had been called into Sheffield. With a cure, the insanity could stop.

He did not understand why Nate had not survived being cured, but he did know that Miss Lewis seemed fine. She did not seem to have any ill effects at all.

If they had found a cure, then he had played an intrinsic part in it, and that made him feel better. If they could stop this virus, which threatened to tear the world apart without even infecting most of the population, then the loss of so many people he cared about did not seem like such a waste. The demons that haunted his dreams might leave. The ghosts he saw every waking moment might vanish.

He might be able to find peace.

The doctor had been chattering excitedly for several minutes, leaning back in his chair and waving his hands around to exaggerate whatever point he was trying to make. The trio of hosts sat on the opposite side of the desk, listening.

Taylor wondered if the other listeners had lost track of the scientific jargon and were similarly playing music in their heads.

'Miss Lewis, are you still following what I'm saying?'

I'm not, Taylor thought, and one look at the young woman to his left confirmed that she was not, either.

She seemed bewildered, but nodded slowly. 'I think so. You're saying that I'm cured, but you want me to stay in the compound, anyway.'

He let out a sigh and gave her a sardonic smile. 'Well, that's a rather simplified version of what I said, but that's the general point. For a start, I said that I *think* you're cured, but we're far from certain. I would like to run more tests before providing a definitive statement. Plus, I think it would be pragmatic to keep you here for observation.'

Her confusion seemed to intensify. 'I don't understand. Did you use some kind of new drug on me? If so, may I ask who gave you permission to use *me* as a guinea pig?'

'It wasn't a drug, ma'am,' he replied sternly, offended that she was not as grateful as he expected her to be.

Miss Lewis seemed to become more agitated and confounded by his statement. 'Then would you mind explaining to me how you got rid of it? I volunteered for tests, under sedation. I did not give my permission for experimental treatment. I assume there was treatment of some kind?'

Norbury noted her litigious tone and visibly deflated. 'Not exactly.' He indicated the two men either side of her. 'This is Christopher Taylor and Timothy Bulling. They are hosts, as you were. It's actually these gentlemen who are responsible for your amelioration. I'll explain the finer details to you later but, basically, Tim's ability is that he can absorb yours.'

She cast a steely glare at Tim with her piercing, green eyes, before returning to Norbury. 'No, you will explain now, thank you.'

He pointed at Tim. '*He* cured you. Let's just leave it at that.'

She glanced in his direction. 'You took it out of me? Are you a healer?'

'No.'

'So, what are you?'

Tim smirked uncomfortably. 'He just told you.'

Lewis turned back to Norbury. 'If I'm cured, why can't I go home to my fiancé and children?'

'It's not that simple,' the doctor explained. 'Before you woke up, we ran some blood tests and you still have the virus in your system. The difference is that it no longer stimulates the brain to produce the side-effect.'

'I still have it? I'm not cured?'

'This is what I'm trying to explain to you, ma'am,' he retorted smugly. 'It's still too early to be certain of anything. You may still be able to infect others.'

She clicked her tongue against her teeth and looked at Tim irritably. 'Has he cured anyone else?'

Norbury's expression turned grave. 'Yes, he has, Miss Lewis.'

She studied the doctor. 'Can I assume, from the look on your face, that something went wrong with the others?'

'There was one man before you, ma'am. I'm afraid he did not wake up.' He waited for her panicked gasp to subside. 'The very fact you're awake and talking to us is an incredibly positive sign.'

Tears formed in her eyes and she struggled to speak. 'Did the other patient die?'

They exchanged dubious looks, but nobody answered the question.

She watched them for a few seconds, before composing herself and taking a lungful of air. She waved her hands in front of her face, as if to dry her eyes. 'How long before I know if I'll be okay?'

Norbury assumed his sympathetic demeanour. He had used it many times before, so knew that it appeared genuine. 'To be candid, we don't know. We have a small, private room ready for you and would like to keep you under observation for a few days to establish a couple of things: first, that you're okay and, second, that you're not contagious.'

She took another deep breath. 'And what happens if I'm not okay or,' she paused and sighed, 'dare I suggest, still contagious...?' She trailed off and took another deep breath.

Norbury waited for a few moments to be sure that she was not going to continue. 'Well, in either instance, we would start trying to find a way to...Miss Lewis?' His face suddenly transformed to consternation and he leaned forwards sharply.

She was flopped back in the chair with her eyes rolled up into their sockets. Her arms were hanging limply on either side.

Leaping up, Norbury slammed a button on his telephone and screamed into it. 'Get a team in here now!'

Tim and Taylor jumped out of their seats, moving to avoid the doctor as he dove over the table. As he reached her, the convulsions began. He threw her to the ground as she fell silent and stopped moving. He checked her airway, pinched her nose and placed his lips over hers, forcing air into her lungs.

The office door crashed open and a swarm of doctors and nurses rushed through with a crash cart. They barged both Tim and Taylor aside as they dashed to the aid of the young woman.

One person grabbed a resuscitation mask and began to give Lewis CPR. Another grabbed the defibrillator.

Taylor turned away. The sight of the frenzied medical team made him shudder, but it was the sound of the alarmed voices that made him feel nauseous. He strode out of the room, with Tim close behind, and waited outside.

All Taylor could see now was memories. Jane in the hospital, covered in blood. Herodotus biting off his own tongue. Nate's legs jerking around violently.

He closed his eyes and tried to block out the noise, but the hysterical shouts stung his brain until he heard them calmly calling the time of death. Tears rolled down his cheeks, but he did not really understand why. He barely knew Miss Lewis.

He knew, of course, that it was the sudden deluge of painful memories that crippled him. He tried to push them back into the darkest recess of his mind, but he was not strong enough. Once they seeped through his emotional dam, they gathered momentum and he could not stop it. He collapsed to the floor in a ball and began to sob. Tim watched him, but did not say anything.

He did not know how much time had passed when Norbury announced his presence by coughing several times into his hand. Both men met his sombre gaze.

The doctor looked at Tim. 'I guess that we still have a lot of work to do before we can use you to cure this.'

His voice was surprisingly even, considering what he had just witnessed. 'Such as?'

Norbury folded his arms. 'We need to find a way to stimulate the brain enough to keep them alive. I can't imagine that it will be especially difficult. We just need to figure out which drugs to use and administer them as you treat the patient.'

'Do you already know what to do? Then why didn't you do it with her!' Taylor's voice was more croak than ferocious roar.

'Not exactly,' he replied softly. 'I do, however, have several ideas. It means running an entirely fresh set of tests.' He eyed Tim directly. 'How do you feel about that?'

'Is she still contagious?' he asked, matter-of-factly. 'If she can still transmit the virus, it seems like a pointless exercise.'

'We'll know about that soon enough.'

Taylor suddenly stood up. 'How so?'

'Because I gave her CPR. If I don't get it, we can be pretty confident that she stopped being infectious after you took the virus from her.'

'Can you guarantee nobody else will die?' he asked angrily.

He forced a smile. 'I'll do everything in my power to keep them alive.' He turned back to Tim. 'Will you help us?'

He shrugged his shoulders. 'I can't see that I really have a choice, do I?'

Taylor's mood became increasingly sombre over the next seven days. He felt powerless as he watched the parade of subjects entering the laboratory. He watched the first, few 'attempts', as Norbury called them, with hope in his heart. It soon became clear to him that these were experiments and he quickly stopped observing.

He was unsure what aspect of the process bothered him more: the convoy of trolleys, the bodies shrouded only by a basic, white sheet, or the fact that Tim seemed so at ease with the situation. He had no proof, but he suspected the subjects were not volunteers.

He had no idea how many combinations Norbury had tried. After each death, he returned to the laboratory to produce another drug cocktail. Once satisfied that his latest creation might be the one, he summoned another patient.

Taylor knew the procedure. Norbury already knew which drugs to try, but he was uncertain of the precise combination. He would formulate a cocktail that worked in a test tube and then try it on a live subject. Tim killed the virus inside the patient as Norbury injected the serum. They died shortly afterwards.

Some were dead within minutes. Others, like Miss Lewis, awoke and were able to engage in lucid conversation before a sudden seizure claimed their lives. It seemed that the length of time they survived did not correspond to how close the serum was to effectiveness. To Taylor, it seemed more like a lottery than science. Norbury insisted the heuristic approach was the only realistic approach available to them and perfectly in keeping with standard emergency medical protocol.

Taylor said it was murder.

He found it difficult to believe that *this* was his destiny. The empty chamber of the Magnum resonated day after day and he thought it was for a higher purpose. Could it really be this? He refused to believe that.

He was alone in his objection, though. Indeed, everyone else in the facility acted as if the deaths were merely part of the daily grind. It was routine to kill several people a day. Taylor could not understand how anyone could think that way.

He wanted to leave. Yet he knew, if he tried, they would stop him. His only escape would be the cure. He pondered trying to fight his way out, but he was heavily outnumbered. He considered sneaking out, but there were eyes everywhere. He was trapped, stuck there until Norbury completed his research.

He tried to talk to Tim about it, but his best friend waved his concerns away, dismissing them as weak and insignificant. Tim agreed with Norbury. This was the only way to stop the virus before it tore society apart. The sooner they found a cure, the sooner the world could return to normal. Tim explained how he felt: it was regrettable that people had to die, but they were already infected, so had survived the lottery of contraction. If they did not help Norbury find a way to cure the illness, it was inevitable that it would escape the compound eventually and then billions might die.

The comparatively small numbers that died in trying to save the world was a price worth paying.

No matter what Taylor said to his friend to try to convince him otherwise, Tim was steadfast in his belief that Norbury was doing the right thing.

After several attempts, Taylor gave up. Tim ignored his assertion that there must be a safer way, without using living, human guinea pigs. He did not seem to care about Taylor's insistence that no organisation, government-sanctioned, or otherwise, should put such little value in human life. It was bordering on evil. But, nobody cared and nobody agreed.

Taylor was alone.

He was also concerned about Tim's attitude. To be so apathetic about the loss of life was simply not like him at all. Indeed, his entire demeanour seemed to be changing. He seemed to be relishing his part in the experiments. He appeared to enjoy the fact that he might be integral in saving humanity.

In some ways, Taylor was pleased about this. Such responsibility might crush lesser men, but Tim had always been blessed with an unnatural confidence, which was probably why he had been able to successfully hide his misery for so long, from those who knew him best.

In other ways, however, he felt unmistakable twinges of consternation in his gut. Tim's confidence seemed to grow with each experiment. He was bordering on arrogant.

He was changing and Taylor did not like who he was becoming.

Taylor spent most of the week on his own. For the first three days, he voiced his opinion about the experiments to anyone who would listen. So they ostracised him. People did not greet him as he walked past. They did not make idle conversation or sit with him at dinnertime. He did not know if this was as a result of some order from Norbury, but he came to enjoy his own company and started to spend his days sitting in the marquee, watching the other hosts sleep.

It was exactly seven days after the death of Miss Lewis that the news arrived. Taylor was sitting on a chair in the marquee, watching a seven-year-old girl sleeping peacefully, when he heard a ripple of excitement outside. People were chattering joyously.

The people here were never happy. It was considered unprofessional.

He walked outside curiously, watching soldiers embracing nurses, and doctors gathered around a young man he recognised from the marquee.

Except, now, he was walking around, apparently well.

Taylor watched the scene for several minutes. There was no doubt about it. They believed they had found the cure.

He stormed away towards Norbury's office.

Norbury had the sofa in his office so he had somewhere to sleep. The dormitories were filling up quickly, as he allowed virologists, neurologists, physiologists, anatomists, zoologists, oncologists, pharmacists, microbiologists, endocrinologists, chemists, molecular biologists, neuroradiologists and pathologists to join his team. He had even recruited some palliative carers, to help make his patients as comfortable as possible, should unexpected, and fatal, consequences occur.

He quite enjoyed the fact he was able to pick and choose his staff. Specialists from all over the world were begging him for the chance to work in the compound. He had assembled the greatest concentration of medical minds in the history of the human species.

Despite the array of intelligence, he had been the one to discover the cure. Of all the possible combinations of medicine, he had unlocked the secret to the virus. He had figured out the precise concentration of the individual drugs and how they should be blended together.

He had beaten The Hero Virus.

As a reward, he had decided to leave the others to check and re-check the solution whilst he got some sleep for only the second time this week. He had seen enough. It worked. He had done it.

He jumped up groggily when the door slammed. It took him several seconds, and some firm eye rubbing, to be able to descry the unhappy figure of Taylor standing before him. He looked up blearily, noting that the time was a little after five a.m. 'What's the matter, Chris?'

His eyes were full of anger. 'Are you infected?'

Norbury sat up straight, yawning and stretching before he replied. 'No, I'm not.'

'I saw that guy walking around with a bunch of doctors. Does that mean you have a cure now?' His tone was stern, almost admonishing.

Norbury reached over and flicked the button on his coffee machine. 'It seems that way.'

'At what cost? How many?'

He rubbed his face again. 'How many what?'

'How many died?' he fired.

Norbury stared at Taylor blankly and wondered why he was not blinking. 'Are you okay, Chris?'

'Answer the question.'

He glanced back at the coffee machine as he spoke. 'I don't know an exact number without checking.'

'You don't even know,' he said in a slow, disdainful tone.

Norbury stood up sharply, throwing his hands in the air. 'What would have me do, Chris? We needed a cure and we had to use clinical trials on infected subjects to get it quickly. You ask about the cost, but I would ask you what the price might have been if we hadn't found one.'

'Did you figure out how it manages to spread even though a lot of these new cases haven't been anywhere near a host?'

'Not yet.'

'Do you plan to run down every case?'

'Until we can figure out how it's finding new hosts, yes. But we *will* stop it. I swear.'

'Does the cure work for everyone?'

'We haven't tested extensively but, so far, it's ninety-eight per cent successful.'

'Two per cent still die?' Taylor inquired, through gritted teeth.

'That's actually very good for something like this. Besides, it's not like we've administered the serum. The subjects we can't help are all allergic to at least one of the ingredients. We can't cure them yet, but we have their medical histories, so we know what we can use and what we can't. We'll just have to find another way for them.'

Taylor's face softened. 'Are you leaving them sedated until you do?'

'Of course!' Norbury held up his hands defensively. 'Chris, do you think I'm some kind of monster?'

'I think you're not concerned about collateral damage.'

He scoffed. 'Do you have any idea what I've seen in my life? I've watched viruses claim thousands upon thousands of lives. I've watched people I care about ravaged by the very bacteria they were trying to stop and die horrid, excruciating deaths.'

He fell silent for a few moments and let out a lamenting sigh. 'I'm very sorry about that, but it shouldn't influence your work here.'

'It hasn't!' the doctor snapped. 'What it *has* done is give me the experience and knowledge to judge a situation. It's regrettable that we've lost patients, but this has probably saved millions, perhaps billions, of lives.'

'You don't know that,' he rebuked tersely.

'You're being myopic, Chris. Either that, or ridiculously stubborn. Christ, look at the state of the world, as people scramble after this virus. You must have considered the effect this would have on the world if everyone had an ability. You only need one per cent of people to use them for the wrong reasons and you have anarchy. Believe me when I say that we've narrowly avoided a catastrophe here.'

Taylor scowled angrily. 'I think it became a catastrophe when we started killing innocent people.'

'You're letting guilt get the better of you. Don't feel bad. We have a cure. That's what matters and it's all anyone will care about.'

'Really?' he asked, raising his eyebrows. 'I wonder if I should test your theory by mentioning to the press that your test subjects were human. I'm pretty sure that's illegal.'

Norbury's expression changed suddenly. His face flashed with anger and his tone became grave. 'I have clearance.'

He paused and failed to stifle a gasp. 'From whom?'

'The UN sanctioned the tests, Chris.'

'Excuse me?' he asked, drawing breath sharply.

'Don't be so naive,' Norbury scolded. 'Everyone wants this problem gone and they want it done yesterday.'

He paused, considering his words carefully. 'I doubt the public will agree with them.'

'I think the vast majority of people will accept whatever it takes to get rid of the fear. Everyone is afraid and people hate fear. They hate that they-'

The office door burst open. They both spun to see Nurse Hooper in the doorway. 'Doctor, why is your 'phone turned off? Never mind! We need you!'

He stepped forwards. 'What happened?'

She did not wait to respond. She had already vanished.

Exchanging a concerned look, they dashed after her, but did not catch up until she entered the marquee.

Taylor looked over the beds he had been visiting every day and rubbed his eyes in disbelief.

It couldn't be!

His eyes barely grazed the collection of several dozen medical staff. They focused on the beds. There remained a patient in each of them.

But every patient was dead.

18

Taylor felt the bile rising from his stomach as he surveyed the macabre scene.

Everywhere his eyes roved, there was pain.

Contorted expressions, frozen features and twisted, angled limbs. Gaping mouths, clawed hands and lifeless eyes.

It was worse than any nightmare he could remember. And he always remembered the scariest ones.

There was blood dripping from many of the beds, pools forming on the floor. The entire marquee stank where many of the patients had evacuated their bowels, presumably in response to the imminent dread of their deaths. The stench of destruction filled his nostrils. It was what he imagined war smelt like.

There were pieces of flesh on the floor, too, haphazardly scattered in random places. They looked like they had been torn from the bodies of the dead.

Large piles of intestines, livers and kidneys sat in the middle of the room, like some kind of horrific ornamental centrepiece.

Taylor reached and found himself dry heaving. He had not eaten in several days, so there was nothing inside of him to vomit.

He looked at the floor for a while and took several deep breaths. He looked back up.

As his eyes absorbed a sight that looked like a battlefield, he felt the dark cloud of death hovering over the compound.

Everything had just changed.

Every, single host in the marquee was gone.

His eyes flickered back and forth, left and right, landing on the cured host he had seen walking around the grounds. His head was lying on the floor next to his body, which had burst open and was charred across the ribcage.

Norbury had also needed several moments to digest the sight. Then he had marched into the marquee and begun screaming and shouting. The horde of doctors and nurses met his orders by scurrying around busily.

Taylor stopped Dr Bishop as he rushed past. He was a tall, portly man with brown hair swept back into a ponytail and a bushy beard spattered with flecks of grey. His usually flushed complexion was ghost-white.

'What happened here?' he asked, his voice little more than an anguished wheeze.

Bishop's eyes showed only discombobulation and panic. 'W-W-We don't know. I walked in this morning for my rounds and found this.'

'Is everyone...?' He could not finish the question, so overwhelming was the anguish.

'Dead?' Bishop squealed. 'It looks like it. We're currently searching for any survivors, so if you'll please excuse me...'

Taylor jumped aside. 'Sure, yes, sorry to keep you. Do you know how they...?'

Bishop did not answer the question. He hurried to one bed, then the next and the next, looking for any signs of life.

Taylor turned and headed out of the marquee. The sun was up now, so he looked around the grounds as he ambled somnambulistically across the field. The crowds still gathered outside. People continued to beg for the virus.

The Hero Virus.

Somehow, he suspected the carnage in the marquee would not change their minds. Perhaps the announcement of a cure would.

Something had to end this madness.

Taylor realised that he was finally beginning to understand what Norbury was talking about in his office. The image of the mangled, twisted corpses was seared into his brain for the rest of his life.

This was what Norbury had been afraid of. It was *this* moment he had dreaded.

The moment the virus showed everyone the depths to which humanity could sink.

He tried to think of an explanation for the massacre, but there was none. Somebody had got into the tent and, it seemed, eaten body parts to contract the virus.

It was not important who it was.

All that mattered was the sobering truth that someone was capable of such horrors.

Norbury was right. Humankind could not be trusted with the powers the virus produced.

As he mused, he saw movement in his peripheral vision.

Turning his head and tearing himself from his rumination, he watched two men run towards the marquee. They were dressed in civilian clothing, just as he was, but he did not recognise them. He was confident that he knew everyone in the compound, especially those who were not in a uniform of some kind. There were so few of them. He had never seen these people before.

The only thing he recognised was the hunger in their eyes.

He veered towards them, quickening his pace to a jog so that he could intercept them as they ran across the field. It was at this point he noticed the large blades each of them carried.

Both of which had blood on them.

Taylor felt his stomach turn. It was them.

It was them!

He clenched his fists and roared. 'Hey!'

They looked at him, now in their path, with rapacious glares. Both men raised their daggers.

Taylor spent a moment scrutinising his adversaries. Both men were quite large, but one was bald and clearly much older than the other, although they had similar features. He guessed they were father and son. They looked at him with rage etched into their faces and Taylor instantly knew what was coming.

The elder of the two grunted as he swung the blade through the air. Taylor lifted his hand and slapped him away. The attacker flew backwards and landed on the grass. The younger man stabbed at Taylor, who narrowly evaded the point of the blade as it sliced through his tee shirt.

Taylor grabbed his arm and used his attacker's own momentum to hurl him forwards. The young man landed on the grass in a roll that carried him at least ten metres.

By the time Taylor turned around, the elder foe was already on his feet and charging. Taylor jumped backwards to dodge the swipe. He instinctively thrust out a fist. It landed on the side of the aggressor's head. His head snapped backwards and eyes rolled up as he flopped to the ground.

Taylor knew that he did not need to hit someone hard to defeat them, but even he was surprised how little effort he had put into the blow. His shock, however, almost cost him dearly. He only just reacted in time to duck under the younger man's diagonal chop. Taylor tossed his fist out whilst crouched and felt his knuckles connect with his enemy's solar plexus. The blow hurled him to the ground, fighting for breath.

Taylor stood up straight and studied the young man, who was writhing in agony. His fight was over. He looked over to the father, who was unconscious on the grass. He was so intent on analysing their threat to him that he did not notice the third attacker until it was too late. He caught a flash of movement behind him, but could do nothing to prevent what followed.

The strike crashed over the rear of his skull.

Taylor felt the blow, but the impact was so mild, he could barely believe it when he turned around to descry the weapon.

A burly woman glared at him in surprise as she clutched a two-foot metal bar. Taylor reached around and rubbed the back of his head. It was a little moist, so he examined his hand. There was a little blood.

The woman seemed to recover from the shock swiftly, gritting her teeth and swinging again. Taylor raised his hand and caught the middle of the bar, stopping it in mid-air. He then pushed it forwards sharply, so the tip of metal cracked her on the forehead. She was unconscious instantly.

Taylor checked in every direction, to be sure of no more surprise attacks, and then rubbed the back of his head again. The strike had pierced the skin and, although he had felt it, there was very little pain. In fact, it was more discomfort than pain.

He looked over the three prone forms as he rubbed the back of his head and he considered what had just happened. There was only one reason he could think of to explain the fact three civilian strangers were inside the compound and attacking him.

They desperately wanted the virus and thought he would stop them from getting it. Which told him that his prior assumption was incorrect.

If they wanted the virus, it meant they did not already have it. They had not slaughtered everyone in the marquee.

So, who did? Perhaps the same person that had let them into the facility.

Taylor walked over to the young man and grabbed his shirt, hauling him to his feet with one hand. He winced and writhed as he moaned in pain.

Taylor pulled him close and spoke only two inches from his face. 'How did you get in?'

He was whining and groaning, but none of his noises resembled an answer. Taylor scowled and tossed him several metres onto the grass, before walking over to the main school building and alerting the first soldiers he saw about the intruders.

He walked back out and continued to stride around the grounds, noting, with dismay, the lack of sentries and patrols that he usually saw whenever out for a stroll. They seemed to be missing from the far side, so he moved closer to investigate. As he came around one of the temporary buildings, he noticed the heel of a boot sticking out from the next corner. He approached cautiously and rounded the corner to find an injured, bound guard, accompanied by another group of infiltrators. Only, this time, there were eleven of them.

And they were all armed.

There was a brief moment as they analysed the startled man who happened upon them. They seemed to pause for consideration, which gave Taylor a vital few seconds to study them.

They were mostly young men, but he noted one young woman and a middle-aged man in their midst. They carried a variety of weapons, from planks of wood and metal pipes, to chains and machetes. He spent a few seconds wondering who was their leader, but guessed a broad young man in a leather jacket was directing their incursion when they all turned to look at him for guidance.

He seemed as reluctant as any of them, but seeing that they looked to him, he growled and raised his fist. The brass knuckles flashed in the sunlight and he charged.

Taylor was not sure what was happening. He was still coming to terms with his predicament when the leader darted at him, covering the few metres in a flash and swinging as he ran. The metal cracked across the side of Taylor's face with a sickening crunch.

His head whipped around and he felt the blow. It felt like someone had just prodded him in the cheek. He turned his head back and watched the surprise spread across all eleven faces with a satisfied smirk.

They all knew the blow he had just suffered should have cut his face open and knocked his teeth out.

Taylor rubbed his cheek and stretched his jaw. The young man responded by swinging his fist again, crashing the brass knuckles against the side of Taylor's head. Again, the force of the strike caused his head to jerk around, but he quickly turned it back to face his latest foe.

He heard a series of gasps and watched as the leader attacked again. This time, however, he caught the forearm and pivoted, keeping a firm grip on the arm and swinging it around. He let go once he was facing in the opposite direction.

This manoeuvre plucked the leader from his feet and tossed him twenty metres into the side of a portacabin. He struck it with a loud thud and dropped to the concrete. Taylor watched with intrigue as the young man slowly got to his feet and smiled appreciatively.

Hearing a shuffle behind him, Taylor spun around to see the young woman rushing at him. She was charging with her long, metal spear held by her waist.

Taylor was too late to dodge it. She was only inches from skewering him. He winced in preparation for the mortal blow. Several thoughts flashed through his mind, but he found it interesting that his overriding emotion was one of annoyance.

He had been so smug he had let his guard down against ten armed adversaries.

In the end, it would be his own stupidity that killed him. And his gift would go to waste.

He felt the cold tip of the blade touch his flesh and then the most incredible thing happened.

The spear snapped.

The tip pierced his flesh. He felt it happen. But only very slightly. As the young woman drove the spear into his abdomen, the blow exacerbated by the speed of her run, her eyes widened with fear as the blade twisted and then snapped completely.

Taylor looked down at his stomach. A small, red patch appeared on his, already torn, shirt, but there was no pain. He looked up at the terrified young woman and realised that the last thought in his head had been about his gift.

He still believed Destiny, God, Allah, or whoever controlled the universe, had given him a gift. Despite what he had seen of late, he still wanted to make the most of it.

He eyed the woman. She had just tried to kill him. He felt the rage bubbling in his veins and instinctively swung his hand around. He caught her across the cheek with a backhanded slap. She flew into the wall and did not get back up.

Taylor could not control his fury. He powered towards the group of nine and waded in with a wayward, swinging punch that did not connect with anyone, but clipped three of the young men. They spun to the floor like a trio of tornados.

The middle-aged man sprang into action next, realising that this freak's intent was to incapacitate them all. He swung his titanium baseball bat at his enemy's head.

Taylor saw it coming and snatched it out of the air. He held it up to his eyes, looked straight down the shaft and then bent it so far that it actually snapped. He tossed both halves on the ground and stepped towards the eldest of the group, grabbing him by the throat.

Taylor watched him struggle for breath for a few seconds as he picked him up. He pulled his victim closer for a moment, staring deep into his terrified eyes, before tossing him backwards.

He crashed into two of the others intruders, landing on them in a tumult of wails and yelps.

He looked over the remaining five faces. By now they all knew they were dealing with a host, so they attacked in unison. Taylor managed to block the machete with his arm and catch the plank with his free hand, but he could do nothing about the chain that whipped across his back, the metal pipe that struck his shoulder or the nightstick in his ribs.

He felt all the blows, but no pain. He saw that the machete had drawn blood on his forearm, but it was little more than a graze, despite the fact he had stopped a full-forced downward chop with it. He snatched the plank away and swung it around, crashing it against the head of the young man carrying the machete.

He watched the victim of his swing flop to the ground as the remaining four opponents prepared for their next assault. Taylor was better prepared this time. He stepped in towards the two holding the chain and the nightstick, thrusting his fists out. The blows only glanced his intended targets, but the power was enough to hurl them back into the wall of the hut behind them.

He turned in time to grab the remaining foes, as one swung a pipe and the other grabbed the machete from the ground. Taylor gripped their collars, picked them up and crashed them together. The clunking sound of their skulls colliding resonated against the wall. He dropped them and they landed in a crumpled heap.

Taylor looked around and saw everyone writhing in agony. He walked out from behind the hut and saw that the leader was still standing and had gathered a new weapon. The brass knuckles remained and he had now added a bayonet to his arsenal.

Taylor strode towards him and the leader skipped to the side, jumping in and swinging both arms. Taylor caught the arm with the brass knuckles, but the bayonet eluded his attempt to block it. The leader rammed it down into his ribcage.

Both men watched as the blade pierced several millimetres into his skin, before buckling and snapping. The leader landed and cast his victim an incredulous glare. Taylor grinned, before grabbing his jacket and picking him up. He swung his arms backwards first and then forwards, releasing the leather as he hurled the leader through the air with all his might.

The young man flew over fifty metres, landing on the angled roof of the marquee and sliding down as far as the vertical wall. He then dropped ten metres to the grass.

Taylor watched him for several seconds, but when the leader did not move, he turned away, focusing his attention on how these people had managed to sneak into the compound. He checked the captive guard had a pulse and untied him.

Moving along to the next hut, he found three other intruders leaping over the corpses of two former sentinels. He disabled them with three swift punches and found the hole in the fence.

This was how they were getting in.

He could see others approaching from the tree line on the other side of the fence and snatched the radio from the closest body. He gave his position and announced the breach in security. Within thirty seconds, seven armed soldiers were defending the hole. A minute later, a captain arrived with twenty reinforcements. They fought back the small crowd of on-rushers and began to repair the fence.

Taylor stepped back and took a deep breath. The situation was getting worse. The marquee was already full of dead patients and now the grounds were filling up with the bodies of both soldiers and intruders.

He felt dizzy and nauseous. He looked around the complex and saw groups of troopers around the marquee. They were carrying the body parts away.

After several minutes watching, he noticed that nobody seemed to be going to the control room. Nobody was trying to establish the identities of those responsible for the slaughter in the marquee.

He would have to do it.

Composing himself, Taylor marched towards the reinforced steel doorway and barged into the control room, formerly the head teacher's office. The man and woman entrenched inside turned to look at him curiously.

'Can I see the footage covering the fence near the shower shed?'

The soldiers exchanged a curious glance before the young man answered. 'I'm sorry?'

Taylor met him with a frigid glower. 'There's part of the fence missing. I want to know who vandalised it.'

The technician knew who was asking and visibly shrank in his seat. 'It went down during the night. Did you just say the fence is damaged?'

He ignored the question. 'It went down?'

When the man paused, the woman replied. 'We've got someone on their way here to fix it now.'

'It's too late. We've already been breached. I'm just wondering who would have disabled the camera and the fence. I'm also curious about how they managed it.'

The remark met stunned gasps. 'Breached? By civilians?'

'Why didn't you report the camera malfunction?'

The male technician stared at him blankly. 'It happens all the time. We didn't think it would be a big problem. That's why we have armed patrols.'

He scoffed acerbically. 'They're both dead. Can I suggest you examine the footage at the point the camera went down?'

The woman spun to the control panel, a glittering array of buttons, LEDs and blinking lights. She started tapping keys on the keyboard and, a few seconds later, the monitor flickered and the image of the area around the fence appeared. There was no activity for the minutes leading up to the time it suddenly turned black.

'That looks like a simple malfunction to me,' Taylor commented. 'What do you think?'

'Hold on,' she said, studying the screen. She rewound the feed and played it back. Then she paused it and pointed at top edge of the monitor. 'What do you suppose that is?'

Taylor peered in. 'I don't see anything. What am I looking at?'

She indicated a sliver of light at the very edge of the screen. 'It looks like a spark to me. Literally one second before the camera stops working, at least one spark comes off it.'

'So what? It was a malfunction.'

She continued to examine the screen carefully. 'Sparks suggest some kind of technological trauma. There was interference of some kind.'

'What sort of interference?' he asked intrigued, casting a disparaging glance towards the male technician, who remained frozen in his seat.

'I've no idea,' she answered thoughtfully. 'It could be anything. But it's not a malfunction. Somehow, this camera was disabled.'

Taylor paused and scratched his scalp pensively. After a few moments, he had an idea. 'Can you check the other cameras to see if there's anything unusual, please? I've got to see how they're getting on. If you find anything strange, report it.'

'To you?'

'No, to your senior officer. Thanks for your help.'

Taylor marched back out of the control room and eyed the hole in the fence. More people had noticed it and the soldiers were struggling to hold them back. He considered intervening for a few seconds, but suddenly had a better idea. He sprinted to the room he shared with Tim. If anyone could fight the crowds back, it was him.

Crashing into the small dormitory, he expected to find it empty and was not disappointed. He suspected Norbury would have enlisted Tim's aid for this crisis. He darted to the marquee and found the doctor.

Norbury was sitting in a chair just outside the entrance, smoking a cigarette. Taylor peered through the doorway to see dozens of people, in full chemical suits, cleansing the horror.

Taylor peered down at him. 'Is Tim in there?'

The doctor looked up at him with a glazed expression. 'No.'

Taylor sighed with relief. 'He must already be helping with the breach. Good.'

Norbury smiled wryly. 'Did you check your room?'

'Like I said, he must be helping with the fence.

The doctor took a radio from his pocket and spoke into it. 'Captain Nolan, are you there?'

A few seconds of static passed. 'I'm here.'

'Are you at the scene of the breach?'

'Where else would I be, sir?'

'Is Mr Bulling with you?'

'No, sir.'

'I suspected as much. Once you've contained the situation, would you be kind enough to search the facility for him?'

'Of course, sir.'

Taylor glared at Norbury, confounded. 'What the hell are you doing?'

He frowned. 'We need to find Tim.'

'Why? He'll be around here somewhere.'

Norbury's face creased into a sympathetic smile. 'I'm afraid I have some bad news about the marquee massacre, Chris.'

He stared down at the doctor intently. 'I'm listening.'

He paused as he decided the best way to say it. After a few seconds, he just blurted it out. 'It looks very much like Tim killed them.'

19

Taylor felt a chasm open in his mind. He felt himself falling.

It was dark. It was cold. It seemed never-ending.

He was spinning, like a toothpick in a whirlpool. He was about to spin down into the abyss in his head, when he suddenly found the strength to reach out and grasp the jagged side. The freefall stopped.

He tried to speak, but the words clogged up his throat.

He could not breathe. He choked, drawing air into his lungs gratefully.

He looked down at where the doctor was sitting, but everything was a blur. It was as if he were two inches from a Monet.

He blinked and images began to form. He closed his eyes and shook his head vigorously.

When he opened them again, the doctor slowly came into focus.

Taylor felt the anger deep inside of him. It started to impair his vision, red flashes covering the world. He wanted to reach out and snap the man before him. He wanted to tear him limb-from-limb. He wanted to grab his head and squeeze until he felt the crumbled skull in his hands and the brain matter squished between his fingers.

He took several, deep, cathartic breaths, forcing the fury back down inside. This was not him. He was not a violent character. He refused to succumb to the temptation of his power.

He needed several more moments to force down the emotion. He gulped heavily and pushed it back. His throat was suddenly arid and the words scraped his oesophagus like the tip of a knife.

'You should be careful what you say, Mike.'

The doctor was watching the powerhouse in front of him carefully and could see the conflicting emotions behind the irate glower. He spoke slowly and carefully. 'I'm sorry, but it's true.'

He wanted to pull the doctor apart. He quelled his desire and tried to keep his voice as level as possible. The best he could manage was a low growl. 'You forget who you're talking to. I could crush you in an instant.'

'I know that,' he replied warily, 'but hurting me won't change the facts.'

He realised that he had clenched his fists and gritted his teeth. Bulging veins and a scarlet complexion beset his exophthalmic expression. 'How dare you accuse him of atrocities after everything he's done to help you!'

Norbury chose his words carefully. 'We've tested twelve corpses so far, Chris. Every one of them has a dead virus in the bloodstream, but no ability. I'm pretty confident the others will be the same.'

Taylor continued to fight the urge to snap the doctor in half. 'Tim has no reason to slaughter all these people. Why would he?'

'I can't be one hundred per cent certain. I know it aggravates him that the ability he absorbs becomes defunct when combined with the serum.'

Suddenly, his muscles relaxed. He felt weak. 'It what? He never told me that.' If Tim had kept that from him, what else was he hiding?

'Did he not?' Norbury watched Taylor's arms go limp. 'Well, it's true. We have to inject the serum before he takes the virus away. The reasons behind it are quite expansive, but the headline is quite compelling. If we save the patient, Tim doesn't get their power. Evidently, he's not happy with that.'

He felt his intestines being pulled in every direction. His brain did not stop spinning for several minutes. He felt sick. He studied Norbury's face and could not find a single trace of doubt or a flicker of uncertainty. He had not known Norbury long, but had managed to gauge two, very important, facts about the man: One, he was rarely wrong; Two, he was trustworthy.

When he managed to speak, all he could muster was a mumble. 'I can't believe he would do this.'

'Who else could?' the doctor pressed, sensing his advantage. 'There are patrols around the marquee all night long. There are cameras covering every square inch of this facility, including the patients. I've checked the footage from the marquee. Somehow, all the cameras managed to spark and cut out before anything happened. Who else could do that?'

He shook his head violently. 'No, no, no. That doesn't prove anything. Why would you think Tim could do any of this, even if he wanted to?'

'Well, the fact he now has about thirty, different abilities that we know about-'

'He what?' Taylor was clasping his head in despair.

Norbury screwed his face up as he studied Taylor, intrigued. 'He didn't disclose that to you, either?'

He fought it. The truth seeped through his wall of disbelief and penetrated his mind. But he fought it. 'I still don't believe it! Tim would never-'

'Believe it, Chris!' he snapped.

Taylor was wide-eyed. His lips were quivering. 'I-I-I can't.'

Norbury felt confident enough to press. 'I suggest you give it some real thought. Really consider the situation. There is only one conclusion you can reach. Go to your room and reflect. Besides, Captain Nolan is going to want to ask you some questions.'

He could not fight it any longer. The realisation washed away his barricade of faith. It was too much for him. He felt his legs buckle and he almost toppled over. Instead, he managed to merely collapse to his knees. He buried his face in his hands and began to sob. 'I gave it to him. I did this.'

He placed his hand on Taylor's shoulder, pathos in his tone. 'No, you didn't. The responsibility for such power lies with the individual who wields it. You carry yours with such humility, Chris. Unfortunately, you're in the minority. Do you see now why The Hero Virus is such a threat to the world?'

He continued to weep and nodded slowly.

Norbury tried to assume an authoritative tone. 'Now, get up and pull yourself together. We're going to need your help.'

The Jeep broke almost every traffic law in existence. Taylor sat quietly in the back seat, trying not to return any of the glares from the four, armed, Special Forces soldiers with him. He knew they were the centre vehicle in the convoy of five. He had long-since lost track of where they were.

He fidgeted in his seat and fumbled with his hands as he stared at the floor. The vehicle screeched around a corner and the momentum threw him sideways, onto one of the warriors. He pulled himself upright and looked up apologetically. 'Sorry.'

The soldier grunted. 'You the 1st Gen?'

He nodded. 'Are you sure he'll be there?'

'We got the call less than an hour ago.'

'How good is your information?'

The warrior scowled. 'We just chase the leads, pal. We'll confirm it before we take him down.'

Taylor chortled as he shifted in his seat. 'You sound very confident.'

'We've got the only 1st Gen in the world with us. Just don't let him touch you.'

He looked over himself, dressed in jeans and a tee shirt. 'How do I stop him doing that?'

'The doc. says he'll need to touch your skin, so we've got a full tac. suit for you. He won't be able to make contact, so you should be able to get in close and use your strength.'

Taylor was unconvinced. 'And if he finds a way through the suit?'

The soldier smiled wryly. 'Let's just make sure that doesn't happen, huh?'

'But what if it does?' he asked urgently, concerned about the lack of a Plan B.

The warrior noticed their passenger's nerves and winked nonchalantly, shaking his rifle as he did so. 'Well, let's just say we're not carrying this hardware because it looks cool, huh?'

Taylor fell silent. He placed his hands in his lap and looked back down, turning the situation over in his mind. He had barely managed a full minute when his telephone began to chime. He looked at the screen. It was San.

He steadied his shaking hands and pressed the button before putting it to his ear. 'Hi, mate.'

'How are you, Chris?' His voice was rife with concern.

The soldier watched Taylor carefully and mouthed his question. 'Dr Namib?'

He nodded once as he replied. 'I'm okay. How did it go?'

'He's coming to the surgery tomorrow morning, before it opens.'

'Let's hope he turns up.'

'He said he would. Look, Chris, I don't know what's going on, but I can't say I'm comfortable lying to one of my closest friends.'

Taylor sighed and pinched the bridge of his nose, hoping it would subside the throbbing in his head, if only to allow him a moment to think clearly. It did not. 'Tim's changed, I'm sorry to say. He's not the same guy he was a few weeks ago. It's imperative that we find him as soon as possible.'

'Just tell me what he's done, Chris.'

He paused and let out a hesitant sigh. 'Look, San, if you trust me at all, believe me when I say that you don't want to know. Do you trust me?'

'Of course.'

'Good. I'm pleased that's settled. What time did he agree to come?'

'Seven a.m.'

'Okay. Just make sure you take your family somewhere else for the day. Someone will drop a car at your house shortly.'

'A car? Why? What's-?'

'Because we need to have your car parked at the surgery, San,' he interrupted tersely. 'He'll be suspicious if it's not there.'

'Oh, Chris! What are you involved in?'

'San,' he admonished, 'please just take your family out somewhere nice and, by the time you get home, this will all be over.'

There was a long pause before the doctor replied. 'Tim trusts me. Whatever he's done, just let me talk to him first, before it goes too far.'

'It not safe, San!' he snapped. 'Do you honestly believe that I would indulge such an extreme course of action if I thought there was another way?'

This pause was even longer, lasting almost a minute before Namib replied sheepishly. 'I guess not.'

'Precisely!' he shouted. 'That should indicate the gravity of the problem we're dealing with here. Please, just do as I ask and everything will be fine.'

The doctor spoke with defeat in his voice. 'Okay, I'll do it. Do I want to know how it goes?'

'I suspect not. I'll speak to you later.' He ended the call with an aggressive stab of his thumb and stuffed his telephone back into his pocket.

Everyone in the Jeep was staring at him. Even the driver watched him in the mirror. Taylor's eyes flitted from side-to-side nervously. 'It's done.'

Captain Nolan was a tall woman, with broad shoulders and an enormous chin. Her eyes were small, beady and distrustful. She was sitting in the passenger seat and turned to examine the man in the back seat with an unwavering, apathetic glower. 'Are you sure?'

Taylor looked her square in the eyes. 'I'm sure.'

Nolan took an encrypted telephone from her pocket and hit speed dial. There was a brief pause as she waited for someone to answer. 'It's Nolan...Do you have Dr Namib in view?...Is he at home?...Excellent. Be ready...Bulling could arrive at any time now...Excuse me?...No, don't worry about that...Why are you asking? I told you your primary objective...Yes, I did...Okay, I'll tell you again. Your objective is to secure the target...No, all other objectives are secondary...Yes, that includes the safety of the Namib family.'

20

The monitor flickered and Taylor shuddered. San's house had never looked so eerie.

The ghostly grey image seemed to pulse in time to the pounding in his head. His clothes were drenched in sweat.

He wanted to cry, but did not dare show weakness in front of his colleagues. He had never before seen such an array of cropped hair, tattoos, muscles and weapons. Even the women looked like they used barbed wire as dental floss.

He listened to the profane banter as they waited impatiently for Tim to appear. He suspected that this might be the toughest collection of people in the country. And they could not wait to sink their bullets into his best friend.

The trailer was half a mile away from the house and looked like the inside of a space station. He guessed it was the same as the trailers he had seen in the school car park. There were monitors, computers, dials and buttons everywhere. Taylor cast his eyes around and could not fathom what any of them operated.

He peered at the screen closest to him and tried to descry the team hidden around the Namib home. He knew they were there, waiting to pounce, but could not see the slightest trace of a single presence.

He could not settle his mind. The depths of his treachery were inconceivable. He was betraying his closest friends. Every time he let the thought into his head, he felt pangs of guilt stabbing at him.

What other choice did he have?

Tim was out of control and San was one of the only people who might be able to talk some sense into him. Not that this factor influenced Norbury or Nolan. They believed that San was a lure. He could use Tim's trust to reel in their target.

Taylor secretly hoped San would be able to prove that Tim retained some trace of his humanity.

But he hated himself for the way he was putting this to the test.

He knew Tim would never hurt San, or his family. And he knew they needed to stop Tim before he killed anyone else. Tim clearly needed help. There was something wrong with him, presumably connected with the virus somehow. If San could halt his rampage, they could get him some professional aid.

Ordinarily, Taylor would not entertain the notion of entrapping his best friend, even after what had happened. But Norbury had invested a lot of effort into convincing him that this was their best chance of getting Tim into custody without seriously injuring him.

Nolan was equally adamant that this was the best plan. She was convinced that Tim would concede to the heavily armed team of elite warriors and that they could avoid unnecessary conflict and potential bloodshed.

That was the only reason Taylor had agreed to their plan.

A hand landed on his shoulder, disturbing his thoughts. He looked at the owner.

It was the soldier from the Jeep. He was sympathetically proffering his hand. 'You okay, mate? I'm Jay, by the way.'

Taylor shook it weakly and nodded sombrely. 'I'm alright, I guess.'

'Just take solace in the fact this is our only option.'

'You can't be sure he'll even turn up here.'

'I've led teams all over the world and the only thing you can be sure of is that you can never be sure of anything. But I'd estimate a ninety per cent likelihood in this case.'

Taylor gave him a cynical scowl. 'Based on what?'

'Dr Namib told him that he thinks he might be infected, yes?'

'So?'

'And then he informed Mr Bulling that he wanted a blood sample to compare his own to, so he could be sure before turning himself in, did he not?'

'That's what they wanted, but that doesn't mean-'

'Strike that ninety,' Jay interrupted. 'I'm ninety-nine per cent certain.'

Taylor squinted suspiciously. 'Even I know how tenuous that is.'

He chuckled confidently. 'Trust me, I've tracked people in every terrain and situation you can think of. The tricky part is figuring out their motivation. Once you know what they want, it's easy to predict what they'll do. Criminals are reliable like that.'

'He's not a criminal!' he retorted vehemently.

'Didn't he kill a bunch of people?'

Taylor said nothing. His eyes merely filled with hate.

'Then that's exactly what he is,' Jay continued, smirking. 'We've established that your pal is travelling around the country targeting anyone who has the virus. He's running out of people. He'll be here.'

'He won't hurt San. They agreed to meet tomorrow morning. There's no reason to think he will turn up here to ambush our friend.'

'Maybe not. But he'll be here and that's what matters.'

'Perhaps he's smarter than we give him credit for.'

The soldier chortled. 'Let me tell you something that will stand you in good stead for tonight. It doesn't matter how smart your mate is or how much he cares about your doctor buddy. He's an addict. He's not the same guy you knew. The addiction has consumed him. It compels him to do extraordinary and horrifying things. He can't help it. It controls him now.'

'You sound like you know a thing, or two, about the subject.'

He indicated a silver bracelet on his left wrist. 'Eight years sober, sunshine. Anyway, I thought Dr Namib was your friend. He is, isn't he?'

Taylor narrowed his eyes sceptically. 'How's that relevant?'

'I'm just wondering why you're not rooting for him.'

'Tim won't hurt him.'

'Believe me when I say that you have no idea what an addict is capable of,' he remarked in a perfunctory tone. He paused and let out a jocund sigh. 'But, I reckon you'll find out if that's true soon enough.'

Taylor threw his hands up in frustration. 'I can't stand this! Why am I even here? I don't need to watch this.'

'You're here just in case.'

'In case of what?'

Jay scratched his head thoughtfully, as if he was choosing his words carefully. 'In case things go wrong. We might need *you* to stop him.'

'And if I can't?' Taylor scoffed, gritting his teeth.

He looked at the monitor. 'Then you need to delay him long enough for us to.'

'But what if-'

Jay's eyes suddenly opened wide. 'Sssh!'

Taylor fell silent and turned back to the screen. The grainy, black and white image followed Tim as he walked down the street, towards the Namib home.

Taylor felt his heart sink. 'Oh, Tim. Please, no.'

Jay winked. 'Told you.'

'Maybe he'll walk straight past,' he offered, half-heartedly.

The soldier stifled a laugh. 'Uh-huh. We'll see.'

They watched the monitor intently, as Tim strode down the street and turned into the Namib front garden. Taylor felt like crying.

Jay pointed at Tim's feet. 'You see that?'

Tim stopped walking, yet kept moving. He was gliding, several inches above the ground.

Nolan was suddenly behind them, radio by her mouth. 'Everybody, wait for my command. Alpha Team, get ready.'

Tim glided down the path and headed towards the gate leading to the rear garden. When he started to lift himself over it, Nolan screamed into her radio. 'Alpha Team, go!'

Taylor watched, transfixed, as figures emerged all over the screen. They were in the bins, in the bushes, under the car and even up the oak tree in the front garden. They burst out of their places and he saw the flickers of several gun muzzles, like fireflies dancing in the night.

The darts sped towards their target, but Tim noticed one of the flashes and pivoted in mid-air. He held up his hand and the darts stopped inches from him. Taylor watched the screen, the fear growing inside of him. The darts hovered in mid-air for several seconds as Tim looked around him.

Discerning the exposed soldiers, he turned the darts around by twiddling his fingers and fired them back with a small flick of his hand.

Nolan saw the darts hit her warriors and reacted. 'Bravo Team, go!' she hollered into her radio. 'Lethal force is authorised!'

'What?!' Taylor screamed, turning towards Nolan, who ignored him. He sat, open-mouthed for a few seconds, before slowly turning his head back towards the monitor.

Soldiers poured into view on every screen and from every angle. They raced across the street, guns blazing. Tim slowly lowered himself to the ground and continued to hold his hand in the air.

The bullets zoomed through the air, but stopped around ten inches from him. After several moments, the collection of ammunition looked like a small, metal insect swarm, which floated peacefully in the air.

Tim twiddled his fingers once more, before flicking his hand nonchalantly. The elite forces dived in every direction, taking cover behind anything they could find as the fusillade tore through the street.

The bullets ripped through cars, piercing metal and shattering glass. They crashed into brick and wood. Sparks flew as they scraped the concrete.

The soldiers managed sporadic bursts of gunfire, but found their efforts returned with contemptuously easy hand movements from their target.

The loud cracks of the battle echoed down the street and lights started to come on in houses all around them. Taylor saw the ghostly visage of his friend in the corner of an upstairs window. Tim saw it, also.

Taylor felt his heart break as he saw the menacing grin spread across his best friend's face. He looked into Tim's eyes and saw the intent he had prayed did not exist. He was there to kill San.

He wanted to drop to his knees and let the dejection envelope him, but he knew he could not. Tim turned towards San and said something, but it was not loud enough for the small microphones to pick up.

Nolan was screaming, but Taylor did not realise what she was saying to start with.

The whole world felt mute and numb. He knew he needed to snap out of his trance. He knew he needed to act.

Nolan's words permeated his melancholy. 'Get Taylor over there now! Backup teams, get into position! Snipers, get ready! Bravo Team, hold him there! Just keep him busy!'

Jay grabbed Taylor's arm. 'Come on, pal!'

He stood up. 'What do you want me to do?'

Nolan did not even try to hide her panic. 'He's stronger than we thought. You distract him. We'll do the rest. If you can, get him to face the moon.'

'The moon?' Taylor asked, confused.

'It's the opposite direction to the snipers. It's darker.'

He nodded, trying to focus on anything other than the fact he was about to try to stop one friend from slaughtering another friend. He raced away, following Jay, who leapt into the driving seat of the Jeep.

The journey lasted thirty-eight seconds. Jay screeched to halt several doors down, away from the flashes and crunches, and Taylor leapt out, sprinting to the Namib home. By the time he got there, the gunfire had stopped. He slid to a halt and cast his eyes over the scene.

There were bodies everywhere. They were mangled, charred and twisted. Taylor's jaw dropped in horror as his roving eyes cruised around the garden, down the street and then landed on Tim, who stood in the middle of the heap of corpses.

He forced the words out as he fought back the tears. 'Tim?'

He was panting loudly, but did not respond. He looked straight through his friend.

'Tim, what have you done?'

His expression was apathetic. 'What are *you* doing here?'

Taylor could not tear his eyes from the scene. He looked at the splatters of blood all over the front of the house and noticed the broken window where Namib's face had been. His eyes flicked back down to the garden and began their panicked search.

It lasted only a few seconds before they locked onto the one sight he never truly believed he would see.

San's mangled body.

On top of a small pile of mangled bodies.

The pile was the rest of the Namib family.

He could have defied Nolan's plan. He could have sent them away or warned them. He felt despair deep in his bones. But not for long.

He felt the desolation vanish in an instant. Instead, there was heat. There was anger. It was raw and dangerous. The white-hot rage coursed through his veins. Every molecule crackled and burned. His eyes flashed and he felt the blood pound through his skull. His stomach tightened and his fists automatically clenched. When he spoke, he found the words squeezing through gritted teeth, his voice a guttural growl. 'Is that San?'

Tim's expression was vacant. 'He's not infected. He lied to lead me into an ambush.'

Taylor took the gloves and mask from his pocket. He fiddled with them for a few seconds before slipping them on. 'I know. I asked him to.'

'You?' he snarled, his face suddenly filling with rage.

Taylor could not work out how he felt, as the pangs of guilt stabbed into his anger. He had never before felt two such extreme emotions simultaneously. He did not know how he was supposed to feel in this situation. He only knew that he wanted to crush Tim's bones. He cast a glance at the Namib family, tossed on a pile of death, and moved his eyes back to his best friend. He found himself roaring involuntarily. 'I never believed you would hurt him!'

'I need it, Chris. You can't understand how much I need it.'

Taylor recalled Jay's wink and the fact Tim had proven the soldier right made him even angrier. The faith he had placed in his best friend seemed like a cruel joke. He started pacing towards the murderer. 'I'm going to break your arms and legs.'

Tim scoffed. 'Don't be absurd, Chris! You're no match for me.'

Taylor's strides quickened as he broke into a run. He was several metres away when Tim recognised the threat as real, lifting himself up a metre in the air and firing a bolt of electricity at his on-rushing friend. His Machiavellian scowl vanished as he watched it bounce away, harmlessly striking a tree trunk.

By the time Tim realised what had happened, Taylor was upon him. He grabbed Tim by the leg. 'Oh, yes, there are a few things you didn't stick around long enough to find out about me.'

Tim's expression filled with a mixture of shock and fear as Taylor swung him around and hurled him into the same tree his electrical attack had struck. Tim crunched into the wood and hit the ground.

He needed several moments to recover from the surprise of failure, by which time Taylor was only inches from grabbing him again. He pushed himself away, sliding on his back along the floor before propelling himself upwards with a ping.

Taylor clutched at thin air as Tim sped away, his fingernails tearing through the fabric of the clothes. By the time he turned around, Tim was hovering out of reach and scanning the area.

Taylor darted towards San's car as his foe began to hurl parts of the Namib rockery at him. The smooth stones crashed down around him, zipped through the air with the tiniest flick of Tim's finger. Several of them cracked against his body and one struck his head with a loud thud. None of them hurt. They did not even leave a mark. They simply struck him and fell to the ground.

Taylor was already crouching down, stabbing his fingers through the wing and door of San's car. He lifted with his legs and tossed with his arms, the underarm swing hurling the vehicle up into the night sky.

Tim tried to move, but reacted slowly. The car clipped him as he swirled away, sending him tumbling back towards the ground as it careered through the front window in a cacophony of screaming metal, shattering glass and crumbling brick.

Taylor pounced, desperately reaching out to grip his enemy. He was quickly surmising that he might have already wasted his best opportunity of victory. Having had Tim in his grip, he should not have let him go.

Clearly, Tim had gained some kind of healing ability. There was no other explanation for how he had recovered so swiftly from his body being slammed into a tree and a car hitting him as it flew through the air.

Tim seemed to realise this, also. He bounced back up into the air and landed in the oak tree, gripping the branches like some kind of frog. He looked down, the disdain clear in his eyes. Taylor looked up at him as he charged and noted the uncertainty.

Taylor hit the tree with his shoulder and clawed at the bark, scraping it away and digging his fingers into the trunk to get a firm grip. Tim could do nothing but watch, as he yanked, pulled and pushed.

Taylor felt objects striking him, but ignored them as an elephant would ignore a wasp sting. He could hear the roots tearing and see the tree toppling. With an almighty heave, he watched the roots ripping through the garden as the sound of creaking, snapping wood echoed down the street. The mighty oak tumbled to the ground, crushing the fence into kindling.

Tim bounded from the tree as it fell, powering through the air and sticking to the remnants of the Namib house. He used one hand to stick himself to the wall as he perched on the upstairs windowsill. He raised his spare hand in the air and flicked his wrist.

Every gun in the garden suddenly lurched up into the air, as if snatched up by ghosts. Taylor looked around him briefly and then back up at his target. He hoped he was as resilient as he thought he was.

The cracking of gunfire sounded louder from such close proximity. It was almost as if there was a series of fireworks going off next to his head. He felt the bullets striking him. It stung. Yet they bounced off his skin and ricocheted around the area, splintering shrubbery, chipping brickwork and piercing metal. Taylor took three large strides to reach the house and swung his fist at it. His knuckles crunched against the remainder of the wall and several large chunks came free, falling at his feet.

He picked up the closest one and spent a moment eyeing his target. Then he tossed it, as an Olympian might throw a shot put. Except this projectile sped through the air as swiftly as a jet-propelled rocket.

Tim saw it coming, but the clump of brick flew at him with such velocity that he could not evade it, even with his heightened reflexes. He pushed away from the building, but the blow crashed him back against the wall and he dropped several metres into the rubble pile beneath.

He landed in a crouch, poised to bounce away as Taylor waded in. Tim somersaulted over his foe and landed behind him.

Taylor spun around in time to see his adversary clicking his fingers. A small flame appeared over his thumb. Tim grinned menacingly and blew on it.

A huge fireball swept through the air. Taylor dived away, but felt the heat as the inferno enveloped him. He rolled away as Tim ran out of breath and then jumped up. He was not hurt, but the fire had burnt through his tactical suit in several places.

Taylor looked at Tim, whose eyes lit up excitedly. He flashed across the ground at an inconceivable pace. Taylor thrust out a hand instinctively. Tim zoomed straight into it.

The strike was marginal. Taylor knew he could have landed a telling blow and had wasted another opportunity to balance the bout in his favour. Without even trying, he smashed Tim backwards several metres. He was about to chastise himself for lacking composure when he saw his adversary getting back up.

Tim's eyes were alight. He was ravenous, desperate. Taylor could scarcely believe his fortune when Tim rushed at him again. The move defied rational thought. It was the manoeuvre of an addict.

Taylor waited until his best friend was upon him before reaching out and grabbing him by the throat. He picked Tim up and ignored the thrusts and scratches. Tim fired electricity and fire at him in quick succession, but Taylor simply turned his head away as they passed by harmlessly.

He pulled Tim in close and inspected the feverish, drooling expression. 'You make me sick,' he whispered, before steadying himself and hurling Tim towards the house with every ounce of power he could muster.

Tim careered through the air with such force that a sonic boom pulsated down the street, cracking any window it did not shatter. All the people amassing to watch, soldiers and civilians alike, winced and covered their ears. Tim crashed through the wall and vanished into the house. The smashing, creaking sounds resonated for several moments, before the house began to collapse.

Taylor looked on, astonished. He had clearly destroyed a load-bearing wall. With a human being.

It was less than two minutes before the house was demolished. Dust clouds accompanied the symphony of destruction as it filled the night air. The spectators did not utter a sound. They did not even move. Most of them questioned the legitimacy of what they had just seen. They looked across at their peers, as if seeking some kind of assurance that this was not a hallucination.

One man had just thrown another man through a house. Which had then fallen down.

They all knew the only explanation for such a sight. The Hero Virus was now their neighbour.

The soldiers quickly formed a cordon as the residents started to move closer to the scene.

Yet Taylor did not move. He realised that he was holding his breath and took a lungful of dusty air. Had he just killed his best friend? It seemed impossible that anyone could survive that.

He was just about to start rummaging through the debris when he saw the slightest of movements. Where the kitchen had once been, pieces of roof tile began to slide away. Then the rubble bounced down the pile and rolled towards the street. Then a hand appeared.

Taylor froze as Tim clambered out of the remains of a wardrobe. He was groaning and lacerations covered his face, but they were healing.

Taylor watched the bones crick back into place and the bloody gashes close up before his eyes. His jaw dropped.

Tim took a deep breath and blew. The ensuing gale took Taylor by surprise. He stumbled backwards and tripped over a brick.

Tim was next to him in a flash and forced him back with a shove of his hand from two metres away. Taylor landed on his back and felt his head being pulled back up, before the invisible force slammed it back into the ground. It did not cause him any pain, but it successfully dazed him long enough for Tim to leap on him and grab the exposed skin on his arm.

Tim gritted his teeth and tightened his grip as he looked down apologetically. 'Sorry, pal, but I need it.'

Taylor could barely hear the words through the grogginess. He felt a sharp pain in his neck and looked around to see that there was a dart sticking out of it. He could feel the effects instantly.

A fog entered his mind. He could not understand how it had pierced his skin, but he knew that he was starting to fall asleep. Was he not impervious to needles?

He tried to focus, but his vision was blurring. He tried to talk, but could only slur incoherent gibberish. He could feel the strength fading from his body.

Tim kept his hand wrapped firmly around Taylor's arm. He noticed the soldiers starting to rush towards him, but dispersed them with one wave of his hand. Screaming men and women flew in every direction.

Taylor could feel a hot sensation where Tim was holding him. It was painful. He had almost forgotten what pain was like.

'If only everyone I took was as powerful as you,' Tim said. 'You wouldn't believe some of the useless abilities I've accumulated.'

Taylor tried to swing a fist, but could not lift his arm. He could feel the snug darkness beckoning him.

Tim was sneering. 'Actually, that gives me an idea.'

Taylor could not even lift his head to see if help was imminent. His arm was burning. He tried to scream in agony, but his tongue felt like a rock. His eyelids slammed shut as he lost the power to keep them open.

Within seconds, he was unconscious.

21

Taylor listened to the music for several moments. He did not recognise the melody. He wondered why he was listening to music he did not know in total darkness. He realised that his eyes were closed. And it was not music.

It was the sound of sirens.

And there was no singing. There were loud voices and they were muffled. He could not distinguish what they were saying. The tone suggested panic, but he was too disorientated to be certain.

He tried to open his eyes, but it felt like someone had covered them in cement. He felt numb all over. The only sensation in his body was the warmth and comfort of the encroaching darkness in his mind. He succumbed to it eagerly.

He did not know how much time passed when the rattling sound filled his ears. The voices were louder this time. He managed to force his eyes open a few millimetres. A bright light sped past overhead. Then another. And another. There were several faces over him, but they were too blurry for him to discern. A sudden, sharp pain appeared behind his eyes, forcing him to close them. The darkness quickly swept in and claimed him.

The bleeping sound stabbed into his head. He could hear soft voices, barely above a whisper. He started to open his eyes, but the light blinded him and forced him to close them tightly.

'He's awake.'

'Sedate Chris again, please.'

'I don't think we should give him any more. He has enough in his system to kill five elephants, sir. '

'Do it now, please.'

Taylor managed to muster enough cognisance to recognise the authoritative voice. It was Norbury. He opened his mouth to speak, but was asleep before a single word escaped his lips.

His eyes opened suddenly and he took a deep breath as he sat up sharply. The only sound was the gentle bleep of the heart monitor next to the bed. There were no voices and no bright lights. It was quiet, there was daylight and his head did not feel as if there were shards of glass stuck in it.

There was a throb behind his eyes and his body ached all over, but he managed to turn his head from side to side, stretching his neck as he did so. He let out a loud groan as he fought the tightness in his muscles. Looking around, he quickly recognised where he was.

Norbury's office.

'We were worried about you.'

He recognised the voice behind him as the doctor and swallowed hard as he tried to speak. His voice was little more than a wheezy croak. 'What happened?'

Norbury stood up, moved into view and indicated the table next to the bed. 'There's water there.'

Taylor located it and took a sip. It quickly extinguished the flames in his throat. 'What happened?'

'Tim got to your skin and managed to get a sedative dart into your neck. Small sips, Chris.'

He swallowed the water in his mouth. 'I think I'm only impervious to objects I know are coming. That's how he got the dart in.'

'I suggest you try to remember that from now on.'

He took another sip of water, feeling better with every passing second. He let out a resigned sigh. 'It doesn't matter, anyway. Tim has my ability now.'

The doctor smiled wryly. 'Well, that's the most curious and interesting part of this episode.'

Taylor swung his legs over the side of the bed slowly and placed his feet on the cold floor. 'What is?'

'Your body rejected him.'

He stared at Norbury, confused. 'Then how is it that I'm still alive?'

'You still have the virus,' he returned cheerfully.

He shook his head. 'No, that can't be right. I remember it clearly. I could actually feel him taking it from my body.'

He was grinning as spoke in a jocund tone. 'It seems that he failed. It looks like he couldn't take it from you.'

'He *couldn't* take it? How's that possible?'

Norbury paused, walking back past his patient and around the bed. 'We're not really sure, truth be told. He tried. That much is evident.'

'Maybe he didn't have enough time. Maybe your soldiers interrupted him before he could finish.'

Norbury was shaking his head. 'We tried to intervene, but we couldn't.'

Taylor suddenly paused, the sense of alarm causing the hairs to stand up on the back of his neck. 'You didn't catch him?'

He rubbed his scalp and smiled ruefully. 'I'm afraid not.'

Taylor winced as the memories flooded his mind. The Namib family, strewn across the ground, mangled and broken. Dead soldiers in every direction. The blood and gore. The carnage. He felt the hot rush of tears behind his eyes and fought them back. 'San and his family? They're...?' He trailed off, incapable of completing the question.

Norbury allowed himself a single, sullen nod. 'Yes, they are.'

'All of them?'

'Yes.'

He felt the grief overwhelming him, threatening to choke him. 'It was all for nothing?'

The doctor offered him a smile of condolence. 'That's not entirely true.'

He could feel the melancholy quickly changing to anger. He threw his hands in the air. 'Your people let him get away! The whole point of this exercise was to capture Tim! They died for nothing!'

Norbury paused and met his patient with a cold glare. 'I'm sorry about Dr Namib and his family, I really am. However, I'm afraid that we don't have time for the luxury of entertaining your guilt. At the moment, they're just names on Tim's list. Personally, I'd quite like to keep that list to as few names as possible. We'll have time to mourn later.'

He scoffed angrily. 'How can you be so blasé about it? Can you really just write them off as collateral damage?'

'For now. We need to concentrate on catching your friend before he hurts anyone else.'

Taylor opened his mouth to retort, but stalled. As much as he loathed the idea, he knew Norbury was right. He spent several moments collecting himself, forcing the despair, agony and ire to the back of his mind. He took several, cathartic, deep breaths. 'Okay, fine. You said it wasn't a complete loss. Why don't you expound?'

'Tim can't take your ability,' he replied tersely. 'That's useful to us.'

He laughed acerbically. 'Maybe we just got lucky. You didn't even know that I can repel bullets until I showed you. Nobody knew that I'm only unaffected by objects I know are coming. After all your research, you are just as clueless as ever. Why can't you just admit that you have no idea what you're doing?'

Norbury scowled. 'My apologies for not shooting you, Chris. It's not a test widely recognised in the medical profession. Although, when you consider it, I would think it's only logical that your skin would be as strong as the rest of you.'

'Do you even have a theory as to why he couldn't take my ability?'

'I do, as it happens,' he returned defensively.

'Well, don't keep me in suspense!' Taylor snapped.

The doctor sighed. 'The anger isn't helping anyone, Chris.'

'I'll worry about my emotional state,' he replied furiously, his face now crimson. 'Your job is to get me the information I need to stop Tim.'

He shook his head and continued to walk around the bed. 'The theory is relatively simple. You're 1st Gen and he's 2nd Gen. You're more powerful than he is.'

Taylor paused to consider it. Maybe it really *was* that simple. 'That makes sense. He can't use the virus to remove it from someone with a more potent strain.'

'There is, however, one major drawback to this prognosis.'

'I'm the only 1st Gen on the planet?'

'Exactly. It looks very much like it's only you who can stop him.'

'He beat me already, or didn't you notice my abject defeat? He was just too fast. He has too many abilities.'

'You'll just have to find a way,' Norbury informed him firmly.

'Why me? You must have access to dozens of specialist military personnel for emergencies such as this.'

'We hit him with five teams, Chris. Three army and two SAS assault teams went down trying to stop him.'

'So, who else is there?'

'Nobody.'

'That's total crap. Get the Americans to help. It's in their interest to stop him, too.'

'I hate to break this to you, but there isn't anyone out there more lethal than the SAS. If they can't stop him, nobody can.'

'No, that can't be true. There are dozens of options. Even the Americans can-'

'You're not listening to me, Chris. They could send five thousand soldiers, but Tim will kill them all. The

Mossad have been in touch and offered aid from Shayetet 13, which we'll be taking up. The Americans are sending a team from Delta Force and a team of Navy SEALs. Russia have sent three Spetsnaz teams. We have people coming over from every country from China to Brazil, but they aren't going to offer anything the SAS can't. You're our only hope.'

Taylor flopped backwards on the bed and let out an exasperated sigh. 'That's an awfully large amount of pressure.'

'Yes, it is,' he replied, without a single trace of sympathy in his voice. 'It's not going to be easy, either, so we need to get to work immediately.'

'Just give me a moment, will you?' Taylor retorted querulously.

'No, Chris!' he bellowed. 'We don't have spare moments. Tim's out there killing people and you're the only person who can stop him.'

He sat up sharply, swaying slightly as the blood ran straight to his head. He was still a little groggy. 'If he has no compunction about slaughtering San, and his family, then he's getting desperate. He's running out of people to take abilities from. Does he know I'm alive?'

'No, I don't think so.'

'Then we wait and ambush him. He'll come to us as long as you have subjects here.'

'I'm not so sure, Chris.'

'He'll have to. He needs to feed his addiction. Taking 20th Gen hosts isn't helping him. They're far too weak. He'll have no choice but to come here, if he wants abilities that are of any use to him.'

Norbury's lips creased into an uncomfortable smile. 'I'm afraid there's a slight complication with that theory.'

'Really?' he snorted irritably. 'There seem to be a lot of extra complications that I know nothing about. What's *this* one, dare I ask?'

Norbury moved back towards his desk and took the glass of water from it. As he took a sip, his hand was shaking. 'Recently, we've discovered several fresh victims with traces of dead virus in their blood.'

'So what?'

He held up his hand brusquely. 'Let me finish, Chris. We tested the cadavers and their blood work matched that which we've seen from our 3rd Gen hosts within the facility. Which means-'

'That he's starting to infect his targets first,' Taylor interjected, aghast. 'He's giving them the virus to farm their 3rd Gen abilities.'

22

Taylor watched the world flashing past far beneath him without enjoying it. The sunshine made everything look ethereal from his vantage point. The lakes, rivers and ponds glimmered brightly, millions of twinkles in every direction. The warm rays stroked the trees and bushes, iridescent with a kaleidoscope of colours. The glass in the buildings below seemed to wink at them as they flew past, the sunshine reflecting off them at varying angles.

Taylor did not appreciate any of it. He was deep in thought. Even the loud thumps of the blades did not interrupt his musing.

The helicopter banked to the left and he eyed the housing estate ahead. The semi-detached houses were arranged in concentric circles, with a circular park at the very centre.

He spoke into the mouthpiece dangling from his helmet, turning to the woman in the adjacent seat in the cockpit. 'Are we nearly there?'

The pilot kept looking straight ahead. 'Affirmative, sir. LZ in sight. We're heading for the flashing lights.'

Taylor peered out of the huge, bulb-shaped windscreen. They were descending and he could now see the street with army barricades at either end. There were police maintaining the cordons, the flashing lights from their vehicles barely noticeable to the untrained eye against the glare of the sunshine.

He gave up counting the army vehicles when he reached a dozen and eyed the swarms of uniforms up and down the street. This was serious.

The helicopter swerved and dropped, causing his stomach to jump into his throat, as the pilot navigated a landing in a garden that did not look like it had enough space. The rotors chopped back a few bushes and shrubs as the soldiers rushed to meet them. They did not wait for the blades to stop turning before they opened the door and greeted him.

Taylor shook the proffered hand and jumped out. The SAS warriors escorted him through the rear entrance of the house. They were talking to him during the short journey, but the noise of his transport drowned out their words. It was not until they were indoors that he could hear them, but they quickly left him with Captain Nolan in the small kitchenette.

Nolan met him with a single, approving nod of the head.

Taylor looked past her towards the medical team in the living room. 'What do we have, Captain?'

'Dr Norbury can explain it better than I can,' she replied matter-of-factly, turning and striding through to the room Taylor was eyeing curiously. 'He's through here, if you would like to follow me.'

There were plastic sheets covering the walls, ceilings and floor. There were three gurneys, two of which had black body bags on. The other had a young woman on.

She was sitting talking to a team of doctors, but seemed shaken and had red streaks down her cheeks. Taylor surveyed the scene for a few moments, before his eyes locked on to Norbury, who was already approaching him.

He seemed almost jubilant. 'Ah, Chris! Finally.'

'What's going on? You said it was urgent.'

He tossed a thumb over his shoulder in the direction of the young woman sitting on the gurney. 'We have three more hosts. Two are already dead, but we found one survivor.'

'A survivor?'

He nodded ecstatically. 'Our searching has finally paid off!'

Taylor waved his excitement away and scoffed loudly. 'I don't know if I would classify it as a great victory. We've been looking for three weeks and have fifty-three more victims. I'm not sure I quite agree with your barometer for success.'

The doctor scowled. 'This woman has an ability already. She can now turn her fingernails into razor-sharp claws at will.'

He stared at Norbury, bemused. 'So?'

'So, this one's different.'

'How?'

The doctor smiled happily. 'She never came into contact with Mr Bulling. She arrived home after he had been here to infect both the victims in the bags. She found them both already deceased. Before she could call the police, she fainted. She woke up this morning. She was unconscious for four days.'

He raised his eyebrows, his curiosity successfully piqued. 'Do you think Tim plans on coming back for her?'

260

'No, why would he? He doesn't even know she exists, or he would have been back to claim her already.'

Taylor paused and considered it for a moment before replying in a low growl. 'I don't understand why you're so excited about this.'

'Don't you see?' he retorted joyously. 'It explains how we have these mystery infections. It explains why we were never able to lock this virus down.'

'Does it?'

He rolled his eyes, laughed heartily and slapped Taylor on the shoulder. 'It goes airborne.'

Taylor's eyes suddenly doubled in size as alarm gripped his heart. 'It's airborne.'

'No, no, not permanently,' Norbury assured him. 'If it were, we would see far more cases than we have. No, it's not airborne. We're running some tests to prove, or disprove, my theory, but I think that, when the body can't accommodate the virus, it can leave that body. It kills the host, but can become airborne for a short period of time to seek a replacement host.'

Taylor's face lit up. 'That makes sense. It was certainly strange that such a complex organism would kill its host and, therefore, commit suicide. How long do you think it's airborne for?'

'It can't be long, or these cases wouldn't be so sporadic. A few minutes, an hour maybe. And it doesn't travel far, either, or, again, we would see a lot more cases.'

He smiled contentedly. 'That's good news. Really, it is. But how does it help us catch Tim?'

Norbury paused for a moment. 'It doesn't,' he replied, frowning.

'Isn't that our main objective?'

'Well, yes, but-'

'Shouldn't we try to hold our excitement until we find him? I mean, he doesn't know about this, does he? Otherwise he would simply fill a room with people and give one the virus. If it kills them, they infect others. If it doesn't, they will still infect them with the same potency of strain.'

The doctor paused, as if an idea had suddenly struck him.

Taylor watched him for a moment before pressing. 'What?'

'You might have just hit upon an idea, Chris.'

'Might I?'

'Indeed. Given what we've discovered here today, we may need a huge number of hosts in a short space of time.'

Taylor suddenly fixed him with a fierce glower. 'No.'

'You don't even know what I'm thinking.'

'Yes, I do. My answer is no. Don't make me come after you, too.'

Norbury met him with an angry glare. 'You haven't even heard what else we've discovered here today. It might make you change your mind.'

Taylor resisted the urge to grab him by the throat. 'Why don't you stop being so cryptic and tell me what's going on?'

'We've made a monumental breakthrough here today, Chris,' he stated gruffly. 'I suspect you don't appreciate just how important it is. Everything up until now is vapid in comparison.'

He held up his hand forcefully. 'I don't doubt it, but all I'm interested in is finding Tim and stopping him. If you have something that can help me do that, I'm listening.'

Norbury analysed Taylor through narrow eyes. 'You didn't even ask who the victims were?'

'Does it matter?' he returned, casting a quick glance in the direction of the black pouches on the other side of the room. He had seen so many of them lately, they no longer struck the chords on his heart. Indeed, they had become part of his daily routine. He met Norbury with a steely stare. 'We've already established that Tim doesn't follow any kind of pattern. His victims are random choices, dictated by chance, opportunity and luck.'

He shrugged his shoulders nonchalantly. 'Okay, well, in answer to the question you have yet to ask, they were her housemates. She shared this house with three other people, all of whom were students at the nearby college.'

Taylor paused, rolling his eyes upwards as he counted in his head, casting his eyes towards the gurneys. 'I thought you said there were two victims?'

Norbury stabbed his forefinger in the air triumphantly. 'Exactly! The fourth person is missing. More intriguing still, it seems as if he packed some belongings and left in quite a hurry.'

'Why?' he asked, intrigued.

'Hazard a guess.'

Taylor scratched his cheek slowly and pensively. 'Do you suspect he's with Tim?'

'I can't think of any other explanation, can you?'

'Voluntarily?'

'Why else would he pack his things up and take them with him? Kidnap victims, so I'm informed, don't tend to have time to throw a bag together. More importantly, they don't empty their bank account before they're taken. Unless Tim can control minds now, too.'

He took a deep breath and exhaled sharply. 'That doesn't make any sense. If Tim wants the abilities, why would he leave one of them alive? We haven't seen any evidence of this before, have we?'

'Not until now,' the doctor returned swiftly. 'The only theory I'm able to postulate, at this point, is that this young man developed a talent that Tim already had.'

'Maybe he liked the lad?'

Norbury shrugged. 'Perhaps. The truth is that we have no idea.'

Taylor suddenly froze as an idea hit him. It was so terrifying, it actually paralysed him for several moments. 'Of course, there's another possibility that you haven't yet mentioned and, to be frank, it's the most terrifying prospect of them all.'

The doctor leaned in towards him curiously. 'Really? What's that?'

'Maybe he's decided that he's bored of simply collecting power. Now he wants more. Perhaps he's decided it's time for him to build an army.'

23

Taylor powered through the corridor, wondering how they had managed to hide it from him for two weeks. Since learning that the virus managed to exist in the air, they had been hiding away. He should have suspected sooner.

He reached the door and hammered his fists into the metal. The array of dents all over the reinforced titanium grew each time he crashed his hands into it. 'Open this door!'

He paused and caught his breath, before slamming his fists into the metal again. The loud clangs echoed down the corridor, drawing several spectators from their respective tasks.

The armed soldier guarding the door found his entreaties useless, although he could not tell if it was because Taylor was ignoring him, or simply could not hear him over the din. He only knew that this man, who was able to create sharp dents in the vault doors with only his knuckles, did not seem calmer, despite his pleading.

The deafening cacophony of metallic thuds was making his head hurt. The warrior continued to try reasoning with Taylor for several minutes more, before trying to gain his attention by lightly touching his arm.

Taylor spun on him furiously, grabbing him by the lapels and lifting him from the ground. 'I said no!' he screamed, foaming at the mouth to such an extent that spittle flew out in every direction.

The soldier dropped his weapon and froze in terror. He stared, wide-eyed, at the monster and ignored the spray covering his face. 'Please,' he begged. 'It's the only way.'

Taylor tossed him aside. The soldier crashed into the wall and slid to the floor, landing upside down. Taylor turned back to the huge, titanium door and swung his fist at it again. It was starting to buckle. Within four swings, he had managed to crumple it enough to slip his fingers through the newly formed crack at the edge. He peeled it open like it was a tin of soup.

He stormed inside, fists clenched, and cast his eyes over the laboratory. Everyone in the room turned towards him. All of them trembled, except for one.

Norbury stepped toward him angrily. 'What the hell are you doing, Chris?'

'What did I say to you?' he hollered.

The people in the room shrunk. None of them had ever seen him this angry before. It was like a red-faced, smaller version of The Hulk.

The doctor approached him fearlessly. He spoke in a calm, even tone, as a negotiator might when dealing with a terrorist. 'We need them.'

Taylor stomped towards him, jabbing his finger into his own chest. '*I* will get him for you.'

He scoffed. 'You're not strong enough, Chris,' he riposted in a perfunctory tone. 'We need them.'

'You're becoming as bad as Tim,' he retorted venomously, turning his finger around and wagging it in Norbury's face.

The doctor scowled, waving the suggestion away vehemently. 'That's total bullshit! I give everyone the choice.'

'What are you going to do if he decides to come here? He'll take their abilities, too!'

'That's precisely what I want!' he answered, a sardonic chuckle escaping his lips. 'The virus I'm using is engineered with serum in it. He won't be able to take their abilities. So, let him come. In fact, this entire plan hinges on it.'

'And if he doesn't? What then? How do we stop his inexorable march to power? I know him better than anyone else alive does and he's smarter than you give him credit for.'

'Then we'll go to him. He's not hiding any longer. We have the element of surprise in our favour. He doesn't know what we're doing here and he doesn't know you're alive.'

'He's not hiding because he knows he's all but invincible!' Taylor returned, gesticulating furiously.

Norbury allowed himself a nefarious grin. 'He'll get quite a shock then, won't he?'

He glared at the doctor, confounded. 'Have you even seen the news today?'

His smile vanished. 'No. Why?'

'Turn on the TV.'

Norbury darted to the nearest table and snatched the remote from it. He aimed it at the screen on the wall and jabbed his finger on the buttons.

The BBC News channel flickered on and the image of Tim appeared. He was standing on a podium outside the

Houses of Parliament, a microphone stand directly in front of him.

Norbury turned to Taylor. 'What's he doing?'

Taylor nodded his head in the direction of the TV. 'Just watch it.'

The doctor turned up the volume. Tim disseminated his grandiloquent message with crisp enunciation. He stared frigidly at the cameras as he delivered every word with aplomb precision. He was almost unrecognisable as the same man who had begged them for the virus. He had an extra fifteen kilogrammes of muscle, his upright posture made him seem taller and he held his head high. His face was clean-shaven, his eyes were cold, but clear, and his hair seemed somehow more thick and lustrous, even though it was short and cropped. Even his diction and language had improved: he looked and sounded smarter than Taylor had ever known him to be.

'I don't want violence. However, it's imperative that the world powers now concede that we have a new species of homo sapien. Humankind must submit to us. I have no desire to hurt anyone, but I cannot tolerate insurrection. It's clear to me now that we cannot trust those charged with the progression of our society.

'As a result, the New Breed will take up the reigns of civilisation. We shall begin here. Therefore, I request that the incumbent Prime Minister resigns his post and allows me to assume full control of state affairs. I realise that this may not be easy to arrange, so will happily assist the process by delaying the start of my tenure until midday on Friday.

'I am also aware that this request may be met with resistance. I truly hope this is not the case but, if this should transpire, I would like to announce my intention to take control by force. I wish to reiterate my hope that we can avoid a highly undesirable predicament by taking the only, sensible course of action available.'

As Tim paused, so swarms of hands leapt into the air. He selected one. The journalist asked her question gingerly. 'How do you plan to deal with any resistance, if you encounter any?'

Tim's booming laughter caused the speakers to rattle. 'Like the army or police? Well, I have several dozen warriors behind me, all of whom posses 3rd Gen abilities.' He indicated a tiny man with scales all over him and a large woman who had fangs. 'I would respectfully suggest that no army in the world may stand between them and their goal. I would also urge the government not to test my theory. There is no need for it to come to that.'

He snatched the microphone from the stand and stepped off the small dais. 'We don't need any more unnecessary loss of life. I should also like to use this opportunity to remind anyone who wishes to contract The Hero Virus that they can begin the process by calling the freephone number or following the link on my website. Of course, there are some provisos, such as unconditional support, in return, but my legal team will fully explain all the terms of the contract before they receive the virus, although-'

'Excuse me, Mr Bulling,' another journalist interrupted, 'but can I ask what you plan to do about the opinion of the people? Maybe they're not willing to accept the fact that democracy is the latest of your victims.'

Tim grinned menacingly. He raised his hand in the air, holding his thumb and forefinger around an inch apart. 'Well, I'll help them see things differently.' He twisted his wrist and the journalist's head spun around with a loud crack. He flopped to the ground.

The crowd suddenly parted as muted gasps and horrified shrieks filled the air. Every pair of terrified eyes stared at the corpse.

Tim continued talking, as if nothing had happened. 'But, I will answer his question. When I want the opinion of the people, I'll let them know what it should be. Any other questions?'

The silent crowd exchanged terrified glances.

Tim chuckled. 'It's okay, as long as you're not interrupting me.'

An awkward impasse ensued, lasting almost a minute, until a large, flame-haired, middle-aged woman tremulously raised her hand.

He turned to her, visibly relieved. 'Yes, ma'am?'

Every face on Parliament Square turned towards her. When she spoke, her voice trembled. 'If the government acquiesces to your demands,' she began apprehensively, 'what will you do next?'

Tim seemed pleased by the question. He moaned thoughtfully. 'That's quite simple, really. I'll fix the problems here before I move on to the next country.'

A young man raised his hand with slightly more assurance.

Tim pointed to him. 'Yes?'

'Which country is next?'

Tim spent several seconds considering his response. 'Erm, that depends on a number of factors: size, proximity, the issues in the country and some others I'm not willing to disclose at this juncture. Let's face facts, please. Our society is chaotic and broken. I'm going to fix it. I'm going to instil some order.'

This time, a number of hands leapt in the air. He selected another woman, who stammered her question. 'W-W-What p-p-problems in this c-c-c-country d-d-do you believe you must c-c-c-contend with?'

He cast her a quizzical glance, uncertain if she suffered from a speech impediment or unadulterated fear, so chose to ignore it. 'Where do I start? The welfare system, crime, education, discrimination, soaring debt, political corruption, the economy...must I continue?'

An ocean of hands pointed to the sky the moment he stopped talking. He selected an elderly man. 'Do you honestly believe you can resolve all the issues in the world?'

He grinned arrogantly. 'Time will tell. Watch me and see for yourself, sir.'

A ripple of excitement shimmered through the crowd. The people crept forwards, treading over and around the forgotten corpse in their midst. Tim selected another from the shower of hands. 'With all due respect, what makes you think you have the right?'

His smile disappeared and he fixed the young man with a stern glare. 'Our government had their chance. Before them, we relied on the royal family and the church. Now is the time for change. It's *our* time.' He swept his arm across the horizon. 'The New Breed.'

'This virus is an opportunity,' he continued, his voice full of lustre. 'It's a chance for us to get it right. Of course, I realise that not everyone will agree. Of course, I understand that this path will be fraught with difficulty, especially to begin with. However, once people learn that they are simply a tiny part of a much larger machine, we can get this to work. We must all appreciate that our individual needs are secondary to those of the entire world.'

More hands. He selected one. 'Forgive me, Mr Bulling, but that proposition sounds vaguely familiar. It's quite reminiscent of remarks made by people like Stalin and Hitler.'

'Ha!' he exclaimed jovially. 'Any easy mistake to make, young fellow. I'm not a Fascist. This is not Socialism. This is not Communism. Have you heard any racist rhetoric? Do I sound like I speak with hate in my heart? We have examples all around us of how a society can function successfully and in peace. There is not room for selfish behaviour at the expense of the common good. Everyone merely needs to accept their place, that's all.'

'Which examples do you refer to?' They were not even waiting for him to point at them as they clamoured for a front row position.

'Ants, bees, wasps...I could go on.'

'You're comparing humankind to ants?'

'Not at all. They're far more civilised than we are.'

'Don't they use a rather primitive version of Communism?'

'I'm not going to get into a political debate right now, but suffice it to say that the state isn't going to own everything, nor are the people going to have an equal share of everything. The free market economy and capitalism will continue.'

'Don't you think that enforcing your will under the threat of violence countermands your message?'

'Can *you* think of any other way?' Tim snapped.

The same young man answered. 'The democratic process, perhaps?'

He harrumphed. 'Which is stale, slow and corrupt. No, this is the only way.'

'What about religion? Does that have a place in-'

The TV suddenly went black. Norbury tossed the remote on the nearest desk. 'I've seen quite enough, thank you.'

Taylor smiled wearily. 'Well, I guess your plan needs to change.'

'Why?'

'You won't be able to stop him. Your ploy is every bit as absurd as Tim's. It's sheer lunacy.'

'No,' the doctor retorted defiantly. 'It will work.'

'He's too strong, and now he has his followers, his New Breed, he's more dangerous than ever. You'll only make him more powerful. I'll find a way to defeat him, I swear.'

'He won't be able to use his ability on them, either. Not with the serum-engineered virus.'

Taylor scoffed. 'How could you possibly know that for certain?'

'We still have his test results, just as we have yours. We looked into it. I didn't just guess.'

'And if real life turns out to be different from the laboratory?'

'It won't,' he declared confidently. 'We've considered and anticipated every conceivable variable.'

Taylor took a deep breath and let out a resigned sigh. He had spent enough time with Norbury to know that he was determined to the point of obstinacy. 'Is there nothing I can say to change your mind?'

He shrugged his shoulders as he held his hands out submissively. 'We don't have any other choice. If you've got something else, I'm all ears, but you don't, do you?' He paused for a moment to see if there would be a reply and continued before Taylor could muster one. 'Besides, we're on a deadline now. You heard him. If we don't act before noon on Friday, he'll end up slaughtering thousands.'

'Again, you don't know that for certain.'

'Do you think Hodgkin, or the government, will submit without a fight? I don't think so. He will have to kill his way to power.'

Taylor shook his head ruefully. 'We might be able to make him see sense. This isn't him. If I can talk to him, then maybe I can change his mind. If not, I'll find a way to take him down. But, if you do this, if you start down this path, there's no turning back. He'll follow his threats through on principle. Do you fully comprehend what you're starting here?'

The doctor nodded his head adamantly. 'We're fighting for our way of life, Chris. We're moving to stop a despot before he can take power.'

'No, you're not. You're about to start the next world war.'

24

Taylor opened his eyes and stared through the darkness, focusing on the bottom of the bunk bed above him. He knew it was empty.

It was reserved for Tim.

He thought about when they had tried smoking behind the rugby club and Tim had vomited. The time they had first gone to a pub and someone told them to try Southern Comfort, their first double date, the holiday to Tenerife.

He turned his head to the side and looked at the small sink only around a metre away. The toilet was in the corner of the room and dripped throughout the night. The light from the dormitory outside, formerly a guidance counsellor's office, pierced the small grill at the bottom of the door. The overpowering scent of onions wafted through the grill from where the resident soldiers had enjoyed hot dogs for supper.

He sighed and turned towards the wall. The memories of the past, few weeks plagued his thoughts. Everything had gone very wrong.

He thought about his Magnum and how many times he had pulled the trigger. Had Destiny really taken everything from him, only to bestow the gift of his ability? Had Destiny then chosen to let him turn his friend into a mass-murdering dictator? Had Destiny played any part in this at all?

He refused to believe that it had not. The only explanation for his pain was that there was some kind of

276

grand scheme. Yet, he was struggling to see the big picture. The names rolled around in his mind: Jane, Herodotus, Nate, Debbie, the boys, San and his family.

The people he cared about were either dead or killers.

He curled up into a ball and the tears saturated his pillow. He knew he could not give up now. If he did, everyone had died for nothing.

Everything would be for nothing.

He had to see it through. He did not know where this journey was taking him, but he had to finish it. If he stopped now, he might never know and he would always regret it.

He stared at the wall as if it were a cinema screen, playing the images over in his mind. It had all been so promising. The truth was that he had felt guilty about his good fortune when so many others were suffering. He had never known how miserable Tim really was. When he got the opportunity to give his best friend the chance at something special, he had not even properly considered it. He jumped at the opportunity to alleviate his own guilt.

He did not understand why. Tim had never even had a real relationship. He certainly did not understand how it felt to lose a wife.

Taylor knew the virus was his reward for having faith. He was not certain what it was he had faith in, but he had no doubt that his misery was part of the scheme. He felt an increasing nagging in the back of his mind.

Tim was intricately involved in the scheme.

He found it odd that his resolve had not yet wavered. The series of events that had started with Jane's sudden death were gathering momentum and, somehow, this voyage was claiming the lives of those he cared about the most.

The only person remaining was Tim.

And he had changed beyond recognition. For all intents and purposes, his best friend was dead, too.

Taylor did not understand why these tragedies had to occur, but he did not want to question it. He needed to see it through. He needed to find the end of the path.

The hollow click had not sounded one hundred and thirteen mornings in a row for no reason.

There *was* a reason. He simply needed to find out what it was. It must be a good one.

Surely, Destiny would not force him to endure so much, and let Tim slaughter so many, unless it was vital to the future of their species.

One hundred and thirteen times that hollow chamber had sounded. That had to count for something.

He tossed and turned as he fought back the images of those he loved, before he eventually gave up on his pursuit for sleep and sat up, swinging his legs over the side of the bed. He stood up and walked to the sink, splashing cold water on his face and eyeing himself in the mirror.

He looked as tired as he felt. He checked his watch. 04.13.

The assault team would enter the New Breed's stronghold in seventeen minutes.

Taylor rooted around under his bed until he located some jeans and a black jumper. He left his private room and crept through the adjacent dormitory, navigating the corridors outside somnambulistically. He reached the kitchen and downed two mugs of coffee, before striding out and making his way to the control room.

It was like walking through an invisible wall of heat. His eyes scoured the rows of computers and screens as everyone in the room turned to examine the arrival. They recognised him, dismissed him and turned back to their workstations.

He puffed out his cheeks and closed the door behind him, regretting his decision to wear a jumper as he surveyed the row of sweaty brows and armpit stains. Then his eyes moved to the transformation this room had undergone.

Taylor could barely believe this had once been a classroom. There was no sign of its previous use. It was now the heartbeat of one of the most important military operations in human history.

The amount of equipment and people crammed into this large room made it seem tiny. Screens covered every inch of all four walls, hanging above the makeshift workbenches, hastily erected from the student's desks. There were laptops, keyboards and tablets strewn all over the room. People talked into their headset, telephone, smartphone or tablet.

Taylor focused on the tantalising aroma of fresh coffee, which almost drowned out the stench of sweat, and nodded to the one person who continued to examine him with a sanguine twinkle in his eye.

'I thought you weren't having anything to do with this?' Norbury asked, a satisfied smirk creasing his lips.

Taylor shrugged his shoulders as he moved towards the filter coffee machine and took the carafe from the plate. 'How are we looking?'

'As expected,' he replied, indicating the largest of the screens displaying a live feed. 'It's not very well fortified. His arrogance has left him exposed. There are virtually no defences at all.'

Taylor poured himself another mug of coffee, before walking over and leaning in to the monitor, studying the grainy image of the townhouse. 'That's not his house, Captain.'

Nolan cast him a stern glare. 'It is now. It used to belong to some banker who donated it to the cause when he joined the ranks.'

Taylor indicated the sentinel on the roof. 'Is that the only guard?'

Norbury was grinning contentedly. 'He did take *some* precautions, at least, otherwise I would be highly suspicious that our protocol had been breached.'

He took a sip from his mug. 'Any idea what he can do?'

The doctor sat back in his seat. 'That's Robin Maybury. He's thirty-eight years old and a former accountant. His ability is that he has natural night vision. Apparently, it's far better than our goggles.'

Taylor chuckled. 'Useful for a sentry. How do you plan on circumventing him?'

Nolan held up her hand as she surveyed the screens. 'Don't worry, Chris. We know what we're doing. Our entire strike force has been hand-picked from the finest military forces on the planet.'

He raised his eyebrows suspiciously. 'Really? I didn't know that.'

Norbury stood up and walked towards the coffee machine. 'We used our secure channels to let our allies know that we planned to attack. Given our depleted resources, we had no option, other than to ask for aid. Once they heard the news, almost every country in the world pledged their support and every one of them sent their best men and women to help. Each of them volunteered for the programme.'

'How many died?' asked Taylor curtly.

'They volunteered,' he replied, pouring his coffee. 'They knew the risks.'

Taylor knew he would not get a straight answer, so let out a cleansing sigh. 'If all these different countries supposedly know about what you're doing, what makes you think Tim doesn't?'

'We have trusted conduits,' a middle-aged man, that Taylor had only seen a handful of times before, snapped. 'We know what we're doing. This isn't our first dance.'

Taylor looked across at him and noted the name Fuller on his chest, along with the red and gold crown on his epaulette. He chortled. 'Fair enough. As long as he can't take their abilities, they know what they're walking into.'

Norbury offered Taylor a refill, which he accepted by extending his mug. 'Why don't you just sit down, relax and enjoy the show? We're about to end this nonsense.'

He sat on a desk at the back of the room. 'You're about to start a war.'

Nolan scoffed loudly. 'This is a pre-emptive strike designed to specifically avoid a prolonged conflict. There won't be a war. Soon, this will all be a distant memory.'

'And if you're wrong?'

'We're not,' Major Fuller growled. 'Please, Mr Taylor, sit back and let us do our jobs.'

'Sorry. I'll just sit here and be quiet, shall I?'

He did not get a response. Norbury returned to his seat and they all focused on the wall of screens. Nolan began to speak quietly into the microphone on her headset.

Norbury sat and listened for a few seconds, before spinning his chair around and peering at Taylor. 'Relax, will you? These people are hardcore professionals. Tim's people are rabble. We'll have our victory in just a few minutes.'

Taylor forced a smile, but could not help lacing it with cynicism. 'Be mindful that *your* arrogance doesn't leave *you* exposed.'

Norbury rolled his eyes and turned back to the screens. Nolan looked across at Fuller, who nodded his approval.

Nolan rolled her chair towards the control panel, hardly able to contain the look of glee on her face. 'All teams, we're a go. I repeat, we're a go. Proceed.'

Taylor watched the screens as dark figures emerged from the bushes in the rear garden. He noticed one screen with the live feed from the garden itself, on which read the moniker Falcon One.

The next monitor showed an image of an alleyway, although he did not know how far it was from the residence. This one was called Kestrel One.

His eyes flickered across the screens with the labels at the bottom of their live images. As well as Falcon One, there were screens dedicated to three other Falcon teams, four Kestrel teams and one for a team known as Eagle. It seemed that only Falcon One, Kestrel One and Eagle were at the scene. All the other seemed to be in the back of different vans, which were, presumably, close by.

He noted that the Eagle screen was from a completely different view, seemingly a rooftop opposite the house.

Nolan's voice had risen an octave. 'Eagle, confirm that you have a clear shot.'

'Affirmative, ma'am.'

'Take it when ready,' she ordered.

A few seconds elapsed before the muffled shot crackled over the speakers. The live video showed Maybury drop from view.

Nolan inhaled sharply. 'Eagle, keep them peeled. Watch that house. If you see anything even slightly unusual, report it immediately. Be prepared to offer covering fire, if required.'

'Roger that, ma'am.'

'Falcon One, Kestrel One, you are clear to advance.'

Taylor sat silently watching the screens. Kestrel emerged from the alleyway and they were two houses away from the front door. They stopped out of view of the guard blocking their path. 'Should we engage?'

'Negative, Kestrel One. Cover the exit.'

Falcon moved towards the rear entrance of the house. They suddenly stopped and zoomed in on another sentry. 'Ma'am,' the soldier whispered, 'we have a static post at entry point four. Request permission to engage.'

For the first time, Nolan seemed flustered. She had clearly not been expecting either sentinel. She looked to Fuller for clearance and it was granted by a single nod of the head. 'Proceed, Falcon One, but maintain silence.'

Another muffled gunshot fizzed through the speakers. This time, however, Taylor could surmise the dart. The guard flopped to the ground and one of the team quickly dragged him into the bushes, securing him with plastic cable ties and a small hood that looked a little like a gimp mask.

'Once he's restrained, give him another dose of sedative and position him near the rear garden gate,' Nolan instructed. 'Extraction Team Delta, you're three minutes away. Move in immediately. Take him to the secure location and keep him sedated. We don't know exactly what these people are capable of.'

'Affirmative, ma'am,' both teams chimed in unison.

A few moments later, Falcon One paused just outside entry point four. 'There's a light in the garage, ma'am. Should we investigate?'

'Affirmative, Falcon One, but proceed with caution. Engage any hostiles in silence. Bulling remains the primary objective.'

Kestrel One suddenly moved slightly. 'Ma'am, the sentry at entry point one has turned his back. We can engage without compromising our position.'

'Permission to engage, Kestrel One, but don't let him make a single sound. Extraction Team Alpha, go to the front of the building now.'

Taylor was shocked how quickly one of the team was able to get to the guard after the dart hit him. They caught him before he even hit the ground. Then he realised that they had not caught him.

The guard was floating. Into the road.

Taylor knew the soldiers had abilities, so did not know why he was surprised to see the unconscious sentry gliding away from the front door. The black van coasted along the road with the side door open and barely slowed down as one of the team lifted the hostage into it using their impressive telekinetic talent. The van was gone without making a sound, the guard safely inside.

Taylor smiled wryly. He did not know if Tim was even able to lift a person with such mastery and precision.

Norbury seemed to sense his feeling and turned around. 'Impressive, huh?'

Taylor shrugged his shoulders. 'Don't get too excited. They're not even inside yet.'

Kestrel One advanced to the door and one of the team managed to silently unlock it from several feet away.

'Evans, is there anyone on the other side of that door?'

Norbury turned to Taylor. 'Corporal Evans has developed X-ray vision, of sorts.'

He smiled. 'Very useful.'

'Negative, ma'am,' the speaker crackled.

'Proceed, Kestrel One.'

Taylor fixed his gaze on the next screen, where Falcon One was sneaking into the garage. It was bright inside and the sound of several darts permeated through the speakers as the cameras adjusted to the light.

He watched the image of several men and women playing cards come in to view. The darts hit all but one, who was up and out of her seat quickly, dashing towards the exit with lightening speed.

The bodies flopped to the ground as she reached the door. Taylor's eyes flitted from screen-to-screen, trying to keep up with the activity. Then there was a sudden, loud crack.

The speakers did relate to the video feeds, but Taylor had not yet worked out what the layout was. By the time he located the source of the sickening sound, the woman by the door was already doubled-over backwards, her spine snapped in half. She fell the ground with a without as much as a whimper.

'Proceed with caution,' Nolan ordered abrasively. 'And try to capture as many subjects as possible.'

Fuller growled. 'Maintain silence, Captain,' he admonished.

Nolan cast him an irritated, sideways glance, before turning back to the wall of screens. 'Yes, sir.'

There was a sudden flurry of activity in the garage and Taylor managed to move his eyes quickly enough to catch sight of a young woman opening the door. Faced with the macabre scene directly in front of her, she opened her mouth to scream. Nothing came out.

The dart landed in her cheek and she was instantly unconscious. Soldiers rushed over to drag her inside and close the door.

Norbury rolled his seat backwards towards Taylor. 'She's a very interesting subject. Her name is Sally Hall and she can silence people. She literally takes away their ability to talk. I'm looking forward to studying her. Her talent is fascinating.'

Taylor ignored him, preferring to concentrate on the screen ahead. Kestrel One entered the house quietly as Nolan told them to secure the ground floor and points of egress until Falcon One were inside. The cameras fanned out in several directions.

'Eagle, do you have a visual on any targets?' the captain demanded.

'Negative, ma'am. It looks very quiet.'

'Maybe too quiet,' Taylor remarked.

Nolan spun around angrily. 'It *is* the middle of night. We expected it to be quiet. That's why we chose this time.'

Taylor shrugged his shoulders. 'Even so, security seems very light.'

The captain turned back to the monitors. 'Noted, thank you, Chris. All teams, proceed with utmost caution. Eagle, keep your eyes peeled. Report anything you see.'

Falcon One arrived in the kitchen to find no activity. They began to spread out and secure the other rooms.

'Kestrel One, you have Falcon One with you. They can secure that floor. Proceed to the first floor.'

Kestrel One moved up the stairs slowly, reaching the landing silently. They moved towards the closed doorways. Carefully opening each one, they found bedrooms on the other side. Darts thumped into the sleeping targets, ensuring they remained in that state.

Falcon One moved into the library, which seemed to be the focal point for the ground floor. It was at the centre of the house and most of the rooms seemed to lead into it.

Kestrel One located the first floor lounge and entered.

Suddenly, the live feeds flashed and became blank. The lights in the house came on simultaneously.

Nolan gasped loudest of the people in the control room. 'What the-?'

Taylor watched the screens. He could certainly see blotches approaching the soldiers. It was difficult to discern what they were, but he assumed they were people.

There were figures slipping into every screen, from every direction.

Nolan need several moments to accept the reality. Suddenly, she frantically screamed into her headset. 'Engage! Kestrel One, Falcon One, fire at will! Eagle, cover them!'

Neither team inside the house waited for her order. They were already in the throes of battle. Gunfire crackled through the speakers over the urgent shouts. Then the screams began.

'Eagle, have you got a visual on the targets?' Nolan hollered. She paused for a few moments. 'Eagle, do you copy?'

The screen with Eagle on it was blank, coinciding with the static from their speaker.

Norbury leapt up. 'What the hell's going on?'

Fuller sighed. 'Isn't it obvious? They're gone. The whole thing was a goddamn ambush.'

25

The black screens flashed and turned white. Taylor watched the panic in the room starting to take control.

Every direction he looked, there were gaping mouths and wide eyes. Nobody knew what to do.

The speakers continued to play the melody of carnage in crisp, clear, digital stereo. The occasional fusillade or muffled dart shot interspersed the shouts, screams, grunts and wails. On one screen, the image returned for a moment. Every pair of eyes in the room turned to watch it.

There was a burst of flames, followed by a splashing of water. Drips landed on the camera lens. Then there was a bright flash and it turned white once more.

Norbury grabbed Nolan by the collar. 'For fuck's sake, get help in there!'

Nolan was frozen, apparently crippled by her own indecision.

Taylor shook his head dejectedly. It seemed that the captain had not even considered the possibility of a battle.

There was a brief lull in the noise from the speakers, but then the sound of breaking bones echoed through the control room, a split second before a blood-chilling scream.

Norbury yanked Nolan to her feet. 'Captain!'

She started blinking and the doctor dropped her back into his seat. Nolan sat up sharply and started to look around, as if waking up from a dream. Her dazed expression landed on Fuller. 'What do we do now, sir?'

He seemed as bemused as everyone else in the room. 'Whatever we can.'

Nolan lurched forwards and started barking into her headset. 'All backup teams, go! Breach the property and engage now! You have multiple hostiles and friendlies, so be careful who you shoot!'

One of the speakers crackled. 'Did you say engage, sir?'

'Yes! Get in there and shoot anyone you don't recognise!'

Nolan sat back and pressed a few buttons on the laptop in front of her. The satellite image of the area appeared where Eagle's live feed had previously been. It showed the dots of each team as they began moving towards the New Breed's headquarters.

Three minutes passed like three hours. The sounds of an agonising and barbaric conflict rattled through the speakers. The screens remained white, except for the odd flash of an image with umbral forms in the background. They lasted seconds, before the feed flashed off again. The noises slowly got quieter and less regular. The battle seemed to be reaching a conclusion when there suddenly seemed to be a huge amount of glass shattering and a host of new voices in the background.

Taylor looked up to see that the dots had converged upon the property. The reinforcements had arrived.

The flurry of gunfire started to crackle through the speakers as the shouts and shrieks began once more.

Norbury turned to Nolan. 'Can they save the mission?'

She shrugged her shoulders. 'Let's hope so.'

The hollering and wailing continued. They could hear one person crying as they begged for mercy. Something or someone silenced them quickly.

The gunshots and crashing continued for a few more minutes. The cracks sounded like broken bones, but it was difficult to be certain of anything when blind. Then, suddenly, everything fell silent.

The screens all flickered brightly and the images all returned. With the addition of the extra teams, there were now dozens of angles to choose from, each of which displayed the carnage.

Every window was broken and every piece of furniture destroyed. Flames flickered in the background, with pillars of smoke billowing out, making their serpentine path towards the exits created by the lack of windows.

There were also dozens of people on the screen. Where their faces were visible, they each carried the blank expression of death. Where the faces were not visible, the view was no less macabre. There were twisted, scorched and butchered bodies on every screen.

Several of the staff in the room vomited into the nearest bins. Some even left the room.

Nolan simply turned white. 'No!' she cried, moving from one screen to the next. 'Fuck! No! Please, God, no! Don't let this fucking happen!'

Taylor's eyes moved from screen-to-screen with a despondent gaze. He could recognise some of the victims, but not all. Some wore uniforms, others did not. After a few moments, his eyes rested on the one monitor that did not have anything grotesque within view. It simply showed the white, artexed ceiling, although there were several burn marks on it.

'Kestrel?' Nolan screeched desperately. 'Falcon? Anyone? Come in!'

The camera pointing at the ceiling suddenly started to move and Tim's face appeared.

Everyone in the room froze, mesmerised as they watched him remove the headset from a decapitated soldier and put it on. 'Hello?'

Nobody dared speak. The whole room seemed to hold their breath in unison.

'Is there anyone there?' Tim asked. His face seemed somehow more chiselled than the day before, his hair somehow tidier, his jaw more muscular.

Nolan looked across at Fuller, who urged her on by raising one eyebrow. 'Hello?' the captain replied, tentatively.

'With whom am I speaking?'

'I'm Captain Nolan.'

'Who else is there?'

'I'm in command of this operation,' she retorted, her voice quivering and squeaking.

'Yes, you sound most authoritative.'

'I can assure you that this is my unit, Mr Bulling.' She sounded no more assured.

'*Was* your unit, Captain. Where's Norbury? Standing next to you?'

'I have no idea what-'

293

'Talk to me, Mike!' he interrupted. 'We need to talk about this.'

Norbury looked across at Nolan with an inquisitive glare, who gulped loudly. His eyes moved to the reticent major, who nodded his head once. He picked up a headset and put it on. 'I'm here.'

'Hi, Doc.'

'What do you want, Tim?'

He grinned into the camera. 'To compliment you, for a start. Your ploy was ingenious and ballsy. I honestly did not expect you to grow an army of super soldiers. It's a good job I have such great sources, or I would have been taken by surprise.'

'How did you know we were coming?'

'I've got a lot of abilities now, Doc. One of which is telepathy. Did you know I can extract whatever information I want from someone's head just by touching them? I ask them a question and the answer pops straight into my head. It's awesome. You shouldn't have sent scouts. Although, I am intrigued about why I couldn't take their abilities. You did something to them, didn't you, Mike? You do love a guinea pig. What did you do to them? Put serum in their blood, or something like that?'

Norbury scowled. 'There are plenty more where they came from, Tim.'

'I'll assume your evasive answer to be affirmation. Is this the best you can do with the tests you got from Chris? You're using the same tactic as me, I see. The problem is, I have an unlimited supply of my blood, whereas you will run out of his. It's a shame he can't provide you with any more.'

'You should hide,' Norbury riposted angrily. 'We're going to come for you.'

Tim scoffed loudly. 'I might not have been able to take their abilities, Mike, but I still managed to kill them all. You can send as many super soldiers as you want. I'll dispose of them with similar ease. But, you know this already, don't you? You had your chance and all you managed to do was piss me off.'

'Only one of them has to get to you, Tim. I have a conveyor belt of these people. I suggest you hide whilst you still can.'

'You'll run out of blood. Chris only gave you a couple of samples before I eliminated him, that much I'm certain of. You'll run out and then you'll be stuck. You won't send 3rd Gen soldiers after me. That's just like sending me fuel. When I figure out what you did to stop me taking the abilities from these soldiers, I'll be able to find a way around it. Send them. Let's find out, shall we?'

'You would be surprised what some of these people can do.'

He laughed sardonically. 'I can move faster than the speed of sound, Mike. I can block electrical transmissions. I can fly. I can cause earthquakes. I can slice a building in half with a single thought. I can pick up cars from a hundred metres away. You can't kill me.'

'Your arrogance is your weakness, Tim.'

His face flashed with anger. 'Your faith in those around you is yours! Now, Mike, it seems that this mission of yours wasn't a complete failure. You've managed to kill or abduct all of my closest friends and followers. I want those you have taken to come back.'

'I don't think so, Tim.'

'What makes you think I don't already know where they are?'

'If you do, why ask me?'

Tim's smile was menacing. 'I'm magnanimous enough to give you the chance to do the right thing.'

'I don't think giving you back your supporters qualifies,' the doctor scoffed acerbically.

'These people came to work for me because I made promises to them,' he returned dryly. 'I have a duty to them and you should not doubt how seriously I take that.'

'We're not going to bring your allies back to you so that they can help you overthrow the government, Tim. We're going to do everything we can to stop you.'

'What makes you think *that* will stop me?' he spat.

'Perhaps solitude will give you cause to reconsider. Divided we fall, remember?'

'I will be marching into Downing Street in a few hours with, or without, my cohorts. They're not integral to my plan.'

'Why do you need them by your side, then?'

'I don't. I *want* them by my side. And, as it happens, I disagree with kidnapping and false imprisonment.'

'But you're okay with murder?'

'Oh, Mike!' he laughed loudly. 'Your delightful naivety would be entertaining, if it wasn't so tragic. This is a new dawn for our species. That should be obvious. The very fact I have to take power by force is proof that I need to.'

'I guess you think Prime Minister Hodgkin should just hand over the reins to the New Breed?'

'Yes, I do, as a matter of fact.'

'Without any kind of vote? We still live in a democracy, Tim.'

'No, we don't. The power of vox populi waned years ago. People are too busy chasing the latest Xbox game or 3D TV to care about the long-term welfare of the world. The people get their opinions from footballers and film stars. They need to learn that freedom is not a right, it's a privilege.

Over the course of human history, millions of people have given their lives so that we can make choices. Yet, when I look at the decisions we make, it fills my heart with melancholy and my blood with anger.'

Norbury scowled. 'The problem is that you sound convincing, intelligent and articulate. You might think that makes your rhetoric more considered. I think it means you should know better.'

'Mike, you're being myopic. I realise there will be short-term unpleasantness, but that will change when people see what it is I want to achieve. We can develop a system where the people can rule, but also understand the responsibility associated with democracy. We all need to work together. Once we have learnt to live our lives for the greater good, I can relinquish power.'

'Pah!' the doctor exclaimed. 'All the dictators in history claimed they would give power back to the people. Win an election if you want to improve things. Don't slaughter hundreds of people and then take power.

Tim, do you even understand that you're a mass murderer?'

'Don't talk to me like this, Mike. You're not as ignorant as the rest of them.'

'You're more Fred West than Ghandi, Tim. You're not George Washington, Mao Zedong or Pancho Villa. This isn't *Braveheart*. You have massacred hundreds of innocent people.'

'An unfortunate, but necessary, sacrifice.'

'Collateral damage?'

'Yes.'

'You killed all these people so *you* could be more powerful. You murdered strangers and close friends with utter impunity. Your motivation wasn't to help the world. It was to satisfy your own lust for power and paranoia. You're Hitler without the greasy hair.'

Tim paused, his jocular expression replaced by a grave, cold expression. 'I'm sorry you feel that way, Mike. I took you to be more of a visionary.'

'If I was, I might have envisioned you killing all my patients, might I not? I might have had some inkling that you were a sociopath. You're right, I am short-sighted. I gave you the virus, didn't I?'

'I'm going to get my people back, Mike. You can't stop me. I suggest you spend your remaining few hours of freedom finding somewhere to hide. I'll be coming for you presently.'

'I'll be spending my last few hours of freedom trying to find a way to stop you, Tim.'

'Then you will have wasted them. So be it.'

They watched him removing the headset in silence. The camera fell to the floor, showing the scorched face of a young woman, before the screen flickered and turned white again.

Fuller was the first to break the awkward silence. 'What the hell was that?'

Norbury turned to him with an innocent expression. 'What?'

'You were practically goading the man! Now he'll probably go after the prisoners!'

'If he can really absorb information telepathically, then he knows where they are. Several of our team knew of the secure location, so it's fair to assume he does, too.'

Taylor interrupted confusedly. 'Secure location? You're not bringing them here?'

Norbury turned to him. 'No. I wanted to, but was over-ruled.' He cast an irritated glance at Fuller.

'You almost dared him to go after them!' the major growled. 'That was cavalier and irresponsible, Mike. You can't be sure he has the abilities he says he does. The man's a liar!'

The doctor was shaking his head adamantly. 'On the contrary, there's no reason to think he doesn't. It's quite clear he has many talents we're not aware of. How else can you explain the fact he knew we were coming?'

'Someone talked.'

'Come on, Major! You know better than that. Besides, why would Bulling lie to us? He doesn't fear us. He was boasting. He knows where they are and he's going to get them, irrespective of what we say to him. We might as well try and use his arrogance to our advantage.'

Fuller paused and took a deep breath. 'There's obviously something going on that I'm not aware of. Explain it, please.'

'We've got more teams,' Nolan interjected sheepishly.

The major turned to face her, shocked. 'Really?'

'Yes,' Norbury answered. 'But we need to get them over there before he arrives. So, we need to get moving.'

'What makes you think we will succeed this time?' he scowled.

Norbury stood up. 'Two things, really. First, they'll have the element of surprise we didn't have here. Second, we'll have Chris with us to help.'

Fuller looked over at Taylor. 'He failed once. Why would this time be different?'

'Because he'll have help this time!' Norbury retorted. 'Now, we need to get moving. If we don't get there first, this will have all been a waste. All those good men and women will have died for nothing. We can discuss this further on the way there.'

The convoy of black Jeeps raced through the town and into countryside. Taylor watched the world passing by, unconcerned that he was the key proponent in an ambush attempt against the man who was once his best friend.

Indeed, he found that he was actually relishing the chance to exact some vengeance for all those who had fallen before him.

He did not know where Tim's house was exactly, but knew it was in London. He had absolutely no idea as to the location of the secure compound housing Tim's colleagues, but was starting to think that it might be in Milton Keynes, as they were speeding down the A5.

If Tim really was able to move at the speed of sound, it should take him about five minutes to get to their destination. At eighty miles per hour, they were ten minutes away. Whatever happened, the chances were that they would arrive after Tim.

On the plus side, that meant that Norbury's team on-site only needed to stall him for five minutes before the cavalry arrived. Taylor did not know who was in the other vehicles. As he peered backwards and forwards, he counted at least ten other Jeeps before the corners of the road obscured his view.

If they were all full, it was a significant force. Even Tim would not be able to combat all of them at once, especially if Taylor could get hold of him.

All he needed was to get hold of Tim and victory was theirs.

He looked over at Norbury and Nolan. He could not imagine more contrasting expressions. Norbury seemed delirious from excitement, whereas Nolan looked like she might vomit at any moment. Fuller sat in the front, screaming into his telephone at someone, but Taylor suspected he was every bit as nervous as Nolan was.

They were responsible for the safety of the nation, for the preservation of democracy and freedom. This convoy was now the last line of defence against a tyrant.

If they failed, nothing could stop the New Breed.

He could appreciate the pressure of such a situation, even if he did not share it. He knew he should have been afraid of failure. He knew the ramifications if they could not stop Tim. Yet, he was not afraid. He did not fear the ensuing conflict. He did not fear the very likely possibility that he could not defeat Tim, even with the help of Norbury's super soldiers.

He realised that he had not been afraid for some time. He remembered being constantly worried about losing the good things in his life. That was no longer true, although he did not know if this was a result of the virus, or just because everything he cared about was gone.

He did know that the emptiness was gone. The ache in his gut had faded and vanished, although he had not noticed it going. It was as if he had simply forgotten it. He had no desire to put a revolver in his mouth and test his place in Destiny's plan.

Yet, his love for Jane had not faded with it. He just felt different. He felt as if he could make sense of the tragedy if he stopped Tim.

Then the true purpose of his life would finally be clear. All along, he had suspected that there must be a reason for his pain, that the events were leading towards his real purpose. How else could he explain the empty chamber in the Magnum day after day?

Now it was clear. He had to stop his best friend. He had to save democracy. He had to preserve freedom.

Otherwise, he had no purpose. Jane had not died to free him from attachment. She had died for no reason at all. Herodotus, San, Nate, their families. Everyone.

If he could stop Tim, their deaths suddenly had a meaning that was worth their sacrifice.

His reverie ended as the Jeep screeched to a halt.

They were on the outskirts of Milton Keynes, at a small carpentry workshop in the centre of an industrial estate. Taylor looked around at the other units. There were people sauntering around, eyeing the convoy suspiciously. Others were busy working and barely offered them a cursory glance.

Their indifference ended when the soldiers began to pile out of the vehicles. They rushed towards the small industrial unit and vanished inside, shouting a series of code words that Taylor did not understand.

Fuller followed their progress on the radio and, three minutes later, the all clear came through. He looked around at the back seat confusedly.

Norbury was already leaping out of the vehicle. Taylor followed him as he darted into the carpentry firm. He was a little surprised to find an actual workshop inside, filled with the scent of fresh sawdust, but Norbury soon veered to a hidden doorway under a tool cabinet.

Down the stairs, Taylor stayed close behind him until they reached a series of plastic panels. On the other side were the New Breed prisoners.

Fuller and Nolan were not far behind. The major seemed elated. 'You see? I told you he didn't know where it was.'

Norbury eyed Taylor suspiciously. 'You know him better than anyone else, Chris. Does Bulling make a habit of making claims that can easily be disproven?'

He narrowed his eyes. 'No. Quite the opposite, in fact. He's changed a lot lately but, he's not here, so...'

Nolan did not appear relieved. 'He might still come yet. We should prepare extra defences.'

Fuller slapped her on the back. 'He's not coming! He's full of shit.'

'He's a murderous scumbag, but he's not an idiot,' Taylor said quietly.

'I agree,' Norbury insisted. 'We should be worrying about why he hasn't turned up.'

The major scowled as he studied the duo. 'You two are never happy. We've successfully weakened the man by taking away his support and all you can do is complain. If he's not already here, it's because he's not coming. If he's not coming, it's because he doesn't know where to go.'

Norbury was wagging his finger. 'I'm sorry, but we're missing something.' As he spoke, his telephone rang.

A few moments later, other telephones started to ring. Within thirty seconds, most of the people in the room had answered their telephones.

Taylor watched and waited as the expressions on their faces uniformly transformed. He concentrated on Norbury, who said nothing, but was the first to finish his call.

'What's going on?' Taylor asked eagerly.

The doctor slowly lowered the telephone, staring straight ahead into nothing as the pallor spread over his complexion. 'The facility.'

'Which facility?'

'The one at the school.'

Suddenly, Taylor understood. It did not matter if Tim knew where the secure location was, or not. 'What about it?' he inquired fearfully.

Norbury seemed like he was about to collapse as tears appeared in the corner of his eyes. 'It's gone.'

26

Taylor stood outside the fence and stared into the school. He had endured the return journey in silence, sitting in the back seat of the Jeep listening to the frenzied conversations of the others.

Their voices full of panic and faces covered with horror, he watched each of them sinking further into dejection with every passing mile.

The moment they arrived, every single member of the convoy leapt from their vehicle and rushed into the compound. Taylor was the only person who did not. He stood in the road and cast his eyes over the scene.

There were towers of smoke billowing from the rear of the building and snaking up into the sky. There was a pile of rubble on the right-hand side, where the wall had collapsed. All the temporary buildings were now kindling, the equipment strewn across the playground and school field.

All but one of the tents was gone. The enormous marquee remained, the roof towering over the school. Taylor could see scorch marks randomly strewn across it.

He walked into the facility slowly, his head pivoting from left to right, twisting up and down. From the front of the school, it was hard to discern the level of carnage. He ambled past the pile of rubble, eyeing the exposed former classroom, now refrigerated storage room. Tim had destroyed every sample Norbury had collected.

Taylor looked across at the playground, where there had previously been several portacabins. He had not been in most of them, nor did he even know exactly how many there had been. It looked like a hurricane had just passed through the compound.

The splinters of wood ranged in size from a couple of centimetres to several metres. He looked around carefully, but could not find a single piece of wood that remained intact. The equipment included computers, weapons, crockery, cutlery, desks and chairs. Such was the mess, he did not even notice the body parts straight away.

He was looking at the remains of a cabinet when he noticed the fingers poking out from underneath. As he focused his attention on them, it quickly became clear that there was no body underneath the small pile of wood. It was not large enough to conceal a corpse. The fingers belonged to a mangled arm.

Taylor turned away and walked further into the compound. Suddenly, they were everywhere: heads, legs, hands, ears, feet and a host of parts he did not even recognise. It was as if he had put on a pair of glasses that suddenly revealed the terrible reality of what he was looking at.

He turned and searched for somewhere to vomit, before it dawned upon him that his stomach's contents were hardly going to make the scene any worse. Doubled over, he emptied everything onto a pile of rubble and wood that had once been the security outpost.

He saw the head far too late. It was the young man who had helped nurse Tim after contracting the virus: Yuri. Taylor turned away again, running towards the marquee, trying not to look at anything.

Everywhere he turned, there was something horrific in view. Tim had literally torn through the entire compound.

He could see Norbury standing outside the marquee with his hands on his hips, glaring at the ground despondently.

Taylor walked over to him and placed a sympathetic hand on his shoulder. 'Hey, Mike.'

'They're all gone.'

Taylor caught a glimpse inside the tent. The gory flashes of body parts, blood and burnt flesh caused him to turn away quickly. 'Did anyone make it?'

Norbury seemed to be in a trance. 'He's scorched their faces and fingertips, Chris.'

He paused as the gruesome concept embedded itself into his mind. He could barely believe that his former friend would do such a thing, yet he knew it to be true. 'Why?'

Norbury shrugged his shoulders, defeated. 'Who knows? The guy's an enigma. Fuller seems to think it's because he doesn't want us to know if anyone's joined him, or not.'

'Maybe, although you'll soon be able to tell if people are missing, won't you?'

He shook his head disconsolately. 'There are too many bits. It will be days before we know who's here and who isn't.'

Taylor looked the doctor up and down. He had not seen abject defeat in him before. 'Are there any survivors?'

He nodded once. 'A few staff. Nurse Hooper made it, at least.'

Taylor allowed himself a sigh. He suspected Hooper meant more to Norbury than the doctor would admit. 'No soldiers left at all?'

'Unless they left with him.'

'So, how many-?'

'Two teams,' he interrupted tersely. 'The one guarding the secure unit and one that arrived here with us.'

'How many were here?'

'Seven.'

Taylor eyed the building behind them. Tim had pulled it apart looking for the soldiers. It seemed they had confronted him, to no avail. 'Two teams aren't going to be able to-'

'No, they're not!' he snapped angrily. 'It's time for you to step up.'

He continued to study the dilapidated building, his earlier determined confidence forgotten. 'Look at what he did here. Seven teams. Seven! What chance do I really have?'

'Better than most.'

'I already tried once. He was too strong.'

Norbury let out a resigned sigh. 'Okay, well I guess I'll just need another sample of your blood before I can get back to work.'

Taylor glowered at him through narrow eyes. '*More super soldiers?* Haven't you learnt anything from this?'

'What are our other options, Chris? You have unimaginable power, yet you mope around and do nothing. At least we're trying something.'

'All you're doing is giving him targets. Why don't you focus on finding a cure instead?'

'Bulling *is* the cure!' the doctor retorted angrily. 'It's in his blood.'

'You had a sample.'

'Not any longer. Besides, that was from before the virus had developed fully in his body. We couldn't use it to synthesise a cure. We did think of that, you know.'

Taylor threw his arms in the air in frustration. 'I just don't think I can do it. If I had help, perhaps. But, alone?'

'You have two teams to assist you. We're already sending them to Downing Street to intercept him, but I think we already know how that will work out.'

'Why send them, then?'

'Because we have to do something, Chris! We can't just let him take power without a struggle. It's our duty to fight tyranny to the bitter end.'

'And when they fail?'

'I use your blood to start again,' he returned dryly. 'I'll probably have to go into hiding, but I'm certain that, sooner or later, one of them will develop an ability that trumps Tim's.'

Taylor rolled his eyes and scowled. 'And what stops them from doing the same thing? You're addicted to this virus, Mike. You might not be obsessed with contracting it, but you're hooked on its power.'

'That's absurd!'

'The only difference between you and Tim is that you collect the abilities in other people.'

'That's not the same as-'

'Where does it end, Mike?'

'When we stop him.'

'Does it? You've done a lot of research into this virus and, other than stumbling onto Tim, I haven't heard much in the way of a cure. I'm starting to think this was all just so you could control it, not eradicate it.'

'We can't cure a virus,' he answered weakly.

'You wanted the effects without the illness.'

Norbury turned away, staring at the ground ashamedly. 'Nobody knew there was a virus in this Pandora's box. It's not as if we opened it ourselves.'

'Yet you don't really want to close it, despite the fact it's tearing the world apart.'

'This could be the greatest gift our species had ever known,' the doctor replied, his tone more assured. 'Would you really spurn it so frivolously?'

'Have you even considered that it's not a gift?' he growled. 'It might be a curse.'

'Bulling told me what you were like before the virus. Do you *really* believe that, after all it's done for you?'

'No, but at least I've considered it. The thought hasn't even crossed your mind, has it?'

Norbury paused. 'Of course it has. Tell me, Chris, if you could give it back, would you?'

'If I could get back everything that has been taken from me, I would give it back in an instant.'

'Honestly?' Norbury seemed sceptical.

'Absolutely. You have no idea what I've been through and what I've lost. This is the only positive to have come from the past, few months. But I think it's very clear that there are few who can be trusted with this power. I like to think I'm one of the few. I believe I was chosen.'

'To do what, though?'

'Well, I was starting to think that it was to stop Tim and preserve democracy and freedom, but I truly don't believe that I can do it alone.'

Norbury stared at him, bemused. 'Maybe that's exactly what you should do.'

'I've tried! You saw what happened!'

The doctor sensed an opportunity he dare not waste. 'Perhaps all this death is for a reason,' he remarked, sweeping his arms out in front of him. 'Maybe you're destined to face him alone.'

Taylor's face lit up. 'Do you really think so?'

Norbury was careful to hide his delight. 'It would make some sense of all this death, wouldn't it?'

He paused for several moments, considering it, and then nodded slowly. 'I suppose it would.'

'I can't pretend to understand all that you've lost. I know you've lost everyone close to you, including Tim. I know you've had to endure more than any one person should ever have to. I think you're right. I think you *were* chosen.'

'Can I tell you something I've never told anyone?'

Norbury nodded and adopted his most serious and trustworthy expression. It was the one he used when asking for more funding. 'Of course.'

'I used to keep a loaded Magnum next to my bed. It had one bullet in the chamber. Every morning, I would wake up and put it in my mouth. Every morning I closed my eyes and spun that chamber. Every morning I pulled the trigger. It never fired the bullet.'

The doctor stared at him, perplexed. Maybe he really had been chosen. 'How many times did you do it?'

'One hundred and thirteen.'

'Holy f-'

'I know.'

Norbury studied the man next to him. It did not matter if he was deluded, or not. All that mattered was that he believed it. The man must have imagined it. Not that he faulted Taylor for that. When a person went through such turmoil, their mind was certain to become strained. 'You *were* chosen, Chris.'

'You think so, too?'

'I do, yes. I think it might be fate that you save us from Tim.'

Taylor suddenly felt buoyant. It was as if Norbury's belief in Destiny's plan had energised him. He could feel the power inside of him, suddenly revitalised and ready to explode. 'What if I fail?'

'Then you will have tried. Nobody can ask for more. Somehow, though, I don't think you will fail. I think this is all part of some grand, cosmic scheme. I believe that you have the universe in your corner. Even Tim can't match that.'

'That's very true.'

'Chris, there isn't anyone else. Either you stop him, or democracy and freedom are resigned to the history books.'

Taylor stood up straight, jutting out his chest. 'You're right, Mike. This is what it's all been leading up to. This is the culmination of my suffering and loss. For me to be totally selfless, I needed to be in a position where I had nothing to lose. Self-sacrifice is easy. If it means you leave people behind, it's not selfless at all. I have no-one to leave behind. I can be selfless. I can follow the path that lay before me.'

Norbury punched the air. He did not believe a word of it, but that did not matter. 'It's up to you to save us. It always was. Now I see how pointless my efforts were. I didn't need super soldiers. I just needed to realise that *you* were the key.'

Taylor continued to puff out his chest and take deep, cleansing breaths. His fear was gone. He was ready to save the world. 'I needed to realise it too, Mike.'

Norbury heard Hooper calling his name and turned away to face her. He allowed a Machiavellian smirk to crease his lips. Had he known Taylor was so easy to manipulate, he would have done it sooner.

The nurse arrived next to them with a radio and cast a curious glance at Taylor, as he stood straight and tall, his chest puffed up and his eyes staring at the horizon.

He thanked her as he took the radio and put it to his mouth. 'Norbury here.'

'Doctor? It's Nolan.'

'What's the problem, Captain?'

314

'Our teams intercepted Bulling on his way through Central London.'

'And?'

'What we expected, I'm afraid.'

'I understand. We have another option now, though.' He looked up at Taylor, who nodded once, a steely determination in his expression. 'How quickly can you get Chris to Downing Street?'

27

Tim closed his eyes and took a deep breath. London smelt cleaner to him than ever before, although he did not know why. Perhaps this was the scent of change. It wasn't the current state of the city, he thought, as he looked around at the damaged store fronts, the result of riots caused by having the virus in the area.

He listened to the sounds of Whitehall. It seemed quiet without the traffic, although the news crews and spectators following him caused enough of a cacophony to rival the largest trucks.

The zephyr swept past, kissing his skin gently. He could feel the warm sunshine on his face and it made him smile. Today was going to be a good day.

He opened his eyes and looked towards the clear, azure sky. His eyes scanned the buildings. Although they were tall, the road was wide, so the street did not have the same, enclosed feel found in most major cities around the world. The bright sunshine made the clean buildings seem even whiter.

It struck him that this was one of the oldest parts of the city, yet it seemed immaculate every time he was here. He believed that every part of the country should be maintained to this standard. The fact this was the tourism epicentre of the country should not be a good reason for allowing other areas to fall into disrepair. That was going to be one of his first changes. A clean country would help it become a happy and productive country.

His eyes followed the delicate, neo-classical lines of The Banqueting House across to the imposing, Palladian features of the Horse Guard's Palace. They moved further down the street to the cordons and rows of armed police lining up nervously on either side of the street, directly outside both the Ministry of Defence and Cabinet Office.

He walked away slowly, his gaze locking onto his target: the tall, black gates that indicated the entrance to Downing Street. He saw the parked tanks and A.P.C.'s, surrounded by armed soldiers, blocking his path. He chuckled to himself.

What did they really think they could achieve?

He craned his neck and looked behind him at the fleet of ambulances around Trafalgar Square. There was little they could do to help the assault team that had appeared from Charing Cross station as he walked casually past.

He had probably dispatched them with a bit more fervour than was absolutely necessary. But they had made him angry. He did not stop to count the aggressors, but it was more than ten, he guessed.

And they had managed to hurt him.

He did not know which of them had been able cut him, or which had frozen his arms. He wished he was able to absorb the ability to create phantoms. It had taken him several minutes to figure out which images were soldiers and which were ghosts.

Regardless, he had left them in a series of twisted heaps. Medical science was not going to be able to aid them now.

He turned back towards his destination and continued walking slowly. The crowds covered the pavements and roads, but they were subdued, as if cautiously awaiting his appearance. He studied the faces.

There was every creed and colour. There were men, woman and children of every age. The entire spectrum of the population was crammed into a small area of London. He could not see any signs or banners of protest. All he could see was apprehension. No, that was not accurate. He could see fear.

It made him feel warm inside.

As he approached the throngs, they began to part. People stared at him nervously. It was as if they were afraid that he might snap their necks at any time.

Why would he want to hurt them? They would soon be his subjects.

He could understand their confusion, but he would prove that he only wanted the best for them. Their dread only confirmed their ignorance.

He continued moving at a leisurely pace through the flocks until he reached the armed police at the cordon. He paused and examined them, but they continued to stare straight ahead. He was not sure what he expected, but he was not surprised when they failed to engage. They were not going to confront him because they knew they could not stop him.

Striding on, he passed through the barriers and grinned when the police closed ranks behind him and started to follow closely behind. As he continued, so the police became soldiers, who eyed him nervously, with twitchy fingers hovering over their triggers. Perhaps these were to be the last line of resistance.

He kept walking and his view of the black gates became clear. The soldiers were positioned all around with a startling array of weaponry. Several tanks had their turrets and main guns aimed directly at the gate. If there was to be conflict, this was where it would take place.

He sauntered forwards, his eyes locked on the closed gates. An old man suddenly appeared from behind the wall of soldiers, blocking his path.

Tim stopped and looked around. The police were concentrating on crowd control, ensuring the civilians did not cross the barriers. The soldiers cast him nervous glances. Even the tank operators sat atop the turrets. He was pretty sure they could not fire the gun from up there.

Did this old man represent all the fight Britain had left to offer? If that was the case, the country deserved to be conquered.

He approached the elderly gentleman as the soldiers moved in around him, leaving him completely surrounded. He studied the last obstacle between him and power.

He was small and had tufts of silver hair over either ear. His wizened face sagged to the point where it almost covered his small, penetrative, hazel eyes. He was in full dress uniform and Tim noted that he was not wearing anything to denote his rank.

The old man stood erect and puffed out his chest, defiant despite the patent fear in his beady eyes. 'Mr Bulling, can I offer you this opportunity to turn around and walk away?'

He sneered loudly, turning his head from side-to-side and analysing the danger. There was no threat to him here. He glowered at the old man. 'Who are you?'

'That's not important,' he declared valiantly. 'What *is* important is the fact that I'm not going to allow you through that gate.' He threw his thumb over his shoulder in the direction of Downing Street.

'Do you think I'm here to ask for permission?'

'I highly recommend that you leave, Mr Bulling. I'm authorised to use any and all means at my disposal.'

'And?' he replied glibly, with a shrug of his shoulders. 'Is that supposed to concern me?'

'It should.'

Tim raised his finger and wagged it once. The old man flew into the gate and landed in a heap on the ground.

He looked around at the soldiers, all of whom stared at him. He discovered a cocktail of expressions: anger, fear, amazement, confusion. He held his arms out at his sides and spun around slowly, lifting himself to levitate a few inches above the ground. 'Come on!' he bellowed. 'What are you waiting for?'

There was a moment of total silence, as the spectators, police and soldiers all seemed to hold their breath. The old man shattered it as he let out a pained roar. 'All units engage!'

Several hundred weapons trained on him in an instant. The muzzles flashed as the loud crack of combined gunshots echoed down the street. The crowds of spectators winced and covered their ears several seconds too late.

Tim raised his hand as a malevolent smirk spread across his face. A ring of bullets quickly formed around him like a tiny, metallic asteroid belt. As the fusillade continued, so the ring became denser until it appeared solid, hovering in mid-air only a foot from him.

His grin widened as the metal fog continued to increase in size and density. Then, suddenly, a large glimmer flashed through the cloud.

Tim saw it late. His eyes widened and the smile vanished, as the tip of the dagger reached his hand. He managed to stop it as the point touched his finger. The spot of red it caused seemed to make time stand still.

Guns stopped firing, jaws dropped and people held their breath. Every pair of eyes moved to the tiny droplet of blood, as it formed and began to drip. The eyes followed it, as it seemed to fall in slow motion. The stunned silence in Whitehall made the tiny splash seem audible. The sound that echoed around the entire world.

Tim Bulling was bleeding. He was mortal, after all.

Like the cameras and eyes all around him, Tim watched with incredulity as the tiny speck of scarlet splattered on the ground, covering an area of little more than two centimetres. He looked up sharply, the anger igniting inside of him.

His eyes moved from left to right, staring at the throngs of armed soldiers who continued to aim their weapons at him. Just as they motioned to squeeze their triggers, Tim flicked his wrist.

The fog of bullets dispersed, zooming out in every direction. The shrieks and wails started piercing the air, the silence of several moments before instantly forgotten.

The soldiers began to shake and jerk as their ammunition returned to them. The police caught the bullets that did not strike the troopers. At the very back were the public. Hundreds of bullets sped into them.

Blood accompanied the pained and panicked commotion as the cloud vanished outwards. The people that could still run did so. They bolted away screaming, fighting and barging their way past the injured and less mobile. The public blocked the path of the police, who tried to escape with them, as the masses demolished the cordons and barricades in their frenzied desperation to put as much distance as possible between themselves and Tim.

The only people who did not try to escape were the soldiers. They rushed to tend to their injured colleagues. Hundreds of people were on the floor wailing in agony. Just as many had suffered fatal wounds. Blood and gore filled Whitehall.

Tim watched the scene with indifference. He saw the ambulance crews and first responders rushing to the aid of his victims. For a moment, he wondered if his temerity was leading him astray. Then he saw more soldiers moving into position and his resolve returned.

Did they never learn?

As one half of the troopers dragged their fallen comrades away from the area, another group of warriors moved in and opened fire.

He did not even raise his hand this time. He merely stopped the bullets, allowing the cloud to return and grow, as he looked around at the carnage he had created with one flick of his wrist.

This was not how he wanted his reign to begin.

He turned towards the gate and the bullets started falling to the ground all around him. He eyed the row of warriors standing in his way, firing their weapons at him. He waved his hand once.

They all flew away in a variety of directions, crashing into one another, the wall or the ground. The bullets continued to fly at him from behind, but they still stopped and fell to the ground a foot from their target.

Tim started to approach the gate slowly. His eyes scanned the huge, fortified, black gate for a few moments as the bullets piled up behind him. His eyes eventually came to rest on the old man still lying on the floor, directly in front of the entrance to Downing Street.

Tim smiled menacingly. 'That's a pretty big gate. I'm going to need to concentrate if I want to open it. I can't do that and protect myself at the same time.'

The old man glowered at him, but said nothing.

'Tell your people to stop firing or I'll force them to.'

He remained defiantly reticent.

'Fine,' he sighed, rolling his eyes and shrugging his shoulders. 'I tried.' He clicked his fingers and a small flame appeared on the tip of his thumb. 'Last chance.'

The old man shook his head once. 'We will never submit to tyrants.'

'Very well,' he replied dryly, turning back to face the fusillade. 'Don't say you weren't warned.' He raised his thumb to his mouth and held it there for a few moments, deliberating over his next move. He had no choice. They had to learn. He pursed his lips and blew.

A huge cloud of flame poured out. Tim moved his thumb from one side of his mouth to the other, toasting everything in front of him.

The gunfire soon stopped, replaced by strident and stomach-churning screams. The smell of cordite quickly faded as the scent of scorched flesh filled his nostrils.

Soldiers were diving in every direction to evade the feather-shaped blaze, but many of them were too slow.

Tim continued to blow for almost half a minute, completing the entire panorama before him twice. Once satisfied that the gunfire had stopped, he smiled and turned back around.

His face suddenly changed as he held both arms out in front of him. He was focused.

The gate started to rattle noisily. The tremors shook the buildings on either side. The clangs and clunks resonated down the streets over the wails of the fallen and the fading screams of the panicked as they got further away.

The gate shook. He gritted his teeth. The gate started to bang violently as it lurched and jumped. Sweat formed on his brow.

The old man got to his feet, his mouth gaping.

Tim brought the gate up with a strident, metallic squeal. The hinges buckled and snapped. The metal twisted and tore, scraping through the Portland stone on either side, showering the area with sparks.

He lifted the gate in the air, ripping it away from the mounts. Drenched in sweat, he strained every sinew as he drew the gate away from Downing Street. He was so focused he did not even notice the old man lunging at him until he felt the sharp, stabbing pain.

He cried out as he looked down at his abdomen. A depressed syringe was sticking out. Tim's eyes met the old man as he backed away so hurriedly he stumbled and fell onto his behind.

Tim was suddenly aware of how vulnerable he was. He eyed the old man as he scowled. 'You shouldn't have done that. What is it?'

He shuffled backwards in a vain attempt at escape, but said nothing, despite the obvious fear in his eyes.

Tim shook his head ruefully and looked up at the enormous, black gate hovering uneasily in the air. Deciding that he dare not waste more time trying to get an answer, he suddenly swung the gate around and dropped it on his quarry.

The huge, twisted, metal spikes crunched into the ground, skewering the old man where he cowered. A spray of red spurted up in the air as the gate dug a huge series of holes in the pavement before clattering to the ground. The screeching of metal on concrete tore through Whitehall and the acrid stench of burnt steel filled the air.

Tim offered the squashed and butchered corpse of the old man a sneer as a bullet zipped past his ear. Spinning around to face his latest adversaries, he felt a pain in his leg and realised there was a bullet hole in it. He looked up, but could not see a single soldier firing at him. Another bullet sped towards him, but he raised his hand to stop it. The lonely bullet paused and hovered directly in front of his eyes. It was soon joined by another. Then another.

Tim looked down at his body as he felt several jolts of pain. He had been shot six times, each time from behind. They must have happened whilst he was tearing the gate from its hinges.

He could feel his body pushing the projectiles out and watched as they fell by his feet with a series of tiny tinkles. He looked down, eyeing them past the syringe that remained in his abdomen. Reaching down, he yanked it out of his flesh and lifted the tip to his nose, sniffing it several times. He had several olfactory-related talents; he could identify every molecular ingredient of any item with a prolonged sniff and he could smell blood from miles away; but none of them helped. The scent was redolent of a thousand others, but mostly stank of his blood. He shrugged his shoulders and tossed it to the ground.

Peering back out towards Whitehall, he now counted seven bullets. He examined them. They were different to those he had seen in such numbers only minutes prior. They were longer and sharper.

There were snipers shooting at him.

He furrowed his brow and focused his eyes on the rooftops of the buildings opposite, zooming in on anything that seemed slightly out of place. He scanned the area for a minute before it bored him.

He turned on his heel and strode into Downing Street, leaving the bullets hovering where they stopped.

The grin covered his face. He had done it. He was in Downing Street. And even he was surprised how tame the resistance had been.

He had expected them to throw everything they had at him. He had expected their full arsenal. Not a few unused tanks and a couple of platoons.

He was almost ashamed to be British. The country deserved to be conquered.

As he paced joyously past the mangled remains of the huge, steel gate, he looked towards Number Ten and realised that Britain was not quite as tame as he had thought.

28

Tim had barely crossed the threshold of Downing Street when the fleet of death opened fire. He saw tanks and drop-side trucks with a variety of guns and rocket launchers mounted on the back.

Now he understood why the tanks out in Whitehall had not fired upon him before now. They were waiting.

It was a trap.

The shells, rockets and bullets raced towards him and he raised both hands to stop them.

But they did not halt.

There were too many of them.

Quickly changing his tactic, he twisted both hands and the ordnance started to explode in mid-air.

His eyes widened as he realised that he could not destroy them all before they reached him. He dug his feet into the ground, bent his knees and pushed with all his strength.

The shower of death bounced back away from him, falling back onto the fleet that had fired them. The series of explosions shook all of London.

Flames roared as the sky turned black with the rain of carnage. Huge chunks of metal, brick, shards of glass, shrapnel, blood and bone filled the sky, falling back to Earth with a series of splodges, slops, clatters and clunks. It was as if God himself had taken death, war and slaughter, put them all in a blender together for several minutes and then tipped the contents onto Downing Street.

Tim winced slightly at the macabre spectacle as it covered the area, spreading across every square inch of the most powerful street in Britain. He eyed the parts of tank and truck, lodged in the neighbouring buildings. Those that had remained intact bounced away, crashing through the brick and glass of some of the most famous and celebrated structures in British history. St James' Palace, Westminster Abbey and Nelson's Column took direct hits, others were just damaged.

A tank had landed in the front of Number Eleven. The entire facade of the house had crumbled.

He sighed. This was not what he wanted.

They would rebuild it all.

It would be one of his first acts as the ruler of this country to return this famous street to its former glory.

Because now it looked like a war zone. This was what he imagined most of the Middle East looked like after the Allied Forces had torn through it, trying to force their own beliefs on the indigenous population.

That would be his second act.

To stop Britain getting involved in wars that did not concern them.

He walked slowly towards the remnants of the fleet.

His eyes scoured the wreckage for the source of the pained wails. He took a moment to watch a serpentine wisp of smoke, twisting a trail towards the sky as if trying to escape from him. Even from fifty metres away, he could study the remains of Britain's last line of defence against him.

He focused his eyes and zoomed in.

He counted one survivor. A young woman lay on the ground next to the dismembered remains of a tank. Her abdomen was bright red and he could see her entrails spilling out from it, stretching out several feet on the ground.

Tim closed his eyes and let out a sombre sigh as he shook his head. She was not going to survive. Even he could not remedy such severely horrific injuries. He opened his eyes and focused on a small spike of metal lying near to the young woman. Without hesitation, he lifted it and speared it through her head.

She fell silent and flopped to the ground.

She was in peace.

For a moment, he paused and enjoyed the relative silence. The symphony of destruction ended as the chunks and fragments of the fleet settled in their final resting places. The only sound was the crackle of the flames. The creaks and moans of the strained and mangled metal seemed to pause at his command, as if sensing his desire for tranquillity amongst the violence.

The harmony came to an abrupt halt when he heard the distant roar of engines. He needed a second to locate it and turned his eyes towards the sky.

They were jet engines.

He could not see them until he focused. Aiming his vision between the rooftops, he caught a glimpse of some triangular specks on the horizon. They were rapidly becoming larger and louder.

The roar started to shake the buildings as the jets boomed towards him. They were already at attack speed, which was far too quick for him to target his powers at such a distance.

As they reached his range, he realised it was too late. There were dozens of long tubes already racing towards him.

Rockets.

At least fifty of them.

The jets zoomed past overhead as he faced the swarm of rockets meandering between the buildings. They were close enough.

Raising his hands, he focused all his energy. They started to explode into the buildings as they flew past, shattering windows, crumbling brick and twisting metal.

Tim felt his heart skip a beat as he realised that he could not get them all in time. Again, he dug his feet into the ground, bent his knees and pushed with all his strength.

Nothing happened.

They should have bounced away from him. They should have rebounded into nearby buildings, crashed into the ground or spiralled away harmlessly into the river.

But they kept coming.

He looked at his hands in bewilderment, then at his abdomen in dismay.

The syringe.

Gritting his teeth, he tried again. More rockets exploded in mid-air, covering London in showers of metal, glass and stone.

But many kept coming, surging towards him at an unfathomable pace. He could do nothing to stop them.

The flock of missiles flew into Downing Street, reaching their target with devastating effect. Tim could only watch them fly into the nearby ground, only a few feet away.

The explosion shook the foundations of every building for miles around. The fireball roared in every direction, toasting the streets of Whitehall and leaving the famous limestone scorched and black.

The impact of the first blasts tossed him into the air. As he fell back to ground, the ensuing explosions blew him back up again. He bounced from one eruption of flame to another, blown around like a feather on a strong breeze.

The rockets continued to explode, throwing Tim from one surge of energy to the next for several minutes. Anyone walking in on the scene would think he was part of a game being played by invisible giants. The only sign this was not a game was the gore.

He screamed in pain. He had forgotten how pain felt. Every fresh blast caused him renewed agony. As the final rocket hit, he was several metres in the air. He seemed to float for a second and it gave him time to look over his injuries.

Half of his torso was missing. He had no limbs. That was all he had time to notice before he plummeted back to Earth.

He fell face-first, hurtling towards the wreckage of the fleet. He crashed into the crumpled metal.

Downing Street suddenly fell eerily silent. The flames were the only sound, roaring above the carnage like the victors that had won the spoils.

A minute passed. Then two, then three. Seven minutes and forty-seven seconds went by before the door to Number Ten started to slowly open. The creaks of the hinges echoed down the street.

A team of fifteen SAS warriors, in full tactical gear, filed out cautiously. They approached carefully, almost apprehensively, meandering through the carnage. They slowly covered the ground between the doorway and the location where they had seen Tim land.

Their weapons were primed as they moved, assessing every inch of the wreckage as they passed. Every soldier looked directly down the sights of the trusty service weapon in their grip. There were ten C8 Carbine assault rifles moving through the scrap metal, as five tripod-mounted M107 .50 calibre weapons set up behind them, aimed squarely at the point their target was last seen.

The ten mobile units continued to approach tentatively, one centimetre at a time. They were twenty metres away when a loud metallic scrape caused them to freeze.

The wreckage near where Tim fell had moved. Only slightly, but it had definitely moved. The SAS team paused and watched for a few moments. Nothing.

The piles of twisted, charred metal were so unstable they would inevitably move. They continued, every bit as tremulous as before.

Suddenly, the remains of the vehicles flew out in every direction. Wheels jumped into the sky, doors spun through the air like Frisbees and a chassis rolled past, crashing into an inferno that had once been a tank.

Tim Bulling stood in the clearing.

The warriors let out a collective gasp as they froze instantly. They needed several moments to process the possibility that this man had survived a direct hit from several dozen Brimstone missiles.

Then they opened fire at the target. All of him. Complete with torso and limbs.

He did not react immediately. It was ten seconds before he realised that he was already under attack. By the time he raised his hands, the C8's had dispatched almost a thousand bullets. The M107's had fired twice each.

The C8 bullets hit him with small sprays of blood, making his body jerk. In truth, none of the warriors expected the smaller bullets to do much. All they needed to do was distract him until the Fifty-Cals tore him apart.

Three M107 rounds hit him. The first hit his chest, causing an explosion of blood as it tore straight through him. The second hit his thigh and took his leg back off. The third hit his shoulder and ripped through it, leaving no shoulder joint and an arm that dangled from a few wiry muscles.

That would normally have been enough to level a small building. But Tim continued to stand there, a vacant expression covering his face. He seemed dazed, confused. They had to press their advantage.

The team continued to fire, the bullets tearing their target apart. He raised his intact arm and held his hand out, but the bullets tore through it, piercing his hand and taking his fingers off.

Then the fourth M107 round hit him. It struck him in the abdomen and managed to knock him from his foot.

He flew backwards and landed on the ground several metres away. They grew back quickly, the bone first, a spindle speeding out from the remaining fragment, muscle forming around it within a second and the skin growing last, like pink ice forming over fleshy water.

The soldiers could only watch in dismay as he jumped up and sped away. They concentrated their gunfire on him, but he was too fast to focus on. He moved so quickly all they could see was a blur.

He circled.

When he stopped, he arrived at their rear, next to the five warriors lying on the ground behind an M107 each. He tore them apart with his bare hands, as his fingernails suddenly became claws.

He had healed completely.

The group of ten spun quickly, training their smaller weapons, but he zoomed away before they could fire. The fusillade followed him as he circled back around the clearing.

He stopped in front of them, at the first soldier in the queue. Tim snatched the weapon from his grip and cracked the butt on his head. Before the remaining nine could open fire, he was already a blur, speeding away behind a pile of wreckage.

Suddenly, the blur passed straight through them, stopping in the middle to snap two necks. This time, they managed to engage before he vanished again, whizzing around to the rear of the troupe. He stopped and his claws decapitated two soldiers. Again, he suffered several precise, close-range gunshots before he turned back into a blur.

The last five huddled together and he appeared directly in the middle. He pushed one away as he sliced and diced the others in a flash. The last soldier emptied his entire ammunition clip into Tim from a distance of less than two metres.

All he could do was watch in horror as Tim's body pushed the bullets out and healed within seconds. His last sight was Tim's claws slicing through his carotid artery.

Tim looked himself up and down. His clothes had been torn to shreds, but his body was completely intact. He smiled. He did not even have a single scratch.

The stolen C8 Carbine dangled by his side as he began to make his way towards Number Ten. He could hear the helicopter approaching, although he could not yet see it.

He disregarded the threat. If missiles could not kill him, he was not in jeopardy.

Tim was about to stride through the remains of the doorway to Number Ten when a stifled moan caught his attention from nearby. He focused his vision to descry a warrior struggling to hide under a panel from a tank.

One of the SAS soldiers had survived, albeit with a nasty incision across the chest.

Tim grinned as he walked towards the survivor and stood over them, glaring down. They tried to ignore him, shuffling slowly towards cover on their stomach, like a worm. He reached down and grabbed them, pulling the mask off in the process.

Tim was a little shocked to find a young woman under the mask, but managed to force out a malevolent sneer despite the surprise.

She croaked and coughed up some blood, but continued her attempt to scramble away.

He studied her injuries. His claws had not just sliced her chest open, but her stomach too. He could see a kidney and, judging by the smell, had pierced her bladder. He looked up at her face, indifferent to her plight. 'What was in the syringe?'

'I don't know. Something to block the virus.'

He looked into her eyes and saw the light fading. She would be dead soon, although she did not seem to know that. She held on to life stubbornly, squirming away from him.

'It didn't work,' he said apathetically. 'You limited some abilities, but not others. You must have known you couldn't block them all, so why bother?'

He could hear the helicopter above him and cast it a quick glance. He could not discern a threat, so he turned back to the woman and leaned in so that he could hear her response over the noise.

She was smiling, her teeth covered in red. 'We knew it wouldn't stop you,' she said faintly. 'But it weakened you.'

'And yet I still won. I destroyed your entire army.'

She laughed, the frothy blood running down either cheek. 'We weren't trying to beat you. We know *we* can't stop you.'

Tim shook his head. He could not have heard that correctly. 'What did you just say? It sounded like you're claiming that you threw all this at me knowing very well I would win.'

Her smile got larger. 'We were just a test. A distraction. We had to keep you busy until our secret weapon arrived.'

Tim's eyes widened and he found himself screaming involuntarily. 'What secret weapon?'

She lifted her arm weakly and struggled to stick out her forefinger in the direction of the helicopter.

Tim turned just in time to see a dark figure leap from it and land in the clearing. He tried to focus, but the wreckage obscured his line of sight.

He turned back to the woman, confounded. '*Another* super soldier? Don't you people ever learn? I'm 2nd Gen and loaded with 3rd Gen abilities. There isn't anything that can stop me now, not even other 2nd Gen hosts.'

She sneered. 'You sure about that?'

Tim gave her a last look of disgust as he stood up and walked towards the clearing. They obviously had one last line of defence. They must have been hiding another super soldier, so maybe this one might actually test him.

He moved slowly around the piles of wreckage and his last obstacle came into view.

He froze. It can't be.

His jaw dropped as he blinked several times. He briefly wondered if this was some kind of trick. Was it a phantom? A hologram? A hallucination? He dispelled each notion as it popped into his mind, leaving only the impossible truth.

It can't be!

Taylor was standing in the clearing.

338

He stared at the figure, a potent cocktail of disbelief and consternation coursing through his veins. 'Chris?'

'Hey, buddy.'

'I killed you!' he roared.

'I guess not,' he replied, shrugging his shoulders.

'It can't be you! I watched you die!'

Taylor smirked confidently, enjoying the astonishment in his former best friend. 'I guess all those abilities didn't turn you into a doctor, huh?'

'Did you come back to life, or something?'

He ignored the question. 'You don't seem too pleased to see me, old friend.'

Tim screwed up his face as he tried to comprehend the situation. 'What are you doing here, Chris?'

'I would have thought that was obvious.'

He tried to understand, but it was unfathomable. He had watched Taylor die with his own eyes. How was this possible? And why would he be standing here? He fought to compose himself. Now was not the time to panic. Not when he was on the cusp of victory. 'Are you here so I can correct my mistake?'

'No, Tim,' he retorted in a calm, even tone. 'I'm here to destroy you.'

29

Tim tilted his head slightly as he studied his friend for a moment. He decided not to waste his energy with words. He yanked the C8 Carbine up and opened fire.

He continued squeezing the trigger until the hollow chamber sounded. The muzzle flashed and the bullets cracked through the air as they sped towards their target.

He could only watch as each one ricocheted off the target until the ammunition clip was entirely spent.

Taylor placed his hands on his hips and smirked, watching the bullets bounce off his body. He barely even felt them.

Tim did not stop pulling the trigger for several seconds. The loud clacking bounced around Downing Street until he let go and dropped the weapon. He continued to examine his foe, narrowing his eyes and furrowing his brow.

Taylor stood in the same spot defiantly.

Suddenly, Tim was a blur, covering the distance between them in a flash. He swung upwards with his fist, throwing all his weight into a bone-crunching uppercut, directly under Taylor's jaw.

However, the broken bones were his. Tim yelped and leapt backwards, eyeing his disfigured knuckles suspiciously as they cracked back into place and healed.

It was his turn to smirk and Taylor watched his hand convalesce in moments with a look of consternation on his face.

Tim set off again, speeding around to Taylor's left, stooping down to pick up another C8. This time, he emptied the clip into his friend's face from only ten or twelve centimetres.

The bullets bounced away, many of them rebounding into Tim, whose body pushed them onto the ground as it healed. He zoomed away again, the blur speeding around a pile of wreckage and returning to the rear of his foe.

Tim jabbed his newly acquired dagger into Taylor's kidney.

Taylor laughed loudly as the blade snapped in half.

Tim paused for a moment, half in shock, half considering how best to defeat his invulnerable enemy.

That was what Taylor was waiting for. He pivoted swiftly and extended his elbow.

The connection was slight. The blow glanced off Tim's shoulder.

He flew into the flaming shell of a tank five metres away. Three seconds later, he leapt out of the wreckage, the cuts all over his face already disappearing.

Tim held his hands out on front of him and flicked his wrists. Nothing happened. He glared at them, perplexed, before looking up at his adversary. 'What have you done to me?'

'Levelled the playing field,' Taylor chirped, taking slow, meaningful steps towards his enemy. 'Many people sacrificed themselves to inject you with an inhibitor. It's blocking certain neurotransmitters in your brain.'

'But I still have some abilities.'

He smiled broadly. 'The virus will fight the drugs. Your talents will turn on and off, but you won't know which will work or when.'

Tim started clicking his fingers repeatedly, like a desperate smoker wrestling with an obstinate lighter. Finally, a flame appeared. He aimed it at his foe, but the flame extinguished itself and the small blaze dropped to the ground short of the intended target.

Taylor took another step forwards as Tim extended his arm and pointed with his forefinger. A jet of water gushed from it, slamming into Taylor's chest.

Shocked by the impact, Taylor took several steps backwards, fighting to stay on his feet, but the water soon dried up. Tim glared at his finger.

He was confused. He was worried.

He lowered his hands, his palms facing the ground, and started to tense his muscles. Taylor approached again, watching his former friend curiously. The ground started to shake.

Taylor looked at his feet and saw a couple of small cracks appear, but the tremors soon stopped. He looked up with a smile before breaking out into a run.

Tim tried to force the ground to open, but nothing happened. Just as his adversary reached him, he darted away, trying to become the untouchable blur. He took several steps at his normal pace. Confounded, he looked up. It was already too late to escape.

Taylor was upon him, swinging his fist. It landed in Tim's chest with a thud.

He flew backwards, vanishing into a pile of metal with a wail of agony.

Taylor stood and watched as his foe hauled himself out of the remains of the drop-side truck. Tim dragged his feet laboriously and wheezed loudly.

Taylor strode towards him and realised the laboured breathing was a result of his blow.

He had not healed.

This was the chance he had been waiting for. If Tim could not heal, he could die.

Darting over, he connected with another punch. This time, he aimed for Tim's face. The crunch of bones echoed throughout Downing Street.

The strike hurled Tim to the ground. He screamed in pain as he landed on his backside and slid for several metres. Taylor ran after him, eyeing the dislocated jaw and depressed cheekbone.

He reached Tim swiftly and watched his former friend cower. Taylor reached down and picked him up with one hand, lifting him into the air.

Suddenly, pangs of doubt started to plague his mind. He could snap his neck and end it in a moment, but all he could see was his best friend, beaten and in pain.

He knew he should kill him.

He knew it was the right thing to do.

Tim had gone too far. He had murdered hundreds of people. He would have taken over the country if Taylor had not intervened.

He had to be stopped.

There was no telling if Tim would stop of his own volition. He was not the man of a few months ago.

But he looked so pathetic. He wheezed loudly, his face battered and his soul broken.

Tim was beaten.

Taylor shook his head violently, trying to dispel his thoughts of kindness and charity. This was not the time for mercy.

This was the time to fulfil his promise, to realise his destiny.

He was the only person in the entire world who could stop the madness. He had succeeded. Now he needed to end it.

He had to find his mean streak. It was in the best interests of the entire planet.

Tim had many chances to stop. He took none of them.

He needed to die. It was the only way to ensure the safety of the whole world.

It was the only way to preserve democracy.

Taylor eyed his best friend and wrestled with the doubt inside him. He knew what he should do. Until now, though, he had never realised how difficult it would be. He had smashed Tim's face to pieces. The facial bones were shattered and cracked. His lungs were clearly starting to fail.

He was almost dead already. All Taylor had to do was squeeze. Yet he seemed incapable of closing his fingers around his best friend's throat.

Then he felt the warmth in his fingers.

He held his friend aloft, but was surprised when Tim started to glow. He felt the heat in his hand. It became unbearable within a few seconds, forcing him to let go.

Tim landed with a thud and flipped onto his back instantly. He bounced upwards, propelling himself ten metres into the air, landing in a crouch directly behind Taylor, who spun around, ready to strike.

Taylor swung his fist, but Tim bounded backwards, putting a distance of several metres between them. When he stopped, Taylor noticed that his jaw had healed.

He cursed himself. He had hesitated. And now it was too late.

He had failed.

Tim was grinning. He raised his hand and flicked his wrist. Taylor was thrown backwards, into a metal panel, which he crushed as he landed on it.

Taylor jumped up and watched Tim become a blur, speeding up a wall as if stuck to it. He stopped near the top of Number Ten. 'I think it's wearing off!' he bellowed, laughing loudly.

Taylor could only watch, powerless, as Tim dropped to the ground and engulfed him in flame. It did not harm him, so he charged through it.

Tim seemed a little shocked that the fire was so ineffective. Other than covering Taylor in sweat, the blaze had no effect on him at all.

He darted away, becoming a blur, just as Taylor lunged forwards to grab him.

This time, he did not retreat. He attacked instead. His fingernails extended several inches and he swiped them furiously across his enemy's chest and face. Taylor raised his hands instinctively to protect himself, although he did not need to. The talons scraped over his skin, sending sparks flying as if they were clawing brick.

Tim retracted them and threw a hand out in front of him, using his telekinesis to shunt Taylor backwards and give him time to think. His mind rifled through his list of abilities. Many of them were useless in this situation. He was rapidly exhausting the abilities that might be able to inflict harm on the only real obstacle between him and absolute power.

He tried his telepathy, trying to force pain into Taylor's mind, but it bounced back and jabbed him behind the eyes. He winced, grateful that he had not used his full power, suspecting that it might rebound.

Taylor's mind was as tough as the rest of him.

He saw Taylor wading back in, so fired out several blasts of telekinetic energy to knock him backwards. Whatever his weaknesses were, Tim did not have a talent to exploit them.

He would have to find another way.

Taylor could see his former friend's mind churning. All he had to do was get close enough to grab him. He would not make the same mistake again. He would not pause. He would end it. He charged again, lowering his head. He was stronger than his former best friend was. He would barge straight through the invisible forces and snatch Tim's life away.

Tim saw Taylor sprinting at him and thundered his telekinesis in that direction. To his astonishment, though, Taylor kept coming. He seemed to charge straight through the barrier. Tim zapped him with electricity, to no avail, and had to leap up in the air at the last moment to avoid the hand that tried to grab him.

He knew he could not let Taylor catch him. If he did, it was over. Taylor was too strong to engage in a fistfight.

He was too powerful. It actually was the unstoppable force meeting the immovable object.

Nobody would win this battle unless one of them made a grave mistake.

And, even then, Tim knew it would not be him. He had no way to penetrate Taylor's defences, no ability that could grant him victory.

He had to leap away again to evade another lunge and he realised that he did not need to get through Taylor's skin to beat him. Taylor might have been invulnerable from the outside, but inside he was just as frail inside as every other person on the planet.

Tim stopped a few metres away and spent a few moments studying his friend. The profuse sweat gave him an idea.

Perhaps he had found a way to dislodge the immovable object.

Taylor swept forwards, fighting the energy that pounded against his body. He was getting closer each time. He could also feel that Tim was getting weaker. Each blast of the invisible force was less emphatic than the last. It was a matter of time before he caught him. Then he could settle this war.

Then, suddenly, he felt a cold gust of air. It was several seconds before he realised that it was not air. It was too cold to be air.

He looked down to see ice covering his body. His eyes moved to Tim and he could see that the ice was coming from his fingers.

Another talent Taylor did not know about.

347

To begin with, he was not concerned. The ice would not affect his skin, just as fire and electricity did not. However, it became rapidly clear that something was wrong.

The cold did not penetrate his exterior, yet he was becoming slower.

He could feel his joints freezing first. His pace slowed from a run, to a walk, to a crawl. Finally, he stopped completely, only a metre short of his target. His head and face were freezing, too. Within moments, a diaphanous sheet of ice obscured his vision.

He realised that he could not move. He was frozen from head to toe. It took him only a moment to realise how it had affected him.

The sweat.

The perspiration all over his body had frozen. His skin was unaffected.

But he remained trapped.

He strained and tried to break free, but could not. His wrestling caused him to pant, his hot breath carving through the ice and creating a small hole from which he could draw air.

But he could not move any of his limbs. He fought to swing an arm or kick a leg, but it was as if he was paralysed. He did not understand why he could pick up trucks, but not crack a layer of ice, but he was learning new facts about himself every day.

His power must have something to do with movement. If he could not move, he had no strength. That was the only explanation he could think of.

Unfortunately, he had discovered this idiosyncrasy too late.

Tim was approaching, gleaming from ear to ear. He strode over casually. 'You can't move, can you?'

Taylor could not respond. He had just enough space to breathe, but could not move his mouth.

He laughed. 'Who would have thought you were so easy to immobilise? All your power means nothing if you can't move to use it. I bet you wish you'd taken your opportunity now, huh?'

He did not even try to reply.

Tim stood in front of his foe and examined the sheet of ice with a supercilious sneer. He moved his face to just a few inches from Taylor's. 'You had me, Chris.'

He could move his eyes, but nothing else. He blinked and continued to strain inside his icy straightjacket.

'You could have finished me off, but you hesitated. You'll regret that.'

Taylor fought with all his strength. His muscles burned, but did not move. He let out a resigned grunt as he stopped, needing a break from the exertion. He was exhausted.

He chortled contentedly and lowered his hands so his palms faced the ground. It started to rumble. 'Don't worry. I'm not going to make the same mistake you did.'

Taylor began to battle again. He tried to move any muscle. If he could generate some heat, he might be able to melt a portion of the ice enough to allow him movement. If he could move, he could use his power. All he needed was a section of the ice to weaken.

Tim was merrily concentrating on the ground. Cracks appeared and the concrete started to crumble. He looked at his enemy's frozen eyes and grinned as a small hole started to appear directly under Taylor. 'Your skin might be impenetrable, but let's see how well your lungs function two hundred feet underground.'

30

Taylor felt the ground crumbling beneath his feet. He tilted to the side and felt the vibration shaking through the ice. He stared through the sheet of ice at the man who was about to kill him.

Tim continued to talk to him, but the ice muffled his voice.

Taylor could not really understand what he was saying, but he could feel the ground shaking and disintegrating. He could move his eyes, so scrolled them down and glimpsed the edges of the hole appearing at his feet.

The pieces of ground appeared to be sliced away in chunks, like Play Doh with a knife. The larger bits were being snapped off and dropped into a swirling mass of rock, like an asteroid belt in a whirlwind.

He looked back up and focused on Tim, who was still chattering away merrily as he stared at the ground. He concentrated on his lips, but still could not discern the words that were coming out. It looked a bit like he was singing.

Either way, he was not paying attention to Taylor. He was also failing to notice the creaking within the sheet of ice. A crack might appear at any moment.

Summoning up every ounce of energy, Taylor fought. He strained, pushed and pulled, desperately trying to weaken the ice. He just needed a chip or a crack, anything that might affect the integrity of the sheet.

The creaks resonated through the ice, bouncing around inside the frozen shell. They sounded incredibly loud from within, as if the entire world was groaning, but Tim did not even look up, suggesting he could not hear them.

A crack reverberated behind him somewhere. He tried to pull his arms down and flex his back muscles, but his arms would not move. He could not break free. He needed something more.

He watched Tim happily opening the ground as he gritted his teeth and tried again. He could feel the sweat forming on his brow and hoped it might help melt his prison, but it simply froze on contact with the ice, increasing the density of his obstacle.

Movement caught his eye and he looked up, noticing that Tim was spinning around to face something, although he could not see what. He could hear Tim shouting, but he could not surmise what he was saying. Then he heard the zip.

A bullet whistled through the air inches from his head. Then another arrived, but this time it pierced the ice, stopping against his hand.

Tim was firing lightning bolts into the distance, his back to his adversary. He could see the bullets strike his friend, as he jolted, temporarily knocked from his rhythm. Taylor could also see that Tim was healing immediately. The effects of the drug they had given him had not lasted anywhere near as long as projected.

He started to pull his arms backwards once more, no longer distracted by the rumbling, cracking ground beneath him. Tim continued to concentrate on firing electricity into the distance. The frequency of the snipers' bullets seemed to be decreasing, so Taylor could only assume that Tim was finding targets to hit.

The bullets continued to fly into Downing Street. For every four or five aimed at Tim, one seemed to come at Taylor.

Taylor suddenly realised what was happening. His allies, whoever they were and wherever they were hiding, were trying to distract Tim and set him free. By mounting an attack on Tim, it seemed that the bullets hitting him were merely wayward.

Tim had not even noticed the cracks in the ice.

Taylor could feel them growing. He could hear the ice weakening with every passing moment. This was his chance.

His enervation forgotten, he searched his entire body for every iota of energy left within him. Summoning every drop, he swung his arm forwards.

It did not move and Taylor realised a terrible truth.

He was drained. His power was clearly kinetic and, without that, he had no strength left in his muscles. He was helpless. He needed to move to re-energise.

But he could not move.

He had failed.

Tim finished firing the bolts of energy from his hands and turned back to Taylor, a smug grin on his face. He looked down at the ground, turned his palms down towards it, and continued.

The ground continued to open up beneath Taylor, the concrete shattered and crumbled, the earth swirling around like a soil whirlpool. The hole expanded from a foot to three feet. Any moment, it would swallow Taylor up.

Bullets continued to zoom past, but those on target stopped only a foot away from Tim's head. A collection began to build up around them.

Taylor looked at his former friend and noted that he seemed to be proceeding with great care. He briefly considered it, but could guess why.

Tim wanted to be certain.

He was excavating with exacting prudence, as if sculpting his masterpiece.

The ground continued to fall away, swirling and spinning beneath Taylor's feet. He could feel himself bobbing from side-to-side, shaking as he teetered over the abyss. He fell a few inches.

Then he felt the block of ice start to tumble.

Taylor could do nothing to prevent his ice prison from toppling down into the stone whirlpool and the gaping blackness beneath. He went over.

As he fell, he realised that the hole was not large enough for him to fit through immediately. It grew with every passing moment and, as he fell face first, he realised his last view of life would be the impending burial.

Why had fate allowed him to survive one hundred and thirteen depressions of the trigger just to subject him to this?

What was the point? Suddenly, Destiny's grand plan did not seem so grand.

He had not properly considered the possibility that he would not survive whatever it was that fate had in store for him. He had always assumed that the universe had intentions for him. He had believed that his misery was for a reason, that his gift had a purpose. All those mornings, he woke up, put a gun in his mouth and pulled the trigger. Surely, Destiny did not put him through such tribulations just to bury him alive without really accomplishing anything.

Or maybe there was no grand scheme. Perhaps everything *was* pure chance. In which case, a painful death seemed much more plausible.

And he seemed to be speeding towards his demise. His failure would be buried in the earth with him.

He started to wonder what it would feel like. Would the pressure crush his lungs? Or would he start drawing earth into his mouth and suffocate?

Suddenly, he found himself cursing his ability, wishing he could take a bullet to the head.

He landed over the black hole, prepared to watch death approaching, when he heard the noise.

It was difficult to discern over the grinding of swirling rock and soil, so Tim was unaware of it, but it resonated around the inside of his ice shell. He did not know where the sound came from, but it was somewhere behind him. He knew exactly what it was.

It was a shatter.

Suddenly, he could move his arms. He pulled them forwards. The ice cracked and broke. He could see the chunks and shards of ice falling into the abyss.

Next, he moved his legs. More ice fell into the hole. His legs were now free.

Just as the hole widened far enough to engulf him, he snapped free. He felt his strength return, washing over him as if it was life itself. No power in the universe could change one fact, however.

He had nothing to grip.

The stone whirlpool swirled around and there was no ledge for him to grab.

There was only one thing he could see that he had any chance of reaching.

Tim was very aware that modern London was a city built on top of a city. There were old buildings, subways and sewage systems strewn across the city, buried just a few storeys down. He was so focused on ensuring that there were no surprises underground that might leave his former friend a pocket of air, he did not notice the shattered ice prison until it was too late.

The hand was already around his ankle. The grip was so firm it felt as if it might break his fibula.

How the hell had that happened? Then he realised. The rock had broken the ice. *He* had freed Taylor.

Taylor felt his legs flopping down into the abyss as he lunged forwards and upwards. His fingers closed around Tim's ankle and he held on tight as his body tried to fall into the chasm beneath him.

He dangled there and his shoulder took the strain easily, as the world seemed to spiral away beneath him into the very depths of hell. His strength had returned. He tightened his grip and watched Tim's face fill with shock.

The whirlpool ceased and dropped into the void as Tim tried to knock Taylor off.

The flames bounced off him and the electricity careered away harmlessly. Tim tried ice again, but he was not sweating. It deflected off his skin and vanished into the gaping hole.

Taylor knew, however, that Tim could use the same tactic as before. As a variety of projectiles, from rock to twisted metal, sprung back off his skin, Taylor yanked on the leg.

Tim lost his footing and fell to the ground, slowly inching towards the abyss. Taylor's weight was going to drag him into the hole. He slid out his claws and stabbed them into the ground. The sparks flew, but his talons managed to find some traction as he flipped on to his stomach and dug his spare hand into a crack created moments earlier.

Tim tried to kick Taylor loose, but he held on tightly. Tim could feel his claws losing their grip as he slid towards the hole. Taylor hung from his ankle, refusing to release his hold, ignoring the kicks aimed at his head from his foe's free foot.

Taylor took a deep breath. If he went down into the chasm, he could accept that fate. Provided he dragged his former friend down with him.

Tim, though, had different plans. He stabbed the toes of his foot into the side of the hole and bounced away, propelling himself into the air several metres and away from the abyss. Taylor kept a firm hold of his ankle, forcing Tim to pull him to safety.

They landed in a heap on top of the remains of a tank, Taylor refusing to release the ankle. They remained sprawled across the twisted, charred metal for only a few moments before Tim resumed his attack. He fired everything he had, hoping his former friend might be dazed enough to incur damage.

Taylor stood up, ignoring the assault on him from a wide variety of elements. He kept his hold on the ankle and ensured Tim's head bounced off as many surfaces as possible as he descended to ground level, dragging his captive with him.

Reaching the ground, Tim started squirming, desperately trying to wriggle free of Taylor's vice-like grip. Taylor pulled his ankle up in the air and squeezed.

He felt the bone break in his hand and watched the contortions of agony in his enemy's face as he screamed. Taylor kept his hold, but released the pressure on the ankle. He could feel the bones snap back into place and heal, the vibrations permeating his palm.

He squeezed again. Tim yelped once more, but the ankle healed as quickly as before.

'I can do this all day,' he said quietly. He broke the bone again.

Tim remained suspended by his leg, his head still resting on the floor, and screamed. He scrambled to escape, but Taylor simply dragged him back.

Taylor picked him up by his ankle as it healed and crouched down to get as close to his victim as possible. He swung his fist.

The knuckles crashed into Tim's face, snapping his head backwards and into a rock on the ground. As Tim's head came back up, it met Taylor's fist.

Images of San filled his mind's eye. San's family naturally followed, before the long list of corpses that Tim left in his wake in his search for power.

Taylor hit him several times and could feel himself losing control. Tim's nose crunched, his cheeks shattered and his eyes popped out. After five direct punches, Tim was unrecognisable. His face was, once again, smashed into pulp, a gruesome canvas of blood and bone.

Taylor paused and took a deep breath, composing himself. As he calmed down, he watched Tim's face ameliorate. He could not control the anger that rose up inside of him as he watched the damage repair itself.

He struck repeatedly, his fist crushing the face under it. His knuckles tore the flesh to shreds within seconds, battering the bones in to dust. When he paused for breath, it healed within thirty seconds.

Taylor could feel San watching over him. He could see Jane smiling at him, hear Nate's laugh and feel Herodotus breathing on him. Everything had led to this moment. This was his destiny. As those he had loved and lost watched on, he would not stop. He would not give Tim another chance to hurt others. He swung his hand, his mind a typhoon of rage, a hurricane of desperation to claim his chance to end the madness, to make sense of his suffering.

Preserving freedom and democracy, whilst potentially saving thousands of lives, might almost justify his pain.

Tim had stopped wailing. His eyes rolled up into their sockets and he became still and silent. Taylor did not care. He continued to swing his fist, crunching it into the mangled face with all his strength, vaguely aware of the fact he was hollering. He did not stop even when he had crushed every bone in Tim's face.

He hammered and pummelled it, only to watch it heal before his eyes. He did not know how much time had elapsed when he realised that there were figures gathering around him.

A familiar voice managed to pierce Taylor's introverted, irate hollering. 'Chris! Chris!'

Taylor stopped mid-punch and looked around. Norbury was standing next to him. Taylor noted that he was panting heavily. He looked back at the prone form beneath him and watched the horrific injuries repair in moments. Tim, however, remained unconscious.

'We'll take it from here,' the doctor said calmly. He nodded his head to signal that it was time for a soldier to rush in with a syringe and inject the contents into Tim's shoulder.

'What are you doing?' he asked, gasping for air.

Norbury smiled confidently. 'Bulling will not get the opportunity to hurt anyone ever again.'

'What did you give him?'

'It's the serum,' he replied with certainty. 'His own ability will absorb it and cancel itself out. He'll cure himself.'

Taylor furrowed his brow sceptically. 'Are you sure about that?'

'There's a strong sedative in there, too, until I'm sure it's working.'

'And if it doesn't work?'

Norbury grinned and chuckled. 'You can keep hitting him until I find something that does work.'

He met the joke with a cold glare. His voice was grave and even. 'That's hardly a long-term solution.' His looked down at his hands, examining the blood as he turned them over several times.

Norbury placed his hand on Taylor's shoulder softly as the soldiers started to drag Tim's prostrate form across the ground towards a van that was reversing into the entrance to Downing Street. 'I'll keep him sedated and isolated until I'm either certain he's cured, or I find a way to cure him. Don't worry, it's over.'

'Is it?'

'You should be proud,' he announced triumphantly. 'You probably just saved the world.'

'For now,' Taylor scoffed. 'But what happens next?'

Norbury sighed. It was clear his cohort was not prepared to rejoice in their success. 'Well, there are a lot of people out there with the virus. We'll need your help, obviously. We'll get Bulling's blood and we already have a working serum. I believe we can counteract the effects of The Hero Virus permanently. Once I've ironed out the details, we can start an inoculation programme.'

'How does that involve me?' he asked, perplexed.

'We'll need your to help us catch the hosts, Chris. I can't imagine that everyone will be willing to give up their ability.'

Taylor eyed him curiously. The reluctance in his tone would have been clear if Norbury had actually listened. 'How long do you think that's going to take?'

He shrugged his shoulders. 'I've no idea. Why? Have you got somewhere better to be?' he laughed, as he slapped Taylor on the back. 'I'd better get back to the compound and get to work on Tim. I'll see you soon my friend.'

'Soon?'

'Indeed. We're going to be spending a lot of time together.' He started away, before halting and turning to Taylor, making a gun with his hand. 'Great work, Chris. I think you're going to be an invaluable asset to our little organisation.'

'Wait, what organisation?' he asked, bewildered.

'Oh, just a little something the Prime Minister wanted me to set up once we'd managed to stop Tim. I'll take you through it later. It's a brave, new world, Chris!'

The doctor pranced away joyously, leaping into the back of the van with Tim and a host of armed soldiers. The van sped away.

Taylor stood in the centre of the warzone, open-mouthed. The remains of Downing Street filled up with soldiers quickly. They set about securing the area, although he did not really understand why. Tim was the only threat and he was gone.

He was gone.

Three, small words that bounced around in his head. He was gone. It was over.

He had beaten Tim.

Now that it was over, now that he had realised his fate, he did not know what to do or how to feel.

Why didn't he feel any joy? Why didn't he feel better? Why had the emptiness not been filled with the warm, fuzzy feeling he had expected?

He watched the army and police flood into Downing Street, scurrying around without any guidance, of any kind, from their supposed superiors. He realised that he now had this problem.

He had no sense of direction.

He did not know what was going to happen next, but he was quite certain he could not carry on like this. He needed less.

Less drama, less action, less hosts, less soldiers, less facilities, less doctors, less politicians.

Less death.

As he watched the clean-up of Downing Street begin, only moments after it had been conquered, he considered his options and the realisation struck him that it was not going to be as simple as he wished it would be.

As long as he had the virus, there would be people who want it from him.

The serum would not work on a 1st Gen strain.

Taylor sat on the edge of a tank and mulled it over for an hour before deciding he had only one option and it would be very unpopular.

He could not tell anyone about it as he worked through the details.

Especially not Norbury.

31

Taylor burst through the doorway just behind the armed soldiers. They spread out in every direction, their weapons raised, capitalising on the element of surprise to subdue the targets with maximum ease and minimum bloodshed.

Taylor stood and looked around the cavernous warehouse. There were rows of bookshelves in every direction, but he could not see a single book. The shelves were full of vials.

Which were full of blood.

He scoured the area for any hint of danger. Beyond the shelves was a small area of tables and computers, which seemed to be a makeshift laboratory. It smelt of dust and the lighting was concentrated over the tables, so the recesses remained in darkness. Other than a balcony that skirted the perimeter of the building, which led to a large office on the second level, the virus factory was surprisingly devoid of features.

It was a basic operation, relatively undeveloped, which suggested they had caught it early.

They had discovered a very sophisticated operation only last month that had seven separate locations, vaults and an armed courier service exclusively detailed to deliver their product. The main headquarters had been a yacht and it had been heavily fortified. In the end, the only option was Taylor, who marched in and tore the operation apart.

Today was much easier. None of the factory workforce was armed and they did not have active security patrols or multiple locations. They even conducted transactions over the internet, which was why they were so easy to trace and their endeavour so simple to unearth early on.

He heard the scuffle of opposition from the far end of the warehouse, but he could not see what was happening and it stopped after a few seconds, so he disregarded it. He would only intervene if the situation required it.

He watched one soldier suppress a resistant young man with the wall of heat she could create from her eyes. He collapsed to his knees with a cry and she swept in with cable ties and secured him.

Taylor looked at her ankle and eyed the electronic bracelet secured to it. He could not see the small vial incorporated into the design, but he knew it was there. All Norbury had to do was press a button and the anklet administered the serum directly into the host via the remote trigger.

The only people in Norbury's unit who did not wear one were Taylor and Norbury himself. Everyone else involved in the project, from the soldiers to the cleaners, had signed a contract to wear the contraption at all times and allow Norbury to dispense the serum if he felt necessary. The soldiers had all agreed to take the serum voluntarily once they had successfully caught all the infected, nullifying the need for operatives.

But anyone involved with the unit would wear the anklet until three months after they had left and would be constrained by the confidentiality agreement for the rest of their lives.

Taylor found a bench, sitting and watching as the soldiers confiscated everything in the warehouse and instructed the clean-up crews how to divide the contents. It would not take long. They had become fast over the past eight months. Every sample of blood and the extracted virus were loaded onto a secure convoy, which would transport it back to the facility for analysis and, probably, incineration.

The computer equipment, including the records of every business transaction, were taken to the investigative department of Norbury's unit, which they would use to find more leads and track down more hosts.

He watched them, lost in thought about his plans, but was suddenly distracted as Norbury plonked himself down next to him.

He slapped Taylor on the back merrily as he looked around, his elation conveyed in his wide grin. 'That's the last one in England. Our sister units abroad report they are all contained, or very nearly.'

Taylor raised his eyebrows curiously. 'How can you possibly know that for certain?'

'Well, we have a few more people to cure and you might have a few more hosts to run down, but the intel. analysts insist this is the last major distribution point in the country. There are no more facilities mass-producing strains of the virus.'

'So, the containment is complete?'

'There will obviously still be work to do where unscrupulous criminals try to sell fake strains, so we'll have to keep an eye on that. Most of them are pure poison. But, other than that, the containment is complete.' He finished the sentence emphatically, with a firm nod of the head.

'How many people left to cure?'

He considered it for a moment. 'Twenty-seven, plus anyone who purchased from here in the last six hours. Just as with the last dozen facilities, these people had access to a strain of The Hero Virus, but it's a weak one. So weak, in fact, that's it's not even contagious. New hosts have to contract it intravenously.'

'The airborne strain, too?' Taylor fought the excitement growing inside of him. He did not dare believe it.

Norbury nodded. 'Oh, yes!' he returned imperiously. 'We haven't seen an example of that for a long time.'

He shrugged his shoulders. 'Let's hope it stays that way.'

He chuckled. 'Indeed. Well, the beauty of this particular strain is that it's not even strong enough to kill someone. We estimate that it's 25th Gen, at the very best.'

'So, you don't really need me anymore?'

'We haven't *needed* you for several months, Chris,' the doctor scoffed. 'We want you here because you know as much about this virus as anyone else in the world.'

'Good to know,' he retorted glibly. 'If the virus is contained already, what happens next?'

'We keep it in a secure, controlled environment and study it. We can learn so much from it.'

Taylor furrowed his brow sceptically. '*Learn* from it?'

'Don't look at me like that. You have no idea about the level of insight we can gain into the workings of our brain. It can help us treat other illnesses. As you know, there are a number of incredible, positive side effects. The implications are endless.'

He raised his eyebrows and scowled. 'Don't tell me you're going to weaponise it?'

Norbury laughed heartily. 'Good God, no! I'm talking about the way the virus binds to our bodies, the way it adapts and interacts with an individual host, magnifying, or even creating, a strength or talent. Presumably, this is an evolutionary means of protecting itself by helping the host survive. Make no mistake, Chris, this is an extraordinary organism.'

Taylor could not sense a dishonest tone, but could not believe that someone, somewhere did not have criminal intentions for the virus. 'What about all your super soldiers?'

'They all want to go home at some point. None of them signed up to do this for the rest of their lives. Once we're confident that there are no more infections in the public domain, I'll cure them and send them back to their families.'

'So, that will be that?'

'That will be that, Chris,' he replied, nodding his head. 'We can get down to the real business of scientific exploration and discovery. That's what all this unrest has been for.'

'Unrest?'

'Okay, chaos,' he admitted. 'But it will have been worth it if we glean a cure for cancer, won't it?'

'Will it?'

Norbury was smiling excitedly. 'Another frontier will fall in the journey of human discovery.'

Taylor paused and studied the man next to him. 'You're really thrilled about this, aren't you?'

'Chris,' he explained, sighing heavily, 'it's every scientist's dream to cross a boundary of knowledge and make the breakthrough of a generation. The list is pretty exclusive: Einstein, Newton, Copernicus, to name three. Maybe Norbury will join that list soon.'

'Don't get too far ahead of yourself, Mike. You haven't even contained it yet.'

Norbury waved it away. 'I have teams out now. It will be done by the end of the week.'

'It's Wednesday now.'

'I know,' he replied, standing up sharply and marching away. 'So, I need to get to back to work.'

Taylor watched him leave and sighed. He had spent enough time around Norbury to know that the doctor truly believed in the altruistic potential of the organism. However, he did fear Norbury's naivety. He knew there were people out there, many of whom might be in the higher echelons of the governments around the world, with perfidious eyes on Norbury's facility and the research conducted within.

He felt a guilty twinge about keeping his secrets, but he felt dreadful about his reasons why.

He opened his eyes again, finally accepting that he was not going to be able to sleep. He was too nervous. He flicked the button on his telephone. 03.05.

The night sentries would have their coffee break in five minutes.

Taylor got out of bed slowly and silently, slipping on some jeans, a black long-sleeved tee shirt and a navy blue jacket. He selected the boots with the softest soles.

Sneaking out of the room, he crept past the sleeping soldiers and down the corridor. Both guards were already in the small canteen at the end of the corridor, sipping coffee and talking about Arsenal.

He darted past the room when they were not looking, rushing around the corner and down the next corridor. He ensured his run was exactly as his SAS colleagues had taught him: heels first, touching the ground softly, smoothly followed by a fluid motion from the rest of the foot until the toes touched the floor.

It was quick, but silent.

He reached the control room and entered the key-code on the locking panel, holding his other hand over it to muffle the beeps. Despite his efforts, and the slightness of the sound, he perceived it like he was banging a drum. He nervously peered over his shoulder and down the corridor. He could still hear the voices echoing in the darkness. He needed to calm down.

After several moments, with no sign of the guards having heard the noises, he continued into the control room.

He looked up at the camera briefly, but could do nothing about it. The soldier who should have been monitoring it was in the canteen. The images were uploaded to a remote server but, by the time anyone saw it, he would be long gone.

Inside the control room, he located the camera controls and switched off the one in the room. Next, he found the fire alarm system and deactivated it. Moving to a panel on the wall, he slid the plastic cover up and his finger hovered over the button as he read the inscription.

SERUM CONTROL.

He paused for a moment, but only a moment. He depressed the button, causing a section of the wall, adjacent to the panel, to slide sideways. This was the panel he wanted.

The name panel.

This panel housed one hundred and eleven small, rectangular plastic tabs, each with a name scrawled on a piece of card and stuffed underneath. Directly under each tab there was a small button. The tabs were in a circular arrangement, around one, large button, which had a very clear inscription on it.

DISPENSE ALL

Taylor took a deep breath, knowing that he only had a few minutes, from the moment he pressed it, to discovery.

He pressed it. He watched the buttons blink several times then light up. It had worked.

He turned and ran.

He dashed through the door and turned left, entering the laboratory fifty-three seconds later. Having watched Norbury enter the key code many times, he had it memorised, so it took less than a second to tap the keys. Taylor recalled a time when Norbury had taken care to change the code to the laboratory daily, but he had become complacent.

It had been the same for weeks now.

Taylor darted into the laboratory, passing through the clean room without even washing his hands. He was not concerned about contamination. He ran into the main laboratory, turning right and heading directly for the refrigerated room. He opened the door.

A cold blast of air swept over him, but he ignored it. The scent of detergent filled his nostrils as he eyed the glass storage cabinets. There were rows and rows of them, stretching back into the chilled, swirling mist that flowed out into the laboratory. In each cabinet was a collection of small vials. In each small vial was a blood sample.

Taylor knew there were thousands of them, all with a case number scribbled on a piece of paper stuck in a plastic tab underneath it. The cabinets retreated into the vapour that obscured his vision, but he knew the room was at least thirty metres long. That would not present a problem.

He heard a panicked shout from somewhere outside. He did not have long.

Taylor was pleased he had elected not to share his secret. He had considered revealing it to Norbury several times, but now he was glad he had not.

The changes had begun after his fight with Tim. He noticed them within a few hours. He did not understand why, but it did seem to add some credence to Norbury's theory that the virus contained rapid evolutionary mechanisms. It seemed to be evolving inside of him. It seemed to have reacted to the fact it faced a superior foe.

How it knew this, Taylor had no clue, but he had heard tales of talents suddenly changing when a host encountered another with a similar, or more powerful, ability. Although, none of these were documented and no empirical evidence existed to support these claims.

Even so, he felt it within him.

His had not changed. It had expanded and developed.

Whatever caused the evolution, he knew keeping it a secret was the right thing to do. In truth, he was quite excited to see how powerful he now was. At least he would get to test one of his new abilities.

Afterwards, he would have all the time he needed to try out the others.

He heard more shouting and snapped away from his deliberations. There would be plenty of time for that later. He was running out of time.

He had to act now, before it was too late. He just hoped he was as powerful as he thought he was.

He clicked his fingers and two, small flames flickered over either thumb.

'Mike!'

Norbury sat up sharply and opened his eyes. The room was dark, but light poured in from the open doorway, causing him to wince. He recognised Nolan's silhouette instantly. His eyes grazed the clock. 03.18. 'What's going on?' he croaked wearily. He could feel the vodka he and Taylor had drunk the night before.

'We've got a fire in the lab.!'

The haze in his head vanished as he leapt out of bed. 'Why hasn't the alarm gone off?'

'It's been disabled.'

Throwing on his gown and slippers, he suddenly froze, his eyes slowly moving up to Nolan as his body filled with panic. 'Disabled? By whom?'

'We don't know yet.'

Norbury sprinted towards the doorway, barging past Nolan, who followed close behind. 'How bad is it?'

The captain was already out of breath, having run to wake the doctor. She panted loudly. 'It's bad.'

'Is it under control?'

'Nearly. Soon.'

They crashed through the closest emergency exit and into the cold night.

Norbury felt his heart sink when his eyes clasped on the towering flames. There were people everywhere; soldiers, nurses and doctors alike; getting water in buckets and unreeling hoses.

Norbury scowled at Nolan angrily. 'What are you doing? Get Jake out here. He'll put that out in seconds.'

'Mike,' she began, but stopped.

'What?'

Nolan took a deep breath and just decided to let the words escape her lips. 'Mike, he's been cured.'

The doctor spun on his heels, grabbing Nolan's collar, his eyes wide and fearful. 'What?' he screamed.

'They've all been cured,' she said morosely.

'No!'

'I'm so sorry, Mike.'

The doctor released the captain and turned back to the raging inferno. He could see the pillars of smoke,

374

snaking away towards the black sky, carrying his dreams with them. 'It can't be!' he cried, falling to his knees.

Nolan placed her hand on Norbury's shoulder gently. 'Mike, you're the site commander. I need your authorisation to request off-site assistance. We need the fire brigade.'

'Yes!' he screamed, the veins bulging in his neck. 'Get them!'

Nolan jogged away, dialling a number on her telephone. She fought to contain her smile. She did not dare hope it was all over.

Norbury glared at the flames licking the night sky, his eyes flicking back and forth as they watched thousands of sparks spiral and dance against the backdrop of stars. He could feel the tears forming. He could feel his gut tightening. He could feel the chasm of despair opening up beneath him.

He buried his face in his hands and began to sob uncontrollably. Everything he had worked for was lost.

It had all been for nothing. He collapsed into a ball and let the misery consume him.

Nobody saw the dark shadow on the far side of the compound as it vaulted over the fence.

32

The fields undulated as far as the horizon, a vast canvas of greens, beiges and browns. Trees and hedgerows skirted the edges of each rectangle, making it look like a huge, homemade quilt. Only the occasional copse, small town or village spoilt the perfect, linear design.

Salisbury Plain changed colour depending on the time of day. In the very centre, hidden by hundreds of tall, imposing tress, was the village of Imber. Only the lonely, grey church steeple rose above any of the trees.

If not for the steeple, it would be impossible to discern the fact that there was a habitation there at all. None of the other buildings were visible from more than a few metres away.

The Ministry of Defence owned and controlled the village and Taylor had no idea how long it had been deserted for. It was private property.

There were no roads leading to it. There was a single track leading from a number of other tracks that eventually led to the B3908 or the A360. It was over two miles to the nearest road and over five miles to the next settlement. The tracks were bumpy, damaged and dangerous.

Nobody had any reason to travel down them.

The Ministry of Defence granted access to the public several times a year, on such occasions as bank holidays and Christmas. He estimated that several thousand tourists visited each time, attending services in the church. Taylor hid himself, and the few belongings he owned, in a sealed basement and was careful to cover his tracks every evening.

Although once used for military training, it had been abandoned in favour of Copehill Down a few miles away.

Only one man, who maintained the church, ever bothered to visit here, on the first and third Thursday of each month.

Very few people knew it existed. It was serene. It was safe.

It was Taylor's home.

Imber was a small settlement, with only a church and about twenty other buildings. There was a range of dilapidated, boarded houses and barns, most of which were two-story, constructed of either limestone or red brick, and tin-roofed. The vast majority were concentrated in a semi-circle, around twenty metres downhill from the church. Only a few had basements and he had spent several days ensuring it now looked exactly like one of the houses that did not. There was no way to find his hiding place unless it was subjected to forensic scrutiny.

He enjoyed running water, but no electricity. He had taken the time to board up all the windows of the house he lived in, so the light from his battery-powered lamps could not be seen at night.

The plain was black at night.

He kept his old Range Rover hidden in the copse on the edge of the village, under a camouflaged cover. He only ventured out at night and had never used the lights until he had reached the main road. He had a detailed map in his head of every track in the area.

It had taken weeks to scout every shop in every village and town within an hour's drive, but more than ten miles away. He needed provisions twice a week, since he relied on a cold, dark hole in the ground as a refrigerator. He had a list of ten stores he visited regularly, all of which either had cameras that were easily avoided, or no cameras at all. He visited them in a strict order, always at different times in the evening, so he was able to avoid meeting the same members of staff regularly.

He did not want anyone to be able to recognise him.

Taylor walked out of the house and felt the warmth of the morning sun on his face. He eyed the jar of dust in his hand, which he left just inside the front door at night to warn him of any unexpected visitors. He also used it to sprinkle dust on the ground in the evening. He had hidden jars all over the village to collect dust. It allowed him to cover his presence whenever he needed to. He could not run out of dust and, as yet, had not developed an ability that enabled him to create it.

He took in the fresh air and eyed the lifeless buildings in the village. A bird chirped and he saw a rabbit staring at him. It stopped chewing the grass on the edge of the tree line and watched him intently. He took a step forwards and the rabbit darted into the trees.

He smiled sardonically. He found it ironic that his only company would not come within thirty metres of him. He sat on the step and watched nature work for an hour.

He loved the fact it was peaceful, but hated how lonely he was.

Taylor sighed as he watched a crow descend and start picking at the remains of a sandwich he had left in the trees. It was ridiculous that he had spent forty minutes ensuring that it was hidden from the road before leaving scraps for the birds.

But he had wrestled with it in his mind hundreds of times. It was the only way. As long as the virus remained in his blood, people would want it. He would not be able to find peace.

Norbury would claim that they might find a cure for him, but Taylor knew better. The research had not revolved around a cure for months before he had left. He could be certain that the doctor was hunting him, along with an unknown number of well-funded, worldwide organisations. None of them wanted him.

They wanted the virus.

A satisfied grin curled his lips as he wondered if they were successfully distracted by him purchasing a ticket to India. When he paid a young man to take the flight and enjoy a free holiday, he thought the matter might have been settled.

He recalled how worried he had been when Marcus went through security at the airport. He was not sure how long the effects of his ability would work, or what the range was, but it obviously lasted long enough to get Marcus onto the flight. He had not needed to alter the perception of any item ever since. Marcus' passport had read Christopher Taylor as far as the security and airline staffs were concerned.

The Indian authorities had allowed Marcus Wright into India. They did not care that he was not booked on to the flight. He gave Marcus enough money to have a free holiday and purchase a return ticket in his own name.

Christopher Taylor went to India and did not return.

Taylor wondered if Norbury was fooled. Probably. Nobody knew that Taylor had developed so many new abilities. The pyrokinesis, matter manipulation, telekinesis and vision manipulation were just the start.

He took the mini binoculars from his shirt pocket and surveyed the horizon in every direction. Nothing but fields, trees and small animals. Just like every other day.

He stood up and moved towards a fallen tree trunk at the edge of the trees, which gave him the most commanding view of the area. Sitting on it, he opened the small bag in his hand and removed the chipped mug. He eyed the plains as he poured himself some coffee from a thermos flask.

The plains were majestic. The tapestry of green, orange, brown and beige seemed incandescent in the brilliant sunshine. The trees and fields seemed to be alive. He eyed the tall hills in the distance and the dazzling reflections from the traffic a little over two miles away. They were nothing more than tiny twinkles. They might as well have been in another world.

He sipped his coffee and made a mental note to check his funds later today. He did not know how much money he had left, but he knew he would not feel guilty about storming another vault, provided he could locate someone else with the same level of criminal enterprises as Daniel Grimes, his previous victim.

That way they did not involve the police, who might trace the money.

He smiled. He often lamented his loneliness, but had never known such serenity.

He wondered how long it might last.

The agents entered the house using the key code on the panel, which was new. Norbury must have ordered the installation to deter local juveniles.

They walked around without any real interest, half-examining the items left behind. After several minutes, as they entered the main bedroom, the young man finally voiced his confusion. 'Why the hell are we here again?'

'Tread carefully!' the elder of the duo snapped. 'Norbury wants us to check for any sign that he might have been back.'

Jarvis eyed the layer of dust covering everything. 'Doesn't look much like it.' He caught sight of the Magnum on the bedside cabinet and pointed at it. 'Was that here before?'

Holmes nodded. 'Uh-huh. Leave it there. He wants everything left exactly as it was.'

'We can't just leave it!' Jarvis retorted. 'This house is empty, so it's a prime target for mischief. What if some kids get in here and find it? Someone might get hurt.'

He waved it away. 'Don't worry, we tested it months ago. The firing pin's faulty. It doesn't even shoot.'